DISCARDING DECENCY

D. Mackenzie Fuller

Anitpodeon
PO Box 552, Mount Eliza, Victoria, Australia 3930
http://antipodeon.com

<!-- Skeuomorph -->

Noun. / skeuomorph (also spelled skiamorph,
/ˈskjuːəˌmɔːrf, ˈ skjuːoʊ-/)[1][2] is a derivative
object that retains ornamental design cues
(attributes) from structures that were necessary in
the original.

PROLOGUE

The tip of the arrow-shaped cursor hovered over the icon shaped like a square; the familiar image was designed with a slight bevel to make it appear to be raised from the flat screen like a button on a machine from a time when machines had buttons. Taipan could have just as easily typed the shortcut CTRL and S, but the muscle memory of decades of computer use compelled him to lift his right hand off the keyboard and click the left mouse button to execute the command. Save.

If Taipan had been using a product designed in Palo Alto or Seattle an algorithm built into the code of the program would have automatically saved the work after each keystroke, a feature that was conceived as a convenience, but secretly captured every backspace and 'on the fly' edit. Instead, when Taipan clicked the on-screen representation of a 3.5-inch disk, his changes were committed to a small solid state memory device with a USB connection commonly known to some as a 'stick'.

His frozen shoulder ached as he reached for a half empty bottle of cheap whiskey, violating the 'Consumption of Liquor Local Law 2022'. Sitting on an old milk crate to use the computer compounded the shoulder injury, but an ergonomically designed office chair was not an option. He stared out the back window of his nondescript white van which came off the production line in Japan around the time when disks in the shape of a save icon were inserted into a drive labelled A.

The movement of the Norfolk pine fronds suggested the wind was blowing from the east. An easterly produced onshore conditions at the front beach, flattening out the waves. On the back beach, the cross-shore wind would have been perfect for Windsurfers. There are no windsurfers anymore. The peak of that trend was around the time the van came off the assembly line and the disks were labelled A. No windsurfers, but the lumpy, messy waves were dotted with black shapes. Even though it was January the waters of Bass Strait between Tasmania and Victoria were colder than usual and a wetsuit with short arms and short legs called a springsuit helped to keep some of the chill off while waiting for the next set.

Taipan watched out the back window of the van as one of the black shapes changed form, splashing before an oncoming peak, standing, and falling off the back of the board almost in a single motion. A tourist. Perhaps someone who only gets to surf the waves at the height of the summer season between Christmas and New Year, someone with seven days off out of a possible twenty allotted for the year by the corporate policy.

He could still remember the day his allotted holidays ended, but he had to think hard to remember what day it was. Yesterday he had watched the start of the Sydney Hobart Yacht Race which always began on Boxing Day, the 26th of December. It was the same day that tens of thousands of Melbournians went to the MCG for the opening day of the Boxing Day Test. For those who didn't care for sailing or cricket there was the opportunity to be obedient consumers, flocking to the sales at the behest of the screaming advocates of the oligopolistic Australian retailers flogging big screen TVs and leather sofas.

His whole body froze as still as his shoulder. The whining hum of a Leonardo AW139 helicopter became louder, passing low over the carpark, moving from west to east... It was a distinctive noise. Not as recognisable as the Eurocopter AS365 Dauphin which the Victorian Police Airwing operated during his formative years, but it was 'definitely' a police helicopter. His fingers played ALT and Tab, then CTRL and T on the keyboard to open a new tab in his browser, keying the URL for the Fire & Rescue scanner from memory. The CFA were responding to some grass fires, a fishing boat was in distress, nothing out of the ordinary for the day after Boxing Day.

He took another drink from the bottle, closed his eyes, and waited. The helicopter didn't circle back. The noise faded away until all he could hear was the occasional shrill squawks of seagulls squabbling over discarded fried chips on the near molten tarmac of the carpark.

Taipan removed the thumb drive from the laptop and closed the lid. He looked at the innocuous device he'd bought for cash at the only remaining local independent newsagent where Tattslotto tickets were the only thing that still sold in any volume. There was no loyalty card or membership discount, no cloud-based wallet that could be tracked. There was a raised eyebrow when he held out a tomato coloured twenty dollar note instead of bringing his phone close enough to the reader to activate the NFT chip. Covid had accelerated to adoption of contactless payment. Only tax-dodgers or spouses hiding transactions from their bank statements would use cash.

He rummaged through a shoebox that held everything from old paper boarding passes, pens, rubber bands, batteries of all sizes, charging cables, +1 glasses, single use coffee sachets from dozens of hotels and envelopes. The kind of envelopes that were designed in the 1820s and still the inspiration for the email icon on your phone. His hands shook as he placed the USB stick inside the envelope.

- # -

Tara Kwong stepped down and out of her pickup and pulled her down gilet around her shoulders to take some of the chill out of the wind. She looked down over the small surfside car park, full of tradie utes, luxury 4WDs and Chinese EVs. *Tourists*.

Her Chinese-born ancestors had arrived in Victoria in 1855 along with more than eleven thousand others seeking fortune in the goldfields in the northwest of the state. Her own fortune was made off the back of a different kind of goldrush, the volatile world of cryptocurrency and virtual assets.

Tara looked to the east. About 500 kms across the sea, the Sydney Hobart fleet would be enjoying beam reach conditions. At this time the year before she had been skippering a Jeanneau Sunfast 3300 yacht, optimised for shorthanded sailing. She slipped her phone out of her pocket and opened the race tracker. It wouldn't be a record year, but if the wind stayed like this, it would be great sailing conditions and a fast race.

She sighed loudly, taking a deep breath of coastal air and wished she could be at the helm of the boat then her field of view shifted closer inshore where the surfers were trying to make the most of a messy beach break. Then she refocussed on the carpark where her gaze came to rest on an old white van, the kind used by backpackers or 'grey nomads' to travel around the Australian coast. Perhaps the inside was converted to carry a quiver of surf, paddle, and kite boards, but the out-of-state plates suggested otherwise. There was something else that caught Tara's eye. A 5G or Starlink antenna mounted on the roof. She watched as a local law enforcement officer approached the van.

-#-

The side door of the van rumbled as someone pounded with a fist on the outside.

"You can't camp here." said an officious voice as Taipan opened the door and squinted at the onslaught of sunlight.

"Just here for a surf," said Taipan, recognising the bylaws officer as Andrew 'Memphis' Smith.

"Tommo?" The by-laws officer was a bit taken aback by the van occupant's identity, that and the overpowering smell of alcohol. "I thought you were in London, or Athens, or Dubai. I can't keep up."

"Back for Christmas. Hopefully get some waves." They both looked out at the ocean. "Pretty scrappy out there today, and the sun's pretty low. Feeding time for the men in the grey suits."

The parking cop was having a rare moment of insight. Someone would have to be suicidal to go surfing while drunk at dusk. "I might need to leave the van here overnight, but I won't be sleeping in it." Tommo adopted the tone of a scolded child. "No camping officer."

Memphis looked around the interior of the van, making a mental note of the opened suitcase, sleeping bag and Coles carry bag full of crumpled hard cider cans. It was too late in the day, and he wasn't paid enough to deal with writing up a local he'd have to see at the pub quiz later. "Yeah, whatever mate. See you round." Memphis rolled his eyes and rolled the van door shut.

Tommo rifled through the shoebox again. It was amazing how much stuff was accumulated when you didn't choose to throw it away. Champagne corks, fridge magnets, bespoke charging cables made by companies who didn't know what the U in USB stood for, and pens, acquired from hotels around the world, from trade shows and hotels and 'bricks and mortar' banks that hadn't replaced the flimsy chain where people signed deposit slips with ink. He picked a pen at random from the 'Grand Excelsior Hotel, Dubai', it didn't work anymore, maybe it never did. He chose another and chuckled – the URL Antipodeon.com was printed along one side, something he'd created as marketing merchandise in a past life. He tested the pen on the lid of the shoebox to make sure it did the job it was intended to do, then addressed the envelope to himself at a post-office box and placed the stick inside. It contained a single file.

Monaghan.pdf

1

The Royal Oak Hotel was restored at great cost last year. The intricate wrought iron decorating the balconies had been painted a shade of white called Cornish Clay from the heritage colour collection making it look like lace from a distance. The interior and the staging materials were modernised. Starched white cloths, silver cutlery and upside-down wine glasses were added on the restaurant tables. The old menu was thrown out. Pub classics like fish and chips and, sausages and mash had been discarded by an Executive Chef who had replaced old favourites with gourmet wagyu burgers and Moreton Bay bugs. Otherwise known as The Royal or the Oak, the pub is frequented by an older crowd, retirees who voted against the republic in the 1999 referendum and against The Voice in the referendum of 2023.

Ray 'Mace' Mason grumbled and muttered under his breath as he looked around the pub for a seat, preferably something with a line of sight to the big screen, made more difficult by his short stature. He wanted to be inside with the benefit of the AC, not out the back under the sprawling tree that gave the venue part of its name. Ray didn't usually have to stand at the bar. This was his pub, his local, his town. He took a freshly poured pot of domestic draught beer off the branded rubber mat on the bar. He didn't thank the kid. There was tension between the ex-federal member and The Royal's casual barman.

"Looks like we will finish off the Pakis before tea, whatcha reckon?" Ray chuckled as a polite cheer echoed around the pub from those watching the cricket on the big screens.

Steve 'Fish' Fisher nodded with a thin smile. He didn't usually work Wednesdays, but the last week in December was a good chance to make some extra money. Fish hadn't seen Ray since the crypto winter, since the value of a chunk of the older man's retirement savings had been wiped out as the price of Bitcoin went from an all-time high to almost half in the space of weeks.

Fish hadn't exactly encouraged Ray to invest his retirement money into crypto, but Ray had watched the university student flashing money around and he wasn't getting it from pulling pints. A good local kid from a middle-class family, Fish didn't seem to Ray like the kind of guy to be selling drugs or stealing jet-skis and flogging the parts. So, one day, Ray had enquired where the money was coming from. Most of what Steve said went over his head but there was something in it. The kids have a term for it. FOMO. The Fear of Missing Out, and Ray sensed he was being left behind.

That was around the time Ray retired. Or as the Liberal party pundit commentating on election night put it, "had his ass handed to him, because he was a corrupt, climate denying dinosaur who couldn't see the meteor of public opinion coming straight at him." That was one of the more positive assessments of his campaign. His post-real-estate career as a federal politician was ended by a 'Teal' candidate in the May 22 election.

Fish hadn't been the only one talking about crypto. 'Ed', his barber of 23 years, talked about it. The Indian bloke who took over driving one of the town's four taxis was talking about it. His YouTube feed was full of dickheads in Dubai driving gold Lambos and that, juxtapositioned against the sort of lifestyle he was looking at in his retirement, funded by investments made by faceless fund managers ate away at him. Fish had warned not to stray far from the main coins and that advice, only to buy Bitcoin and Ethereum was probably the only reason the two men could even look at each other. That and the fact that Ray still owned one of the largest properties in Victoria.

"That mob of curry munchers who bought the taxi company would do a better job than these clowns," said Ray, lapping up the laughs from a few of his remaining gang of acolytes. The barman, who had been given compulsory diversity training, had given up trying to soften the racist language from guys like Mace. Most of the time he couldn't help laughing, though he would say that he was laughing at Ray not with him. He just stacked up clean pint glasses and let it go.

"Hey, speaking of bloody foreigners buying shit, I'm thinking of putting Monaghan up for sale, see if I can flog it to a Russian or a raghead, get a tax break and buy a few more Airbnbs." Ray wanted everyone to know he was the beneficiary of the perks of white privilege and his generation, but he didn't want them to know he was basically broke.

- # -

The sprawling Monaghan property with its tower was the kind of local landmark that featured on the front page of glossy local tourism brochures. It's anachronistic in the way colonial properties often are. Oak trees instead of natives planted on either side of the driveway to create an avenue leading to a partially ruined mansion imagined by a late Victorian architect in the Italianate style. The original lease was over 16,000 acres, but the Grice brothers couldn't make the property work through the depression of the early 1840s. The owner who built the decaying red brick building, complete with tower purchased 2000 acres from the Crown, paying 10,000 pounds in cash in 1895.

Alfred Mason arrived in Melbourne in 1863, aged 25. He was a savvy businessman who built a varied industrial business. In 1891 he became a member of the Legislative Council and later in 1910, accusations of political corruption coincided with his suspicious disappearance from the property's beach during a family picnic. Perhaps because of an inherent sense of immortality, he left no will, his sons and daughters could not agree what to do with the property, so they sold it off to divide the money between them.

Since then, the property has been subdivided so that the current area is 888 acres, including a creek, beachfront and a headland that the locals call The Point.

Ray had employed every bit of cunning and malfeasance at his disposal to bring the property back into the family, from bribery and corruption to starting a bushfire in one of the back paddocks. Ordinarily for a property of this size and significance there would be double page colour glossy ads in the property section of The Saturday Age newspaper. Ray had fixed that. Brown envelopes full of 'jolly green giants' were exchanged at shady meetings in the early hours at the Embassy Taxi Cafe in Melbourne's Spencer Street. The large wooden AUCTION sign that had been erected by the roadside outside the Monaghan driveway was destroyed by hoons who were happy to use it for shotgun target practice in exchange for a fistful of 'pineapples' and two bottles of Bundy OP. The replacement sign met the same fate and was never replaced. A middle-ranked officer of The Department of Jobs, Skills, Industry and Regions signed off on a soil test that showed the groundwater to be contaminated with arsenic and lead which would require significant clean-up investment if the land was to be used for farming or growing crops. Ray made sure that report was distributed widely, especially on overseas property portals that were aimed at foreign property investors.

On the day of the auction, an anonymous benefactor had offered a free breakfast at the Royal Oak Hotel for anyone who wanted to protest the sale. The donor had hired a 36-seat bus that coughed black smoke from the exhausts as it idled outside the public house waiting for the NIMBY types who had been radicalised through a letter writing campaign to the local paper. One of Ray's agitators handed out placards and signs, designed to play on the ingrained prejudice and casual racism of the mostly Boomer crowd. Ray's was the only bid.

#

Tara's deck shoes squeaked on the polished wooden floorboards as she approached the Oak's bar, looking for a space away from the ranting old white guy who looked vaguely familiar. She paused and looked around, taking in the newly framed portrait of the newly inaugurated king above the daily special written on a chalkboard in Alexandria calligraphy font - $50 for pan-fried sea-bass and a glass of Chardonnay. The crowd was not looking at each other, but rather the test match cricket on the big screen TVs.

"Where ya gunna to host your famous Australia Day party if you don't have it at the big house?" Fish asked the cantankerous old git.

Ray looked around the pub, then directly at the woman who had just walked in and shook his head. "Not many of us left around here." He made no attempt to lower his voice. "You know what I mean. Proper Australians who understand why the Union Jack is in the corner of the flag, why the queen, sorry king, is on the $5 note and why we celebrate Australia Day on the 26th of January."

Fish followed his gaze and addressed Tara. "You lost? You need something? The restaurant isn't open yet." He said it in a way that made Tara feel instantly unwanted. She took another look around the bar and shuddered as the slobbish guy with the beer-gut leered at her as if she was a hooker in Patpong road. She shook her head, turned, and walked back out the front door, wishing she could do it more silently as her non-slip soles announced her retreat. She clenched her fists so her nails dug into her palms, wishing she couldn't hear them talking about her.

"You would, wouldn't you, even though she's a chink. Me love you long time." The creepy old guy put on a generic Asian accent as he added the trope and got extra laughs from Fish and the regulars who thought they knew where it came from but had never actually seen Kubrick's Full Metal Jacket.

Memphis nearly knocked Tara over as he barrelled into the Oak. He was still in uniform, still on the clock, but this couldn't wait. He nodded to Fish who picked up a schooner glass and began to fill it with VB from the tap. Memphis tapped Ray on the shoulder.

"Mace, he's here. I just saw Tommo, you know, Travis Tompson, down at the surf beach carpark. That camper with the internet thing on top and he was inside working on a laptop." Memphis took a break from giving the news to gulp down half his beer.

"Slow down, did you actually see him, or did you just see the van?" Ray's mood had changed, his afternoon in the pub watching the cricket ruined by the interruption.

"I spoke to him, he was half cut, the van stank of alcohol, reckon he's sleeping in it." The bylaws officer took out his phone, parking fines were all backed up with time stamped photos these days and Memphis wanted evidence if he had to write Tommo up for camping or drinking alcohol in public or whatever other violations he could find. "See, that's the van."

"Ok, ok." The heat in Ray's face was almost turning to steam in the air-conditioned space. "Leave it with me. Don't write him up, we need to handle this quietly, don't want to spook him."

- # -

On his printed birth certificate, wherever that is, his name is spelled Travis Thompson, so inevitably, his nickname at the local public high school was Tommo. It never sat well with him. Tommo is a name for the kind of guy who plays centre half forward in the Aussie Rules team and has a dozen close mates who are thick as thieves. Travis Thomson has never been a team player. He always preferred solo pursuits, like surfing and computer hacking.

In Australian society, you can't choose your own nickname. There is an unwritten, not so secret algorithm that shortens a name and adds 'o', hence Tommo. But the o is not compulsory. Steve Fisher, the casual barman at the Royal Oak Hotel is just Fish. Other nicknames can be opaquer, like cockney rhyming slang, with several degrees of meaning and derivation baked in. Andrew 'Memphis' Smith, whose life plan didn't turn out the way he wanted and ended up as a Bylaws officer, got his nickname because he mis-sang the words to Toto's song 'Africa' in the Royal Oak Hotel one New Year's Eve. Until that night, Smithy thought the lyric was 'As sure as Kilimanjaro rises like a memphis above the Serengeti...' No one really remembers who was the first to call Smithy Memphis. Even fewer know the actual line from the song. But Memphis stuck.

Tommo shuffled along the cliffside track from the surf beach carpark towards the Pier Hotel. The easterly wind helped sober him up a little, but not as much as the encounter with Memphis. He really didn't want people to know he was back in town, much less a gossiping ticket inspector who thought he was Javert.

The rules for walking on a beach path were displayed on a sign on a pole sunk into the sand and secured with a concrete foundation. Here, somewhere on the 59,000 kilometres of Australian coastline, with not another soul in sight, he was forbidden to drop litter - that one was fair enough. He was banned from walking a dog without a leash or riding a horse. He wasn't allowed to go fishing without a licence, he couldn't camp or light a fire, he couldn't chop down trees or take any vegetation away, and he wasn't allowed to fly control-line model plane – at least that's what he thought the symbol represented. Then there were the laws relating to alcohol.

"To protect against alcohol-related behaviour and
to enhance community health and wellbeing,
consumption of alcohol is prohibited, Fines apply.
Alcohol may be confiscated by the police."

What is alcohol-related behaviour? He took a sip from the plastic Coke bottle that contained the remainder of his whiskey and cola, a ruse designed to circumvent the nanny-state laws. A month earlier, he had opened a can of Mamos lager on the streets of Athens and reflected on the relative permissiveness of the Greek capital compared with the beach path, where having an open container of alcohol in public was an offence. These laws were supposed to be a show of civility, a way to separate us from the animals - except that the seagulls could shit on the signs and fly away without punishment. The prurient laws mirrored the times the state was named after: Victorian to the core.

Stopping on the path where the fence had fallen away due to a landslide, he found yet another warning sign. This one less preachy, just a stick figure falling to its death and the words – 'Unstable Cliffs'. He looked over the edge at the rocks below and wondered if the height was enough to sustain a fatal injury or if he'd end up being airlifted into the waiting arms of his pursuers. A blue heeler nudged against his leg, growling as if to say, "Don't do it." Smart dogs, Blueys. More emotional intelligence and empathy than most people. Tommo ruffled the dog's head as the owner caught up to her four-legged, casual social worker. He tugged his Pilote baseball cap down over his face as he recognised her as one of his mum's old neighbours. She reached down and clipped a leash onto the dog's collar, so she didn't fall foul of the laws posted on the signs.

"Leave the poor man alone Max," she tugged the dog away as he whined and dug his paws into the sand wanting to wait beside Tommo to make sure he stayed on the land side of the path.

Maybe coming back was a mistake. The dog walker looked back over her shoulder as if she'd just cottoned on to who he was. "Fuck

Tim Minchin and his fucking Christmas song." Tommo's lower lip trembled and his eyes watered speaking to a pelican as its large, webbed feet skidded along the flat water of the front beach to land beside the pier.

- # -

Some say that the inspiration for the Mos Eisley Cantina was the Pier Hotel. It's only Tommo who says that and he's been saying it since he celebrated his VCE results with the high school class of 1995. Whenever he walks through the doors of the public bar, the words spoken by Alec Guiness as Obi Wan Kenobi come into his head… You will never find a more wretched hive of scum and villainy. Which is a bit unfair to the venue mostly inhabited by surfers, tradies, backpackers and a few digital entrepreneur types who escaped Melbourne during the Covid pandemic. It would be hard to make an argument that this small-town hotel could be the home of intergalactic smuggling and rebellion that Tommo assigns to it in his mind, but then again, it's about as far-flung from the empire as Tatooine.

'The Pier', like many pubs in Australia, is imaginatively named for its location opposite… the pier. The establishment goes through owners and managers like the country goes through modern day Prime Ministers. After failed incarnations as a gastro-hotel, a gay bar and cabaret and an Irish theme pub, the current offer is a return to the basic bar, bistro and beer garden formula that never fails. Like the Star Wars cantina, the Pier features a wide range of characters. It's probably the only bar in the world where Tommo would rub shoulders with a guy like Archibald 'Kelpie' Prince.

Archie sat alone in the beer garden at the back of the hotel facing west. He sank down into the canvas sling of one of the deck chairs that were usually used to watch outdoor screenings and checked the weather app on his phone. It was a specialised app, designed for surfers. As well as the basic weather forecast - the temperature and the probability of rain, it also used readings from offshore buoys and complex models to predict the size and direction of the ocean swell. He scrolled down the screen and a puzzled look came across his face. The weather should be hot and dry, but the forecast was for rain and thunderstorms for the next week. The waves wouldn't be any good with an easterly, not at the main back-beach. But maybe at Kelpie's.

"Strange weather isn't it," Tommo said, casting a shadow over Archie's screen before pulling up a deckchair of his own and slumping into it. "Are you thinking Kelpie's?"

"Hey Tommo, when did you get back into town? I thought you were hiding on a yacht in the Med or something." The ex-pro surfer looked up and acknowledged Tommo's arrival before putting his phone away. "You had better not let Mace see you. You kicked that bull-ant nest hard, and they are still in a biting mood." He looked up at the sky. As the day had worn on, a pillowy cumulonimbus cloud had formed as it might at a tropical latitude. "Kelpies could be a go, but it's a long paddle if you don't have a ski and you know it's technically Mace's private property." He laughed and shook his head at the irony of what he just said.

The way they tell it in the Pier Hotel, Archie was the one who discovered Kelpie's, but the truth is, his people had been fishing on that beach for thousands of years. 30,000 give or take. He knew the wave would be there, at least on some days, when the conditions were just right. The aerial photography that had always been prohibitively expensive, was now available to all, democratised through the satellite view tab on Google maps.

Archie only really had two choices in life. AFL would have been the obvious one. But instead of training with a Sherrin on the local oval, he was paddling to the outermost break on a three fin Trigger Bros thruster surfboard he found in a skip behind the caravan park. A tourist, one of the 'all the gear no idea' types, bought a $500 surfboard and tried to use it for two days before giving up and throwing it away.

The tourist's lack of commitment to the cause was Archie's awakening. He felt at one with the sea, and as it turned out, he was a naturally gifted surfer. After receiving a wildcard entry into a local competition and winning at the age of 15 he was awarded a lucrative sponsorship deal that allowed him to go pro. The footballers saw the inside of some of Australia's larger stadiums. Archie got paid to fly around the world and surf at iconic beaches.

It was the death of surfer Mark Foo at a wave called Mavericks south of San Francisco that gave Archie the idea for the spot now known as Kelpie's. To the west of the main break where he learned to surf there was a headland. In keeping with efficient place naming traditions, it was called 'The Point'. The Point, as Tommo had alluded to, was private property, and recently tied to an international scandal involving political corruption and alleged sex trafficking. Long before that, it had been the land of his people. Now, everybody knew who owned the headland and the pristine beaches beyond it - Ray Mason.

One day, when the wind was blowing from the east and the Windsurfers had taken over the main break, Archie decided to paddle around the point to see what was on the other side. He figured that on the opposite side of the headland the wind would be offshore, and the surf would be clean and rideable. The paddle took nearly two hours. The wind helped push him west, but a rip dragged him a long way off-course and out to sea. He probably should have told someone at the lifesaving club or the pub that he was going, but the origin story of the discovery of Mavericks was in his head. The tales of Jeff Clark, paddling out under the alien-like dishes and towers of the Pillar Point Air Force Station in California combined with a kind of hubris drove him around the point to where the wave should have been.

Archie's nickname, 'Kelpie' had been given to him because of the nameless cattle dog that used to follow him around. The dog appeared around the time of the surfboard. Perhaps in a similar manner, dumped after the holidays. He loved that dog but couldn't take him on the professional surf tour. The dog ended up being adopted by the crowd at the Pier Hotel as a kind of mascot.

The surf spot on the western side of the Point was given the name The Kelps. Archie would say that it was because of the treelike seaweed that floated just below the surface of the water and washed up on the beach. He said that out of a kind of modesty. Despite his success as a professional surfer, having won several prestigious events and achieving the world number six ranking, a surf spot named after him just didn't feel right. The Kelps, named after the giant brown underwater trees, became just Kelpies. Archie never used the possessive apostrophe.

"I'm sure we could just jump the fence and sprint over The Point. It's not like Mace has cameras or security patrols," mused Tommo. "And the law says that the beach and sand up to the high-water mark is crown land."

"Ah yes, the Crown Land Reserves Act of 1978," Archie scoffed with contempt. "195 pages including special provisions relating to certain reserved land for horse racing or greyhound racing or purposes connected therewith." He took a deep breath, trying to edit the rant that was about to come. "We use words like crown land all the time, but no-one, well no-one except me and maybe a couple of students of Victorian state law, actually knows that the text of this particular document begins with the words, I shit you not, Be it enacted by the Queen's Most Excellent Majesty, though the Queen isn't the monarch anymore, it's King Charles the tampon instead."

Tommo couldn't help laughing. Were it not for the Netflix series The Crown, most people would have forgotten the incident involving the former Prince of Wales that Archie was referencing.

- # -

Tara put as much distance as she could between herself and the crowd at the Royal Oak Hotel and wondered how it was that she came to be in this particular town for the holidays. Last year she had been in the middle of Bass Strait with one other person on a racing yacht and now she felt like she was in one of those tourist theme-park towns that was designed to give an immersive historical experience like Sovereign Hill or Westworld.

A bit of nostalgia was fine. She was a child of the eighties, that were fashionable again, though it was confronting to hear the kids talk about Hall and Oates and Cold Chisel the way she talked about James Taylor. She watched a group of twentysomethings cross the road in bare feet, carrying surfboards under their arms and briefly wished she could be that carefree, but she was still shaking with anger from the run-in with Ray at the pub.

She thought about turning around and confronting the sexist, racist creep at the bar, but she didn't want him to recognise her. Of course he wouldn't. Even though Tara was one of the management consultants at Quantum Strategy Partners that helped the man draft tax legislation that benefited the richest of her company's clients, he would only remember the men on the team, the ones with the right school ties.

Pushing her earbuds into her ears, she grinned to herself as the algorithm did its thing and cued 'Misfits' by Cold Chisel. Maybe preference theory had been perfected. The music streaming service knew her better than anyone else. She hummed along…

Well youth is my advantage
Anonymity my reward
While the world's being measured for a uniform
It's my luxury to be ignored

In her corporate attire, her expensive custom-tailored suits and designer heels, waiting in line for her flat-white under the soaring glass tower in Melbourne where she worked, she looked the part, but here, in this enclave in her branded polo shirt and capri pants, she was a tourist. Maybe if she wore a different top and exposed the longhorn tattoo low down on her back, they might treat her differently, but probably not.

She needed this break. She was tired. Tired of keeping up appearances, tired of playing the conscientious, corporate ladder climbing Australian born Chinese girl. She was tired of being asked if she liked anime or K-pop or what her favourite Pho cafe was. She didn't want to go back to work, and she didn't need to. She never had to work again, but how would she explain that she had no job to her parents and the tens of millions of dollars in her offshore bank account?

In October of 2008, Tara was taking her exams in her final year of a business and finance degree at the University of Melbourne. While business hasn't really changed in 2000 years, finance was becoming increasingly complicated. The nature of money was changing. Digital currencies had the potential to have a large and unpredictable impact on world economies and power structures, if only someone could work out how to fix the double spend problem.

The tomato coloured plastic $20 note that Taipan had used to buy a USB stick could only exist in one place at any time. That note, with a serial number and a multitude of anti-forgery mechanisms, could only be held by one person or entity at any one time. But a digital currency, a virtual $20 could be cloned and copied and spent over and over and over again. Just as Tara was finishing her exam essay on the impact of dividend policy on shareholder value, a whitepaper began to circulate. A whitepaper authored by a mysterious and anonymous academic which proposed a solution for the double spend problem. A whitepaper that became the blueprint for Bitcoin.

Two years later, in October, as Tara was finishing her management training program with a 'masters of the universe' styled consulting firm, QSP, the price of Bitcoin doubled from $0.1 to $0.2, but it was a fringe idea, not a serious investment.

About a year after that, her brother Kam gave her 1000 bitcoin.

At least that's what he told her. At the family Christmas get-together in a park in Williamstown, as her father cooked sausages and prawns on a coin operated BBQ, Kam handed her a USB style stick and told her it was a gift. She didn't ask any questions. Her brother had been talking about a website called the Silk Road, which as far as the media was concerned was an online black market for all kinds of shadiness. It was. She knew that because some of her clients used it for that purpose.

As she rose through the ranks of QSP, she was well aware that she was complicit in the business of money, weapons, drugs and all manner of other activities that were illegal if a 23-year-old on a website did it but tolerated if it was a state actor.

If the flash drive did contain 1000 bitcoin, then it would have been worth about $13,000 Australian dollars, but she had no way to check. The technology was a bit over her head. She forgot all about the stick until she was cleaning out her mother's backyard shed in October of 2021. There was a 45-litre plastic tub filled with shoeboxes in turn filled with old mobile phone chargers, an original Kindle with a 6-inch electronic paper display and 250 MB of storage, and there was the drive. A month later, the sale of 500 Bitcoin was written into the immutable ledger of the blockchain. The total transaction value was just under $35 million US dollars or $45 million in Australian money.

Tara sat down on a park bench style seat and watched a homeless drunk in a Napster t-shirt talking to a pelican about drinking white wine in the sun. She took out her phone and scrolled through Instagram. Maybe it was her GPS, but images and reels of the town's beaches, sailing club and pubs filled her feed. Maybe the algorithm had found a connection other than her tangential relationship with Ray Mace Mason. *Am I really that easily influenced?* Is that why she chose an Airbnb in this random seaside town rather than do the Sydney Hobart Race? She doom-scrolled through images of her peers behaving badly on superyachts and exclusive bars, pausing on a photo of a full glass of Aperol Spritz staged against the sunset.

"I need a drink," Tara said, addressing the pelican who had given up listening to the ravings of the lunatic and perched on top of a lamppost. She almost tripped over a chalkboard sign advertising Quiz Night at the Pier Hotel.

- # -

Tara Kwong's deck shoes squeaked on the worn floorboards as she entered the Pier Hotel front bar. No heads turned. She made her way out the back to the beer garden and looked up at the looming storm cloud that had been building all day. All the sturdy wooden picnic style tables were occupied with groups. The benches attached to the tables could only fit 2 per side, 3 if you were close or thin. The only other seating was low slung folding deck chairs.

Tara looked towards the sound of laughter where two men sat on the movable chairs beside each other. She guessed they were of a similar age, mid-forties. One a white Australian with greying hair who she'd seen earlier and assumed was a drifter and the other could be Aboriginal. She felt a tap on her shoulder.

"You look a little bit lost. Are you on your own? Want to join us?" said a bubbly voice with a softened west coast American accent. Tara stiffened slightly. "It's the holidays, and it's quiz night. 10 more minutes and it will be standing room only out here. Grab a seat." The owner of the voice picked up a folded chair in each hand and walked towards the two men Tara had been watching. The dark-haired Californian looked back over her shoulder at Tara. "Come on. I'll introduce you."

Tara stood rooted to the spot. An introvert, she didn't make friends easily. The place was filling up. She could go back inside and sit at the bar, which didn't really appeal. She could swing by the IGA, pick up a bottle of wine and drink it alone on the balcony of her

Airbnb. *That's just sad*, she thought. The woman with the American accent and the wide smile patted the spare deckchair beside her and beckoned Tara to join them. So, she did.

"I'm Marta. I'm married to him." She pointed at Archie who rolled his eyes. Marta was always picking up strays. "That's Archie. I'm about the only one who calls him that, everyone else calls him Kelpie." She pointed at Tommo. "And that's Tommo." She realised as she said it that she didn't know Tommo's real name. Tommo looked uncomfortable, like he'd been unmasked, but he nodded. "Tommo graces us with his presence once or twice a year but spends the rest of his life searching the globe for meaning that he could find at Kelpie's." Tommo opened his mouth to respond but then checked himself as Marta glared at him. Marta looked at Tara expectantly.

"Oh, I'm Tara. Hi." It felt like the first day at school or a new job. Marta saw the discomfort cross Tara's face and continued.

"It's okay, I was new too once," Marta said, "I met Archie at a surf comp in Hawaii, but I'm from Huntington Beach. It's about 30 miles from LA. That's about 50ks I guess, I will never get used to metric. There are a lot of things about this place that I will never get used to."

A woman wearing a short leather jacket that seemed out of place in the casual beer garden handed Tommo a few sheets of A4 paper and some cheap biro pens. "The prodigal son returns. Welcome back Tommo, it's been a while. I assume you will be playing the quiz." She looked at Tara and raised an eyebrow. "Looks like you have another ring-in tonight. Good to see a bit of diversity. Welcome luv."

Wednesday night was quiz night at the Pier Hotel, and it was a big deal. Those who were in town for longer than just the holidays competed in a rolling league. Last year the ultimate prize was 6 tickets to Bali, albeit on a budget airline. The quiz was MCed by Babs, who was the lead singer of local live music duo Babs & Daz who would play in the band room after the serious business of trivia.

"Sax and Violins or Art and Fishing Intelligence?" Tommo was already laughing at his own idea of a joke as he looked to the others before writing the team name on the first answer sheet. Until recently, the quiz team names had been a way to make quiz host Babs say politically incorrect things as she read out the scores, but a scandal about inappropriate boat names at a local yacht club had led to a heated debate about what was offensive or just a joke. The boat name scandal had somehow made it onto the ABC news website and into the pages of The Age newspaper.

"Art and Fishing Intelligence?" Archie snorted into his beer. "Did you just make that up, or have you been waiting all year to spring that on us?"

"I see what you did there. Very clever. I actually like it," Marta said. "We've used the other one for ages and I don't think anyone got the joke, but I don't think any of us know the first thing about fishing. Maybe Tara does. Are you a fishing expert Tara?"

Tara shifted in her seat. A few moments ago, she was looking to have a relaxed summer's evening and now she had been roped into a trivia quiz with a group of friends who obviously knew each other very well. But if she was honest with herself, she was there for the quiz. Tripping over the chalkboard out the front of the Pier Hotel had provided her with a short-term distraction from everything else that was happening and if Marta hadn't asked her to join their team Tara probably would have played on her own. "The closest I have come to fishing is Red Dead 2," she said, referencing a popular video game. "I know that if you are looking to catch something in Ringneck Creek, crickets are your best bait." She laughed nervously, hoping that she didn't sound too geeky. Tommo gave her a knowing look before he was distracted by a booing from several of the tables.

Ray 'Mace' Mason, self-appointed team leader of Royally Flushed and his fellow quizzers from the Royal Oak Hotel held up their arms to the hostile crowd and sat down at a reserved table. The rivalry between The Royal and the Pier was like Holden and Ford or Collingwood and Carlton. Tara flushed and tried to hide her disdain.

Tommo seemed to sink into his chair and turn his face away from the new arrivals.

"You knew they would be here mate," Archie said to Tommo. "Ray and the guys from the Oak are always here on a Wednesday for the quiz. They never win, they don't know anything about music or popular culture after 1970, but they show up just to annoy us. You better keep your head down." He stood up and fanned out a stack of brightly coloured cards. "Marta and I won last week and we have vouchers. And you two," he nodded to Tommo and Tara, "get the benefit of all our hard work. Aren't you lucky Tommo, I bet you couldn't afford a round anyway. Let's get the drinks in."

"I'll help," Marta said and winked at Tara as she left her alone with Tommo. The two of them sat awkwardly and silently for a moment. Each had a feeling that they had met before. Tommo was wearing a grey shirt with a logo of a blue stylised cat's head with green eyes wearing headphones.

"What's the story behind that?" Tara nodded towards the shirt and Tommo smiled self-consciously.

"Ye-ah. Amazing how things become retro and forgotten so fast isn't it. It's Napster. I know it looks like I bought it from an Op-Shop, but I think it might have been my very first online purchase." He looked at her to see if the brand would register, not wanting to insult her knowledge of early MP3 music piracy sites or her age. She nodded without giving anything away. "I was advising Trevor Stone's company about some namecoin he wanted to create, you must know Trevor, he's all over the news these days, Sydney socialite who got lucky with other crypto early on, anyway…"

Tara did know who Trevor Stone was. He and his company were one of her firm's biggest clients, but he was also the owner driver of a 100-foot racing yacht with the casually racist name of 'Didyabringyagrogalong' that nearly cut her own boat in half on a congested Sydney Harbour. A sociopath and a bully, that was her opinion of Trevor Stone.

"There was a website that was like an early precursor to Meetup. It was about as nerdy as you can get." Tommo's eyes looked slightly upwards as he remembered the details of the event. "Anyway, long and boring story short, we met up in a Star-Trek theme bar in Pimlico, and the only way these programmer types could interact was after three pints each. I used Napster a fair bit, but someone said they had merchandise on their site. So, I must have bought it online, because one day it just arrived in the mail. They must have been shut down shortly after that. I don't know, maybe it's worth something, maybe I should keep it in a glass case, not wear it to the pub."

"Does all your clothing have an origin story?" Tara asked. Tommo looked down at his black, unbranded board shorts and grinned. They had been given to him by an accident and emergency nurse at a London hospital after his jeans had been cut off following a drunken incident in the Thames River.

"Maybe," Tommo said. He hadn't told anyone about the events in London and didn't want to. Babs saved him from going into details.

"Round one," Babs called the quizzers to attention. "In The News, and the first question is: Name the management consulting firm that is under investigation for corruption due to an anonymous whistleblower." Tommo felt a flush take over his body. Archie and Marta looked at him.

"You used to work there, didn't you Tommo," Marta said. "What are they called? Quantum Strategy Partners? Helping all those drug cartels and arms dealers and despots launder money and avoid tax." Tommo shrank even further down in his seat and nodded. He looked over at the table where Ray Mace Mason sat. Tara followed his gaze and stayed silent. She looked back at Tommo again and made the connection.

There had been a whistleblower. A senior consultant had leaked documents which had ultimately led to a corporate and political scandal. Tara's firm, QSP, the one that apparently also employed Tommo, had won a bid to act as an outsourced arm of the government and write legislation relating to taxation while at the same time it advised its clients, like Trevor Stone, about how to use the same legislation to avoid paying tax. Ray Mason had been the minister responsible, but he was the star pupil of the new school of shameless denial. The politician who had given him his surname who built the tower at Monaghan would have resigned, but Ray doubled down and went to the election in defiance of all advice. He had lost in a landslide.

She remembered the internal investigation that followed at the firm. The normally toxic culture of power plays and backstabbing had been taken to another level. It was one of the times that she was thankful for their prejudice. They assumed she was a 'company man' since she wore the QSP t-shirt at the corporate fun-runs and volunteered at the university job fairs. They assumed she couldn't risk losing her job and her culture wouldn't look kindly on her bringing her employer into disrepute. Some of which was true. She remembered there were some resignations and some terminations, but they never found the source of the leak, or at least they never announced it.

Tara realised she was staring at Tommo. He didn't look familiar. Why would he? There were hundreds of people who worked for the company across 5 floors in the CBD. She had probably stood next to him at Upstate Coffee or jostled with him for space on the number 48 tram. She may have even swiped left on his Bumble profile, just another guy in a dark grey suit. Did he recognise her? Was she the enemy?

"Where is he? Where is that piece of shit?" Ray bellowed as he got up from the table spilling his team member's pints, soaking their laps with beer. Memphis, the small-town parking cop, who'd informed the team leader he'd seen Tommo's van earlier in the day tried to hold the red-faced ex-politician back but was swatted aside. Archie stood, making eye contact with the approaching thug.

"Ray. This isn't the time or the place. This isn't the Oak. You're

on enemy territory here, man. Back away. Don't make me drop you."
Archie's intervention gave Tommo time to get up out of his seat and
brace for whatever happened next. Ray pointed at him over Archie's
shoulder, smouldering.

"We know it was you Tommo." Ray was steaming. You're a
smartass, but not smart enough. You had to come back for Christmas
to see your folks. You could have stayed hidden. You could have kept
running. But we got you now." A few of the Pier regulars were
standing beside Archie now, forming a wall between Ray and
Tommo.

"Seriously Mace, mate. Back off. Either sit back down, lose the
quiz like you always do or walk away," Archie said in a low,
authoritative voice. The crowd, Babs and Tara looked on, saying
nothing, and then everybody jumped. A crack of thunder like a
gunshot broke the silence. A moment later, raindrops the size of wine
grapes exploded on the tabletops in the beer garden, and everybody
scattered.

- # -

Tara groaned, woken by sirens. She didn't want to open her eyes.
She didn't want to know what even the smallest amount of light would
do to the ache at the back of her skull. She mentally worked down her
body. There was pain in her left breast. If she were standing in front
of a mirror, she would see teeth marks around her nipples. She
shuddered as her mind wandered lower. Another ache. One she hadn't
felt for a while. One that would remind her of the night before with
every step she took today.

She shuddered again with a mixture of pleasure and pain, rolling
to her left to try and find a cool spot on the sheet, expecting to be
blocked by a body in the way. Just as her mind had pieced together
how she would look if she opened her eyes, she began to do the same

thing with the bedroom of the Airbnb she had rented. Her dripping wet clothes would be strewn all over the floor along with a pair of unbranded board shorts and a grey Napster T Shirt.

She rubbed one arch of her foot vigorously with her heel, scratching an irritating itch that hadn't been satisfied. Her feet were covered in bites, not the consensual kind, but rather from mosquitoes or some other bug that inhabited the Pier Hotel beer garden at dusk. She pressed her head against the pillows on the other side of the double bed. There was the faint scent of sandalwood and mint, but mostly they smelt of the sea, but there was no body. She looked at her watch. 4am. The sirens faded into the distance, and she went back to sleep.

- # -

Tommo had no idea how he made it back to the van. He only had fragments of memories. Each round of the pub quiz had prizes; shots and pitchers of cocktails and other things he wouldn't normally drink. The 'Art and Fishing Intelligence' team of Tara, Archie, Marta, and Tommo had been doing well, mainly due to Tara's encyclopaedic knowledge of everything except cricket. Then Ray Mason found out Tommo was in the venue and Archie had put himself on the line for him. He has a memory of divine intervention. The storm clouds decided to end play with a torrential downpour, and then nothing.

He wanted to piece together and relive the next part of the night, but his survival instinct suggested he should address more pressing matters. The van was full of smoke. The smell of burning plastic and rubber filled his nostrils with a toxic mix that made him gag and retch and cough. His eyes watered and stung. He could hear sirens approaching. He reached out and touched the metal wall of the van. *Hot. Not good. Not good at all.*

In the cabin of Pumper Tanker 86, the fire crew were being

bounced around on the poorly maintained road leading to the surf beach carpark. They were guided by a flickering light on the horizon. It wasn't the streetlights, they had all been taken out by kids throwing stones, and it wasn't the sunrise, it was too early for that.

"FireCon, Pumper Tanker 86 is turning out for vehicle fire at Surfside carpark off Stingray drive. Code 1."

"Roger 86. Fire reported at the end of Stingray drive. We've had a couple of calls on this one. Vehicle is described as an older model HiAce campervan. There are no reports of anyone in the vehicle."

Tommo grabbed in the darkness and found a beach towel. He wrapped it around his hand and pulled on the white-hot metal handle of the side door of the van. He could see the red and blue flashing lights getting closer and he did not want to be around when they arrived. Too many questions. He took a deep breath of sea air and lunged back into the van's burning interior to grab a backpack and the USB stick, then bolted for the stairs to the beach. Stumbling in the uneven sand, vision blurred, feeling his way through the tea-tree and the spinifex, he made a path around to the far side of the car park. He ducked down behind the dunes and scrub just in time to watch the van explode. He wasn't up to date on his insurance, but that was the least of his worries. He crouched and pressed himself against the sand and hoped no one or thing was in the path of the shrapnel.

"FireCon, Pumper Tanker 86 On Scene. Now known as Surfside Control. Message."

"Surfside Control. Go ahead."

"Firecon, Surfside Control. Explosion has destroyed the vehicle. Residual fire is contained. We are conducting an initial search of the wreckage to determine if anyone was inside, but chances of survival of occupants is highly unlikely."

"Surfside Control. Understood, please confirm if you need AV"

"Firecon, negative, no occupants found, vehicle looks to have been empty at the time. Please notify Victoria Police of suspicious circumstances."

Tommo was wide awake now, adrenaline coursing through his body. He'd thought he was paranoid. It was a management consulting firm and a politician, not the Mob. He thought they might have roughed him up a bit or sued him or ensured he never worked again, but he never thought they would try to kill him. Mace had threatened him in front of fifty people at the Pier Hotel, but 49 of those people knew that Ray Mason had short-man syndrome, all talk and bluster like one of those rat-like dogs that people carry in bags. *Memphis?* He knew where the van was parked and he was in Ray's pocket, but would he risk his deadbeat job to burn someone alive? Or had he taken Tommo at his word and thought the van was empty when he set it on fire?

Despite the early hour, the sirens and the noise of the explosion had begun to draw a crowd. Kids mainly who figured they could get a few extra thousand likes for a viral video on their social feed. The volunteer firefighters tried to keep them away, mainly to protect the scene for the police. The burnt-out hulk of the van smouldered, and Tommo hyperventilated as he imagined being cooked inside.

He unzipped the grab-bag and took a quick inventory. It was an ingenious Chinese design he'd found on Ali Express, or maybe it had found him. Opened out flat, the bag was a suit carrier, and it contained one suit and a couple of collared shirts. Zipped into a duffle shaped tube it also contained jeans and cargo pants, one pair of each. A pair of boardshorts, a rash vest and two polos. That combination could get him through almost any door or gate anywhere, from boardrooms to building sites. He'd need to buy shoes, but if he was lucky, he could pick them up cheaply in Aldi.

Something gnawed away in the back of his head. Tara. He sank down into the sand and opened the Linkedin app searching for her profile. She was way out of his league, a stranger who appeared out of nowhere and had invited him back to an Airbnb owned by Ray Mason to get out of the rain. His phone loaded the screen, and he stifled a cough. She was one of them. She worked for them. Still. To this day. She hadn't said anything when Marta brought up his past. She hadn't said anything after Mace had threatened him. She hadn't mentioned it in her bed. Instead, she'd asked him to bite her. Was she supposed to have kept him there so they could find him?

He couldn't go to his parents now; he couldn't go back to the Pier or knock on Kelpie's door. They'd be watching them all. This was the most expensive week to book accommodation anywhere in Australia, and that's if there were any vacancies two days out from New Year's Eve.

He rolled onto his stomach and looked over the crest of the dune towards the car park. The police had arrived and were dispersing the crowd as the fire-crew began a cleanup that would take several hours. He couldn't see anyone who might be there to check if the job had been done. No Ray, no Memphis, no Tara. He rolled back onto his back. His heart was still pounding as epinephrine pumped through his bloodstream. In a panic he checked the side pocket of the bag he had rescued from his temporary address. The pocket contained his passports. He could run. Again.

2

Tommo had to make some quick decisions. He couldn't help grinning as his inner logic mimicked old eighties text-based adventure game.

```
Look East

To the East is the town and the beaches filled with
holidaymakers enjoying the summer in their brightly
coloured beach houses. The surf beach is patrolled
from sunrise to sunset.

Look South

To the South is the vast and dangerous Southern
Ocean. A small tinnie with no engine is chained to
the fence of the sailing club.

Look North

To the North there is a single road, Stingray
Drive. It is the only way in or out of the car park
where police and fire crews are on scene following
a van explosion.

Look West

To the east there is a vast private property. There
```

is an old, barbed wire fence with a sign that says,
'Trespassers will be prosecuted'.

If Mace was behind the van fire, there is no way he would have done it himself. He would be tucked in bed, sleeping soundly, having rationalised the act through some kind of conscience bypass. The last place Ray would expect Tommo to go would be through Ray's own Monaghan property. Tommo looked at his phone, glancing at the battery level before bringing up the maps app. He calculated that it was a 4-kilometer trip as the crow flies - through the barbed-wire fence, which was more of a joke: just a few strands of old, rusty wire that wouldn't pose a problem. Then over The Point, leaving Kelpies to the left, and through or over the creek, hopefully not too deep. From there, he could skirt across the southern edge of the property to the fire track on the other side. As long as there wasn't a fire, the dirt road would be clear for the 10-kilometer hike north to the old highway. That would be far enough away to plan his next moves. 14 kilometres in thongs across the scrubby, coastal terrain would take him nearly three hours—plenty of time to think.

Go West

- # -

Tommo never chose management consulting. It's not the career that he imagined while playing with Matchbox cars in the creek as a kid. The first job he remembers wanting to do was National Park Ranger, something about being outside all the time rather than being in an office wearing a tie. At his high school it was expected he would go to university and get 'a real job'. He did work experience as a civil engineer, but on a muddy retirement village construction site near Dandenong he was laughed at for considering it as an option. He remembers it to this day.

"You'll never be an engineer kid," a tradie said on a smoko. He had nodded towards a suit and hard hat making a site visit. "Maybe an architect."

Tommo didn't have the maths to be an architect or a pilot. His first choice was journalism, but through some kind of pressure, peer or otherwise, he amended it to Commerce at the University of Melbourne. That's the first time he even knew there was a job called Management Consultant.

He gamed it, the aptitude and personality tests, the interviews, the roleplaying, and he got lucky. He was in the right place at the right time, because he had added computing to his studies and things were about to go digital. Somehow, he managed not to be completely brainwashed at the initiation and indoctrination training camp in the USA. Even though the glossy brochures said Quantum Strategy Partners wanted mavericks, it was a cult. He wore the suits in the right shade of blue or grey, he listened to the '6 Habits of Effective People' tapes in his car and read Sun Tzu's 'The Art of War'. He cranked out the cookie-cutter reports using find and replace to change the names of other clients with similar problems and a growing part of him wished he had become a park ranger.

As Tommo's career at QSP progressed, he struggled more and more with the nature of the work. Some people worked for tobacco companies, some people worked for online gambling companies, some people worked for pharmaceutical companies that faked drug tests, some people worked for banks and payday loan companies who preyed on the elderly and vulnerable. He worked for them all. And he was rewarded handsomely for it.

He was paid not to rock the boat. It was a Faustian pact, an understanding that whatever he did for the firm he was being paid, in part, to keep his mouth shut. His salary came in the form of a PAYE slip every month which, ironically, he paid the requisite amount of tax on. But there were also fringe benefits. Tickets to sporting events and a black AmEx for 'no questions asked' entertainment expenses.

Tommo was read-in on a few of the firm's greyer projects and activities. In contravention of his employment contract, he had been collecting documents and saving them off the secure network. It was an insurance policy of sorts. He had imagined himself being called to testify in front of a future Royal Commission and asked under oath what he knew and when. While his superiors would have no problem holding the line and answering, 'no comment', they would just as easily throw him under the bus.

And then he was invited to the party at Monaghan.

It was the 26th of January, Australia Day and his various worlds had circled around and brought him back home, in a helicopter. Specifically, a black Airbus H130 helicopter chartered from Essendon airport carrying several members of the firm and Trevor Stone, one of their biggest clients. They had been invited by local member Ray Mace Mason. Since Ray had re-acquired Monaghan, he had held an annual party and invited the whole town to a kind of perverse charity event. While putting on a spread and an open bar, he'd collect money for a group who purported to send it to starving children overseas, but administrative expenses meant that the cost of the party were always covered and then some.

Monaghan was designed for that kind of show-off event, the main house and tower looming majestically against the cloudless night sky. Its façade was illuminated by strategically placed spotlights, casting intricate shadows. On the sprawling lawn, marquees and gazebos had been erected, offering secluded alcoves where guests could enjoy their personal definition of fun. Beside the shimmering pool the bar was open.

Dressed in a tailored suit and an open necked bespoke shirt with monogrammed cufflinks Tommo felt like an imposter as he ducked his head and quickly moved from under the helicopter blades. He hadn't been home in a while, and this was not the look he was intending for a reunion. He need not have worried. The crowd was different that year. More wealth, the showy kind. Crypto-bros and hedge fund types rubbed shoulders with trust-fund kids from Melbourne's leafy inner suburbs. There was something else. It had the feeling of an end-of-season football trip. The guestlist was all male. As Tommo took it all in and looked around, he realised that the female servers and bar staff and 'hosts' all had a look about them. They weren't in the country on work visas.

Mace had been confused at first, confronting Tommo as soon as he'd cleared the chopper "Who invited you? Locals aren't really on the guest list this year." Tommo's partner had put his arm around his shoulder, having done a few lines on the way.

"Raaaay. Tommo is on the team. He's a good man." They walked through the big house which had the vibe of a rave and out to the setup in the back garden. What followed was a Bacchanalian event that Tommo wished he'd never witnessed.

A couple of weeks later, buried in a small article in The Sun.

```
On the Run: Illegal Immigrants Vanish Amid Visa
Scandal

Authorities have launched a manhunt for two young
women in their twenties who have reportedly gone
missing after issues arose regarding their visa
status. The individuals identified as are believed
to be illegal immigrants who have fled from
authorities and are currently evading capture.

The two women were reportedly last seen south of
the city of Melbourne on Australia Day, the 26th of
January.

The disappearance of the two individuals comes in
the wake of investigations into irregularities with
their visa documentation.

"We are actively pursuing all leads to locate these
individuals," said a spokesperson for the Victoria
Police. "We urge the public to remain vigilant and
report any sightings or information that could aid
in our efforts to apprehend them."
```

The girls' photos were also published, but Tommo was almost positive that the two women would never be found. This was a cover-up, and he knew that he could no longer live with himself as the so-called elites seemingly got away with anything. A few days after The Sun article, a semi-influential political blog claimed it had been provided information about corruption and illegal activities at the highest level of government and implicating Quantum Strategy Partners.

Tommo resigned a week or so after the party. He explained in his exit interview that he'd been approached by Antipodeon.com, a Web3 startup based in Dubai to be their CEO. He would not have to pay any tax and he'd get half his salary in cryptocurrency and a great stock options package. The way he spun it was that he'd met the founder of the company at the party hosted by Ray Mason. There was nothing to raise any red flags with the firm. Several of his team had left after Covid and consultants with his CV and network were regularly head-hunted by start-ups. The domain name antipodeon.com had been purchased in the back seat of an Uber on the morning after the night at Monaghan. Tommo had built a simple WordPress site and set up a matching Linked profile which was enough to satisfy the HR people at the firm that the company making the job offer was real - Web3 start-ups were known for being secretive with key personnel hiding behind Bored Ape NFTs. The day The Sun article came out he was checking into an apartment-hotel in the Barsha Heights precinct of Dubai.

He had planned to run last time. The backstory for his resignation had been carefully worked out, and contingencies put into place. They trained him well. How to use the system, how to bend the rules, how to take advantage of privilege and owed favours and quid-pro-quos. He knew how to use cryptocurrency and offshore jurisdictions to move money and he'd had a head start. He made sure he was out of the country before he leaked the information that ultimately led to Ray Mason's downfall and a big hit to the brand and reputation of the firm.

- # -

Something, a rustle, or a squawk broke him out of his trip down bad-memory lane... He stopped still, locking eyes with a 3-metre-long brown snake, coiled on a sun warmed patch of the track. The sun reflected hues of copper and bronze as it basked undisturbed. Until now. Despite growing up in the Australian bush, Tommo could count on one hand the number of snakes he had seen in the wild. Tommo and the snake maintained the standoff, the snake's sleek body undulating slowly, mesmerising and menacing all at once. The enormity and rawness of the bush gave it a kind of dangerous and uncertain ambience. If he could get it to bite him, he'd be done. It wouldn't be a nice way to go though, respiratory failure from neurotoxic paralysis or kidney failure from envenoming would not be quick. The snake flicked its tongue tasting the air and its demeanour changed, its body tensing. Tommo stayed as still as he could, taking a deep breath, all he could smell was summer in the bush, a potpourri of plants that only grew south and east of Wallace's line. He knew the snake could smell him with its tongue. He waited for the creature to make its move. It did, relaxing and slithering away into the underbrush with sinuous grace.

Getting his breath back and waiting for his heart to return to some kind of new normal, he knelt by a small creek that trickled alongside the overgrown fire track. Tommo thought about the difference between this narrow dirt road and the 16 lane Sheik Zayed freeway that Dubai was built on. He was clear of Mace's property and making good time. He filled his water bottle and took a sip, hoping there were no dead animals or toxic waste spills further upstream. As a kid, he'd never thought twice about drinking the water from the creeks and he wished he didn't need to second guess it now. Hitching his backpack higher on his shoulders he stayed on the shady side of the track as the sun rose higher, grateful for the canopy provided by the gum trees, trees that were absent in the UAE. The wind blew from the east as it had been forecast, through the tall eucalypts and he wondered if Archie had made it to Kelpie's.

- # -

Tara watched the steam rise from the Nespresso machine provided by her Airbnb host. The grating, pulsating noise of the pump sounded more like a jackhammer in her sore head. The 'Superhost' with a 4.4-star rating had not provided Ibuprofen. She picked up her coffee, blowing across the top to cool it and looked out at the pier.

It had been a strange start to her time away from the city, but she had stuck to her plan: to be more impulsive and less worried about what other people thought of her. Then she'd had an encounter with the drunk homeless guy in the Napster T-shirt, who turned out to be a management consultant at QSP and possibly - though she wasn't sure - the person responsible for the chaos she'd dealt with at work for two years. The same guy she'd brought home, slept with, and shared a few of her kinkier desires with. Now he was gone. Which was okay, in a way, because he'd spared her from this moment and the inevitable conversation about "last night."

"Absolutely nothing wrong with a holiday fling," she said to the pelican who was waddling out along the pier towards the fishing boat that had just tied up. "And now, I am justifying myself to a bird."

Taking out her phone she paused before opening Instagram, wondering if her actions the night before had already impacted the algorithm in some way. She gasped leant in as she was presented with a shaky, dark video of a van on fire. It was the van in the carpark, the van she'd seen a parking cop knock on and have a conversation with someone inside. There was no other coverage, yet which probably meant that no one had died. It was too far for the Melbourne news media to come for just a fire. They could just buy the social footage and use it with a voiceover.

Tara's shoulders slumped a little as she moved between apps on her phone to her calendar and realised how deeply her routine was built into her day-to-day behaviour. She was on holiday; her calendar was blank until the 2nd of January when she was expected to 'fly the flag' for QSP as they sponsored some forum in Melbourne. That was days away and she wasn't good with being idle. She looked out the window and down to the left where the Australian flag and a burgee fluttered on a pole above the sailing club. They might accept visitors, but there were no big boats, just off the beach stuff, like A-Class cats and Tasers so it might be hard to get a sail. Turning up to the sailing club here would probably be like turning up at the Royal Oak Hotel. Sailing clubs were not really known for diversity. Picking up a local glossy tourism magazine she flicked through the 'Top 5 Things to Do': Learn to Surf at the back beach, visit the winery, fish off the pier, visit the art gallery, play mini-golf. The list hadn't changed in 25 years, maybe 50 years. She called Marta.

"Hey. It's Tara. You said last night that maybe you could show me around, give me the locals version of the tour, the one that doesn't include mini-golf?

Marta sounded surprised and on edge. "Oh Hi. Yeah. Um. Look, this is going to sound weird and presumptuous, but I need to know, we need to know, Archie and I need to know if Tommo is with you." There was concern in her voice, fear even.

"No. He's not here." She flushed and bit her lip and struggled through the awkwardness. "He was here, but he's not now."

"Shit. Shit." Marta relayed the message to Archie. "He's not with her. Fuck Archie, what if he was in the van. They've put it on a truck and taken it away. What if his body is inside it?"

Tara began to shake as she put the pieces together. The parking cop and the van, the sirens in the middle of the night, the Instagram video, the confrontation in the pub between Tommo and Ray. The empty spot on the bed beside her. She felt sick.

Marta was sobbing. "Listen, come meet me at the Shark Byte Cafe later. Please let us know if you hear from Tommo." She hung up.

Tara sat on the edge of the bed in a stunned trance and stared at the number he'd scrawled across the top of one of the pub quiz answer sheets and left beside the bed. He'd roughly signed it with a T and an X. Tara added the number into her contacts and composed a message.

`Are you okay?`

She didn't know what else to say. She waited and watched the screen looking for the tick that said it had been delivered and the second blue one to confirm it had been read. Neither tick appeared.

= # -

The farmhouse style kitchen of the Monaghan mansion house was filled with the scent of fresh coffee. Ray Mason watched a pretty girl who didn't even meet the definition of age appropriate via a calculation shared by perverts online – 'half your age minus 7'. Perhaps 10 years younger than that, she had no idea about the formula or what the fuss was about, as she warmed up croissants the way he had instructed her to. She was his alibi for the previous night. He opened a paper copy of The Sun, flipping through the pages for any mention of what happened at the surfside carpark. Nothing. The fire and the explosion were timed to be too late for the edition of the paper that made it this far in time for delivery. *Is no news good news?* He hadn't had any updates.

Last time he had been blindsided. He never thought for a moment that someone on the inside, one of the chosen few who had received an invitation to his party, would rat him out. The cover up had been expensive, not just financially, he had to call in a bunch of favours that he would have preferred to keep for a rainy day. A rainy day like the day of the leak, because once that was out there it had been every man for himself. QSP closed ranks, the crypto-bros scattered to hide behind their NFT avatars and the trust fund kids had lawyered up, the 'suppliers' had gone to ground. Ray had been so focussed on his strategy of denial in Canberra that he hadn't even known that Tommo had resigned from the firm and disappeared abroad.

After the humiliation of being soundly beaten at the election, Ray had taken refuge at Monaghan, but he was not used to being beaten or idle. A Google search for 'Private detective in Melbourne' had returned no less than 16 results in the city centre alone. He'd picked one based on the name which made him laugh out loud - 'Fair Dinkum Dicks'. Nick the private dick had seen Ray coming and took a big cash advance to find Travis 'Tommo' Tomson. To Ray's disappointment, it turned out that Fair Dinkum Dicks speciality was helping small employers bust their workers claiming fraudulent workers compensation benefits. Their expertise in white-collar crime ended with staking out the local Centrelink and taking photos of guys who claimed to have a bad back playing golf on Wednesday afternoons. Nick refunded Ray half his retainer after admitting that he didn't have the skillset to unpack the complicated corporate ownership structure of the company that had hired Tommo away from his management consulting gig.

Two weeks after Ray fired the private investigators, he walked to his post office box and took out a sheaf of envelopes. Among the electricity bills and bank statements and mail-order catalogues he found an A4 envelope from Nick. Spreading out the enclosed documents on his usual table at the Royal Oak Hotel he found something that shocked him. In the source code of the HTML of the Antipodeon.com website there was a commented out piece of code:

```
<!-- website designed by Pilote Media -->.
```

Attached to the printout was a Post-it note. Scrawled in Nick's handwriting the note said, Pilote Media owned by Travis Thomson. Stapled to the screenshot was another printout, a copy of a profile page and there in the top left-hand corner of the page was a picture of Tommo. But it was too late. Tommo was offshore and there was nothing that Ray could really do about it.

But now that Tommo was back in town, in his town, there were things he could do about it. Tommo was a liability. He could testify to all manner of behaviour and actions that Ray and others had been involved in. Tommo had to be taken care of.

Then there was the girl. The Chinese one who had been at the Oak and then at the quiz and was renting one of his Airbnbs. The booking said her name is Tara Kwong and her Linkedin profile says she works for QSP. A call to his former policy guru confirmed that she had worked on several projects that were under investigation. The jury was out on Ms Kwong, but for now at least he knew where she lived while she was in town.

Ray's phone buzzed with a notification. A motion-capture camera had registered movement on the southside of the property. He made a note to turn off the messages from the cam, it was almost always wallabies or wombats, sometimes snakes. Deleting the message, he smacked the ass of his alibi as she bent over the table with his breakfast.

- # -

Tracking North, just before he hit the old highway, Tommo came across a small clearing in the bush. He'd forgotten about this place, but standing there with just a backpack transported him back to scout camps as a boy. This was the first place he slept in a tent without adult supervision. *What happened to those kids?* They'd stayed up late, played campfire games and joked about spending the night in a million-star hotel. The tents weren't really needed though. Nestled into the wattles and the banksias was a small 'cattleman's' hut.

Constructed from rough-hewn timber logs and weathered to a silvery-grey patina by the elements, the hut blended almost seamlessly into its surroundings. Its steeply sloping roof, patched together from mismatched corrugated iron sheets, was designed to withstand rare snowfalls and frequent torrential rains. A sturdy stone chimney jutted a foot above the roofline, adding a touch of rustic solidity to the structure. Inside, rough-hewn furniture, handmade from native timber, bore the marks of countless years of use, each piece a testament to the craftsmanship of early settlers, one of whom was buried 500 meters away in a forgotten, nameless grave. A wood-burning stove sat beside the stone fireplace. Above, a loft provided additional sleeping quarters, accessible by a narrow ladder.

Tommo's phone signalled with a beep that the battery was exhausted, and it shut down as he pushed the heavy wooden door open with a loud creak. He looked around the cosy, and familiar space. Lifting the lid of a footlocker he found cans of beans and corn and even sausages. There was also bottled water, a few teabags and a jar of Nescafe. He worked his way through the cupboards and discovered a pile of freeze-dried meals, some of which he reckoned he'd left behind after a camping weekend 40 years ago, but some were still in date.

Rummaging through a plastic tub he found what he was looking for, a solar powered phone charger. He needed the phone to send a text.

- # -

Taras heart beat faster as her phone beeped. An SMS.

Change of plan. Meet at the Pier. Archie.

She checked the messaging app. Still no ticks, her message to

Tommo remained undelivered. Grabbing a wide brimmed Akubra hat, she walked briskly towards the weatherbeaten wooden wharf. Archie was standing at the end looking out to sea. He turned towards Tara as she walked towards him.

"Nice Hat… Marta had something in the diary she forgot about, but I thought we should have a chat." Archie's voice was that perfect mix of casual and serious. Like a QANTAS pilot. "You okay with that?"

Tara nodded and asked, "I guess he's still missing?"

"He is." There was an awkward silence. "So, I Googled you, found your LinkedIn profile, which means Tommo probably did too. Which raises the question, why didn't you say anything last night." He held up his hand. "Don't respond to that yet It's best when introverts think before they speak. I know, from experience." Tara flushed and shuffled front one foot to the other. "I found another profile. Seems you do some offshore sailing. Short-handed. Respect. One of my old sponsors was big into sailing as well as surfing. I've done a few corporate gigs, met a few offshore sailors and I reckon you need to be a bit unhinged to do that." He looked back out to sea. "When I was at Nazare or Jaws, I had a guy with a ski, helicopters with divers, all kinds of rescue measures, but you just sail off over the horizon with a radio."

"Yeah. I wish I was alone on a sailboat in the middle of the ocean about now," Tara said.

"Ok, let me try an analogy," Archie took a deep breath. "You and Tommo were on the same yacht. He thought the course was too risky, too close to the rocks, but worse than that, the captain and the afterguard have a kind of hubristic Icarus thing going on, to mix my metaphors." Tara listened and nodded to show she was following along. "Tommo jumped ship and tried to send up a flare and that made him a mutineer. Now you. You found yourself in the middle of the storm and you rode it out. The ship's damaged, but the captain is still sailing it the same way. You're not in the afterguard, you're rail-meat.

You're there so the helm can point higher in the gusts and maybe clear the reef." Tara made a mental picture of her clinging to the rail of a racing yacht in the worst storm she could imagine. "You can jump ship, maybe they will throw you a lifeline, maybe if you grab it, you get keelhauled over the rocks. Maybe they deploy a life raft. In the inquiry they'll say they did all they could, but they aren't about to stop the boat and come back for you. You can hang on. Keep riding out the storms and hope they reward you for your loyalty. Whatever happens it's going to be scary. Survival conditions."

"I'd never met Tommo, until last night. I had no idea he worked at the company." Tara implored Archie with her eyes, she wanted him to believe her. "I've only met Ray Mason a couple of times, and I wasn't at the party. You know. The one they say the girls disappeared at. "

Archie's phone chimed with a ringtone saved as wave.mp3. He looked south and seemed suddenly eager to end the conversation.

"Well now Ray has seen you and Tommo together, so you're going to come under some pressure to explain yourself. What happened to Tommo's van shows that people haven't forgotten. Add to that, you might not know this, but that Airbnb you are staying at is owned by one Ray Mason. So, we don't really know what side you are on. You might be one of them." Tara stamped her foot and held his stare.

"I can't prove the opposite," she said.

- # -

Tommo got busy. He unpacked the backpack onto the long communal table in the hut and did a mental inventory. As well as the clothing, there were a few thumb drives, debit cards, charging cables and travel plug adapters and cheap magnifying reading glasses, and a hammock. He had a portable hanging bed but he had no keys. The only key he had was for the van and that was tucked inside of the leg rope of his surfboard which was now a charred lump.

Depending on where he ended up, he might need shoes. You couldn't even go into the Royal Oak without shoes. It said so, on a sign beside the door to the pokies. His sunglasses were probably melted to his surfboard and would need to be replaced. His noise cancelling headphones, perhaps the ultimate piece of long-haul travel kit had been cremated. Everything else was just stuff. He pitied the people who were lured by IKEA or Crate and Barrel and tricked into the purchase of candle holders or throws. You just didn't need cushions or more than one decent frying pan or anything from an 'Innovations' catalogue full of everything you never wanted.

What if he stood up to Ray and whoever else was out to get him? He didn't have the resources he used to. Archie had been right, he could barely afford a round at the pub, let alone splash out on a new pair of Bose headphones. He was basically unemployable, apart from the fact that he didn't fit the profile for a diversity hire, and his old boss wasn't about to write him a reference, his skillset lined up perfectly with the capabilities of AI. Even his overseas experience was discounted by fresh faced so-called recruitment people who said companies preferred candidates who understood the local market. Who was going to loan him money? He only possessed one piece of ID that had a residential address on it, his driver's licence which happily didn't have to be renewed for another 7 years. He would have to start again. He did have an interest in Archie's Pilote brand which gave him some beer money and sometimes mates threw him a bone and got him to build small websites, but it was hand to mouth.

He was in the right, but did that matter anymore? It used to be that even rock stars had a moral compass, they wrote political songs championing the environment or land rights or religious persecution. Now, the musicians came from reality TV and wouldn't dare to endanger their merchandise deals or the opportunity to put their names on a vagina scented candle. None of the traditional media could afford to do investigative journalism, they didn't want to jeopardise their advertising revenue or be seen to be favouring one political party over the other. Even if they took on the role of speaking truth to power, the shameless set would cry 'fake news' and come up with a suitable distraction. What was the point of calling them out again? He'd made his stand. His conscience was clear. What was he going to gain from crying wolf again? He suddenly felt tired and helpless again. If they killed him, they'd be doing him a favour.

The result was always the same. He'd been at rock bottom, and he'd run. He'd booked a ticket, boarded a plane, found a place to start all over where no-one knew him. He could run again. He wouldn't even have to leave the country. There were plenty of places he could hide in plain sight or get totally lost. He felt a tear run down his cheek. Running that time was not the right call. He should have stayed. He should have faced the music. There was no way he could do this on his own, but it wasn't anyone else's fight. There might be a way. His phone had one bar of signal. Enough to send an SMS.

Operation Skeuomorph!

Between whatever time he made it back from the van and when it blew up it couldn't have been long and he'd been awake ever since, running on adrenaline. He'd half walked, half run about 14ks and it was catching up with him. He picked up the hammock made of the same thing they make parachutes from, took it outside and strung it between two conveniently spaced gums. It was shady enough that he wouldn't burn for the second time today. He tested the anchoring of the hammock and took a look around the campsite, weighing up the chances of being discovered, if he could afford to close his eyes. One more job. He found some rope and some old cans and made a rustic tripwire alarm. Then he climbed into the swinging bed and it rocked him straight to sleep.

- # -

She did her best thinking on the boat. Tara had no boat. *Why did I come on a break with no boat?* She walked towards the sailing club, working out her way in, doubting they would have a reciprocal membership of RORC which she was a member of having done a couple of Sydney to Hobart races and the Fastnet. Archie's words bounced around in her head as she walked – *"we don't really know who's side you are on." Do I have to pick a side?*

She stood by the boat park and watched a couple of A-Class catamarans being rigged. The clink, clink, clink of metal and rope halyards against masts soothed her like a giant wind chime. A girl in her teens, white zinc smeared across her face like warpaint, smiled as she wheeled a Laser down the beach on a small trailer.

"Probably no spare spots today being school hols and everything. If you are looking for a sail, there are a couple of old Hobies for rent down at the resort."

"The resort?" That hadn't come up on Tara's Instagram feed. The girl laughed at Tara's look of confusion.

"The Aquarius. It was built back in the 80s as a timeshare. Kinda old and shabby, but they have an ok beach club and it's the only place you can rent stuff. I worked there last summer. Sail fast." She made the shaka salute with her hand, three fingers curled, her thumb and little finger outstretched as she slipped her boat off its trolley, pushed the hull into deeper water, climbed aboard and sheeted in.

Thirty minutes later, dressed in a pair of boardshorts and a bikini top covered by the dustiest, ugliest lifejacket she had ever seen, Tara pushed the twin hulls of her Hobie beach cat into deeper water. The boat accelerated quickly over the waves of the shore break as she pulled in on the mainsheet, one hull lifting out of the water, reducing the drag. Now she didn't have to think, she could just become one with the boat and the wind and let her unconscious mind work the rest out in the background.

She could end the break early. It was probably too late to find something else for New Years Eve, but she could go to Ballarat and be with her folks. Did she care what an ex-surfer thought about her? She didn't owe him anything. Did she care about Tommo? They had shared a few hours of drunken fun and she didn't wish him any physical harm, but he could end her career. Was she in danger from Ray Mason? She could just go to the cops. What would she say?

Tara smiled from ear to ear and gasped as a dolphin's fin broke the surface of the water just off the port bow, moving at the same speed in the same direction. She became more daring, sheeting in harder, lifting the hull higher out of the water. The dolphin responded by leaping clear of the water.

Maybe it was time to resign from QSR. She didn't need the money. People like Tommo had made a stand and listened to their conscience. What would she do if she didn't have to commute into the city or work late nights? She could start her own business. It wasn't too late to start a family. It wasn't her move to make. She didn't have to be forced into making any decisions yet. The only decision she had to make now was whether to tack or gybe to head back towards the shore.

- # -

Time rolled around like a cut-scene in a video game. Tommo woke to the sound of crickets. He felt like he was in the game Tara had referenced at the Pub Quiz, like Arthur Morgan, late in the final chapter, camped in the wilderness with only tinned goods to eat. The animated depictions of eating food were very well observed for the most part, eating stew with a spoon from a bowl and shaking the dregs out of a coffee mug, but drinking from a can as if it was a pint glass seemed a little lazy and it wasn't clear how the outlaw opened them.

Tommo used a Swiss Army knife to saw around the lid of a tin of creamed corn then, because this wasn't a video game, used a spoon to eat from the can. He took a swig of water from his trusty canteen. No. Wrong game franchise, that was a different protagonist in a post-apocalyptic wasteland.

Like Red Dead Redemption's Arthur, Tommo had a journal. Forgotten in one of the many useful pockets in the backpack was a Moleskine notebook. He used to write every day, even when he was living the same day over and over again in Dubai. Wake, gym, Careem to work, meetings, lunch, meetings, bar, video games or Netflix, sleep. He liked to think that one day, if he ever stopped moving around, he would have a library or a study with all his Moleskine notebooks lined up in chronological order. His phone was still charging, slowly now that the sun was low, about to disappear completely from the clearing. He had nothing better to do than read the pages and see if there were any clues to what he should do next.

Today was one of those days that makes you wonder
if the concept of a fair go is dead. Networking.
The usual mix of champagne, small talk, and
schmoozing with the elite crowd including Trevor
Stone. He's got everyone fooled. Certainly
charming, cleverer than he looks, and he looks like
a predator, and entitled one at that. He's not just
another tech bro. He's dangerous. He's the kind of
guy who knows the rules don't apply to him, who can
get away with anything because he has the money and
the power to make it happen and his million
Instagram followers love him. While he pays QSP a
million bucks a year to keep his accounts looking
clean, they aren't going to tell anyone that the
business is a scam.

Tommo flipped further through the old diary.

Big data breach today at one of the biggest health
insurers. QSP is in the running to do an audit of
the systems and recommend solutions. Trever Stone

is bidding to replace current systems with a
blockchain solution, but it seems like vapourware.
Definitely some backhanders going on somewhere.

Tommo closed the book and looked down the track. *Where are you Bondy?*

DISCARDING DECENCY

3

Claudine 'Bondy' Seaton-Bond's tomboyish nature earned her the nickname 'James' at the Roedean School in Brighton where she boarded while her parents moved between British embassies during her formative years. After being expelled from a string of prestigious boarding schools, she had worked on superyachts in the summer and taught skiing at high-end French and Swiss resorts in winter. She'd been a nanny for a minor Saudi royal family and personal assistant to the partner in a hedge fund, all roles that required a certain amount of discretion and secret keeping. Only a couple of old school-friends call her James these days. Many of the superyacht captains she worked for were ex-navy and just used her surname.

Then one summer she found herself on a yacht chartered as a spectator vessel for the 31st America's Cup in Barcelona. While Australia had no team entered in the regatta, there were Aussies everywhere and so Bond became Bondy in an ironic nod to the infamous Australian entrepreneur who had funded Australia's victory in the 1983 Cup campaign. She remembers exactly who had given her the nickname Bondy, one of the Aussies in town for the regatta was Travis Thomson.

Bondy stood beside her Land Rover across the street from the

Shark Byte Café and watched trouble walk through the door.

- # -

The Shark Byte Cafe was a 'hybrid experience.' The front half was a cafe designed for the laptop worker crowd: large tabletops, power for chargers, and free Wi-Fi. The back half of the store was filled with Kelpie's branded surf gear along with the kinds of gifts you would find showcased by PR firms in the colour weekend supplement of the broadsheet newspapers: artisan scented candles and soaps, perfumed with native flowers, local organic wines, mostly peppery Pinot Noir varieties, and a collection of lavender products from a farm up the road. On the walls were a couple of her own framed photos and watercolours of the local landscape.

Holding her Pilote branded travel mug in both hands, Marta surveyed the store from behind the glass display case that doubled as a till. The bell above the door jangled as a male figure entered the store. Instinctively, something made Marta glance at the time stamp on the CCTV monitor beside the register. The figure was wearing a baseball cap, the brim pulled down to cover his face from the cameras and moved with purpose towards the changing rooms at the back of the shop. Marta didn't know whether to laugh or be enraged. The cap was red, with large white letters on the front panel reading MAGA. She watched him warily as he rummaged through the rack of sale items, grabbing a hoodie and bringing it towards her at the counter.

"My nephew will kill me if I don't get him this brand," the man said in a not quite right southern drawl, placing the hoodie on the glass topped case beside the till. Marta's heart was thumping in her chest. She put on a fake smile and folded the hoodie into a neat square.

"Will that be cash or card?" The man's demeanour changed as he heard her accent. His face reddened to match the hue of his cap and his lip curled as he pushed the hoodie away in disgust.

"Not enough that you people have to infest the States, you're fucking here too," the man snarled, "I thought the Aussies had a system for keeping your kind out." Marta tried to breathe deeply as her nails dug into her clenched palms. The bell above the door rang out again and she breathed a little easier as she recognised a striking blonde woman who she knew could handle herself.

"Fucking spics, coons and dykes," the archaically ebullient American spat as he pushed his way past a life-size cardboard cutout of Archie from back in the day.

"I hate it when I feel like I have to apologise for a whole country" Marta said, "It's one thing to have your opinions in Alabama, but I'm not sure we have to hear them on the other side of the world."

"You don't need to apologise to me babe." Claudine said with both arms outstretched. "But you do need to give me a hug and then make me a double espresso." The two women stood in an overdue embrace. "So, this is where you and Archie ended up,"

"This is where all the magic happens." Marta swept her hand as if revealing a prize on a gameshow. "Archie and I bought it just before the pandemic, which was a stroke of luck, because the remote work thing really took off and all the surfing events around the world were cancelled. What are you up to? I haven't seen you since you were with Tommo. Is that why you're here? Has he been in contact?" Claudine slipped a card out of her back pocket and handed it to Marta with both hands the way she had been taught in Japan.

"A printed business card. That's so old school." Marta said. "Claudine 'Bondy' Seaton Bond, Concierge?" She took out her phone and scanned the QR code on the card.

"It's French, and it sounds better than fixer or troubleshooter"

"Oui? It's French, is it? So is Fuquoo," Marta joked in a bad accent. "We lived in Biarritz for two years. I hated it." She scrolled down on her phone. "BA0001.com doesn't give much away."

Bondy shrugged. "I probably don't need a website. Most of my business comes through referrals. And sometimes... I help out lovable muppets who get themselves in too deep with people they really shouldn't." Bondy put on a Pilote baseball cap and looked in the mirror. "Where is he holed up anyway?"

"Archie can take you to him, but you'll have to wait. We haven't had a swell like this since before Christmas and he gets a bit crazy if it's too long between waves. Did you bring your board?"

Bondy walked over to a rack of mini-mals. "7'2 might work for me," she said, running her fingers down the rail of a glistening fibreglass custom surfboard. "But I really shouldn't be having fun. When this thing with Tommo is all over and done with, maybe I'll buy this bad boy, if Archie signs it." She took the cap off and placed it on the counter. "I'll take this now though."

"Where are you staying? You can crash with us if you like."

"I'm not staying. The plan is to pick up Tommo, take him back to Melbourne or somewhere clear of here for a few days, then we can make a proper plan. And now I've told you too much."

The bell over the door chimed and Archie walked in carrying his surfboard. He smiled with recognition as he saw Bondy and gave her a hug with his spare arm.

"Sorry, sorry. It was epic and as you once told me Bondy, the world isn't going to spin off its axis in the next couple of hours."

"And if it does, we have bigger things to worry about," she finished. "But we do need to get on the road. There was a guy in here earlier who was not a tourist, reeked of private security. Marta, save that CCTV tape for me, will you?"

- # -

Tommo heard the percussive clatter of his rudimentary warning device. It was the kind of alarm that the Famous Five or the Hardy Boys would have rigged up. He had strung a few empty tins across the track and dropped a few stones and old nails in each. The rattle was loud enough to be heard over the birdlife and the creek. The engine noise of Bondy's restored Land Rover County grew louder, pulling up just outside the clearing.

"Cuppa tea?" Tommo quipped in a bad English accent. Bondy flicked her hair behind her ear and closed the distance between them quickly. Archie stayed in the car and gave them a moment to catch up. They hugged in silence for a minute and then Bondy opened an Esky and handed Tommo a cold Corona. They both laughed.

"I'm missing something obviously," Archie said.

"It's a long story," Bondy offered. "But basically, it's our shorthand estimate of the size of a job or a problem."

"I hope you brought a couple of cases then." Tommo clincked his bottle with the others.

"I would have, but someone has to drive and I'm not letting you behind the wheel of my baby." The men watched with awe and amusement as Claudine finished the beer in two long gulps. "You know what they say about that stuff. It's like having sex in a canoe."

"Fucking close to water," the men said in unison.

"Are you packed?" Bondy was already getting back in the car. Tommo was all ready to go. He lifted his only bag and threw it on the back seat of the Land-Rover. She looked him up and down as he slid in the front. "Still not in the habit of wearing shoes I see?"

"Good luck guys, let me know if you need anything." Archie waved them off as Bondy slowly navigated the 4WD only track.

"What took you so long?" asked Tommo as he looked over at the driver's seat.

"I was on a boat in the middle of Bass Strait you dickhead," Bondy replied, slightly annoyed having cut short her post race celebrations in Hobart to come to his rescue.

"Oh right, how'd you do?" His mind flashed back to the night of the quiz and the van fire and the missing bit. Tara.

"I was on Trever Stone's boat. Good result but it cost him a fortune. We blew out the spinnaker just past the heads. He should have paid more for his bowman."

Tommo was seeing a name start to repeat itself. "How do you

know Stone?"

"I don't really," she became defensive. "Yacht Racing is a small world though, always the same faces. Though we haven't seen your face in the beer tent in Cowes or at The Bugle for a while."

"Still living the nomadic life, I see? One gig at a time?" He couldn't keep up with her travels. Her Instagram feed was full of airport codes that he had never heard of like YNB and SKB.

"Yeah, but it's not as much fun as it looks on the socials. Scratch that, sometimes it is a lot of fun, and it's more fun than being broke and hunted by the Illuminati or some cabal." She looked over at Tommo and sighed with a mix of pity and affection, "You look like shit. You're a good-looking guy… when you shave."

"My suit is in the bag. I don't have a tie though. Ooh, can we stop and pick one up? Wait, I think David Jones does 'Click and Collect.'" There was silence between them for a while.

"Weird isn't it." Bondy pulled her sunglasses down as she shared her latest insight. "Suits and ties are still seen as a proxy for status and power and trust. The good old class-system at work. Us and them." She accelerated to pass a semi-trailer full of fast-fashion. "Just be glad you're not a girl." Silence again as they passed cars packed full of beach gear and paraphernalia heading off on summer holidays.

"Do you care where the money comes from?" Tommo asked.

"More and more. I guess that's why I am here. It would be nice to create something or know that what I am doing is making the world a better place, but who can afford to think like that? That's the capitalist bargain." She flipped the shade down as the sun sank lower. "In the immortal words of David Lee Roth, money can't buy you happiness, but it can buy you a yacht big enough to sail right up next to it."

"Jeff Bezos must be a huge Van Halen fan."

"Perfect case in point… Once you get to a trillion dollars or so, you can afford to save the planet."

Tommo looked down at his phone as it found a proper data

network and chimed with a new message from an unknown number. He decided not to open it for now.

"Where are we going?" Tommo asked as the skyline of Melbourne appeared like a grey Tetris piece on the horizon.

"Docklands. I have a small place there. Why?"

Tommo looked down at his dirty bare feet. "I'm guess I'm gunna to have to buy some shoes."

- # -

"I like what you've done with the place." Tommo laughed as he walked around Bondy's sparsely decorated Docklands apartment wearing nothing but a towel.

"If you are going to be a smartass, I will call Ray Mason personally and drop you at the gates of Monaghan in a hogtie," she called out from the bedroom. Tommo looked at the fridge and browsed the magnets that were the only sign of personalisation. He picked one of the souvenirs off the door and inspected the representation of a Greek temple. Underneath it read Aegina.

"I think I bought you this one." He remembered the hot bus ride and the sound of cicadas.

Bondy pushed past him to get to a bottle of Pinot Gris. "Will you put some clothes on please? We are not sleeping together, not today, not ever again." Her eyes roamed up and down his body, which hadn't changed much except for the beer gut. He was probably in better shape than when she met him on a superyacht in Barcelona. She considered the implications of them falling into bed as if the last time they saw each other was yesterday. "Having said that, you do know what I like. Do you know how long it takes to go from 'Likes long walks on the beach' to 'Choke me'?" She sat down on the couch and poured two glasses of the wine. "You don't have to wear shoes. Just put on a pair of shorts and a top. We have work to do."

Tommo padded into the only bedroom and slipped into a pair of boardshorts and a polo shirt. He looked out the window at the Melbourne skyline from the defunct Star Ferris wheel to the stadium sponsored by Marvel beside the station he knew as Spencer Street – it was Southern Cross now. The shape of the city had changed a lot since the Rialto tower was the tallest building. There were changes at ground level too. More Asian influence. More money. More poverty. Returning to the living room he sat beside Bondy on her functional, no-fuss, couch and picked up a glass.

"What do we know?"

"Jesus. You're the Quantum Strategy consultant mate" Bondy rolled her eyes. "Let's start with Mason. He took the biggest hit. A very public humiliation. He lost his power and privilege and he's the one who knew you were back in the country." She refilled the glasses, stood up and took another bottle out of the fridge.

"He also has the most still to lose," Tommo added. "Monaghan is worth a bunch, but it's not liquid. He gets cash from his Airbnbs, but again, not enough to fund his lifestyle. There must be something else he's into.

"See, now you're thinking like one of them." Bondy paced around the small living space between the coffee table and the kitchen, sipping from her wine glass. "Let's stay away from that part of the world for a couple of days. Archie and Marta can be our eyes and ears for now." She sat back down on the couch. "You know QSP better than me, but chances are they burnt Mason, and they've moved on. Unless you have something that is more than you had before, something that implicates them in criminal activity. They won't be wasting much time on you. But it seems we have an insider. Your new girlfriend." She grinned.

Tommo frowned. "Girlfriend?"

"I had coffee with Marta, Tommo, I know everything that's happened to you and the rest of the town for the last two years, right down to the fact that you spent the night before your van blew up in the bed of a woman you'd only just met." She grinned back at him. "Which is the other reason you are sleeping on the couch."

"Oh. Tara." Tommo rose from the couch and paced the same pattern around the floorspace.

"She could be an asset babe. She is still on the inside, and they can't sack her. They could haul her in and make her tell them if and how she is involved, but she's an Asian female and she could take them to the cleaners if they tried to get rid of her."

"She could also help them get to me." They swapped positions again, Bondy pacing, Tommo sitting.

"We can test her. Give her some red herrings and see where the information ends up, but you will need to talk to her. Has she reached out?"

"She might have. I got a message from an unknown number, but it's vague."

"She works in the city, so maybe we can arrange a meeting up here, away from the scene of the crimes." Bondy squatted in front of Tommo, lifting his chin to meet his eyes. "And then you have me." He nodded and smiled. "And I have white skin, blonde hair, blue eyes and great tits." She shook her shoulders, and his eyes dropped to her chest. She lifted his chin again. "You know, of all the men I know, and certainly all the ones I've slept with, you are the one that seemed least interested in my breasts."

"I'm a leg man?"

- # -

Alone on the back porch of her Airbnb, Tara refilled her glass and looked out at the moon on the water and the reflection of the pier in the sea. Her hour-long escape on the rented catamaran had refreshed her and exhausted her at the same time. She looked down at her phone. The message to Tommo still had only one tick. Delivered. Not read.

Her thumbs moved over the keypad.

```
It's Tara. Hope you are okay. I want to help.
```

This time, the delivered tick appeared immediately. She waited. A second blue tick appeared. He'd read it. *Would he want my help? What help could I actually give? Why am I getting involved?* She knew the answer to the last one. Her unconscious mind had worked away in the back of her head while she was cavorting with a dolphin, watching it swim under the netting of the catamaran and leap out ahead of the hulls as she gybed her way back to the beach club of the resort. She was done with doing what people expected of her. She was done with pretending to be something she wasn't. She wanted to be with people who did the right thing because they wanted to, not because they thought they had to.

She swiped to the email app on her phone. 1 unread work message marked urgent from her boss, a calendar invitation, for the next morning, in the office, in the city. No dial in or videoconference link was included. The subject line: Security Breach

- # -

Bondy pushed Tommo back on the couch and thought for a second about straddling his lap. His phone pinged. The same number as before, but this time it said it was Tara.

"It says it's her." Tommo showed the phone screen.

"Okay, so how do you want to play it? I think we should stay in the city. Safety in numbers, use the crowds to our advantage," Bondy advised, looking over his shoulder at the phone.

```
Tommo: I'm OK. In the city. I'll be off grid for a
couple of days.

   Tara: I need to go into the office tomorrow for
```

an hour. We could meet? 5pm?

Tommo: 'meeting' sculpture, Docklands. We can take
a walk. I'll send you a pin.
https://maps.app.goo.gl/8v78TowH9Wrojdau9

Somewhere in the back of his head, the paranoia was coming back. *Why does she have to go to the office in the middle of her holiday?* He felt his head nodding. Each nod got longer as he willed himself awake long enough to see if she replied. He didn't make it, he was out, crashed on the couch. Claudine smiled, pulled a light blanket over him and kissed his forehead.

- # -

Tommo waited beside the modern sculpture titled 'Meeting 1'; eight bright red moulded figures squatting in a circle. Bondy sat on a nearby bench and pretended to be busy with her phone as Tara approached. Tommo almost didn't recognise the woman he'd only met once and briefly. Her hair was tied back in a single ponytail, she wore fitted suit trousers and jacket over a pale blue collared shirt. She was all business except for her shoes. She had changed out of her heels in the car park and slipped into the deck shoes she lived most of her non-corporate life in. Hers were weathered and worn in, his were stiff and shiny and new, having been purchased 20 minutes earlier at the outlet mall. He extended his palm, gesturing like an usher toward the path along the banks of the Yarra River, pointing in the direction of the CBD, against the flow of the famously brown water. At first, neither of them spoke. "It must have been important," he began, "to summon you from your holiday into the mothership."

"I can't really talk about it. You know how it is. You of all people know how it is." She stopped and turned to him. "I'm going to resign. It's been coming for a while, but it's never too late to do the right thing, is it?" A smile came to her face as she watched an electric party boat glide silently up the river. "I told them today that I am going to leave. I think they think it's a play for a promotion or more money."

Tommo's head was spinning. They began walking again in step. "You said you wanted to help. I know you can't give them a reason to fire you, so you can't tell me anything that is privileged, but I need to know if they are still after me, or whether Ray Mason is acting on his own."

"They are worried about more leaks and if you are holding anything back. If there is more to come out? Who would be implicated? Hey!" She cursed as a delivery guy on a silent electric scooter, in custody of someone's chicken parma, came up from behind and swerved around them at speed. "I don't think they would sanction premeditated murder on Australian soil, it would be simpler just to pay you off. If you have more material."

"The stuff I have relating to the firm is not criminal. It shows that most of them are ethically bankrupt, but people know that by now. There was a cover up relating to the party at Monaghan, but only some of the guests invited were from the company. My guess is that there is more to be found in Mason's files." Tommo shivered as one of the the tower's shadow grew longer and swallowed up the sunlight on the path.

"What if he was forced to sell it?" Tara spoke her thoughts out loud, and Tommo stopped in his tracks. She kept going. "Interest rates are going up. The cost of utilities is through the roof. The upkeep of Monaghan must be pretty steep. I'm sure he doesn't do the mowing himself." Tara's enthusiasm grew. "What if we work out where his cash is coming from and squeeze until it dries up. A few 1-star reviews of his BnBs on Tripadvisor, maybe even a ransomware con." She smirked, revelling in being able to be part of the plotting.

"Okay, let's try and keep it legal," he cautioned. "Coincidentally, the person I am staying with could probably arrange something like a ransomware attack. I'm sure Mace pays half his bills by phone."

Tara turned and began to walk back in the opposite direction watching the planes over the Bolte Bridge on the inbound flight path for Tullamarine. "Maybe I'll buy Monaghan." She was only half joking. Tommo laughed out loud and then checked himself. He really didn't know that much about her. She was certainly not predictable, which made her hard to trust completely.

Claudine was waiting for them as they made it back around the distinctive pineapple shaped apartment block beside the sculpture. She held out her hand to Tara. "Hi. I'm Claudine, but Tommo calls me Bondy." She shook Tara's hand firmly. "You must be Tara." She looked at Tommo and raised both eyebrows in approval. "Punching above your weight again, aren't you?" She watched Tara flush red then continued. "I've booked us a table for an early dinner. It's just a pub in Port Melbourne that does a good steak. It's not far. We can get an Uber." Bondy laid out the plan as a fait accompli. "You'll be joining us won't you Tara, I want to know all about you."

Holding up a carpark ticket like a 'get out of jail free' card, Tara backed away from Tommo's friend who was obviously an ex. "I need to rescue my car from over there" She pointed towards the small mall of shops that backed onto a newly opened Marriott hotel. "I can make an early dinner. Send me the address and I'll meet you there." She hated this part of town. It was soulless and empty and that was on a work-day in rush hour. On the Friday before the New Year's Eve holiday weekend it was like a ghost town, shops shut, a lone underpaid security guard forced to make an hourly sweep to move on anyone who didn't have a reason to be there, and no-one had a reason to be there. She liked Tommo, and she liked that she could be useful to him. She was still playing some of her cards close to her chest though, and with the arrival of Bondy, she felt a little intimidated and to be honest, jealous. *I wonder if Ray Mason plays poker*, she wondered, slipping into a fantasy world where she imagined taking him to the cleaners, having to bet the ranch to save his pride. The ranch with Monaghan written on the gate.

- # -

The imprint above the door says the Railway Club Hotel dates from 1875. It's a local's pub, known for its steak nights. Tara parked her car, entered the building, and scanned the crowd. Tommo and Bondy were drinking beer at the bar, the blonde's hair thrown back as she laughed at something Tommo had just said.

"I blame the Consorzio del Vermouth di Torino." Bondy nodded to the barman to order another round of pints, increasing the order to three to include Tara without asking what she wanted. "Nobody wants to drink vermouth, they never have. I think it was Churchill who said about his dry Martini - Glance at the vermouth bottle briefly while pouring the juniper distillate freely." The grinning English girl put her arm around Tara and guided her into the spare barstool beside them. "So glad you could make it babe, next time we should do just the two of us and leave this sap to his own devices." She barely took a breath before continuing her Negroni rant. "The pundits say that a Negroni is an acquired taste which is a bit like saying that an arty film that nobody understands or wants to watch is critically acclaimed. In other words, it's an affectation. It's a way to signal your Instagram followers that you are sophisticated, while telling everyone else that you have no taste at all." Bondy took a long drink from her fresh beer. "If you want to have a classic cocktail that challenges a barman, order an Old Fashioned," she continued. "They hate it, especially if it's busy."

"I was told never to mix whiskey with anything." Tara had grown up thinking that all spirits were mixed with Coke. "I was at Bourbon and Beefsteak. You know that infamous 24/7 bar in Sydney's Kings Cross. I'm not sure if it is even there anymore. Maybe they killed it with changes to the drinking laws." She took a long sip from her beer, matching Bondy's pace and recounting the tale from her formative past. "Don't get me started on the puritanism of Australian lawmakers… Anyway, the lesson was there are only two things that you put in Whiskey…" She paused. "Water."

"Or more whiskey" Bondy finished her sentence for her. She held up her glass to touch it together with the others in a toast, leaning across and whispering in Tara's ear. "We are going to be friends. I can tell."

Tara felt like she was being vetted. Bondy was obviously very protective of Tommo, and it was clear why he would have reached out to her for help. Nothing seemed to phase her. She had an effortless 'I don't give a fuck' kind of confidence that came from a total sense of security in all things. Tara thought when she got money, she would be able to care less, but because it had arrived out of nowhere, she assumed that it would vanish just as easily.

"Tara had some thoughts about a plan of attack. A few campaigns if you will, to destroy Ray Mason for once and for all." Tommo cut into his rib-eye, which for some reason was called a Scotch Fillet in Australia.

"Oh, do tell." Bondy leaned in conspiratorially. "He sounds like a pervert. The bad kind, not the kind you wish you would stumble across on Tinder." She winked at Tara. "You know what I mean girl." Tara turned bright red. "What does your profile say? Hmmm? Shall we see if you come up in my feed? I'd swipe right on you."

Tommo tried to move the conversation on. "All Mason has left is the property. What if we could force him to sell it?"

"Yesterday, you were almost incinerated in your sleep, and today, you want to go on the offensive against an unknown enemy. I can't imagine he'd go down without a fight." Bondy was sceptical of the plan.

"We need to know where he gets his funds," Tommo continued. "He's mixed up in something dirty and it might even be taking place on the property. Can we fly a drone over it or something?"

"Technically, you can fly a drone over private property as long as it is 30 meters away from people," Tara said. "In Victoria, I'd need to refresh myself on the Privacy and Data Protection Act" She looked directly at Tommo. "Luckily we aren't in NSW, there are about 12 laws relating to drones and privacy including the Caravan Parks Act and the Workplace Surveillance Act." The other two looked at her and did a soft clap. She continued despite their mocking. "Even if Ray saw a drone flying over his property, as long as we didn't publish photos of him or others, he would struggle to find the pilot."

"Marta has a drone that she uses to film Archie with for his YouTube channel," Tommo said. "It wouldn't look suspicious if you went in over the point. You could say it got caught by the wind."

"You must have gone that way yesterday for your escape," Bondy said, bringing up Google Map satellite view. "Did you see anything out of the ordinary?"

Tommo cast his mind back. "I did actually. There is a gate on the opposite side. It opens out onto the fire-track. Very old gate with a very new padlock. There were tracks too. Single tread, maybe a dirt bike. But if they are taking things out by bike, they can't be big payloads."

"Right." Bondy was taking charge. She fed Tommo a cooked cherry tomato from her plate making Tara frown unconsciously. "We do a bit of recon, see if there is anything out of place at Monaghan. Some of that can be desk research and maybe we get Marta and Archie involved." She emptied a bottle of Mornington Peninsula Pinot Noir into her glass, looking at Tara. "You brought your car, you've had enough." She continued with her summary. "Tara, keep an ear out for what QSP is doing and if you want to do some forensic accounting, go for it. I'll look into some of the more morally challenging activities like how we could swindle or trick him out of some money. See if he is vulnerable on the crypto side." She put her arm around Tommo and pulled him close as she looked right at Tara. "Our boy keeps his head down. Stay in town for a day or two, not do anything to piss off the firm or draw attention, like being arrested or ending up in A&E."

Tara had been hoping that she could tempt Tommo back down

the coast. She didn't really want to be alone for New Years Eve, but it made sense that he lie low for now. Bondy looked right through her and smiled back at Tommo.

"You can't stay with me for long mate, you'll cramp my style. Oh, and I think I should spend some time down south, I could stay at the Oak, get on the inside. None of you can do that."

4

Lying on his back on the stock-standard display home couch he strained to hear something. Anything. Tommo felt unnerved. There was no distant white noise of waves, no shrill birds, not even the sound of a ticking clock. Then, through the wall, down the hall, the ping of an elevator helped to remind him that he was in an apartment building in the glass and concrete wasteland that was Docklands.

He'd vaguely clocked the sound of the door earlier. Bondy was off on her morning run, which meant he was alone in the flat. Getting up with a slight groan, he opened the fridge and chuckled. Nothing perishable, nothing that could go off. He considered opening a bottle of champagne before closing the fridge and finding the coffee in the freezer. He spooned the grounds into a retro stovetop espresso maker, screwing on the top and placing it on the smallest electric element. A few minutes later, the silence was replaced with bubbling and hissing as the pot told him his coffee was ready.

What now? This one-bedroom apartment was already beginning to feel like a prison. *Surely I don't have to suffer the torture of linear television.* The Aussies had beaten Pakistan with a day to spare at the MCG, so there was no cricket to watch. Tommo opened the EPG and scrolled down the schedule shaking his head. The world was so small.

Pawn Stars and Pointless, yet more Midsomer Murders and MasterChef. One entry stood out. Spicks and Specks, an ancient music trivia quiz hosted by Australian comedian Adam Hills was on its 900th repeat. The Bee Gees had released a song of the same name in 1966, and it seemed highly appropriate given the events of the night before. According to Reddit, which made it irrefutably true, spicks and specks is:

> ... an old Bronx derived term referring to past women & girlfriends in your life, that at the time, you may've cast aside as light weight, unimportant etc but on years later reflection you wonder where they are now and could've had a more meaningful positive impact.

As if on cue, Bondy came through the door, glistening with sweat from her 'quick' 10kms and holding a newspaper. "What are you watching? Is that Adam Hills? He looks about 12." She stood and looked around to see if he'd trashed the joint while she'd been away, nodding at the coffee pot. "Aren't you resourceful? Sorry, there is no milk. If you want a flat white, we can get one delivered."

Tommo shook his head at the concept of being able to summon a single cup of coffee on an app and have it appear. "I've given up exploitation, remember?"

"Oh, get off your high horse, you could become a door-dash driver, make some money, one takeaway at a time." She dropped the paper on the kitchen countertop, took a bottle of water out of the freezer and rehydrated. "I'm taking a shower, no peeking."

Tommo held up his hand to stop her. "Hey, you got a laptop or a computer I can use? Mine burnt up. I can't just sit and watch TV for the next couple of days. Maybe I can dig deeper or go over what I have with a different lens."

Bondy returned from the bedroom with a Mac. "I know you're a Windows guy, and an Android guy, but the beautiful people like me use Apple." She posed with the laptop like a 70s trade show model.

"It's a kind of virtue signalling, like putting the right books in your Zoom background." It didn't really matter, everything Tommo needed was accessible via a browser. As the computer booted, he nodded with approval as the VPN loaded. Bondy stood over his shoulder, still in her jogging gear. "I remember some of the things you taught me. There is a Tor browser too, in case you want to get really dark."

The screen became his world. The box he sat in made no difference. It could be a cubicle in a cavernous internet cafe or a table at a Starbucks or the tray table of an A380. It didn't matter if there was no sound, or if the sounds were being compensated for using noise-cancelling headphones. With the smell of coffee and a hint of Claudine's post run sweat in his nostrils, he began to work.

- # -

The old farmer squinted at Tara, a bemused smile tugging at the corners of his mouth as he watched her bend over to inspect the motocross bike he'd listed for sale on the Gumtree marketplace. It wasn't every day that someone like her showed up at his farm, especially not dressed like she'd just stepped out of a fan convention for 'The Dukes of Hazzard'. She wore short denim shorts, a chequered shirt tied at the front, revealing a hint of her midriff, and a well-worn Akubra hat. The look was distinctly Australian with a twist of Hollywood flair, completed by her scuffed RM Williams riding boots. Despite the outfit, she seemed more prepared for a show-jumping event than for straddling the Yamaha dirt bike she was now examining with a critical eye.

The man's brain was trying to reconcile the Asian face with the authenticity of the hat. Undeniably genuine. The Akubra was decades old, the brim faintly creased and worn from years of use, each wrinkle a testament to the countless times it had been pulled down to shield its wearer from the harsh Australian sun or sudden downpours. Around the base of the crown, the leather band showed signs of wear, its rich brown hue mellowed by age and exposure to the elements. It was the kind of hat that spoke of long days in the outback, of cattle drives and campfires, not something you'd expect to see on someone who looked like - her. His brow furrowed even more when she spoke.

Her voice carried a broad Aussie accent that didn't match the image he'd unconsciously formed in his mind. "Been stored inside or out in the open?" she asked, brushing some dried mud off the bike's front headlight as if she was a professional appraiser.

The farmer shifted his weight, still trying to wrap his head around the scene. "It's been under a tarp in the shed," he replied, his voice tinged with a hint of sorrow. "It was my son's, but he moved away."

Tara nodded, seemingly satisfied with his answer. She straightened up and reached into her pocket, pulling out a thick wad of fresh 'watermelon' $100 bills. Without hesitation, she began counting out $2,000, the slippery notes snapping neatly as she placed them in his hand. "What do you call these? Jolly Green Giants? Bradmans?"

The farmer's eyes widened as he looked down at the money. He'd heard about these new bills but had never held one himself. "I've never seen one before," he muttered. He held one of the plastic notes up to the sky to check for the multiple anti-counterfeit measures. Suspicion briefly clouded his face. "You better not be trying to pass me fake bills, love."

Tara laughed, a light, carefree sound that put him somewhat at ease. "I just want to get on the road," she replied, switching to a playful southern drawl that caught him off guard. Before he could say more, she had already moved to the back of her pickup, expertly attaching the trailer as if she'd done it a thousand times. To her, it was routine - trailers were trailers, whether they were loaded with a bike, a boat, or anything in between. The farmer stood there, watching in disbelief as she secured the bike onto the trailer with practised ease.

When she was done, she turned back to him, offering a quick wave. "Thanks, mate," she called out, her tone now back to its original Aussie lilt. Then, without further ado, she climbed into the driver's seat, fired up the engine, and pulled away from the farm, leaving the old man standing there, the notes still clutched in his hand.

As Tara drove down the dusty driveway, she couldn't help but grin. The bike was hers, and now she was headed for the clearing and the hut that Tommo had described in his story of escape. Her mission was clear: check out the gate and the tire tracks, see what she could learn about the mysterious goings-on at Monaghan. She reached over to her phone, syncing it with the truck's Bluetooth. "Let's see what the AI gods have chosen for this drive," she said in anticipation. The streaming app selected a song from its vast library, and as the first notes filled the cabin, she rolled down the driver's side window, letting the wind whip through her hair. The beat kicked in, and she couldn't resist - her voice joined the music, belting out the lyrics as if she were at a karaoke bar at a Hen's night.

> *"I'm gonna aim my headlights into your bedroom windows*
> *Throw empty beer cans at both of your shadows*
> *I didn't come here to start a fight,*
> *but I'm up for anything tonight*
> *You know you broke the wrong heart baby,*
> *and drove me redneck crazy"*

- # -

A flock of parrots scattered from the trees around the clearing as Tara revved the 450cc engine. It had been a while since she had ridden something with this much power and that was this high off the ground, but she was sure it would come back to her, like… riding a bike. She had swapped her felt hat for a helmet found in a plastic tub in her Mum's shed, a detour she made last night on the way out of the city.

She accelerated gently down the track with no name towards the sea in the opposite direction that Tommo had walked, speeding up as she grew in confidence. The vegetation became a green brown blur, her vision focussed on the surface of the track, looking for holes and bumps and obstructions. She whooped as the bike became airborne, launched into the air off a tree root atop a crest. *Why do I work in the city again? Why did I give up motocross riding?* On the left-hand side of the road, the wild bush gave way to unkempt grass fields bordered by native pines planted as a wind-break and a simple rusted barbed wire fence. Tara slowed the bike so she could keep a look out for the gate and the new padlock Tommo had described. And there it was.

Dismounting her ride, Tara bent down to inspect the tire treads. They were recent. The pub quiz had been abandoned because of the torrential rain that had filled the dams and birdbaths around the area. The puddles on the road where she stood had evaporated almost entirely leaving the surface softer than it would normally be at this time of year. The tyre tracks had been made after the rain. After the rain, but before Tommo had used the track, because any vehicle would have had to pass through the clearing to get to the highway. Tara compared the imprint with the tyres on the bike she bought earlier in the day, same thickness, same tread pattern. A dirt bike. Which would mean that the payload would have to be transported in a backpack. *Pills? Currency? Cold storage wallets? What is light and valuable?*

She inspected the padlock that secured a gleaming metal chain around the gate and its left post. The metal was shiny, the paint intact. New. Like the chain. What Tommo hadn't said was that it was a combination lock with 3 tumblers, which would be useful if multiple people had to use the gate, you wouldn't need to keep cutting keys. *A padlock on a gate. So what? She laughed. What am I doing?*

She looked around the area as she thought she should. *That's what they do on NCIS and CSI. That's when the clue that would solve the whole case would magically appear. The rider would have forgotten to close the backpack fully and an obscurely branded chip packet that could only be bought in a certain store would be found in the bushes.* And there it was, a bright flash of orange among the dried leaves and grasses. Samboy, BBQ flavour. Available everywhere.

- # -

Bondy rode the lift from her apartment down to the garage and studied the three options she had available to her. She hadn't bought the small flat for the view or the floorplan, it was the spaces in the basement that she needed for her toy collection. She desperately wanted to choose the Buell Hammerhead 1190 motorcycle, but if surfboards and dirt roads were going to be involved it would be the least practical. Similarly, the Abarth 595 painted in the traditional Ferrari colour of Azzurro La Plata would get her there with a smile on her face but not be flexible enough for the assignment at hand. The obvious choice was the fully restored British Racing Green 1985 Land Rover 110 County, the car she had rescued Tommo with.

A nice sounding young man from The Royal Oak had called to say that there had been a cancellation and if she wanted the room, she could have it. It was earlier than she had planned to go back, but Tommo was right - what was she going to do in the city on a holiday weekend? She had left him upstairs with the paper opened to an article about an upcoming conference in Melbourne, her laptop and instructions not to empty her bar.

Thank goodness for the colonies, she thought as she slipped into the driver's seat on the right-hand side of the vehicle and gripped the wheel. For a moment she was transported back to summers on her grandfather's farm in Havant, in Hampshire. He'd let her sit on his knee and steer from the age of 8 and as soon as she was able to reach the pedals, she was allowed to take the 4WD into the village on the narrow country roads to the Royal Oak.

Getting around the laneways and fields of Hampshire was one thing, getting out of Melbourne given the extensive roadworks relating to metro tunnels and other grand infrastructure projects of 'The Big Build' was quite another. The GPS was rerouting her normal drive via Shepherd bridge in Footscray rather than over the Westgate Bridge. Claudine tuned into her daily music streaming mix which was a combination of Oz Rock, Britpop and 90s film soundtracks, punctuated with an annoying ad for personalised advertising that didn't have any personalisation at all. She called Tara.

"Hello?" Bondy's number came up as unknown on Tara's phone.

"Hey Babe, it's Bondy, just wanted to tell you that I am on my way down, I'll be staying at the Oak, and we should catch up, maybe do dinner together." There was silence on the line as Tara processed the information.

"Um…" Another silence. "Yeah, I'm... Maybe. Sure. Okay." She couldn't think of a plausible excuse for why not.

"Great. We won't do it at the Royal, maybe just get some fish and chips and eat them on the sand on the beach. Something simple. Or your choice, I steamrollered you last night, so you choose. I'll text you later."

- # -

Tara thought it sounded like a date. She couldn't figure Bondy out at all. *Is Tommo's ex hitting on me?* Slipping her helmet back on, Tara took one more look around the area surrounding the locked gate. She hadn't gained any new information, except for the timing of the bike. If they wanted anything more, they would have to find a way to do surveillance. It didn't matter that this had turned out to be a dead end, she had rediscovered her love of tearing along empty bush roads at literally breakneck speed.

Her head tilted as she heard the distinctive chatter of a trail-bike engine from the property beyond the gate. It would be over the hill, and she would be in line of sight in less than a minute. The race tactician in her took over. There was no cover, but the rider would not be able to hear her bike over theirs, so Tara hit the electric ignition and revved hard causing dirt to spray out behind her as she aimed for the cover of the bush while planning her second move. They would have to stop and open the lock, get the bike through the gate then relock. *A minute? Two?* One minute would give her 125 metres at 75kph, which was the maximum speed she calculated would be safe for this part of the track with the tree roots corrugating the surface. She would have to get off the track and let the rider pass, else he would see her on the road ahead. *Not the right.* The creek is not where she wanted to end up. She skidded to a stop and wheeled her bike into a gap in the scrub, keeping low. Her pursuer was in top gear as they came onto the straight part of the road toward her hiding spot. The engine note gave no indication of slowing. The doppler effect gave her comfort as the screaming din was loudest as she saw the blur of the other bike pass her and then the peacefulness of the wind in the trees returned punctuated by the ping of bell birds.

It was too risky to follow. If she was spotted it would raise suspicion with the other rider, but she had learned that the tracks from the other day were not a one-off and that the gate was being used regularly. They had to get onto the property, which meant they would have to trespass, or be invited. She called Tommo.

- # -

He was high on the hill, looking over the bridge to the MCG. Way up on high, the clock on the silo said 28 degrees. Tommo remembered that he had to get to Officeworks before it closed. None of the independent printers were open on any Saturday, let alone on the long weekend. Bondy had left The Age open for him as she hurriedly left for the coast. The article she'd seen brought home just how out of the loop he was.

```
Trevor Stone Announced as Keynote Speaker at
Controversial Forum

Trevor Stone, the Sydney based tech entrepreneur
has been confirmed as one of the key speakers at
the Quantum Strategy Global Forum making its much-
anticipated debut in Melbourne, Australia from the
2nd to the 5th of January.

Stone is a prominent figure in the Sydney social
scene, known for his extravagant lifestyle and
larger-than-life persona. Born into old money, he
grew up in the lap of luxury, surrounded by the
opulence and privilege that comes with being part
of one of Sydney's oldest and wealthiest families.

Despite his outward success however, Stone remains
a controversial figure, with many questioning the
source of his rapidly increasing wealth and the
ethics of his business practices.

Hosted at an undisclosed location, the Quantum
Strategy Global Forum promises to be a gathering of
the world's most influential leaders, policymakers,
and business tycoons.
```

Stone. That name kept bobbing to the surface like dead fish. Tommo had to get into that event somehow. He had been trying to work out a way to get into QSP, to know who they were talking to, who they were dealing with, but this much better. They were the main sponsor. This was the perfect event that the normally clueless marketing department would spend big on to get to the movers and shakers and mend some of the credibility and trust they had lost as a result of his own actions. But now he had a problem, only had a couple of days to find a way into one of the most secure and exclusive events on the corporate and government calendar.

The phone rang. *Strange. No-one ever rings anymore. They send texts.* The caller ID read Tara. "You sound out of breath. Where are you?"

"I've had a busy day," Tara panted as she spoke into phone above the distinctive call of whip birds. "I bought a bike. I checked out the padlock on the gate and I just missed being mown down by a courier coming out of the property."

"Wait, what kind of bike, that's like a 25km ride." He didn't know why he was surprised.

She kept an ear out for more traffic. "Trail bike. Off Gumtree."

"You and Bondy are like sisters. Yachting, motocross bikes, extreme sports." He changed tack. "Hey thanks for being a good sport last night. Bondy is..." He didn't finish the sentence, because he didn't know how to end it. "Why are you checking out the padlock and the gate?"

Tara was confused by the question. "Because that's what we agreed, last night. That was the plan."

"I'm not used to people actually executing a plan." He laughed, checked his watch, and began walking back towards the city, his shoes crunching on The Tan.

"We might need Archie's drone. You can't see over the hill from the road," Tara said. "Also, we need a way to tail the bikes that are coming out of the property, but it will be difficult, they are fast and can go pretty much anywhere."

"Good work Miss Fisher," Tommo teased as he stepped aboard a tram and checked to see if it was in the free zone before swiping his Myki pass. "I gotta go, I'll get in touch with Marta, she's the drone operator, Archie just smiles for the camera." He watched out the window of the empty tram as it trundled past the floral clock and the Arts Centre spire, over the Swanston Street bridge. "Oh, one more thing. Are you going to the QSP Forum next week?"

"I think the firm gets a few passes." She had thought about going so she could keep her options open "But it's just a lot of backroom deals and parties. Not really my thing." She was lying.

He could hear that she was being evasive. "It would be useful.

You could be our eyes and ears, maybe get an extra pass 'for a friend' or a new potential client. Actually, you know what? I'll ask Bondy. She was on Stone's boat for the Hobart, she can probably blag us a couple of tickets. Talk soon." He didn't want to push her too hard, but he also knew that Tara's competitive streak might push her to beat Claudine to the punch.

If neither Tara nor Bondy could come up with passes, he would have to get in another way. Running through his tried and tested ways of getting access to events that he wasn't on the guestlist for, Tommo calculated the odds of getting into the Forum and close to the players. Getting a media pass was usually the easiest option, but he would need to build a bit of a backstory, print some business cards, and maybe forge a press credential. Marta had a production company which, alongside Archies' YouTube channel, produced various podcasts and newsletters. She wouldn't mind writing him a letter as the commissioning editor saying he was working on a feature about climate change and sea levels or something that lined up with both the content of the event and her titles. The media pass would get him into the conference sessions but might not provide access to some of the more exclusive streams or side events. Tommo decided to register for media access anyway.

Option two would be to use someone else's ticket to gain access. He probably couldn't pull off passing for Tara, but there was no shortage of forty-something white guys in suits that had registered. This was a show-off ticket, especially if Trevor Stone was involved. A quick search of Linkedin and X had revealed people who were Stone groupies who had to tell the world that they would be there. Faked business cards would be required, but some of the companies were public and there were no secrets on the internet. Even a Google image search had brought back thousands of results showing photographs of actual business cards and their designs. The secret to the method was to find someone who said they were going but wouldn't show up or someone who wasn't known by everybody by their face.

Both strategies required the full, no questions asked self-services of Officeworks, the nearest of which was on Elizabeth Street near the Royal Arcade.

- # -

At the Shark Byte Cafe, a seasonal crowd filled the couches and benches. The laptop carrying remote work folks had been replaced with city types who had very strong views about the way they liked their coffee. It was not the vibe that Marta and Archie were used to, but these few weeks allowed them to charge a little holiday surcharge, and it helped them through the winter lull. Marta concentrated on the large computer monitor in front of her. The satellite layer of Google Maps illuminated her face. She had been poring over the map for longer than she could afford, meticulously calculating the range of her drone and strategizing the perfect launch point. Every detail mattered - where to maintain line of sight, where the drone could capture the most revealing images of the activities inside Monaghan. She zoomed in on the screen, her eyes narrowing as she focused on the area around the gate that had been investigated by Tommo and Tara in their missions up and down the fire track. Something unusual caught her attention, a faint pattern in the dirt that seemed out of place.

"Hey, Archie," she called out, her voice turning heads. "Take a look at this."

Archie, who had been reading a faded paper surf mag from the eighties, rose and moved to her side. He leaned over her shoulder, peering at the screen as she pointed to the spot in question. The two of them had spent countless hours working together, and there was an unspoken understanding between them, a shared intuition that often led them to insights others might miss.

"What does that look like to you?" Marta asked, her voice slightly higher than normal, changed by the prospect of a discovery.

Archie squinted, his eyes focusing on the screen as he pressed a little closer to her, his breath warm against her cheek. "Tyre tracks?"

"Yeah," Marta agreed, nodding. "But look closer. They're in pairs, not from a motorbike. Something heavy must've made them, heavy enough to leave an imprint visible from aerial photography." She traced the shape of the tracks with her fingertip, following their gentle arc on the screen. "And they curve to the left, which means…"

Archie finished her thought, his voice picking up on her unspoken conclusion. "We need to see what's at the other end of that road."

Marta nodded, her fingers using the mouse to pan the map, following the dirt road as it snaked toward the ocean. The further she went, the more isolated the area became, with the landscape becoming more rugged, the cliffs steeper.

"There's nothing down there," she murmured, her brow furrowing in frustration. "Just a turning circle." They both leaned in closer, as if squinting at the screen could somehow bring the blurry image into sharper focus. The satellite imagery was of lower resolution in this remote area, offering only vague outlines of the terrain.

Archie's eyes flicked to the date stamp at the bottom of the screen. "2023. It's a recent shot. Too bad they didn't capture the vehicle itself. Whatever made those tracks had to be a heavy-duty vehicle, maybe a pickup with four-wheel drive. Mace has a Hilux, doesn't he?"

Marta nodded again, her mind racing as she considered the possibilities. "You couldn't launch a boat down there. The cliffs are too steep, and the water would be treacherous unless the weather was absolutely perfect." Her voice trailed off, her thoughts drifting to the unsettling memories that had haunted the area in recent years. "They never found those poor girls' bodies," she said quietly, her tone darkening. "The ones from the party. The media said they were last seen in Darwin, but…" She let the sentence hang in the air, unwilling to voice the grim thoughts that had crept into her mind. The implications were too disturbing, too final. Archie didn't press her, but both were aware of what she had left unsaid.

"We need to see what's at the other end of that road," they said in unison.

- # -

In full tourist mode, Bondy floated into the Royal Oak Hotel. Her espadrilles made soft scuffing sounds that were drowned out by the roll of her cabin size case on the polished wooden floorboards. She took off a white sunhat and tapped her foot impatiently at the 'Reception' area. From there, she could see into the bar. A man sat watching the horse racing, with a fat Labrador - who looked like the owner - lying at his feet. She guessed he was in his seventies. He had a familiar look, the kind that reminded her of every politician, CEO, newsreader, and cop of his generation and racial profile. There was something else about him, though: the permanent scowl that shouldn't belong on the face of someone with the freedom to sit with their dog in a pub. *Ray Mason in his natural habitat.*

Fish left the bar unattended and walked towards the guest at reception. "Checking in?"

"Claudine Seaton-Bond" she said, putting on her posh English accent. "I think we spoke on the phone."

"Yes." He fell into her trap, his eyes dropping into her deep cleavage. She made a sound to encourage his eyes back to meet hers and he continued sheepishly "Um. Can I see some ID?"

Bondy weighed up whether she wanted to have this fight. She decided to go with polite annoyance, "Why do you need identification?"

Fish shrugged. "I guess like, so we know that you are not using a stolen credit card?"

Reaching into her bag to retrieve her British passport, Bondy shook her head and muttered under her breath. "What a great experience. Start with the assumption that your guest is a criminal."

"Also, can you please just fill out this form?" Fish asked. Claudine scanned her eyes over the document; date of birth, home address, email address, mobile number, and a declaration that she would abide by all the hotel rules.

"Why do you need my date of birth?" She was trying not to let her annoyance turn to anger. "It's on my ID".

Fish shrugged again and stammered, "It's just policy I guess."

"But I can lie right? It's not a legal document." She challenged him as she wrote down an email she had created just for spam and the kind of cafes that asked for all her personal details in exchange for 10 minutes of free Wi-Fi. The barman took the form without reviewing her responses and slipped it into a drawer.

"I will just need a credit card for the room. You get a 20% discount on food in the restaurant and also, a free welcome drink at the bar." Claudine smiled as she handed over a Mastercard loaded with the exact amount for the room. Something was a bit odd about this check-in. Maybe it was because it was a pub in a small town and not a 5-star global resort, but she was glad she'd taken the precaution of using the prepaid card.

"Once you are settled in, I'll get you that drink."

Twenty minutes later, Bondy took a seat at the bar. The local man with the dog raised his unkempt eyebrows in surprise as he heard Bondy order a cider from the tap. "I picked apples for a season when I was backpacking," she explained. "Sounds like there is a bit of a shortage of seasonal workers these days. The visa system is a mess."

Mace's face brightened as the topic of migration was brought up. "Bloody immigrants. It's a real problem."

Bondy sipped her pint and grinned as he took the bait. "Seems like the problem is that there aren't enough of them," she taunted.

"All the same. Murderers, thieves, rapists," he snarled. Bondy felt sorry for the dog. "Lazy. All looking for handouts. We don't need those kinds of people."

"People like me, you mean?" Her question was met with a blank stare of confusion. "I'm an immigrant. I'm here taking an Australian's job."

Ray could not reconcile her description with the woman who he thought could be the poster child for 'real Australians'. "Nah, you're not an immigrant."

"I have a foreign passport. I'm here on a visa. Not sure what else you would call me."

"Yeah well, whatever. You know what I mean."

Bondy did know. He meant that that he pined for the days of the 'White Australia' policy and that he'd forgotten or never knew that the recipe for the Royal Oak's chicken parma, arrived with post war immigrants from Italy not out of a Jamie Oliver cookbook. And for the sake of his soapbox he conveniently ignored that his favourite croissants and baguettes from the village bakery were cooked by a Vietnamese pastry chef and his Airbnbs cleaned by Filipino labour because the Protestant work ethic hadn't been passed onto Millennials and no locals would do that job.

Ray was becoming more wary of this cocky stranger. "So, why are you in town?"

"Well. I'm looking for potential property investments for a client," Bondy said. She'd prepared this answer on the drive down. "They are looking for something big, with a lot of land that they can turn into a winery or perhaps one of those boutique countryside hotels with a kitchen garden and 5-star restaurant." She sipped her pint, making sure he clocked the Rolex Submariner watch on her wrist as she studied the lines on his face for his reaction. "You know like Raymond Blanc has."

"Not many of those properties around here. Only one really, but the owner might be open to serious offers." Ray was being cautious, but he smelled an opportunity, if not to sell the family farm, then to take this bratty blonde for as much as he could. "I'm Ray Mason. I own the only property that might meet your needs. It's called Monaghan." He opened a battered wallet stuffed with paper receipts and took out a dog-eared card. "Give me a call and I can arrange a viewing."

"Claudine Seaton-Bond." She shook his hand and took the card and slipped it into the back pocket of her shorts, drawing his gaze down. She smirked, turned, and walked away looking over her shoulder. "I'll call you."

Ray waited a couple of minutes and then went over to the reception area, opening the drawer, taking out Claudine's registration card, folding it in half and slipping it into his back pocket. *Who are you, Miss Seaton-Bond?*

- # -

The city was empty, eerily so. The trams were still running, but there were no cars or trucks or electric scooters delivering vegan wraps to bankers and other white-collar workers who had three days off. Most of the shops were closed, with signs written in marker pen taped to the doors advising of the holiday opening hours. Holding his sustainable paper Officeworks bag, Tommo slowly wandered towards the stop for the number 86 tram. In the bag was a laminated credential from the Yachting Journalists Association, a printed copy of a letter on Marta's production company letterhead outlining his assignment and business cards in the name of Brian Tompson, Freelance Journalist. There was another set of business cards with the logo of a middling investment bank and the contact details of Andrew Butcher, Senior Private Banking Advisor, who had never uploaded his picture onto his Linkedin profile. As a backup, he'd also picked a secretive security operative, Paul Shaw from Oasis Sentinel. All his preparation for the Forum was done.

He stopped to look at the deals displayed on the window of a travel agent, tempted by Thailand and Vietnam. It had been 25 years since he was a carefree backpacker, one of the first westerners to travel independently around Laos and Cambodia. Tommo re-focussed his eyes, not on the glossy picture of Hạ Long Bay behind the glass, but the reflection bounced back. Someone was watching him. On any other day, a man in a pair of jeans, a retro pastel t-shirt and a baseball cap would just be another face in the crowd, but it was a bit too hot for jeans, and the tee was tucked in, which seemed a bit off, maybe ex-military. The man worked out. The short sleeves of the shirt were bulging. If the tucked in tee didn't confirm the military background, then the sand-coloured combat boots did. *You're being paranoid again* Tommo thought to himself but stopped again to scan his eyes over the wares on display in a camera shop and confirm that the man was following.

The sprawling Southern Cross station was a block away. Tommo kept the same pace he had before, wondering if his pursuer had the same familiarity with the city's grid layout. His heart started to beat faster as he walked down Collins Street. If you believed the media, stabbings were on the rise. The word spate was used in a way that assumed a level of education far higher than that of the intended audience. A random stabbing in the CBD would not seem too out of the ordinary and it would give ammunition to the pundits who were convinced that crime was out of control. He had no idea how adrenaline worked. Did it run out? Did you need to rest to rebuild stores? He figured he had used up all of his store with the van fire.

A plan formed in his mind: to cross Spencer Street against the red light, up the escalators, through the Metro ticket barrier, hoping his tail would not have the required Myki card, down onto a platform, up the other end to the walkway that connected the station to the stadium with the roof and from there, he'd work it out. *Is there a Big Bash game tonight?* The crowds would give him some cover.

A tram conveniently hummed along the rails in front of him, providing a temporary mirror to check behind without looking over his shoulder, the guy was still there, about fifty metres back. Tommo squinted to try and work out what was written backwards on the chaser's t-shirt, Mount Eliza? Sprinting across the road, using the red 'do not cross' figure as an excuse to speed up, Tommo fumbled for his ticket. Moving quickly up the escalator two steps at a time past the Hungry Jacks and the Water Tower clock he'd never noticed before. He pressed the card against the reader and walked towards the far platform as if he was late for a train, still not daring to look back. Down and out to platform 16A, the furthest he could go, swerving in one door and out the next under the high undulating roof that made him feel like he was in a hall of a mountain king without the Edvard Grieg soundtrack. He had no idea if he was being followed as he crossed over the tracks via a footbridge and headed south.

Mount Eliza? They can't have sold many of those shirts. The suburb on the southern outskirts of Melbourne where his uncle lived had a population of about 20,000, many of which were Australian Collies. *It could mean something, or it could be another red herring.*

Leaning up against a concrete pylon in a carpark in the bowels of the Marvel stadium, Tommo took a few deep breaths. He was confident that the tail was gone, but he was surprised he'd been located so quickly. Probably an app on his phone. Almost every single phone on the market uses the same chipset, made by Qualcomm and those chips collect information, in real time, including GPS location. Every time an app is downloaded and the 'Do you accept, yes or no' is presented in the terms of use, access to his location data is shared with hundreds of 'partners'. It could be his bank application, or the app he uses to conveniently top up his public transport pass or one of the ubiquitous messaging apps required to keep in touch with far flung contacts for 'free', the cost being his location being broadcast.

That was probably the how explained, but not the who. It all seemed a bit too digital and sophisticated to be thought up by Ray

Mason. QSP were consultants, they didn't really get into tactics, which is why Tommo had been surprised when Tara had told him she was getting things done as planned. He would have to run, again. Bondy's place was probably being watched, but he had to retrieve the last of his worldly possessions that weren't in a storage unit, and then what? *Where can I go?*

Tommo walked around the block where Bondy's apartment was three times before he went inside. It was going to be a quick visit, grab his things, 'borrow' the laptop. He needed the computer to explore the only flimsy lead he had, Mount Eliza. The shirt was such an incongruous detail. *Did they WANT me to see it?* Was it designed to throw him off the scent or tempt him down the Peninsula? He rolled the dice and did a search.

Ray Mason, Mount Eliza.

Nothing. A presentation to students at the management college and another at the local footy club pie night. Not a good enough reason to trek down towards Mornington. Tommo paced around the small flat feeling hunted and a bit useless. He needed a new phone, preferably one old enough to be able to remove the battery and go off the grid. Try another search.

Trevor Stone, Mount Eliza.

It was more than nothing. The purchase of a sprawling property, between the Nepean Highway and Port Phillip, complete with racehorse stables and training facilities had been reported a year or so ago. The buyer, Stone Casinos. *Is that the game? Race fixing and rigged betting?* It wasn't very innovative, but it could be lucrative. Then again, a rich kid buying a horse racing stable wasn't exactly scandalous. Tommo's mind kept tumbling questions around in his head. *If the establishment in Mount Eliza is linked to the people who are trying to silence me, why would they signal it? Was it just a mistake on the part of the guy who had followed me, the only clean shirt he had when he got the call to go and track a guy in the city?* It wasn't much, but it was something, a couple of dots that could be joined together.

Glancing at the clock on the microwave in Bondy's kitchen, Tommo grabbed his bag. He could crash with his uncle Graham who he hadn't seen for about 12 years. He began retracing his steps, back in the direction of the station. From memory he could take a Frankston line train to the very end and then the number 781 bus to the place Australian Crawl had used for inspiration in several of their songs in the eighties.

- # -

Bondy was waiting for Tara when she got back to her rented accommodation. Tommo's ex leaned against her Land Rover and enjoyed the look on Tara's face which was one of surprise and some wariness. "You look cooked."

"Why are you here?" Tara asked. She wasn't expecting to see Bondy until later.

"Well, you're going to hate me, but Marta and Kelpie say that someone needs to check out the other end of that track you just came back from." She brushed a stray gum leaf out of Tara's hair, flattened by the bike helmet. "I can go on my own, but I think it would be better if we both went." She showed Tara a piece of A4 paper, a printout of the aerial photo.

"I think I've had enough of this caper for one day. This is supposed to be my holiday. I don't even know why I am getting myself involved."

Bondy inspected the trailer on the back of Tara's truck. "Someone is very motivated to get things done."

"Can we do it tomorrow?" Tara wanted a bath, full of mineral salts and a large drink. "That photo could be three months old and whatever is down there is going to be there tomorrow."

"Yeah, I guess you are right," Bondy started to get back in her car. "Did you give any more thought to what you wanted to do for dinner? Table for two or a takeaway? Have a think..." She revved the engine and left Tara standing on the nature strip, helmet in hand, slightly bewildered.

She didn't notice the white Ford Ranger parked discreetly down the street. Why would she? It blended seamlessly into the urban landscape, one of countless identical trucks that dotted every road, parking lot, and driveway across the country. With over sixty thousand sold that year alone, the Ford Ranger was as common as it was inconspicuous, a workhorse vehicle favoured by tradies, school mums and weekend warriors alike. Its 182 grams of carbon dioxide per kilometre driven, barely registered as a concern in a world where utility and price, mainly price, trumped environmental impact. It was the very ubiquity of the vehicle that made it the perfect choice for Ray's gopher, Memphis. A truck that wouldn't attract a second glance, especially not from someone with other things on her mind.

Memphis sat behind the wheel, eyes trained on the rearview mirror, his hand gripping his phone. He watched as the two women met on the street, their interaction brief and tense. He waited a beat, his gaze focussed before he picked up his phone and dialled Ray's number. The call connected almost immediately.

"Yeah, it's me," he said, though the introduction was redundant. Ray's caller ID would have already displayed his name.

Ray, lounging by the pool at Monaghan, answered lazily, his attention only half on the call. He watched with languid interest as a nubile girl, barely 18, if that, glided through the water with effortless grace. She was everything he liked - youthful, eager to please, and, most importantly, easily controlled. His thoughts were divided between the phone call and the mesmerising sight of the girl doing laps.

"They met," reported Memphis, "and talked… But it was like a two-minute conversation, and the Asian one didn't look very happy."

Ray was impatient, "Do you think they know each other?"

Memphis considered the question, recalling the way the women had interacted. "Well, the Pom knew where to wait, so it's unlikely it was a random meeting."

Ray grunted in acknowledgment, his eyes tracking the girl as she reached the pool's edge, pulling herself up and out of the water. Droplets clung to her skin; her breathing only slightly elevated from the swim. "She's a bit of an enigma is Ms. Bond." Ray kept his voice low, as if sharing a secret. He fought to keep his composure as the girl, fully aware of his gaze, stretched indifferently, allowing him to admire every curve.

"One more thing," said Memphis, sensing Ray's distraction but pushing forward with the report, nonetheless. "The chink's been riding."

Ray's interest momentarily spiked. "So, she likes horses? She looks like the type to ask Daddy for a pony," he quipped, eager to wrap up the call and return his full attention to the girl now posing provocatively in front of him.

"No." Memphis corrected, his tone serious. "She's got a trail bike. A big one, like the ones your guys use."

The mention of the trail bike gave Ray pause, a flicker of concern crossed his mind. "They are not my guys, mate," he snapped, irritation creeping into his voice as the girl moved closer, her wet body twerked inches from his face, teasing him with every slow, deliberate movement. His patience was wearing thin with both.

"Okay, get out of there. Don't get seen," Ray ordered curtly before abruptly ending the call. He leaned back in his lounge chair, his focus entirely on the girl now. With a satisfied smirk, he switched his phone to capture video, of every sultry twist and turn.

- # -

In the Pokies Section of the cavernous underground Mail Exchange Hotel, on the corner of Bourke and Spencer Street, Declan Sharp leaned his phone up against the blinking one-armed bandit and watched the blue dot that was Tommo's location move around the map of Melbourne's Docklands area. Things were not going well. Silly mistakes were being made, and a bunch of amateurs were in danger of wrecking the plan.

Ray Mason was becoming a liability. He had panicked and acted rashly when he'd learned that Travis 'Tommo' Thomson was back. Now, instead of spending the week in a winery in Franschhoek, Sharp was chasing a bunch of pesky kids like a Scooby Doo villain. *Maybe it's time to throw Ray under the bus. A sacrifice for the greater good.*

Declan had lost Tommo after the van fire, where everything that could have gone wrong had gone wrong. He hated working with fools. The intel from Ray Mason's loser traffic cop said there would be no-one inside the vehicle. *It was meant to be a warning, not a hit. It was meant to scare him.* Tommo's phone had pinged off a tower in town with a 6 square kilometre range which was a lot to cover while being inconspicuous. New phones were easier to track because the user couldn't remove the battery, and as long as there was a charge, the phone could be turned on remotely, but Tommo had disappeared off the grid as his battery emptied.

The background check into Tara Kwong had not revealed anything out of the ordinary, except she seemed to have come into some money recently and her spending habits had become a bit more lavish. Other than that, she was squeaky clean. She did have a tendency to gamble though, he'd found an online poker profile and a betting account. Her job at Quantum Strategy Partners meant she could be pressured through her employment contract not to reveal confidential information that related to projects she worked on and there were other strategies to make her behave that would be simple enough to enact. QSP had already called her in and reminded her of her contractual obligations. She had responded by indicating that she would resign, but there was no letter yet. It seemed like a bluff.

And then there was the wild card. Claudine Seaton-Bond, aka Bondy. She was either a glorified party planner or a sort of freelance executive assistant. He'd seen her first at the Shark Byte Cafe. She seemed to know the surfer's wife. He'd tracked her to the old fire track, which was worrying, because up until now it had been a good way to get things in and out of Monaghan without using the main driveway and gate. Then he'd followed Bondy and Tommo back to the Docklands and he had picked up Tommo's phone again. Bondy wasn't a completely unknown quantity. She came with impeccable references. He knew some of her clients. Clients who valued secrecy and discretion. *Maybe she can be turned.*

One thing was working. He had managed to separate Tommo from his support group and isolate him in the city, where he was least comfortable. Declan watched the blue dot move back towards the station over the road and then disappear from the screen. "Where did you go? Where are you going?" He had no idea that the answer was written on his t-shirt.

- # -

With his back to Frankston station, Tommo waited at the bus stop for the 781. This scene hadn't really changed in 50 years, and it wasn't one that would appear in the Visit Victoria campaigns on social media. Even as a 15-year-old, visiting his cousins, he had never felt unsafe, but they were different times with different dependencies, different drugs with different effects on the downtrodden locals. A burger joint, a charity shop and an unemployment centre summed up Frankston quite well. The destination board on the front of the bus before him flicked around to 788. *That will do.* Even though this service could take him to Portsea at the very end of the Mornington

Peninsula, it took a detour off the Nepean Highway at Mount Eliza Way.

As the bus climbed Olivers Hill, Tommo looked out of the window over the bay to the grey Lego block silhouette of Melbourne about 40 kms away as the seagull flies across Port Phillip. It seemed like it was a world away.

He stepped off the bus in the middle of the village in front of the post office. He'd travelled less than 10kms, but the variety of shop fronts were vastly different here, real estate agents and hair salons mostly. When he was 15, Tommo spent three months in Mount Eliza with his cousins, on the wrong side of the highway, while his parents took an extended trip of a lifetime to Europe. Back then the shops never used to open on Sunday. This was the edge of suburbia denoted by the fact that a call from here to the city used to be charged at local rate, while 1 kilometre on in Mornington, per minute subscriber trunk dialling (STD) rates were applied. The boundary also meant shops could open on a Sunday outside the suburban boundary. It seemed very arbitrary, different rules depending on the postcode.

In the window of Sotheby's real estate agency, a big flat screen TV scrolled drone photography of vast tracts of land in 3930 that would be entire communities just up the road. The men who stole the land from the original inhabitants also stole the names, Moondah and Earamil and Moonyong which are still used by the local private schools as the names of houses. *I wonder how many of those kids running for Moondah on sports day know they are wearing the name 'black snake' on their shirt?*

Tommo had always felt different here. In contrast to the 2023 G Wagons parked on the street, the bedrock of the mountain is from the Ordovician age, the second oldest series in the stratified rocks of the earth. At 500 feet, it's not really a mountain, though just a little bit higher than Mount Martha further down the bay. His calves still burned though as he started the climb along the concrete footpath alongside Wooralla Drive with the Peninsula Grammar school on his right. On the left, an estate that local kids thought was a haunted house, hidden behind towering Monterey pines, was being carved up into parcels of suburbia. The roads were bitumen now. When he was here in his teens, they were all dirt.

This used to be the 'wrong side of the highway'. The gravel roads and small bungalow style houses didn't measure up to the architecturally affected street layout of the Ranelagh estate beside the bay, overdesigned by the same man that planned the national capital Canberra, Sir Walter Burley Griffin. Tommo's shoes crunched on the smooth white pebbles of his uncle's driveway. I probably should have rung ahead, he thought as he peered through the windows with the curtains drawn, a pile of junk mail in the box suggesting no-one had checked it for at least a few days. The dog next door was home. It began to bark, fulfilling its purpose to alert the neighbours of a stranger's presence. He slipped the latch on the side gate and went around the back. The BBQ had been covered in a way that only happened when it wasn't in use for more than a day, a timer had been attached to the garden tap so that the sprinkler would switch on and off without human intervention. The dog stopped barking, sensing that Tommo had some kind of right to be there.

His uncle picked up after the first ring. "Hello?" Tommo was using a new 'feature phone', a term dreamt up by some marketer with a peculiar sense of irony. There was a new sim too, so his uncle would not recognise the number.

"It's Tommo, I…"

"Tommo, how are you mate? Merry Christmas. How's Athens?"

"Ha. Well, I'm in Mount Eliza. Mountain View Road to be precise."

"No kidding. You should have given us a heads up. We are down the foreshore. The fortieth year in the same spot. You know. You came down a few times." Tommo's uncle was a creature of habit.

"I don't have wheels. It's a long story."

"Ah… Well, the house is all locked up. You could crash one night at the shed on the beach, I'll send you details of where to find the key. Else you could get back on the 788 and come down here to Rosebud."

The bay beaches were famous for their wooden beach boxes. Some were not much bigger than a phone booth and some were large enough to store small boats and all the other stuff needed for a day at the beach. Most were brightly painted, some with Instagrammable designs painted by artists. "Kunyung beach, right?" Tommo said, casting his mind back to summers with the cousins. "That might work well for me actually." Though it would mean walking all the way back down the mountain. "Hey. Do you remember anything about a big property purchase recently, down near Manyung? Buyer was that Trevor Stone guy?"

The booming horn of a container ship making the turn in the channel near the McCrae lighthouse could be heard in the background during the silence created as his uncle thought back. "There was an article in the local paper, a few letters, but a rich family buying a big property in Mount Eliza isn't really news." He paused. "If it had been a Chinese buyer, all hell would have broken loose, but old money from Sydney? They are more upset by the noise from the chopper when he comes in and out… Listen, I know you're in some kind of trouble, and I'd love to help," his uncle said. "But it's not the best timing, you know. This might be the last year we do this camping lark."

"That's okay. It's a shame we couldn't catch up, but I need to do a few things." He kept it vague.

"We've gone all mod-con down the beach, there are solar panels which power a little bar fridge and there should be a few cans in there so you can have a couple of frothies."

"Thanks so much. Hope you all have a happy new year." Tommo was already leaving depressions in the stones of the driveway as he retraced his steps back towards the sea.

It was hot. He hadn't looked at the forecast, but heat was expected at that time of year. Maybe a few degrees over the average of the years before and a few more degrees over the average for the year before that. The stifling temperature of the Australian summer seemed to be against him as well as everyone else. Even though it was downhill, the walk became a trudge through the upmarket village. He sneered with resentment and bitterness; the atmosphere of wealth and privilege was oppressive. The air was thick with the cloying scent of floral bouquets, and pretentiousness. The immaculately dressed residents' flit past him, their laughter and chatter grating on his nerves like a screeching cockatoo. Every pristine storefront, every meticulously manicured garden, was a reminder of the things he now remembered he despised about this place - the superficiality, the materialism, the hollow facades of happiness, success, and climate change denial.

By the time he had picked up some provisions, bachelor picnic chic, at the Woolworths, open until 8pm on a Sunday, and walked down the steep slope of Kunyung road, and the even steeper track below the primary school to the sand, the beach was mostly empty. The red cliffs, stepped access, and jagged rocks underfoot at the shore made it a quiet beach, even on the busiest days.

His feet sunk deep into the uncompacted sand. There was a beach today at least for now, at low tide. There was always a beach when he was a kid at all tides. Stopping in front of his uncle's beach house, he smiled at the new paint job. The small hut-like building used to be painted 'Cobalt-Embrace', a single shade of blue from Dulux that could be used on wood and metal. Now, in keeping with the need for social media one upmanship, the double front doors had been painted by a Banksy impersonator. Either that, or a generative AI had been used to create something in the style of a very well-known street artist and it had been re-purposed for the doors of the beach hut. If Tommo had written the prompt, it would have gone something like:

```
'A large, intricate stencil artwork depicting Errol
Flynn as Robin Hood, clad in his iconic green tunic
```

and feathered cap, facing off against Elon Musk as
Prince John. Musk, dressed in a regal, mediaeval-
inspired robe with a Tesla logo emblazoned on it,
stands atop a pile of gold coins, symbolising his
wealth and power'.

As homage, or as blatant copyright infringement of the artist
known as Banksy, the colour palette is primarily black and white, with
hints of blue and red for accents. Tommo laughed as he thought about
how his year 9 art teacher would have waxed lyrical about the
juxtaposition of Flynn, a symbol of the romantic era of piracy and
Robin Hood, someone who stole from the rich to give to the poor to
fairly distribute wealth, and Musk, a representative of the usurpers to
the throne. Whether you were a fan of Australian Crawl's Errol, or a
Musk fanboy the image was bound to end up on your Instagram feed.
Tommo unlocked the hut and smiled, transported back to summers
with his cousin's fighting over the inflatable surf mats and learning to
sail on the red hulled Fairy Penguin dinghy *Probably not allowed to
call a boat that anymore.* He grabbed a green can out of the fridge and
connected his phone to a Bluetooth speaker, cueing up a pop rock
band formed by local boys. He sipped his beer as he made a ham and
salad roll to eat as the sun began to set on the other side of the bay to
the lyrics of Boys Light Up.

Let me tell you about my mountain home
Where all the ladies' names are Joan
Where husband works back late at night
Hopes are up for trousers down
With hostess on a business flight
Taxi in a Mercedes drive
I hope that driver's coming out alive
The garden it is Dorsetted
That lady she's so corseted
She's got 15 ways to lead that boy astray

- # -

The two women sat side by side on a wooden seat facing the ocean with the setting sun at their back. Each had a cardboard tray wrapped in butcher's paper on their lap. Despite the rhythmic crashing of waves on the beach and the calls of gulls on the wind, there was an awkward silence between them.

Tara began. "I heard you did the Hobart on Didyabringyagrogalong. What's he like?"

"Who? Stone? He's an asshole." Bondy said dismissively "He's exactly how he appears on TV- smug, entitled, he's not even a very good sailor. The boat is always full of paid gold medal winning Olympic rockstars and helms with 24 Ocean Races between them." She tore open the parcel like she was playing the game at a kid's birthday party. "I haven't had a dim sim for years." She bit into the domed end of the deep-fried parcel and swore. "Fuck... hot hot hot".

"Some people think he's a genius, like everything he touches turns to gold," Tara suggested as she tore off a triangle of paper to protect her fingers from the scalding batter encasing her disc shaped potato cakes, blowing on it, having learned from Bondy's schoolgirl error. "But it's not hard to do when you can just keep pumping money into it, it's like doubling your bet every time you lose, eventually you'll at least break even."

Bondy mimicked Tara's use of the wrapping paper to grip her cabbage filled dumpling. "He's smarter than he looks. He uses that buffoonish private school rugby player thing to hide a kind of deviousness." She nudged Tara in the ribs with her elbow. "And he has a thing for Asian girls. Do you want an intro?"

"I'm not Asian." Tara blushed and waved her hand over her chips to try and suggest her flushed face was due to the steam rising from the cardboard box. "Anyway, I'd never date a guy like that. It's got to feel hollow, winning a race but knowing you've paid for it. But I guess he doesn't think like that."

"I'm sorry," Bondy said. "You're about as ocker as they come.

Don't think I haven't noticed that tramp-stamp on your back." Tara smiled a little. "Though a real Aussie girl would have a dolphin on her ass that she got in Kuta beach on Bali."

"How do you know I don't?"

"Really?"

"It's ironic. And I happen to like dolphins," Tara grinned, rumbled. She handed Bondy a large opaque gym branded water bottle she had emptied a chilled Pinot Gris into earlier.

"Crazy huh," Bondy said, sucking the wine through the attachment designed to stop the sports drink bottle from leaking. "That we can't have a glass of wine with our fish and chips without being fined. Now that is un-Australian."

"Why are you helping Tommo?" Tara asked, looking out at the ocean in the hope she might see her new sea-mammal friend who she cavorted with a few days earlier. She looked back at Bondy to search for signs of dishonesty in the other woman's face.

"He's a friend. You know. A real friend." She avoided Tara's gaze, but only because she felt vulnerable which was not something she was used to. "He helped me out when no-one else would. That's what real friends are for." Claudine paused, deciding how much of the story she was prepared to share. "It was after we broke up. I had a fling with a guy. Got pregnant." She sucked on the water bottle, almost inhaling the wine inside. "The guy was gone, calls went to voicemail, then the phone was disconnected."

Tara put her hand on Claudine's knee. "You don't really have to tell me the rest, I can probably work out what happened."

"No, it's okay." A rare tear ran down Claudine's cheek. She wiped it away quickly with the back of her hand, leaving a smear of grease from her fat fried dinner. "Yeah. So I knew that I didn't want to have a kid. Tommo was there. Drove me to the clinic, waited, took me home. He didn't really have to."

"He does seem to have an unusually strong moral compass," Tara said, thinking back to her curtailed night with him. They hadn't used any protection. She squirmed a little.

"Yeah, but he's not a dick about that either. You know, he's not preachy. He's not like one of those vegans that tries to make you feel bad because you had egg-based mayonnaise on your chips." She changed the subject. "So, I spoke to Ray Mason earlier. At the Royal Oak. He's even more turgid and repulsive than I imagined."

Tara squeezed a lemon segment over her crispy battered piece of flake then lathered it in tartare sauce. "A bit of a legend in his own head, but hardly a criminal mastermind?"

"There is something off about him. Something we are still missing," Bondy said. "Anyway, I fed him a line about sourcing a large property for a client. I don't know if he bought it, but it will check out if he does some basic due diligence. He said he could arrange a viewing."

"Pack your pepper spray." Tara shuddered. "When are you thinking you would do that? Are you headed back to the city next week?"

"I haven't decided yet. It depends what we find tomorrow, "She sucked on the teat of the water bottle for more wine, but it was empty.

5

She remembered why she didn't do dirt biking anymore. It really hurt. Tara shivered and rubbed her bare arms and revelled in the early morning peace as she stood on the nature strip. It was the last day of the year, and no one was hurrying to get out of bed, not even the dog walkers or the joggers or the fishermen. She heard the distinctive custom grumble of Bondy's Land Rover come closer.

"Here you go." Bondy handed over a coffee in a Royal Oak branded paper cup. "Ready for a little road trip?"

Tara took the offer of caffeine as she fastened her seatbelt without thinking. "A few more hours of sleep might have been nice." Tara was not a morning person.

Bondy accelerated, pushing Tara down and back against the custom racing seats. It wasn't a classic restoration job. "I need to get back before noon. I have arranged a viewing of Ray's place. It's an opportunity to get inside that we aren't really going to get any other way." She slowed and turned into the fire access track. There was a new obstacle. The crude steel pole on a hinge which had been open on the last few visits was locked closed. "There are some bolt cutters in the back. I had a feeling we might need them today."

"On it," Tara said as she clambered down from the 4WD and

retrieved the tool from the boot. The padlock, which looked like it was designed for a school locker, or a garden shed, offered no resistance and dropped to the ground. Tara pushed the end of the steel pole in an arc and propped a Y shaped branch against it, ushering their ride through the gap.

"Are they just taking precautions because it's a holiday weekend or are they suspicious?" Bondy wondered aloud. "The track should be maintained by the council or the local CFA. It's not private property."

Tara had been doing 80 kilometres an hour down this stretch of the dirt road on her bike. It looked so different half the speed. "If we worked out that the track was being used, maybe the CFA did too." She pointed beyond the windscreen. "That's the gate. There is no need to stop, let's keep going to the end."

Despite its Dakar Rally style improvements, the Land Rover needed all Bondy's off road experience to navigate the track. "I really wouldn't want to do this in a fire engine," she commented. "You only come this way if you absolutely have to."

The single lane road eventually opened into a cleared, flat space on the clifftop just wide enough to turn a vehicle around so it could go back the other way. "What are we looking for?" Tara asked as she took a moment to take in the uninterrupted view to the southern horizon.

"Hard to say, but we might know it when we see it," Bondy said, joining Tara and looking out to the ocean, her view lowering to the base of the cliffs. "Archie was right, there is no way that you could land a boat down there, even a rib would get ripped up on the rocks" She scanned the clifftop for signs that anything had been disturbed by activity in either direction.

"The tracks came from the property," Tara said, so maybe they were dumping something. It's expensive to get rid of waste these days, especially if it is hazardous."

"It's probably not a byproduct of a process, else there would be frequent trips and more tracks." Bondy scouted around the area. "I really hope we don't find a grave or a body." She shuddered.

"Looks like there was a fire over there. Maybe a campsite?" Tara kicked over a few rocks and watched several species of poisonous spiders scurry for new cover. Stones were arranged in a rough circle and charred logs and what looked to be the remains of a wooden pallet lay at the centre. She picked up one of the rocks and examined it more closely. "They're lucky no one died. These rocks are the kind that could contain air or water inside." She dropped the rock back into its place "Heat it up enough and boom." She mimed pieces of exploded rock flying in all directions.

"How do you know that?" Bondy queried. "I heard that smooth river rocks might have water trapped inside, but we are nowhere near a river."

Tara knelt and brushed the rock with her finger. "I went camping with my brother. We watched those Yogi bear cartoons where you make a stone circle, so we thought that was how you did it." She shuddered "Around one AM we heard these huge loud bangs and then bits of molten rock started melting their way through the nylon walls of the tent. Scary." She picked through the remains in the centre of the fire site. A few empty beer cans had been left behind, which was unusual. Most people who ventured this far away from civilization would take their rubbish with them, having had the 'Keep Australia Beautiful' anti-litter campaign drummed into them for the last fifty plus years.

Tara bent down to collect the cans for her home recycling bin when she noticed something else in the fireplace. She brushed away the excess ash from a piece of cardboard that hadn't been fully consumed by the flames and photographed the branding with her phone's image search function – 'Diletta', specifically the 'Diletta 900i'.

There were only 1,130 results and the top one astonished her. The Diletta 900i was a passport printer, compact and portable with the ability to churn out 270 documents an hour complete with moder security features such as digitally printed photographs, security ink, machine-readable code lines, biometric data contained in 2-dimensional barcodes, and contactless RFID chips.

"What have you found?" Bondy was beside her, looking at the screen. "Wow, that's not what I was expecting, but it might explain a few things." She squatted down and poked around the fire for any other evidence of what was burnt. "You can fit a lot of passports in a backpack, and they must be worth, what do you think? 50,000 bucks? 100K each for the right buyer?"

Tara was busy on her phone doing more searches. "OK, so this could be just a coincidence, but the manufacturer of this printer has delegates registered for the QSP Forum on Tuesday." She was starting to piece together other parts of the enterprise but wasn't ready to share her thoughts with Bondy or Tommo just yet.

"Maybe we can put in an order," Bondy joked. "Can anyone just buy a passport printer?" She was getting back in the car. "Come on, let's go. I have to get back for my tour of Monaghan, and now I know what to keep my eyes out for."

"Maybe I could be your client," Tara said as she was jostled in the front seat. "It would be a good cover story if they start to wonder why we are spending time together."

"Not sure how that would work. I'm sure they pay well at a place like QSP, but enough to buy a property like that?"

Tara tried to keep an offended look off her face as she reached up and grabbed the Jesus bar with her left hand, her knuckles white as the Land Rover nosedived into a large pothole. "Let's call it family money." Her brother had given her the Bitcoin originally. "And I'm not a bad online poker player. It will check out if they do any digging."

"I'm not sure how Ray Mason will react if you show up," Bondy said "It might make him suspicious. We can keep the cover story if we need it later."

Tara liked the idea of owning Monaghan.

- # -

"You know the garden's full of furniture, the house is full of plants," Tommo hummed as he left footprints along the waterline of the sandy beach where they would be washed away in minutes, leaving no tracks. He'd had the best night's sleep in a while, no assignation attempts, the repetitive wash of the gentle shore break more comforting to him than the absence of all sound at Bondy's apartment.

His heart pounded - not from being pursued, but from the three large tablespoons of Nescafé instant coffee and sugar foamed into a frappe in a cocktail shaker. According to the story, a worker at the 1957 International Trade Fair in Thessaloniki had found himself without hot water for his usual brew, so he shook cold water and sugar together with the dehydrated coffee to create a drink still popular in Greece today, though coffee's third wave was beginning to dent its popularity. Walking south, with the sun on his left and Schnapper point and the locally famous Mornington pier on the right in the middle distance, Tommo worked his way through the Australian Crawl Mount Eliza discography in his head rather than turning on his phone to stream a playlist. It was early. Nobody on the beach. Just a few tinnies and fishing canoes propelled by pedal power on the flat waters of the bay.

This is it. Just before the point was the half kilometre or so of the Stone owned property's beach access. Flotsam, mostly plastic packaging, some driftwood and seagrass marked the high-water line. Public thoroughfare and access on one side and private property on the other. Razor Wire. *Someone's hiding something.* He stood on the damp sand, the early morning air smelled of summer and seaweed. It was going to be another hot day. He studied the beach house to the left. The floor-to-ceiling windows were tinted. For all he knew, someone might have been standing behind them, looking out at him, though he had expected he would have company if that were the case. Modest for a billionaire, the house was built from locally sourced materials. It had a calmness with its reclaimed wood and natural stone façade - features not in keeping with Stone's flashy nature - but perhaps it had been built by a previous owner. The creek was his way in. A trickle. It hadn't rained for a while. He pushed through the imported pampas grass, a weed, but he was grateful for its cover, even as the sawtooth leaves cut his skin. The cameras mounted on the beach-house did not face the creek, and he had just worked out why. Once a meandering ribbon of water, the creek had been diverted under the property using a storm water pipe with a diameter of five feet. A heavy, rusted metal grate secured the drain's concrete opening. Water echoed like a strange panpipe out of the darkness as Tommo grabbed the grate with both hands, braced and used his weight to try and budge the grill. It groaned but didn't move. Another 3-dial combination lock. He spun the dials back to 000. 001, 002, 003 - only 999 combinations. He could guess. *The street address of the property? The last 3 digits of the postcode, the sail number of Stone's yacht?* 126, 930, 111. Click. The lock sprung open and Tommo looked to the sky in thanks to the fates. *A win is a win.*

Sitting on the concrete lip of the drain, looking down at the gentle eddies in a shallow pool by his feet, watching the tadpoles, he weighed his choices. *How far does the drain run inland? Is there a similar opening on the other end? What if there is a flash flood?* Climbing up onto the top of the outlet Tommo surveyed where he was in the grounds. The main house was beyond the stables. He'd need a uniform of some sort to divert suspicion.

The ground beneath his feet rumbled gently. A noise like muffled thunder grew louder away to the right of his position. The rhythmic beat of racehorse hooves upon a dirt training track reverberated like a drumbeat through the stillness. It was a working farm. He kept low, using old tree trunks and hay bales and wrecked horse floats as cover, crouching behind a discarded corrugated iron water tank as the horses approached on their next lap of the track.

Just beside the stables Tommo found a small building designed to act as a kitchen, lunch-room, bathroom and changing area for the workers on the property. The locker room was a gritty, utilitarian space. A row of battered metal lockers lined the wall. Each door hinted at the personality of the man who used it, a kind of public collage of magnets, stickers and magazine cutouts that professed a love of fishing, horses, muscle cars, country western music, even anime. A long wooden bench, worn and scarred, stretched out in front of the lockers. More insight into the men of the place scratched into the varnish.

Turning his attention to the lockers themselves, Tommo slowly opened a slightly ajar door crudely labelled with the name "SHARP" like the object that had scratched into the paint to make the jagged letters. A neatly folded pair of black leather rifleman gloves sat on a shelf above another bracket of neatly laid out, mostly illegal, knives. Taped to the inside of the door were newspaper clippings. Tommo stifled a gasp. The articles detailed the scandal of the party at Monaghan, the disappearance of the two girls and speculation about what happened to them. A chill ran down his spine. Using an open palm to make space between the garments draped on coat hangers, goosebumps rose on his arms as he revealed the same Mount Eliza T-Shirt he had seen in Melbourne. One blue, one orange, one black. Rooted to the spot, he felt like he was so close and yet still so far away. Snapped back into reality by a door slamming nearby, Tommo grabbed a polo shirt off a hanger, the farm's logo was embroidered in the top left corner and the Stone Casino brand was similarly stitched onto the right arm. This was crew gear, not available to the public. It would be enough to pass as an employee if challenged. Whoever Sharp was, he had also left a keycard on a branded lanyard hanging next to his trophy articles. Tommo slipped the credentials over his head.

He scanned a cluttered bulletin board for anything that might be useful. An old Pirelli calendar hung beside Post-it notes and race schedules, handwritten 'for sale' ads for fridges, cars and 'free to a good home' posters for puppies. He shook his head as he found a faded yellow card – `Creek Drain lock code, 111`. Lifting the calendar he discovered a laminated fire escape plan. He ran his finger over the names of the buildings on the map of the complex, main house, stables, maintenance… server room. *Bingo*.

Grabbing a toolbox, conveniently left behind to help with his ruse, he found the maintenance shed and the control panel for the sprinkler system. He reprogrammed it it to cause a distraction on the other side of the training track and to draw attention away from his new target. Then he moved with stealth, using the memorised map in his head, towards the place he hoped held all the answers.

Tommo's luck was holding up. Sharp's keycard unlocked a heavy metal door revealing a concrete staircase down to an original basement. He descended as the air grew warmer, humming with the sound of AMDs, a three-letter acronym for air movement devices, otherwise known as fans. Same number of letters, perhaps one of the most redundant TLAs invented by people who used jargon as a defence mechanism, to make them look smarter than they really were. He pushed open a heavy oak door and stepped into the server room, into the heart of a hidden digital empire, maybe.

The air was thick with the scent of hot metal and ozone. The old stone walls surrounded rows of blinking servers. Some of Tommo's suspicions were confirmed as he spied Crypto mining rigs, their fans whirring and whining as they solved equations to produce the amorphous source of digital wealth. The rigs were cobbled together from high-end graphics cards and processors, their tangled wires snaking across the floor like electronic vines. The LED indicators bathed the room in a soft, pulsating light casting shadows against the walls. An artificial Arora Borealis of blue and red and green. Frowning, he tried to find evidence of surveillance cameras. Maybe it was oversight, maybe it was arrogance, but there didn't seem to be any security at all.

In the corner furthest from the entrance, a desk cluttered with monitors and keyboards stood as a command centre. Tommo kept an ear out above the din of the machinery for footsteps as he tried to decipher the various graphs and outputs on the dashboards on the monitors. Most of it was operational - ambient room temperature, GPU utilisation, power consumption, a few warnings of individual machines outside normal parameters. His shoulders slumped. On the face of it, there was nothing illegal going on here. The locker with the clippings was more interesting than the hidden data centre. Using a reinforced, underground cellar for a crypto-mining operation or an offsite backup location made a lot of sense. *This is not enough. I need more.* His frappe fuelled fingers stabbed at the keyboard, as he tried to guess the admin password. He typed 1. It was as good a guess as any. But it didn't work. He laughed. *They wouldn't be smart enough to use 1 as a password.* He typed the most common 6 letter word in the English language 'Number' Still no joy. *No surprise.*

- # -

The Monaghan driveway was a combination of gravel and brick, a long straight run beneath the oak trees in their full summer greenery ending in a circular parking area with a turning circle designed for stagecoaches or carriages. But for the sounds of cockatoos the building could be situated on an estate in Surrey. Bondy parked her Land Rover in front of a weeping wych tree and next to a battered Toyota Hilux. Her car matched the house, the other vehicle, despite its Japanese origins, matched the place.

With her back to the mansion, she looked out at the view that stretched all the way to the sea about three kilometres away. Most of the land had been cleared of trees to allow cattle to graze and on the last day of December the grass had been bleached to what Marta would say was Hex #9EA26B, which had more green in it than other years which was more like straw or #C4DC8A. Early English painters had struggled to capture the colours correctly, painting the landscape with the same palette that they painted Surrey. These days you could use the press of a button on an eyedropper icon to sample millions of colours from a photo or get generative AI to paint you a picture in the Heidelberg School style, allowing you to rip off the learnings and studies of Arthur Streeton or Frederick McCubbin.

"Hey there," a perky young voice called out behind her. Bondy turned and stared at a dark-skinned girl who she imagined was Ray Mason's granddaughter or niece. "The view is even better from the top of the tower," said the teenager, opening a tin of Cadbury favourites.

Bondy picked through the tin and chose a brightly coloured shape she hoped had a caramel centre. "I'm Claudine. I'm here to have a look around the property on behalf of a potential buyer."

The girl looked puzzled. "There's no way Ray would sell this place, it's like been in his family for ages."

"Run along now Amara," commanded Ray, appearing in the doorway, dressed for the poolside in a garish Hawaiian shirt and boardshorts that exposed a bit too much thigh. The girl pouted but bounced away waving and disappearing around the side of the house. Bondy raised her eyebrow, looking for Ray to justify the presence of the young houseguest. Ray shrugged. "What can I say? There are a lot of girls with Daddy issues who want nice handbags and shoes for their Instagram."

"She's a girlfriend?" Bondy shuddered a little.

"Sure, let's go with girlfriend," said Ray without any hint of shame or impropriety. "If they swipe right, I'm not going to say no." He held the front door open and made a waving motion. Bondy's eyes rolled back in her head then switched to roaming around the entrance hall as if comparing it to a list of requirements but actually making a survey of surveillance cameras.

"How many buildings are there? A place like this must have a few barns, some stables?" Bondy was keen to find the location of the printer and any other operations.

Ray wheezed a little as he began climbing a steep staircase. "Let's go up the tower and you can see the layout."

From the top of the tower, where a sun-faded Australian flag flew in the northerly breeze, Bondy grasped the red wrought iron guardrails and looked around to see how the property was laid out. So as not to arouse too much suspicion, she started with the view behind the house, the formal English garden framed by Golden Ash and European Beech trees and beyond that, various pieces of rusted old farm equipment arranged in a kind of collection among the long grass. Her skin crawled as she looked down to see the girl, now topless, lying by the pool's edge drinking sparkling wine from a plastic flute. The area on top of the tower was cramped and Bondy could feel Ray in her personal space. She could smell beer and tooth decay on his rasping breath, the stair climb highlighting his lack of fitness. She contorted her body to move past him to the other side without touching or brushing against him.

To the west there was a collection of primitive shelters, sheds with corrugated iron roofs and open wooden frames, no walls. There was a large feed barn, which had no front doors so Claudine could see inside and determine it was not the centre of operations. She could see three more structures that predated the main house, built with brick in various states of repair. There were no visible power lines to any of them. Then a glint caught her eye and made her squint. Another building, barely one room in size with tiny windows and chimney, perhaps a kitchen of sorts. Installed on the rusted tin roof were shiny black solar panels. Clever. Keep the excess power consumption off the grid. She pointed at the black cells.

"I didn't have you pegged as a greenie Ray," she teased.

"I'd burn my own coal if it meant I could keep the bills under control," he replied.

"There are no cables running to the house though," Bondy noted.

Ray bristled and became defensive. His eyes looked up and right, searching for a plausible lie. "It's a trial. A lot of the main house still has the original wiring, so we use it to heat the pool in winter."

"More houses should have towers." Bondy didn't want to dwell on the smaller building or make it a focus. "I think I've seen enough of the grounds for now. Is there a study or an office? My client would move their business here and work remotely most of the time." She followed Ray back down the staircase.

Ray held the door of a study open. "I'd prefer you didn't go inside." The descent of the stairs had taken almost as much out of him as the climb. "It's my private study and there are some personal documents and the like lying around." Bondy's eyes scanned the room, building a photograph in her head that she could go back to later. She noted the cluttered almost cosy space filled with the accumulated appurtenances of a lifetime lived in a paper age. Books, the kind that have never been read, but bought to make you look clever, lined dusty shelves, alongside stacks of papers and files precariously balanced on every available surface. On the desk, amidst the chaos, her graphical memory list was made easier by a sleek, fit for purpose, custom gaming laptop. Its illuminated keyboard cast a vibrant blue glow against the aged wooden desktop. *That's not a Harvey Norman Boxing Day special*. Inserted into one of the USB ports was a branded cryptocurrency cold storage wallet.

"My client may want to pay with Bitcoin," Bondy said, thinking quickly. "Would you be willing to consider that?"

Ray seemed eager to move on with the tour. "I might have thought that your 'client' would offer me suitcases full of cash."

"What are you looking to get? 25 Mil, 30? That's a lot of suitcases and a lot of scrutiny. One click of a mouse and we can ping you the money and the way the price is tracking, you could make some big gains. Or I know someone who can provide an offramp."

"What the hell is an offramp." Ray was frustrated, but he had dollar signs in his eyes, or whatever the currency symbol for bitcoin was. He stopped walking and turned to Bondy. "Look, I'm not interested in a tire kicking exercise. I think that your buyer needs to show some commitment, something that would make me want to continue this conversation."

"No problem. Just give me your wallet address and I'll have a few BTC deposited."

"I assume BTC is Bitcoin? How do I find my wallet address?"

"I'm sure you have advisors who can help you, maybe someone at QSP?" Bondy probed for more information about who Ray might be in league with. "If you can get me the wallet address, I can get the client to show you how serious they are about buying the property."

Bondy felt a new emotion as she did catch sight of a very personal document, a colour photocopy of the photo page of her passport. She barged past him and grabbed the piece of paper, holding it up and waving it under his nose.

"Why do you have this?" she raged. "Making a copy of someone's ID is against the law. Last time I checked, the recommendation was for a $50 million fine for not storing private data correctly."

Ray tried to pull Bondy back from the desk where she was fumbling to open a manilla folder on top of a pile. "You need to leave. You're on private property and I'm in my rights to call the police." Bondy was already on her phone, her thumb poised over the third 0 required to summon the emergency services.

"You want the cops here?" Their eyes locked in a game of chicken. "I wonder what they would find in the stable building out the back. Maybe they could check your 'girlfriend's' ID while they are here and see if she's of legal age." She could see his face changing, his anger turning to show a new emotion, one that was rarely seen on Ray's face, fear. "Even if you've paid off the local station, my guess is that if forging of documents is involved, it would be the AFP that you'd be talking to."

Ray was conflicted. He knew he had compromised the operation and revealed more than he should have, but his greed was overtaking him. He wanted all the money or Bitcoin or whatever he could get from this woman. He'd known it was a risk inviting her here, and he'd planned in advance. "Let's go this way, have a seat, we can work something out, I am sure." He checked himself and thought better of putting his hand on the small of her back.

As she entered the kitchen, Bondy's head spun, and her skin felt clammy. She felt Ray's breath on the back of her neck and then... darkness.

6

The Airbnb was quiet, save for the whirring of various device fans and the local soundtrack of gulls circling above and cicadas in the trees. Tara looked at her phone in expectation and hope. It had been too long since Bondy had set off for the big house. She should have been in touch by now. A loud knocking on the door startled her out of her pessimism. She'd forgotten to eat; she'd forgotten she had ordered a curry. She'd forgotten she was barely dressed, a sarong knotted around her waist over her bikini, not leaving much to the imagination. *Too late to change now.* She opened the door and found herself staring at the courier. He was ruggedly handsome, like Tommo might have been 20 years ago, with a devil-may-care smile and a hint of stubble.

"Thai Green Curry for Tara?" his eyes wandered down her body and back up again with no hint of shame.

Tara flushed a little but enjoyed the attention from the younger man. "Yeah, that's me." She reached out for the paper bag and her hand brushed his. A tingling shock ran up her arm as a fantasy formed in her mind and she leaned in unconsciously. Was it not for the neighbour's dog barking at the seagulls… Tara snapped back to the present, the bag holding the plastic containers of curry and rice in her hand.

"Enjoy your meal," he gave her a look, perhaps a little disappointed that the dog had broken the spell of the moment.

"Thanks. You too," her cheeks burned as she heard her own voice. She hurriedly closed the door on him, turning, leaning back against it, her heart pounding. *Seriously, Tara? The food delivery guy? You're such a cliche.*

She poured the green curry and chicken over the steamed rice and toyed with the floating cubes of tofu with a fork before putting down the cutlery and picking up her phone. Still nothing from Bondy. Tara dialled. The phone connected, and rang, and rang and then Bondy's voice chirped.

"You've reached BA0001 concierge services. Please leave a message and I'll get back to you."

"Hmmm," Tara hung up without leaving a message. She stabbed at the chicken pieces in the spicy broth and lifted it to her mouth but all she could taste was cardboard. And then the phone rang. Unknown caller. "Hello?"

"Hello Tara." She recognised the voice. The Australian drawl, laced with a lascivious edge that made her move the phone away from her ear. "Your phone number was on the booking, but I am not calling about your accommodation."

"What do you want then, Mr Mason?" She was used to putting on this voice. The professional tone with just a hint of disdain. "If it's not to do with the property, then I can't imagine what would be calling me on a Sunday, let alone New Year's Eve."

"I need some consulting work done." Ray was being vague. "Off the books. I seem to remember that you were QSP's top crypto person. I need to allow someone to pay me using Bitcoin."

Tara's fingers gripped the phone more tightly as she thought through her play. She leaned back in her chair, using a calculated silence, making him wait. "Go on."

"Time is of the essence." His voice was strained, desperate even. She made him wait again. She waited until she heard his intake of breath, the breath he needed to speak. But she spoke first.

"Well," she said, "It's too difficult to explain over the phone. And…" *No way am I meeting you at Monaghan alone.* "Maybe we could meet somewhere public? The Royal Oak perhaps?" There was another silence, this time on Ray's end.

"No. Too many ears. Do I need my computer and Wi-Fi?"

Ray would be old school. He wouldn't trust something he couldn't touch, so that meant a cold wallet. "Do you have a USB type device that your crypto is stored on? That's all I need. We could meet at the picnic table in the park opposite the sailing club."

"That works. In an hour or so?"

"See you there." As she hung up the phone and stared at her barely touched meal, her mind was racing. She'd forgotten about Claudine and Tommo. She didn't need them. She could take down Ray Mason on her own, at least wipe out his crypto assets, or divert them. She had to look like a good team player though. She dialled Tommo.

"The number you have called is disconnected or not in service" an AI voice answered.

"Where are you both?" She composed a message to Tommo and hoped he would get it when and if he turned his phone on again.

- # -

He had given up on guessing passwords. The server room's constant mechanical whirring and humming changed and the solid concrete walls conveyed a new sound, a different constant mechanical chatter, the chop chop chop of helicopter blade tips. Tommo strained to listen. The most common helicopter in these parts was the distinctive red and yellow Eurocopter EC120 operated by Lifesaving Victoria. The bird would fly along the edge of the bay shark spotting and giving beachgoers a sense of safety. As the whop whop whop came closer, he knew it wasn't the lifesaving helicopter or the Leonardo AW139 of the Victoria police airwing.

How do they cool this place? The stone walls would keep heat from the computing power in as much as it would insulate from the sun outside. Tommo looked up at the ceiling. No AC ducting. He paced around the space until he found a grill set into the floor. He placed his open palm over the grate and felt cool air drifting up from below. *The Creek.* Exploring the room's floor more carefully, he found what he was looking for. Another grill, but this one was made for maintenance. He tugged the cover aside and climbed into the shaft, pulling the grate back over his head once inside, then down fifteen or twenty rungs of a ladder towards the sound of the running water below. It was pitch black darkness inside the pipe. He squatted and put his hand in the water to get a sense of which direction it was flowing. He had to crouch as he slowly made his way along the inside of the underground watercourse. The ambient light in the tunnel became brighter and as he came around a wide bend he squinted into the bright, blinding sunshine at the entrance. The grill was still open, still unlocked, which was lucky because he wouldn't have been able to reach or tumble the dials on the padlock from this angle. He could hear the helicopter again, but it was the sound of the engines powering down and the blades slowing. It was on the ground. If the passengers were headed to the beach house. He wasn't free and clear yet.

His skin stung from cuts he'd sustained from the first pass through the sword grass. He shuddered at the thought of another run of that gauntlet. *What if I go North?* Tommo tried to picture the aerial photographs of the area that he had studied the night before. *The old management college should be deserted today.* He crossed over the Gunyong creek and pushed through the dense scrub. The twigs and bark scratched at his skin, but didn't break it the way the long grass did.

His next goal was the Moondah gatehouse on Kunyung road, a heritage listed building that looked to him like it was designed by the same architect as Monaghan. In fact, the Mount Eliza gatehouse was a copy of the Picturesque Castellated Tudor Revival gatehouse, the main entrance to the Governor's Domain at Parramatta Park outside of Sydney. According to the heritage listing documents:

```
...the design for this 1885 gatehouse was derived
from an English architectural pattern book of 1878
titled The Englishman's House from a Cottage to a
Mansion by C. J. Richardson.
```

The version that Tommo had climbed toward, over the paspalum grass, was slightly simplified, featuring quoining only around the openings and less ornate wrought ironwork in the gates, which had been firmly locked shut. *It was going so well.* He had stood back and grinned. The gatehouse, built strong enough to keep out a marauding army, propped up a flimsy, temporary fence. Even Tommo, far from the peak of fitness, could scale the fence, assuming it didn't collapse beneath him. *Perhaps I want them to know I'm here in Mount Eliza.* Tommo had tumbled from the top of the fence into a conveniently planted copse of agapanthus before jogging toward the Nepean Highway. He took out his phone and pondered the consequences of his actions. If whoever was tracking him was in Mount Eliza, they would be on him quickly. If they were still watching Bondy's place in the city, perhaps he could lure them down the Peninsula as he travelled in the opposite direction. *Was Trevor Stone in the helicopter?* Tommo looked at the position of the sun in the sky to get a sense of the time. *Surely Stone would spend NYE on Sydney Harbour, not an obscure empty beach on Port Phillip.* He pressed his thumb against the power button and waited while the phone went through the boot-up process. It found the data network immediately, connected and pinged several times as backed up, undelivered messages and alerts came through.

```
Tara: I'm starting to worry about Bondy. She hasn't
```

come back from her meeting with Ray.

Tommo didn't want to keep his phone on longer than absolutely necessary. Normally Bondy could handle herself, but it was probably an error of judgement to have gone to Monaghan alone. His thumbs typed out a response.

Tommo: Meet me at the same place as before, near the red circle. 7pm.

He waited for the tick that confirmed delivery and then held his thumb against the on/off switch until the screen went black. Breaking into a jog, he headed for the nearest bus stop, hoping that the 781 or 788 or 785 would appear over the hill and he wouldn't have to wait out in the open for too long.

- # -

Despite the generous pay packet, Declan Sharp was not enjoying his job. Tommo's phone hadn't reappeared which meant he knew he was being tracked and had found a workaround. Meanwhile, Ray Mason was in danger of compromising the whole operation. Declan had strongly advised Ray not to meet Claudine Seaton-Bond, and if he did, to choose a neutral location and under no circumstances invite her to the Monaghan property. Normally the words 'strongly advise' were a euphemism for "do not do this," but Ray had ignored the order and organised to meet Bondy.

"You know better than to call this number." Declan's voice was cold and menacing. "All comms are to be through the encrypted chat tools." He heard heavy breathing on the other end of the phone.

"Sorry Mr…" Ray checked himself. *No Names.* "But… well…" He was sweating. "I should have taken your advice, but it's just that…"

Declan was already on the way to his car, a rental, parked within eyeline of Bondy's apartment. Tommo hadn't come back last night, at least not while the stakeout was in place. "What have you done? Actually. You know what? Don't tell me. Not on an open line. Send a message. Use Telegram. Stick to the protocol" He ended the call. "What a melt." He entered the car and cursed again. Without a sunshade over the windscreen, the vinyl seats had become molten. He lowered all the windows and cranked the AC as high as it would go as he waited for the messaging app to ping.

> Mason: The girl is secured in the stables. Her car has been returned to the pub car park. Her phone has been turned off and placed in a signal blocking pouch.

Not Good. Not good. Declan summoned all his military training to try and calm himself inside the furnace created by the hatchback being parked in the sun. There was a plan for this eventuality. Ray Mason had to be dealt with. Another ping from an incoming message. The old politician was getting impatient and desperate.

> Mason: ???

> Sharp: Stay where you are. Do not contact anybody. Do not let anyone onto the property. Do not let anyone currently on the property leave.

Placing the phone in a dashboard holder, Declan tentatively touched the steering wheel and hissed as it burnt his fingers. The phone pinged with a different tone, an alert from the tracking app. He picked it up again and opened the map. *What the*... The blue dot that represented Tommo's location was uncomfortably close to one of the operation's assets. Zooming in he watched as the tracker moved away from the Mount Eliza property that housed a crypto-mining site and other activities, some legal, some not. As suddenly as the blue dot appeared it vanished. He wants us to know he's there. *What did you find Tommo? How did you find it?* Punching the steering wheel, Declan climbed out of the car. He kicked the front tire as he walked in a circle and tried to prioritise the threats to his employer.

The men down on the Peninsula were horse trainers and farmhands. None of them had been read in on the current situation. None of them were familiar with what Tommo looked like and finding him now that the phone was off again would be difficult. The helo was already down there, one of Trevor's mate's girlfriends in hiding from her abusive husband. Drama he didn't need. The facility was secure. There were no alarms or alerts, no messages from the motion sensing cameras at the beach house, no unscheduled visitors let past security at the front gate.

Had he time to do a thorough audit of the security systems he would have seen his own badge used to open the door to the server room, but that scenario never entered his head as a possibility. If he moved in that direction now, he would signal to Tommo that the location was important. No. Chasing Tommo was not the best use of his time and effort.

Tara seemed to be towing the line. There had been no deviations from her expected behaviour since the meeting with QSP on Friday apart from the purchase of a dirt bike, reported by Mace's flunkey, Memphis. Once Declan had gone a bit further back into her past the bike didn't raise any flags. VicRoads showed a motorcycle licence issued in her name when she was 18 and a registration for a road-legal motocross bike. So, she was having some kind of pre-midlife crisis. Nothing for him to worry about. Let her enjoy New Year's Eve alone, crying into a bottle of wine.

Somehow, Declan had to work Bondy's kidnap to his advantage. At least Mace hadn't killed her. She wasn't a faceless backpacker or migrant worker; she had rich and powerful friends who would fund investigations into her death. The only option was to let her think that the part of the operation run out of Monaghan was the extent of it, that

Mace was a pervert who had a thing for teenage girls and helped to acquire them for others. Declan could use Bondy to throw Ray under the bus. It would be her testimony that would sink him, the organisation could be kept out of it. He had to rescue her. If he freed her from Ray, then she might trust him. Owe him even. *Yes. That could work.* He got back in the car, condensation forming on the windscreen, frigid on the inside, baking hot outside. Perhaps it was delirium caused by the heat, but he began to hum a tune his mum used to play when he was a kid. The Duke Ellington orchestra with Ella Fitzgerald singing… "Do nothing 'till you hear from me". His version was less jazzy and terser.

Sharp: Do absolutely NOTHING until I get there.

- # -

Tara sat in her truck, fingers drumming lightly on the steering wheel, eyes fixed on the wooden picnic table across the road, with the sailing club beyond. She was still a little bit flushed, part green curry, part encounter with hot green curry delivery guy and, part telephone exchange with Ray Mason. She'd packed a small bag with a little black dress and a pair of heels, prepared for the low probability chance she ended up somewhere formal. Not knowing how she was going to spend New Year's Eve, not having a plan still made her uncomfortable. Her phone vibrated against the dashboard.

Tommo: Meet me at the same place as before, near the red circle. 7pm.

Tara: Okay.

That would give her time to complete her meeting with Ray. She had come to expect the lack of receipt. There were no ticks. Not delivered. Not read. He was there and then he was gone, but she had other things to worry about.

Ray looked different. The bravado and cockiness that he had when he held court at the Royal Oak seemed to be gone. He wore a sweat-stained white polo shirt that rode up over his belly full of beer. He had a small black backpack slung over his shoulder and in his left hand, he clutched a small object. The cold wallet. He looked to be alone. He paused at the picnic table, scanning the area before sitting down, facing away from her.

Grabbing her laptop, Tara climbed out of the truck, crossing the road with a light, confident gait as if her mojo had already flowed from him to her. "Mr. Mason," she said politely as she approached, her voice now the same professional tone she used with clients she happily billed but had no respect for. She didn't offer her hand.

"Tara, thanks for meeting me." Ray was also playing a character.

"Of course," she replied smoothly, taking a seat at the table and setting her laptop down. "This shouldn't take long, I just need to get the wallet address off the device, do you have it with you?" Ray nodded. He placed the USB cold wallet on the table between them. Tara reached for it and plugged it into her laptop while they held eye contact. She worked quickly, expertly, bringing up the interface for the wallet. "All right," she said, her tone brisk and professional. "I don't suppose you remember the 12 random word recovery phrase for this device, do you? Every crypto wallet has one, you probably would have had to write it down somewhere, because it's usually words that don't go together."

Ray frowned. "Yeah, yeah. I got it," he took a crumpled yellow Post-it note out of his jeans. "But I was told never to give this to anyone."

Tara put on her 'silly Asian girl' smile and turned the computer around. "You can just type it in. I won't look." She widened her smile as she began two apps in the background. One a keylogger and one that recorded the screen as a video.

He typed with his forefingers only. One finger, one key at a time.

It took a while as he looked from the note to the screen to the keys. Tara pretended to be looking out to sea until he turned the laptop back around, so the screen faced her. She handed him a cheap plastic pen she'd stolen from The Aquarius Resort. "You will need to take this down; this is the address you need to give to the person sending you Bitcoin. Ready?" She read from the screen "B for bravo, C for Charlie, the number 1, Q for Quebec, V for victor, 3 …"

"How much is in there?" Ray asked, prepared to be disappointed "I mean I know there is minimum 10 bitcoin, but what's it worth today?"

Tara gave a soft laugh. "Right now, 10 bitcoin is worth $422,651 and ninety cents. That's US dollars, so 640K in Kangaroobles, give or take."

Ray exhaled, visibly relaxing. "It's not what was when I bought in, but it's not bad as a rainy-day pot eh?"

Tara took the drive out of her laptop and slid it back across the table. "I'm happy to help." She lied. "Though there is the small matter of my fee."

A sneer came across Ray's face as his act dropped. He reached into the backpack and placed a brick sized package on the table. "None of your funny money. Just a lovely bunch of non-sequential pineapples."

Tara stood, closing her laptop with a decisive snap. She steadied herself against the table and picked up the package without looking inside. Ray was blinded by his prejudices, he couldn't imagine this dutiful corporate servant doing anything but taking orders, but this was her world. The fifties were nothing compared to what this session was going to cost him. She watched Ray slink off out of sight and thought about Claudine. Bondy hadn't been mentioned by either party during the consulting session. Tara didn't want to seem to be worried or accusative. While heading out of town, away from the seaside on her way to meet with Tommo, she decided to make a detour past the Royal Oak. She wasn't sure what she was expecting to find, but it wasn't Bondy's unique ride parked at the back of the carpark. A sense of confusion and disorientation came over her.

"Call Bondy," Tara instructed the hands-free system in her truck.

"Calling Bondy" it answered dutifully and the sing-song melody of dual tone multiple frequency chords for each of the number's tones played through the speakers. "You've reached BA0001 concierge services. Please leave a message and I'll get back to you."

A horn blared impatiently behind her, the truck stationary in the middle of the road across from the pub. Tara accelerated. Stick to the plan. Go and get Tommo. The drive needed a playlist, something new, filled with new discoveries. Surprise me. The streaming service offered its next algorithm curated selection…

'I think I hear the sounds of then,
And people talking,
The scenes recalled, by minute movement,
And songs they fall, from the backing tape.
That certain texture, that certain smell,'

She was two years old when that one was released, but it spoke to her. She knew all the words. She'd never seen lightning crack over cane fields, but she knew a few awkward blocks that faced west with long diagonals and slopes, and she knew what it felt like, to lie in sweat, on familiar sheets, or unfamiliar, in brick veneer on financed beds. She squirmed. That line reminded her of the man she was on the way to meet.

- # -

Tommo was looking at the bay again, out of the Metro train's window as it trundled over one of the new overpasses built as part of the level crossing removal project. He had his earbuds in. He tapped his foot unconsciously.

'Out on the patio we'd sit,
And the humidity we'd breathe,
We'd watch the lightning crack over cane fields
Laugh and think, this is Australia.'

He was worried about Bondy. Not worried, concerned. Maybe she was playing mind games with Tara, but there had been no messages to his phone when he'd turned it on. If she was winding-up Tara or testing her, she would have let him in on the plan. Maybe. He wasn't sure who was on whose side anymore. Maybe they had underestimated Mace. The guy had his back to the wall, he was desperate. *Had she pushed the wrong button? Hit a nerve that made him snap?*

So far, his return journey to the city had been uneventful. The wait at the bus stop had not been more than 2 minutes. The 781 Ventura bus had whisked him along Old Mornington Road past Toorak College and then down the sweeping slope of Olivers Hill with views of Mount Dandenong and the 'Ming Wing' on the distant horizon. Back to the dilapidated shopfronts in front of Frankston station. He'd wandered into the burger shop and been assaulted by the unique smell of old chip fat and fried onions as his shoes struggled for grip on the greasy linoleum floor. No doubt, the hamburger with 'the lot' would have a fried egg, a slice of beetroot and a pineapple ring. *No time for nostalgia, or food poisoning. No sign of a tail.* If he had been followed, his shadow was much more skilled than the guy in the t-shirt, Sharp. "Who is Sharp?"

- # -

If Melbourne had a native species of tumbleweed, it would have rolled down the empty streets of the Docklands, had there been any wind to propel it. There was not. Tara sat in her truck, parked in sight of the statue of crouched red figures where she had met Tommo a few days earlier. There were only a few hours left in 2023. The first 8500 or so hours in the year had been forgettable, unremarkable. The last 120 hours or so had been a surreal, improbable adventure. A familiar shape appeared from behind a wall and paced around the art installation. Tara waited to see if anyone else appeared, but the whole suburb felt like one of those horror films where the entire population vanishes without trace or explanation, like a modern day, city reboot of 'Picnic at Hanging Rock'.

"Hey." She hadn't seen him since the steak dinner at the pub, when Bondy had fed him cherry tomatoes off her plate and made jokes about Ray being a pervert, not the 'good kind'.

He turned. His face had aged significantly more than the couple of days that had passed. "Hey. Thanks for coming. You've kinda been dumped in the middle of all of this haven't you." They hugged. Both assumed a platonic posture, but both were transported back to the quiz night as they embraced.

"Claudine's car is parked at the Royal, but her phone is going straight to voicemail. What do we do now?" Tara asked.

"Short of calling the cops, there isn't much we can do," Tommo extracted himself from her arms and backed away reluctantly. "They won't do anything immediately though, she's only been 'missing' for a few hours." His line of sight followed an incoming Emirates A380 over Bolte bridge on approach to the main airport. "New Year's Eve, they will be stretched thin with yobbos disobeying the public drinking laws. A rich girl who hasn't answered her phone… well."

"Maybe we… I should call the Oak and see if she is there," Tara suggested. "Do you think they would give out information about a guest?"

"It's worth a shot." He shrugged. "Tie it into New Year's somehow?"

Tara nodded. She looked up the hotel on Maps and dialled. And waited. It rang out. *I wouldn't want to work in a pub on New Year's*

Eve. The crowd, the noise, everyone thinking they're entitled to special treatment. The inevitable mess at the end of the night. She dialled again. It rang and rang until finally, someone answered.

"Good evening, Royal Oak Hotel…. Before you ask, no you can't reserve a table, we are fully booked for tonight and tomorrow?"

The exasperation in the voice caused Tara to change her approach slightly. "Hi. I just left the carpark, and it looks like someone has left their headlights on. It would really ruin the night if someone found a flat battery. It would be a long wait for the RACV. It's a Land Rover."

"Yeah, I know the one. One of the guests. Haven't seen them though. They aren't in the bar or out the back. Maybe they went for a walk or something." There was a sound of crashing plates and glasses in the background. "Sorry, I got to go. Thanks for letting us know." The line disconnected.

"Nothing?" Tommo already knew the answer.

Tara shook her head. "She's not at the hotel or in the bar."

"There isn't much more we can do at the moment. Bondy's smart, maybe she's gone off grid. They might be tracking her phone the way they tracked mine."

"That makes some sense. If she is trying to scope out Monaghan because she learned something from Ray. Maybe her phone is in the car at the pub. So, we just wait, I guess." Tara's gaze was on the yachts moored at the small jetties by the side of the river. There was no security to be seen. The experiences of the last few days were making her bolder, bringing out the rebel that the corporate world had quashed. With a hint of wildness in her voice, she pretended to make it sound like a joke. "What if we just… took one of these?"

Tommo turned to her; eyebrows raised in surprise. "You mean steal a boat? And just sail off into the bay?"

"Why not?" Tara's eyes glinted. The idea was getting more appealing the longer she considered it. "They don't look like they are even locked. Not big enough to have AIS. We could disappear for a bit. No one would be looking for us on the water and… I do my best thinking on the water."

Tommo shook his head. "I'm already being hunted. Who knows what charges they are going to pin on me when they catch me. And you want to add Grand Theft Sailboat or piracy?" He was objecting, but there was a part of him that wanted this adventure though. To have her as his partner in crime.

Tara was already walking out onto a floating pontoon where an old yacht, set up for long-distance, shorthanded cruising was tied up. She looked around, but Tommo was the only one watching her, so she grabbed the shroud at the widest part of the hull and stepped aboard.

Tommo followed her, but stayed on the dock as she looked to see if she could gain entry to the cabin. He didn't want to encourage her, but he heard himself offering advice. "Check the table in the middle there, lift the lid, it's a cold space. If it is anything like the boats I used to sail on, it will be full of beer cans, half empty sunscreen bottles and the key."

She was one step ahead of him, lifting the top of the table and rummaging around, grinning from ear to ear as she held up a rusty key attached to a ring designed to float.

"What's got into you? Are you high?" Tommo felt like a 5-year-old stealing apples off the neighbour's tree, except the stakes were much higher.

Tara paused and looked at him quizzically. "You've never been joyriding? Ever?" She tested the key in the lock that secured the main hatch, her eyes gleaming with a mix of nostalgia and defiance. "You know," she confessed in an unrepentant tone, "I used to steal cars and bikes and tractors all the time growing up. It was just a bit of fun, something almost everyone did, well if you were a boy, in the town where I grew up."

Tommo was taken aback by her admission. "You used to steal cars? For fun?"

"Yeah," Tara replied, a small smile playing on her lips. "Not much to do. No one really locked anything. So, we'd 'borrow' things.

Sometimes for an hour or so, occasionally longer. It was a kind of rite of passage, I guess. Something to do to feel alive, to shake off the boredom. It wasn't just me, though I was the only girl. I guess I did it to fit in."

Tommo nodded slowly as he watched her head disappear into the main cabin of the yacht. He spoke louder so she could hear him. "Yeah. I guess that initiation kinda thing existed for me, but it was mainly pranks. You know, throwing rocks onto tin roofs or writing swear words on the footy oval using pesticide."

The front hatch flipped open from inside and Tara stuck her head out. "The old folks probably knew what we were up to, but they turned a blind eye. As long as we weren't causing real trouble, they let us have our fun. I guess they figured we'd grow out of it eventually, or maybe it just wasn't worth the paperwork." Her tone shifted to the task at hand. "Looks like all the sails are onboard."

Tommo shook his head. "You're not a juvenile in a hick town anymore. We get caught 'borrowing' this boat and we do jail time. Come on, it was a fun idea. But we can't just go on the run. I know. I've tried it."

The hatch flipped back down, and he heard it being sealed shut from inside. Tara's head reappeared and she locked up and replaced the key where she found it. She stood behind the wheel, pretending to steer, imagining a 15 knot south-westerly filling the sails. "I reckon we could get to Devonport or Warnambool, maybe Eden if we went left out of the bay," but her bravado was fading as the reality of their situation, fuelled by Tommo's conscience, killed her fantasy.

Tommo helped Tara off the yacht and back onto the private jetty. It rocked on its floats as her weight was added to his. "Let's head back in the direction of your cottage. It's New Year's Eve. Everyone is going to be distracted." He really didn't want to spend the night in Bondy's box of an apartment. "We could swing by Ray's place and maybe see if there are any clues to where Bondy got to."

Tara looked over her shoulder at the yacht with a shrug of

disappointment but kept walking towards where she had parked.

- # -

Tommo smiled over at Tara as she drove. It wasn't the vehicle he imagined she would have driven, but then he hadn't imagined her as a teenage joyrider either. He'd pegged her for an EV type, but inside the cabin, with her hands on the wheel, she seemed confident and controlled. Neither seemed to want to break the silence, but it became increasingly uncomfortable.

"We could just stay in," Tara offered. It was a place to start the negotiation about how they might spend the last night of the year. "Watch whoever they have dragged up for the Sydney harbourside concert and pop a bottle of bubbly at midnight?"

Tommo watched the reflective stickers on the wooden roadside posts lit up by the headlights. "We could. Seems very romantic. And we never really talked about that night." He could feel her blush even though he wasn't looking in her direction.

"On the other hand, it is New Year's Eve. Don't you want to be around people?" She didn't really know what her own preference was. She had resigned herself to being alone.

He shrugged. "Look at how the last time worked out. I'm not sure I want to be seen by all the locals at the Pier Hotel. I guess there is some safety in numbers. Archie and Marta will probably be there."

She hesitated. He wasn't making it any easier. *Choose one.* She gripped the wheel harder. "You're thinking about Bondy," she said with a hint of jealousy that she wasn't expecting. "Maybe having people around would be better."

"Why don't we start at the pub," he countered. "Have a drink with Archie and Marta and ask if anyone heard anything about Bondy on the grapevine." Tommo studied Tara's face for her reaction as he laid out the plan. "They'll probably do a shit town version of fireworks at 9pm, then we can head back to the cottage for Midnight."

Biting her lip unconsciously, Tara nodded as she glanced at the dashboard clock. "The IGA will still be open. How about I pick up a few supplies for later while you check out Bondy's 4WD parked at the Oak?" She braked instinctively and nodded up ahead. The darkness was pierced by blue and red flashing lights. The two lanes had been restricted into one by traffic cones. Every car could be stopped and the driver subjected to a random breath test. "I guess we won't be going in the front gate of Monaghan. Too many eyes."

- # -

The Royal Oak was heaving, in a way that only a pub where the average age of the patrons was around 65 could manage. It wasn't a pub on nights like these, it was an old-time music hall cum ballroom, minus the cum. Tonight, there was an energy that made the patrons think it was 1970 again. It was one of those evenings when the good stuff would be flowing, no Australian sparkling wine, no this was a night for Piper Heidsieck. The VB would be swapped for Crown Lager, a local kind of bar one upmanship.

Tommo wasn't interested in the goings on inside The Oak. While the patron's attention was focussed on the amateur swing band, Tommo was focussed on the carpark where Bondy's unique ride was parked away from the overhead lights. For all the upgrades, Tommo knew that the concierge was an old-fashioned, practical girl. Fumbling around under the wheel arch, Tommo found what he was looking for - a small box, attached to the undercarriage by a magnet. He used the key, not the fob, not wanting the headlights to flash or the horn to sound the 'unlock' tone. He slid into the driver's seat and took a deep breath, then turned the key in the ignition one click, just enough to activate the GPS history. Sure, enough the car had been driven to Monaghan at the scheduled time and then 45 minutes later it had been driven back to the pub. He opened the glove compartment and found a small, leather-bound notebook. He knew what it was from their time together. It was a diary. *Bondy wouldn't have taken it in her handbag to the meeting with Mace or trust it to the hotel safe.* Tommo held the book in his hands for a moment and then replaced it unopened. He ducked down in the driver's seat as two shadows emerged from the back entrance of the pub. The shadows were arm in arm, giggling like school children. Tommo held his breath as they approached. Cheryl, the membership secretary of the art gallery and Geoff, the used car manager at the local dealer. Both were married, but not to each other. *No. No. Not here.* Tommo looked to the heavens in silent prayer to a god he didn't believe in as the man pinned his panting partner in adultery up against the side of the Land Rover. All Tommo could do was wait it out, and wish for the merciful intervention of beer-induced impotence.

- # -

In the surprisingly busy, but dimly lit IGA carpark, Declan Sharp sat in the driver's seat of his hire car, methodically changing the batteries in his favourite torch. Negative end down, positive end up, all the metal contacts bright and shiny, no chance of failure. The small interior of the car was flooded with a bright, almost blinding light. The petrol guzzling rumble of an approaching engine made him look to the side mirror to avoid the light. A pickup truck pulled into the space directly behind him, the headlights making the inside of his car like daylight. The driver's door of the truck opened, and he watched a figure exit quickly then, sprint towards the supermarket's entrance. *That's Tara Kwong.* Even in low light, Declan recognised her. He estimated he had about two minutes, maybe less, before she would return. That was all the time he needed.

His hands moved with practised efficiency as he rummaged through the worn pilot's case resting on the passenger seat beside him. It contained all manner of tools and gadgets — each one with a specific purpose, even the ones that were rarely used. His fingers were searching for something specific. Finally, he found it: a handheld printer, small and compact, perfect for the task at hand. Steadying himself with a deep breath to induce a calm enough to efficiently deal with the urgency of the situation, he connected the device to an app on his phone via Bluetooth, then he typed out a simple, four-word message. Then he placed a piece of spare paper under the printhead and watched the letters slowly materialising in neat Arial font as he moved the device from left to right.

His eyes darted back to the front door of the supermarket. Tara was still inside, now at the checkout, her focus entirely on the transaction. Declan's heart rate remained steady as he folded the paper, slipping it into a plain, unmarked brown envelope. There was nothing distinctive about it, nothing that could lead to the identity of the author. He approached Tara's truck with practised stealth, envelope in hand. In one fluid motion, he slid it under the wiper blade, ensuring it was securely in place, but not so tightly wedged that it would go unnoticed. He allowed himself one last glance towards the supermarket. Tara was still inside, but the clock was counting down as the staff urged the straggling customers out of the store, now 10 minutes after the advertised closing time.

Returning to his car, Declan turned the key in the ignition. He eased out of the parking space with the care of a teenager trying to pass his licence test the first time. His movements unhurried, careful. It wasn't until he was clear of the car park that he finally turned on his headlights, headed towards his next destination - Mason's mess.

- # -

Giving the kid closing the sliding door of the IGA a wink and a flash of upper thigh, Tara managed to negotiate her way inside just before closing. She'd made a list in her head. Champagne, or perhaps

Australia sparkling wine given the brand above the door. A bunch of grapes, a wedge of Danish blue cheese and a packet of water crackers. She was glad she only had a minute or two as the underpaid staff ushered her through the store back to the registers so they could get to their own celebrations. The less time she had to think about being alone with Tommo at midnight while his ex-girlfriend was missing, the less time she had to dwell on the spinning moral compass in her head. Placing her items on the conveyor of the checkout, she laughed softly at the impulse items displayed before her. *Someone understands this market.* Next to the sunscreen were condoms and headache pills and cheap sunglasses. She added one of each on the moving belt and made a shrugging gesture to the cashier. "Happy New Year."

The cashier was desperate to get out of her gaudy uniform so she could head down to the beach where a bottle of 'Bundy' waiting for her. She ignored Tara as she scanned the items and nodded to the card reader. Tara held her phone over the pad and waited for the beep. *I should have used cash. Do they take cash?* She hurriedly shoved her purchases into a paper bag that cost her more than the generic Ibuprofen.

Walking back towards her truck, Tara took in the atmosphere of the small coastal town as the locals and tourists prepared for the annual celebration of the calendar ticking over to the next year. A secular event in multicultural Australia brought together more people on a common date than any other day or festival. She creased her brow as she approached her parking spot and found a brown envelope tucked under the wiper blade. *Surely that traffic cop isn't handing out fines tonight.* With her breath held, she opened the envelope and took out a small, unremarkable piece of paper. The text printed with a generic inkjet in a default Arial font. One line.

We have the British girl

She was being followed. They did know where she was. Moreover, Claudine wasn't just missing, she had been taken, presumably by Ray Mason or his associates. A romantic night alone with Tommo probably wouldn't be the wisest course of action.

- # -

Claudine awoke from her drug-induced slumber to a reality far less harrowing than the nightmarish visions that had plagued her unconscious mind. For what seemed like hours, she had been left alone, confined to the unforgiving floor of what she gradually recognised from her 90-degree perspective as a converted stable. The roughness of the concrete beneath her made her shift uncomfortably, trying to alleviate the atrophied muscles in her shoulders and the bruises where her hips rested on the floor. The pungent scent of stale straw and harsh chemicals filled her nostrils, making her wrinkle her nose in distaste. They were not farm chemicals. They were bleaches and inks and printer toner. Her wrists, forced behind her back, were bound tightly with coarse hemp rope. Each movement only aggravated the stinging abrasions on her skin. The same type of rope bound her ankles together, further limiting her ability to move. She knew this kind of rope all too well, common on farms, plentiful, and strong enough to hold even the unruliest of animals.

As her eyes gradually adjusted to the dim, muted light that filtered through the small window, made in a time when glass was expensive and used sparingly, she took in her surroundings with increasing clarity. The room offered little in terms of comfort or escape. The muted glow from outside suggested the sun had recently set. *Must be about 8:45.* The twilight gave the room a dark romance feeling. Dark because, the external door remained firmly closed, with only a sliver of light creeping underneath.

Mace panicked. He's losing it. Bondy's anger simmered. It

wasn't born of fear but of frustration and indignation. She wasn't scared. What infuriated her was the chain of events that had led her to this moment. She cursed herself for the naïveté that had led her to accept the chocolates from that seemingly innocent girl and felt sick that the laced sweets even existed. The memory of finding a copy of her passport in Ray's study just before she had blacked out confirmed some of the suspicions about the nature of the operation, and Ray knew it. *He's not going to kill me.* There was no point in speaking aloud.

The light outside dimmed further as the sun dropped below the horizon. It was blue hour, a photographer's favourite when the sky is neither fully day nor fully night. Back in England, it would have been different - the sun setting a full 8 hours earlier at around 4pm, the evening chill creeping in. There, at this time of year, fire was something to be welcomed, not feared. She shivered at the thought of the flammability of her temporary prison. A tinder box. Then her thoughts drifted to where she could have been, Constitution Dock in Hobart, mingling with triumphant offshore sailors, surrounded by stories of varying truth. But she was here, waiting, waiting for Mace, a washed-up politician now not much more than a common pervert. Waiting for the scared old man to come to his senses or for his string puller to instruct him to release her. *Who pulls your strings, Mr. Mason?*

- # -

Tara took a deep breath as she stood outside the Pier Hotel, mentally preparing to go inside. She had changed into her little black dress and heels, perhaps a little bit overdressed, but she didn't care. She cared less about what people thought about her with each passing day. Each time she was prejudged or underestimated she became more resolved to just be whatever she wanted to be. She enjoyed the looks as her heels clicked on the wooden floorboards, the sound drowned out by the mixed crowd's revelry. The music was turned up and there was a party atmosphere. Tara made her way through the bar and out to the beer garden where she'd met Tommo for the first time. It seemed like a lifetime ago, but it was only the night before last.

"Hey, we saved you a seat," Marta called out and waved as Tara stood at the edge of the beer garden and looked around for anyone she knew, which was a small list. The wave was acknowledged with a nod and Tara made her way towards the group - Marta, Archie, and Tommo, who had secured a picnic table, which was a good thing, because the little black dress would not work well with a deck chair. Marta wore a pale blue dress that showed off her tanned shoulders. It wasn't quite as formal as Tara's, but she looked like she had made an effort, unlike the two men.

"I must have missed the memo," Tommo said as he looked Tara up and down appreciatively.

"It's a tradition of mine," replied Tara, shuffling next to Archie on the bench.

Marta came to her rescue. "You look amazing girl, no need to justify dressing up for a party." She poured a flute full of sparkling rose from an ice bucket and handed it to Tara. "What shall we drink? Old and new friends?" The men raised their pints.

"May you never lie, cheat or steal," Archie preached. Marta sighed. It was one of Archie's favourite toasts, but she quite liked it. "If you may lie, may you lie in the arms of a lover." He smirked and nodded at Tommo and Tara who both squirmed on the bench. Marta laughed. "If you must cheat, may you cheat death." They all looked at Tommo who nodded and raised his glass higher. Tara's smile thinned as she thought about the note left on her truck and hoped Bondy was okay. "And if you must steal, may you steal time…" The glasses clinked together, and they all drank as they processed the message of the toast in their own way.

"What have you done with Bondy?" Marta asked Tara. There was a joking tone in her voice. "Did you scare her off? Pay her off? Maybe you wanted Tommo all to yourself at midnight."

Tara visibly shuddered. She reached into her small black clutch bag and took out the note and placed it on the table. "I don't know where she is, but I have a bad feeling."

"Where did you get this?" Archie placed his hand on the slip of paper before it blew away. He picked it up and examined it, turning it over as if there was something extra on the back that had been missed. "Is it a ransom play? Do they want money?"

"Or an exchange," Tommo said bleakly. "Maybe they want to do a deal. Me for her."

"Maybe you should turn your phone on," Marta suggested. "The one they have the number for. The one that they are tracking." She upended the bottle in the ice-bucket.

Seeing a chance to get away from the intense scrutiny, Tara offered to go to the bar and get another bottle. "Same again guys?" She stood up and backed away slightly.

"I'll come with you." Marta rose too and put her hand around Tara's shoulders. "I'm sorry. I didn't mean to accuse you of kidnap!" She laughed, and hugged Tara closer. "Are we good, girl?"

Archie waited until the women were out of earshot, but he leaned over the table, closer towards Tommo "If they are looking for an exchange or a ransom, then they will keep her alive." He lifted his drink to his lips and emptied what was left. "Looks like they are keeping an eye on Tara too though."

"I was with Tara though," Tommo said, looking over his shoulder. "Why did they wait until she had dropped me off to slip a note under her windshield?" He shrugged. "Unless she is in on it. Nah I don't know. Nothing makes much sense at the moment."

Tara and Marta walked towards the bar, the clinking of glasses and the lively chatter of the crowd filling the air. Tara felt a surge of relief as she stepped away from the tense conversation about Bondy. She was still worried, but she knew that worrying wouldn't help.

"I'm sorry about before," Marta said, her voice soft and genuinely apologetic. "I didn't mean to be so accusatory, but this time of year is stressful for me at the best of times. Makes me remember how far away I am from home. You know, family."

"It's okay," Tara nodded, "It's hard to trust people right now, especially someone you don't know. Do you get back to the States much?"

"I used to. We used to. Before Covid. The lockdowns in Victoria were brutal for people with family overseas - or even in another state - but things are getting better. And we have WhatsApp now, free video calling, so…." Her voice trailed off as the barman looked at her impatiently.

Tara raised her hand. "I'll get this." She ordered the round and turned to Marta as they waited. "I'm putting on a brave face," she confided. "That note scared the shit out of me. I work in an office; I'm not used to being stalked and threatened."

"You don't have to be part of it." Marta took the bottle and Tara picked up a pint of beer in each hand. They began working their way through the crowd, back out to the garden. "You don't know any of us really, though I kinda hoped that we could be friends, I can't remember the last time I made a friend - that wasn't one of Archie's."

"Let's see how this thing works out, I like this place. I could see myself spending some more time here. Maybe even buy a place." The crowd were all standing now, facing away from the pub.

"9:30. Family Fireworks," Archie said. "It won't last long. The RSPCA and the dog lobby are trying to get them banned altogether. But for now, we get a couple of minutes of Oooh… and Ahhhh." He turned and looked skyward as a whistle accompanied a fine light trail upwards. The gunpowder, invented by Tara's distant ancestors detonated and exploded into a familiar multicoloured rainbows and everything was forgotten for a while.

- # -

Ray Mason stood atop the tower at Monaghan, with a sardonic grimace on his lips. The fireworks display in the distance was a pathetic spectacle compared to years gone by, a feeble attempt to cling onto a sense of community in a world that was rapidly descending into selfishness and chaos. He had sent his latest temporary diversion packing, her whining, and complaints a grating annoyance that he had silenced with a generous dose of Molly. Enough to bundle her into an Uber without fuss. There was no time for his favourite brand of pleasure now.

The fixer was on his way, a harbinger of the organisation's displeasure with the way he had handled recent events. Ray reached into his pocket, his fingers closing around the USB crypto wallet that Tara had so diligently configured. The balance was substantial enough to provide for a lifestyle he had grown accustomed to, but it would fund an even more lavish existence in the countries just to the North and West. He didn't want to start over, but his choices were rapidly diminishing. He had realised, as he walked away from the park, that he had no idea how to navigate the technical realities of cryptocurrency, how to convert the Bitcoin into tangible wealth, but the QSP consultant had confirmed it was there. He reached for his tumbler of the single malt he reserved for special occasions. The tasting notes say:

'Barbeque sweetness and a crack of black pepper is complemented with rich fruit cake and dried fruits. A drop of water opens the smoke and fruity sweetness from the wine casks, bringing a beautiful balance as notes of apple and pear grow with the dram.'

But all Ray could taste was bitterness. His view alternated from the sky in the distance to the main driveway below. Sharp should be here by now. Even with the NYE traffic, he should have arrived an hour ago. Ray resisted the urge to send a message, his remaining pride refusing to allow him to appear weak or vulnerable. The fireworks exploded in a final, far-off barrage.

In the distance, Claudine could hear the detonations. She couldn't see the fireworks, but she could feel them through the ground. *The family fireworks. 9:30.* She counted the explosions to keep her mind active in the darkness She imagined what each firework might look like based on its sound; how big, what colours, and what the effect might look like from the ground below? As quickly as the muffled drum-like performance began, it was over. Bondy writhed on the floor, trying to get comfortable before falling into an uneasy sleep.

- # -

Declan's drone buzzed high above the Monaghan property. The mechanical hum of the four rotors were drowned out by the cicadas and crickets and the din of mosquitoes around the pool, drawn to the Tiki lamps that contravened the Total Fire Ban order that had been in effect all day. He piloted the device in a grid pattern from his phone until he saw an orange shape on the otherwise black screen. A heat signature. *There should be three. Mason, one of his lodgers and the target.* A frown crossed Sharp's face as he zoomed in closer on the main house. There was only one highlighted form. *Too big to be a girl. It has to be Ray.* The shape seemed to be slumped in a chair in the room the plans said was the study. *Maybe his guest is in the basement. Sick bastard.* Resuming his search pattern, Sharp hovered over one of the outbuildings which had once been stables. There was another figure. Not as bright, but discernible as lying on the floor, consistent with being tied up. *Ms Bond, I presume.*

The flying surveillance kit returned to Declan's position on the fire track. It had been the scene for more activity in the last two days than the previous two years. Declan stowed the drone in its protective case and checked his backpack. This bag had seen more action than most men. In the main compartment, a tangle of black paracord lay coiled, ready to be transformed into a climbing rope or lash logs together for a raft. *No guns. Too noisy.* Instead, nestled in a dedicated, padded compartment, was a sleek, black combat knife and a small handheld crossbow. He checked off a mental list as he worked through the contents of the backpack, deciding what to take and what to leave behind. He needed his favourite torch, with fresh batteries within easy reach. In a smaller, zippered pocket was a multi-tool, a first-aid kit and, a worn, leather-bound notebook, its pages filled with cryptic notes, coordinates, and sketches. *Sometimes analogue is still the way to go.* He still hadn't found what he was looking for and there was a moment of dread at the thought of having lost his talismanic Zippo lighter. He rummaged around at the bottom of the waterproof bag until his fingers brushed over the familiar shape. Familiar to his fingers, but not quite the familiar shape that most knew. This trophy had sharper corners, dating from 1933. The object filled him with a sense of comfort. It was more than just a tool; it was a companion, and it never talked back, and it always got the job done right.

Declan slipped the lighter into the pocket of his tactical cargo pants and slung the backpack over his right shoulder. Rather than fumble with the combination padlock, he vaulted the gate and made his way towards the outbuildings, stopping occasionally to look through a handheld thermal monocular. No guards to be seen, just a few possums moving through the treetops and the flicker of the Tiki torches. He weighed his options.

With less than an hour of the year remaining, no-one would report a fire to the authorities unless it posed a direct threat to life or property. The house, a sprawling monstrosity, was a monument to wealth and privilege. He felt no remorse for its potential destruction, but it would undoubtedly attract excessive scrutiny. Scanning the publicly available photographs of the grounds, gleaned from Instagram posts of various parties and garden open days, he pinched in on a solution. The giant pin oak tree, a sentinel of the estate, ancient, gnarled, and majestic would be his target. Its destruction would constitute a significant event. It would draw attention and might even precipitate Ray Mason's arrest. A thrill accompanied the plan, a sense of calculated risk. The oak would burn.

Sharp moved quickly, hunched over, moving from one shadow to another. There were no guards. Ray's disobedience in relation to keeping the monitoring equipment active now worked to help the intruder sneak across the property undetected. The owner's delinquency, not paying his gardeners, meant that there were piles of tinder-dry leaves at the base of the nearby trees. Declan worked to stack the leaves and twigs and branches around the base of the tree. He wanted it to look like arson. Glancing occasionally in the direction of the main house, he stacked heavier logs around the base like in a pyre. It would be Ray's funeral.

Sharp acted out the next bit like an ASMR video. The distinctive, almost musical metallic click as his collector's edition Zippo lighter was flicked open. The distinctive 'schnick' of the flint striking against the steel wheel then a hiss of fluid being ignited. In slow motion, he moved the lighter towards the wick of a Tiki torch as a suspenseful Wagner-like soundtrack played in his head. He kept his eyes on Monaghan's front door as he knelt and touched the torch to the dry leaves. They caught immediately and began to crackle. His eyebrows were nearly singed, such was the ferocity with which the tinder started to burn.

A few things needed to happen for this plan to work. The tree had to catch fire. Despite the dryness of the wood, the surrounding fuel would have to burn long enough to get into the trunk or to ignite the lower branches. For the kindling to do its job, the fire could not be extinguished too soon. So far, so good, but the noise and the light of the fire would intensify, drawing attention. Sharp kept his eyes on the fire and the front door as he retraced his steps back towards the stable to free Ray's prisoner.

- # -

Tommo and Tara sat in separate chairs on the balcony of the rented cottage. Archie and Marta had made their excuses not long after the early fireworks, so rather than spend any more time in an increasingly rowdy pub, Tommo had suggested a slow walk back to the Airbnb. They had snacked on the improvised picnic items sourced by Tara from the independent supermarket, and now, Tommo was ready to pop another bottle of bubbles at the stroke of Midnight.

"This is less awkward than I thought it would be," Tara said, "But I am a bit of a lightweight when it comes to Champagne."

Tommo kept one eye on the live stream of the festivities around Sydney harbour as the year drew to an end. "Yeah. Despite everything, I do like hanging out with you." The announcer on the telecast was joined by performers and random celebrities as they began the countdown. "Stand up," he encouraged.

"10, 9, 8..." The coverage switched to an ariel shot. There were boats of all shapes and sizes dotted around the harbour, waiting for the coat hanger bridge to be lit up. "3, 2, 1... Happy New Year," said Australia in unison. Tommo popped the cork of the bottle in his hand and turned to Tara,

"Happy New Year." He leaned in to kiss her.

"Let's hope it's better than 2023" She followed his lead. As their faces drew closer, Tara suddenly pulled away. "What's that?" She gasped and pointed.

Tommo followed her gaze and the direction of her finger, towards a distant glow against the night sky. "Someone wasn't looking at their watch. Trust Mace to let off illegal fireworks?"

Tara shook her head. "I'm not sure. It looks too... muted for fireworks. And the way it's flickering, it's almost hypnotic. More like a bonfire."

Tommo nodded, a sense of unease mixing with his anger "Could be a bonfire. But they are illegal this time of year too. Like that's going to stop a guy like Mace who thinks he is above the law."

"It's really high. It's higher than the tower. Is it the building? The mansion? That's a really big fire. We should call 000," Tara said, fearing for Bondy.

- # -

"FireCon, Pumper Tanker 86 is turning out for smoke reported at Monaghan property. Code 1."

"Roger 86. You're turning out to a fire reported on the Monaghan estate. Reported by the owner as a tree fire. There is a high risk of the fire spreading to the main dwelling." The new year was 3 minutes old, and it was already shaping up to be one of the worst bushfire seasons on record. The volunteers who had just finished a non-alcoholic toast at the country fire station were set up to handle burning eucalypt forests and dry grass fires, so a tree shouldn't be a problem.

"FireCon, Pumper Tanker 86 On Scene. Now known as Monaghan Control. Message."

"Monaghan Control. Go ahead."

"Firecon, Monaghan Control. This tree is a 30-metre-high Pin Oak burning out of control. Multiple spot fires burning around the base of the tree. Request assistance."

- # -

She tastes sand, and paperbark and composted eucalyptus wood. She tastes blood, biting her own bottom lip, stifling a squeal of pleasure, and cursing the owner of the footsteps creaking on the floor above her. Her eyes are not accustomed to the darkness. There are probably snakes down here. He pins her face down under his weight in a grove of Redgum stumps that support the weight of the General Store. His bulk is between her legs so she can't close them. With beer on his breath, he whispers a string of racist and misogynistic names into her ear. Each word a retrovirus designed to attack her ideas about empowerment and equality. The offensive words join the war between her head and her molten core. He makes her repeat them. "What are you?" She manages to say two of the names out loud. The war is about to be lost to her body... and then she is woken by sirens.

Claudine's head pounded, and her mouth was parched. Something had woken her. *Someone is here.* She felt herself being lifted from behind - strong arms sliding under her shoulders and pulling her into a sitting position on the floor. Her panic surged as a leather-gloved hand pressed over her mouth, and a low, firm voice she didn't recognise whispered in her ear.

"I need you to listen very carefully." instructed Declan Sharp. "I am going to cut the ropes. I am going to guide you through the smoke and the chaos outside and then we will have a further chat. I am not going to hurt you. I am a friend." Claudine groaned and squirmed. Sharp pressed his hand tighter over her mouth and continued with his instructions. "I need to keep quiet. The police are here, but we don't want to be troubling them right now. The main thing is to get out of here without being noticed. Understand me?" Bondy quivered as the blade of a hunting knife appeared in her peripheral vision. "Stay still. I'll answer all your questions once we are away from here. Ready?" Bondy nodded her understanding and agreement as Sharp worked quickly with skill to remove the ropes. "I'll give you a minute. Do some stretches. Try and get the blood moving. It will hurt like hell, but you need to able to run if needed." He took an aluminium water bottle out of his bag and opened the top in front of her. He drank from it and then handed it to her. "It's just water. Drink."

A kind of survival mechanism had kicked in. Bondy listened to the man's instructions and followed them one by one. *Cute for a Saffa,* she thought as she glimpsed his vaguely familiar face. She winced as the blood forced itself into the skin that had been restricted by the ropes. He helped her to stand and let her lean against him on trembling legs.

"We have to move quickly," Declan whispered, his voice urgent. He supported her weight as he helped her navigate the dark spaces. The smoke and steam from the burning tree filled the small rooms and made breathing difficult. He scowled. The wedge he had placed against the door to keep it ajar had moved. He tried the handle and lost his cool. "Locked."

Claudine's heart pounded in her chest. She looked around the dimly lit stable, her eyes scanning for any potential exits. The only door she could see was the one they had just come through. She had been unconscious when she was brought in, so couldn't contribute much.

Declan surveyed the room. "This was a stable. There should be a way to get feed in and out without going through the front door all the time. Look up, is there a mezzanine floor? Yes. Okay. Now we need to find the ladder. It will be against a wall."

Claudine wasn't in the mood to jump out of a window nearly 12ft off the ground. "Let me try and pick the lock. Do you have a paperclip or a piece of wire in that bag of yours?" She knelt and tried the handle as Declan looked through a small, zippered storage pack. He handed her a large still paperclip.

"That might work, but you can check out the upper floor if you want, just in case we need another backup." She opened out the clip into a long stiff piece of wire and guided it into the lock. She stifled a cough as she breathed the acrid smoke into her throat. "The smoke must be getting in here somehow. She felt around inside the lock's mechanism with the wire.

Leaving his bag by her side, Declan disappeared back into the room where she had been held. He scanned the room, looking for a ladder, some way to get up onto the floor above.

The lock clicked and the handle turned in Claudine's hand. She looked at the bag beside her. Her rescuer was not back yet. She could make a break for it. No. He was a fit guy, and she didn't really know which way she was going. He would catch her quickly. She picked up a piece of wood and threw it into the back room. It landed against the wall with a thud and Declan was quickly back beside her, slipping into the straps of the backpack and helping her stand. He made a military style signal with two fingers, past the door to the darkness beyond.

Ray had a garden hose in his hand, the trickle of water aimed at the blazing oak almost evaporated before it splashed against the crackling, spitting trunk. The intense heat crackled and popped, echoing through the garden. Embers danced and whirled in the air before landing on dry grass and kindling and starting smaller fires around the tree. Then there was a hiss as the more powerful fire hoses were aimed at the impressive, though imported tree. The fire, fuelled by centuries of growth and resilience, was a formidable opponent and new fires sprang up in all directions, fanned by a hot northerly wind. Ray's attention was focussed on survival for himself and his beloved family home. He was too distracted to notice two dark figures moving quickly away from the stables.

In the heart of the inferno, amidst the towering flames and billowing smoke, the volunteer firefighters battled with grim determination, their faces streaked with soot and sweat as they fought a losing battle. The pump on the truck sucked water from Ray's pool, but it was a snowflake in hell kind of match up. The tree could not be saved. All efforts were now on the spot fires and protecting the mansion.

Ray stood and looked on at the chaos, his heart heavy with a combination of disbelief, sorrow, and fear. He watched helplessly as the tree was reduced to a towering black totem. Stunned into silence, he remained rooted to the spot, like the tree had been for hundreds of years until the colour on ground changed, his silhouette now surrounded by alternating red and blue lights. The police had arrived. Ray turned and saw the officers conferring with the firefighters, one of them held a charred Tiki torch. They nodded towards Ray and pointed. He watched as if in slow motion as the police walked with purpose towards him.

"Happy New Year Mr Mason," the taller one said with no hint of irony. "The fierys say that there is no danger to the main house." Ray's shoulders dropped. He waited for the rest. "They also reckon that the fire was deliberately lit, but they won't be able to do a proper investigation until there is some daylight." Ray kept his mouth shut. *Where the fuck is Sharp?* The young cop continued in a professional and respectful tone. "Now, we know you have some enemies Mr Mason, so when you get a chance, we would like you to come down to the station and give us a list of people you think might have done this." His tone became more serious. "It is of course a day of Total Fire Ban, and there is evidence that you might have… contravened that law." Ray stiffened, but he remained silent. "It's late, and you are a well-respected member of the community, so let's sort it all out when we've had some rest, eh." The two policemen paused and looked over Ray's shoulder, past the stables to the farm track that led over the hill.

"Is there anyone else on the property tonight sir?" asked the more junior of the two uniformed men. "It looks like a torch or a lantern out there."

Ray's head was bowed. Contrite. He didn't want to give them any reason to do any more looking around tonight. He didn't look over his shoulder or turn his head. "No. I'm the only one here at the moment." he stammered. "There are some old garden lights up there. Activated by movement. Probably a rabbit or a roo." The cops nodded.

"Don't leave town," quipped the more senior officer. It was meant as a joke, but Ray felt like the walls were closing in. Paranoia was beginning to set in. He wasn't going to sleep tonight, even if he finished the bottle of BBQ and black pepper flavoured scotch.

- # -

Soot was floating out of the sky like black snowflakes, the way they did after the cane fields were burned up north. Tara's fingers stroked Tommo's forearm in an attempt to calm him. Several police cars had raced past the cottage on the way to Monaghan. "Stay here. You can't do anything tonight." She pressed herself up against him. "Whatever happened up there, Ray is going to blame you for it. It's only been a day since the pub. Your van fire gives you a motive for revenge."

Tommo pulled away from her and typed into his phone. He cursed the pop-up ads that stood between him and the page he wanted. The tinny speaker hissed with radio static. "They broadcast the radio for public safety purposes." He was breathing heavily. The relative peace and celebratory nature he had experienced earlier in the evening had been replaced with a mixture of stress and fear. There was a crackle, the sound you hear before someone speaks.

"FireCon, this is Monaghan Control. Message."
"Monaghan Control. Go ahead."
"Firecon, Monaghan Control. Tree fire has been extinguished. There is no damage to the structure and the occupants have been informed that they can return inside. Police are on scene and the fire will be treated as suspicious. We are packing up and will be on scene for another 10 minutes then returning."

Tommo worked through the implications in his head. It's just a tree. *Ray is alive.* There had been no mention of any casualties or other suspicious behaviour, but that would be on the encrypted police channel, not the one for fire and ambulance. Tara was right. *Ray will try and pin this on me. He has an alibi and can prove where he was. He'll get away with it again.*

"Don't worry about Mason," Tara said. "He's not a threat anymore." She took Tommo's wrist again and tugged him towards the door. "At the very least, having the authorities on his property means he can't do business there until the investigation is finished.

Come on, get off the balcony. Don't advertise where you are."

Tommo didn't fight. He let Tara lead him back inside, but then he stiffened. "What if it was Bondy?" Tara looked at him confused.

"That's ridiculous. What about the note?" She was too tired to think.

"She could have escaped. She could have somehow got away and set the tree on fire as a distraction so she could get away." It was more of a hope than an argument. "She gets away from Ray and then works out a way to get the cops to come to the property." It was a rationalisation. One that would get him through the rest of the night. Tara didn't correct him. She guided him gently towards the bedroom as her phone vibrated in her pocket. She took it out and couldn't hide the gasp when she saw it was a message from Bondy.

```
Claudine: Happy New Year! I'm fine! I'm just off
the grid for a bit. I'll be in touch soon. X
```

Tara read it out aloud. "Happy New Year, exclamation mark. I'm fine, exclamation mark. I'm just off the grid for a bit. I'll be in touch soon. And then there is an X." Tommo pushed his bottom lip out and raised his eyebrows. Something was off. He was also tired and emotional and a little drunk, but there was something not quite right about the syntax. "She's okay Tommo," Tara almost pushed him through the door of the bedroom.

7

Tommo hadn't slept well. Bondy's Docklands apartment didn't agree with him. Too quiet. And now that he was alone inside it was worse. She had been called away, summoned to Dubai. The deal was that he could stay until the QSP summit was over. He had two days. The clock was ticking. Despite the climate-controlled atmosphere of the apartment, he had a kind of unease that came with the calm and silence at the eye of a storm, the way the wind dies just before the skies rip open again.

The details of Bondy's escape from Monaghan were still shrouded in mystery. By the time Tommo woke up just before noon on New Year's Day, the concierge was on the road having been requested in the Middle East for an unnamed client. He'd slept on the couch in Tara's rental accommodation. After a passionate kiss at Midnight was interrupted by the fire at Ray Mason's property, Tara had become stand-offish, polite and professional, but seemingly uninterested in a more intimate relationship.

Marta's community grapevine and WhatsApp group had pieced together some of what happened on the night of the 31st. The police and fire brigade were investigating how the grand old oak tree outside Ray's mansion house had been set on fire. Ray himself had been taken into custody by the local police, partly on suspicion of arson, and partly because of his involvement in something more salacious. The rumour mill gossiped about a teenage girl who had been picked up by police in the Melbourne suburb of Richmond. Rather than face drug charges, she had done a deal to tell all about her relationship with Ray. Further investigation of the Monaghan property had found evidence of a criminal operation relating to the production of fake passports and that matter had been referred to the Australian Federal Police. Quite how the network of busybodies on Marta's chat group knew so much wasn't too much of a mystery. It was almost impossible to keep a town secret before social media, let alone now. In light of what the speculation and whispering of events were, Claudine's sudden trip to the UAE didn't seem like a coincidence.

Tommo felt a bit like the dog that caught the car. There was a chance that Ray could wiggle out of his legal trouble, but the AFP were not the local coppers. It would take some time though, for the investigations to be completed and the charges to be brought, and the case to come to trial, but in the meantime, Tommo had mixed feelings. There were too many unanswered questions.

He stared at the webpage. Layers of incredulity piled up behind his eyes and made him squint as he read. The youth's shorthand would have been WTAF. Instead of simply refreshing the page, he shut down the entire browser and restarted it, carefully typing the URL again, just in case he had somehow been duped into following a parody link to 'The Interlude'. The venue for QSP's summit was supposed to be a tightly kept secret, known only to those with an invitation. But, in reality, everyone from the drivers to the security teams, dealers, and high-end escorts knew the location.

He had to wonder exactly which drugs were being taken by those who decided to take Melbourne's most notorious prison and turn it into a corporate retreat. Perhaps the marketing folk, so jacked up on some hipster variation of a Latte, had looked for synonyms of sentence or term and found 'Interlude' to be ironic, slapped themselves on the back and submitted the nomination for a branding award immediately. But they didn't stop there. A new visitor to the Interlude's homepage is welcomed by a kind of d-grade porn video. A single woman, walking alone, barefoot in the darkness, looking over her shoulder, then alone in a pool at night, then for some inexplicable reason she's riding a bicycle. Of course, the whole thing is in slow motion. He shivered as she watched it play out and then almost spit his coffee across her screen as he read the accompanying copy.

```
The Interlude was created to encourage people to
pause for a moment in time and immerse themselves
in a new environment – something unique, something
extraordinary, and a step away from the everyday.
You'll take a walk in someone else's shoes, uncover
hidden stories, and connect to a region renowned
for its creativity and eclectic energy.

With over 170 years of history, The Interlude is
much more than just its stunning bluestone walls
and tranquil underground pool. It's a place to
share and connect with others over breakfast in our
restaurant or provoke discussion around the evening
fire with a wine from our extensive selection.
Reset and realign in our peaceful Reflection Garden
for meditation at sunrise.
```

That's not why QSP had chosen the venue. Or maybe it was. What better place than the temporary home of Robert David Bennett and Mark 'Chopper' Read to host the sociopathic alumni and misanthropic client base of one of the world's most secretive criminal enablement companies. The place where Tara still worked.

-#-

Tara refreshed her screen. Ray Mason's Bitcoin wallet had not seen any activity since she had given herself access and complete admin rights. She briefly paused before hitting the 'transfer' button thinking through all the implications of her action. Ray was in custody. There was a high probability that the cold storage wallet would be seized as they executed the warrant for a search of Monaghan. The device couldn't be hacked. She had changed the pass phrase already, so even if they somehow compelled Mace to talk, they wouldn't get in. A record of the transactions she was about to make would be written into the blockchain irrevocably. Those transactions could be traced. The destination wallets could be monitored. But it was her job to bury needles in haystacks and she was good at it.

She pushed her chair back and stood up from the impractically small desk in her cell. The brightness of her screen doubled the available light. This place gave her the creeps. Sliding the door of the tiny wardrobe open, Tara felt a weight settle on her body. She felt heavier as she flicked through the dark coloured suits she had packed for the summit. Dark grey, dark blue… her corporate uniform. *Suck it up Tara, it's a first world problem. Just a few more days.* The thermostat of the air conditioning clicked, and the room became colder, making her skin crawl. What if this had been Andrew Kirby's cell?

She paced back to her company laptop and paused over the enter key. Once Claudine had resurfaced, it had been relatively easy to act as a client via the concierge's BA0001.com website and pay a premium to have the job in Dubai begin urgently. Tara had bought Bondy a one-way ticket on Emirates Business Class through a shell company and removed her from the playing field, at least until the summit was over. Tommo had shown his hand. He wasn't convinced that the fake passport scheme was the extent of the operation, or that Ray was the head of the snake. Tara was sure that Tommo would try to infiltrate the summit somehow. She was looking forward to seeing how he would manage it without a ticket.

Tara's watch vibrated as she received a 10-minute reminder about the opening address of the event by Trevor Stone. With a click of the mouse Ray's Bitcoin redistributed itself at the speed of light around the world. From her QSP computer with the IP address of 'The Interlude' incorporated into the hash of the block, cryptocurrency was sent to a range of wallets, including one belonging to Travis Thompson.

- # -

Tommo's phone pinged while he was riding the number 34 tram to the corner of Bell Street and Sydney Road, the closest stop to the old Pentridge Prison. Confusion set in. Exactly 1 Bitcoin had been deposited into his account. He'd dabbled in cryptocurrency, but it wasn't very useful in his day-to-day life. He certainly wasn't expecting a payment. Maybe Bondy had felt sorry for him and sent him something to get him back on his feet. He couldn't think of any other explanation… unless of course he was being set up.

Keeping his head down, he hurried along the footpath, cursing at the silent cyclists who should be using the designated lanes on the road and not bullying pedestrians out of the way. It was quiet. Everyone else was still on holiday or in holiday mode. Tara had not managed to get him a pass for the QSP Summit, so he was left with a few ruses to get him past security. He could be a 'content creator', an alternative media pundit who would help deliver the 'right' narrative for the QSP spin doctors. He could be in the security business, something specific and obtuse like an advisor to superyachts in the Red Sea, hard to verify, but the kind of person who would be at an event like this. Or he could take a chance based on the ongoing investigation at Monaghan. *Would the representatives of the passport printer manufacturer show their faces?*

Standing in front of the imposing stone gateway, flanked by two turret-topped towers he was about to try and break into a prison. The weathered bluestone facade was infamous, the feature of countless true crime tales. The sign above the gate was a reminder of the origins of the colony, "PENAL ESTABLISHMENT PENTRIDGE." The clock on the right tower facing outwards seemed out of place. *Why would anyone want to acknowledge the passing of time inside the walls in hours?*

Taking a deep breath, he straightened and put on his 'master of the universe' bravado. *Walk with confidence and carry a clipboard.* Tommo didn't have a clipboard, but he had an old QSP branded lanyard and a plastic pocket, arranged so the credentials were hidden against his chest. He was dressed in a way that could get him into almost any restricted area, from F1 paddock to exclusive night-club - expensive jeans, a collared shirt, and a blazer. Not too formal. Not too casual. Just the right amount of 'Who are you to tell me what I should wear.' He walked quickly towards the first line of defence - lowly paid security guards, maybe a temp job for the summer, probably about 3 hours of training maximum. Basically, just window dressing in ill-fitting suits and snap-on ties - the same way supermarkets have a 'security' person at the front door to deter old ladies from shoplifting. He made eye contact early, nodding his head, not slowing. *Never slow down.* He could see the calculation they were making. 'Do I want to be a hero? What if this guy is someone super important? He looks the part. Let someone else deal with it.'

8:58 am. The keynote was advertised to begin in 2 minutes. He could use that. The organisers would want the session to look full and what kind of person would turn up first thing in a prison on January 2nd unless they really needed to be there? His eyes scanned the badges laid out in alphabetical order by surname as if trying to find his own, but he was really making notes on the titles and companies of the registered guests - mostly the usual suspects. Specifically, he wanted to see if there were companies or individuals who had been around when he first blew the whistle. Had any of the bad actors resurfaced?

Another underpaid, undertrained event employee watched him.

"Are you okay? Can I help find your badge for you?" She was polite enough, in that, obsequious 'people can hear your smile in your voice' kind of way she'd been told to use. Tommo reached out for the one he wanted - Paul Shaw from Oasis Sentinel.

"Found it. Just in time." He held it up. "It's that way to the main room, right?" He looked at an invisible watch on his wrist, "Don't want to miss the main act, do I?" The girl didn't care. Her part of the customer experience was done. She took her phone out of her pocket and started scrolling through Tik-Tok.

Shaking his head, Declan Sharp watched from the edge of the registration area. He had intel that Tommo might show up at the summit. The strategy was to lure him in and keep him close, but maybe they had made it too easy. The summit came at the worst moment. The last thing Declan wanted to be doing was babysitting because it meant that he couldn't be managing the situation at Monaghan. Most of the plan had worked. Ray's penchant for drugging young girls had finally came back to bite him, but not everything had been predicted. Bondy, whose kidnapping and restraint had led to a significant allocation of time and resources to rescue - was gone. One moment Sharp had been dropping her back at the Royal Oak and the next minute she had checked out and vanished. Maybe she'd been spooked by the whole experience. He couldn't blame her for that.

- # -

Tara sat in the front row. This was not a hotel ballroom used for wedding receptions and shampoo brand launches. This was a macabre stage, a place of violence and criminality and man's worst instincts. Her lanyard, branded with some obscure vendor to the wider security community, felt like a hangman's noose dangled around her neck. All the guests wore them. She wondered how many felt like it was a dreadful homage to the last man hanged in Australia on this site. She sat dutifully where she would be in the line of sight of the speakers and her bosses. She wanted them to see her, bright eyed and eager to learn at the feet of the speakers. She even had the notepad and pen, provided by different fawning vendor partner, ready in her lap to be seen to be scribbling down insights.

The energy in the room began to change. A hum of expectation, like a group of teenage girls waiting to see a boy band come on stage. Tara looked around and took into the theatre of it all. Theatre was the best word. The speakers crackled with static, and the bashing of piano keys began to ring out with the intro to Robbie William's 'Let Me Entertain You'. A set of double doors swung open, revealing Trevor Stone framed by a spotlight. He moved like a boxer at a prize fight, raising his fists to the crowd. The murmurs and applause dictated by his celebrity increased. Tara rolled her eyes without trying to be too obvious. Should she rise to her feet and participate in the ritualistic reverence?

"He's not the messiah, he's a very naughty boy." She smirked, quietly quoting the great Monty Python. To her right, a senior partner, a man who probably made ten times her salary, stood, clapping earnestly, his eyes fixed on Stone like a disciple awaiting divine wisdom.

Stone lapped it up. He took his time moving towards the slightly raised stage, each step calculated and confident. She watched him, looking for any trace of the genius that these people claimed to see in him. All she could see was a carefully crafted image: the slightly too shiny, tailored suit, the hair styled with a slight hint of 'I just fell out of bed' ruffledness, and that smug half-smile that he wore as if he owned the air they were all breathing. He stopped occasionally to brush shoulders or drop a word with someone who he knew would consider it a privilege. Tara watched it play out as a barely acknowledged venture capitalist eagerly thrust out his hand. He was offered a token, almost dismissive pat on the shoulder instead.

"Good to see you," Stone said and the VC beamed as if he'd just been knighted. Stone was shadowed by an entourage of sycophantic yes-men and overpaid lackeys; carbon copies whose presence fed the egos of both parties. The courtiers of Trevor Stone, scrambling for the king's attention. He made a dismissive gesture towards the podium. The entourage barked as one at the event producer and the offending lectern was carried away. Blame was allocated and assumed. The room fell silent, waiting for the brilliance they'd convinced themselves was about to pour forth.

Tara shifted in her seat. She turned her head left then right and saw nothing but adoration. *It's a cult.*

Stone squared his shoulders, using the adoration to feed his ego. He sang along with the song, "Grab yourself an alibi." His face scanned the crowd, his gaze lowering to the front row. Tara held eye contact. She let a playful smile spread across her face and he almost dropped his guard, but he took another breath and began to speak.

"Well," he began, "it's good to be among visionaries."

The room erupted into appreciative chuckles and nods, people leaning forward in their seats, waiting for his next scrap of insight. He let them, but his eyes moved back to the front row where Tara, once again made eye contact and held it.

Tommo wasn't in the back row, but he was far enough up and out to the left that he blended in with the rest of the crowd that looked mostly like him. And there was Stone, a tech-world deity making his grand entrance and hoovering up the attention. Tommo scanned the crowd for another face. There, right up front like the teacher's pet. Tara was rising to her feet when the others did, but it seemed performative, like it would be noticeable if she didn't. Just before Stone began to speak, he looked down. He looked right at Tara and his face changed, a micro expression. Tommo couldn't work out what it was. *Recognition? Do they know each other?* The crowd cheered the first line of the speech and Stone looked at Tara again. *Is she flirting with him?*

From his post next to the sound-mixing desk, Declan scanned the room. The task was simple: keep the flock from getting too close and ensure the man of the hour got his drug, the unquestioning worship from his fans. Tara didn't stand immediately. She followed to fit in. But that was okay, she didn't fit the description of a typical Trevor Stone tech-bro. Tommo's lack of enthusiasm for Stone's entrance was also noticeable. Sharp was looking at Tommo. Tommo was looking at Tara. Tara was looking at Stone. Tommo had a feeling he was being watched. Slowly turning his head, he stiffened a little. Declan Sharp and Travis Thompson's eyes met for the first time since Tommo had noticed Sharp following him through the city.

The friendly crowd had their eyes glued to the stage where Trevor Stone could say no wrong. That's not to say he didn't. His speech was peppered with half-truths and boasting that had no facts to back it up. The hot air filled the space. The audience watched the performance through the screens of their phones, hoping to go viral with the portrait streams from all angles.

"I get you," Stone began. "They are trying to replace you. I'm not talking about manual labour; you are not the kinds of men to get your hands dirty." He took a sip of water from a plastic bottle. The room was full of single use plastic. "They have trained AI using your ideas, your experience, your insight. They have fed it on your expertise, and they are going to use it to replace you." The crowd nodded. They didn't understand the technology or how it worked, but they knew it was a threat to their particular brand of overcharging. The crowd got busy with their fingers, posting to social media the instructions from the stage "Delete AI off your phone. Make them accountable." Stone wove in various conspiracy theories, projecting as he called for action against his enemies. "AI is a tool of the deep state. They are watching your keystrokes, recording your searches. They know what videos you watch, even if you don't hit the like button." Phones in the room pinged as the echo chamber amplified his comments as he marshalled his discontented troops. "Soon, they will replace your money with digital currency. They will only let you spend it if you have been good."

What's your angle? Tara thought as she pretended to nod in the front row.

"Today, the AI spits out market analysis that you created." Stone laughed a little. "Well not you. Your eager to please first year associates and interns. But soon the AI will be used to frame you. Deep fakes of you with that cute thing from compliance that you won't be able to defend yourself against." The crowd streamed it live to the wider disaffected white male tribe. Of course, AI was a strawman, a euphemism for them - women, immigrants, poor people, the whistleblowers, anyone other who dared to defy his status quo.

Sharp kept his eye on Tommo. His amateur team of casual workers was in place. The rear exits were covered by a more capable lieutenant called Winters. There were two more exits, one each side of the stage, but crossing the front of the room would create a spectacle and no-one wanted that. Tommo looked deceptively relaxed, shoulders slouched, and one arm draped casually over the back of the seat beside him.

"Eyes on," Sharp whispered into the comms. "Second last row, towards the left. He knows I am here. No sudden moves. We keep him boxed in."

"Copy that," Winters replied. His elevated breathing was audible through the earpiece. "Rear exits are sealed. Awaiting your instructions."

Sharp considered for a split second, eyes flicking to the exits near the stage. If Tommo made for those he would be in full view of the crowd, but worse the spectacle would divert attention from Trevor Stone and that would have consequences. "Hold position. Let's see how he plays this. Be ready to move on my mark."

Stone's rehearsed speech was wrapping up. He'd got all the meme stuff out; he was building a punchline of sorts. The crowd could sense it. He was lapping it up, using their energy to get away with more and more outrageous lies. Tommo was on the move, heading towards the stage. Sharp tried to get into Tommo's head. *Where are you going? What are you doing?*

Tommo hugged the wall. He wasn't the only one who wanted to get to Stone, to shake his hand, to get a selfie, to shove a business card into his hand or try and pitch the next unicorn idea. The audience prepared to rush the stage, like the passengers on a budget airline trying to get a seat or a space for their bag in the overhead lockers. Stone was used to it. If they didn't crowd around him, he'd be disappointed. Despite his success, he needed the positive feedback.

"Boss?" Winters' voice crackled urgently in his ear.

"Stay put. He's hiding in plain sight. Using the crowd for cover. Don't let him out of your sight. If you lose visual contact, report immediately."

Sharp began moving, working his way through the crowd at the back. He kept his eyes locked on Tommo, who was now close enough to stab the keynote speaker, but Tommo held back, not really wanting to be caught on camera in the selfie frenzy.

One audience member didn't join the group hug. Tara sat in her seat in the front row and watched. She made sure Stone saw her unmoved. He'd made eye contact several times during his oration and she'd smiled, even brushed her hair behind her ear flirtatiously.

"Winters. Front exits. Don't make a fuss," Sharp marshalled his deputised troops, breaking into a swift walk. He shoved through the suits closing the distance as Tommo backed slowly towards one of the forward exits. He kept his pace casual. As he moved toward the exit he tried to get Tara's attention, but her head was turned towards Stone.

Sharp reached the front row just as Tommo neared the exit. He caught the hint of an imperceptible smirk as his target pushed the door open and disappeared into the hallway beyond.

"Winters! Where are you?" Sharp was sprinting now. But he already knew. Tommo was now in a labyrinth of service corridors. He yanked open the door with a scowl. Nothing.

"Get me a schematic" Sharp muttered, clenching his fist. "Find out where these come out… Amateurs."

- # -

Tara stood near the bar, holding a glass of wine but not really drinking it. She was one of a handful of women in the place, but still invisible to most of the men. She had been seen though, by the only man that mattered. The room buzzed with the energy of investors, tech enthusiasts, and hangers on, all of them jostling for a moment in Stone's orbit. He moved through them like a magnet being dragged through iron filings.

Stone was wrapping up a conversation with another undifferentiated suit when he saw her standing there, alone, not making any effort to join the crowd of rats lured by his pipes. He straightened and began to move towards her. Tara noticed his approach but didn't shift her posture. She took a small sip of her wine.

"You're not having any fun." It was a statement. Her lack of enthusiasm was an affront to him.

She turned her head just enough to meet his eyes, offering a polite but indifferent smile and raising her glass "Happy New Year," she replied coolly.

Stone blinked. He couldn't read her. He was used to a flirtatious comeback or a glowing comment about his speech. This, though, was something different. "I see," he said, easing into his practised charm. "You seem... difficult to impress."

"I'm easily impressed… by impressive things." The challenge in her tone was unmistakable, a direct affront to his usual routine.

She wasn't following the script, and it intrigued him more than he cared to admit. "Most people are," he replied smoothly, leaning casually against the bar as if to indicate he had all the time in the world. "But you don't strike me as most people."

"Is anyone at this event most people?" Her voice was dry. She didn't give him the satisfaction of a laugh or even a change in expression. Instead, she turned her attention back to the room, watching the others as they jockeyed for his attention. She was making it clear that he didn't captivate her the way he did everyone else here.

Stone slowly realised he had a worthy adversary. "I suppose I should be grateful for the honesty," he conceded, his eyes fixed on her, trying to read between the lines. She couldn't help laughing.

"You're joking right?" She mocked him, her eyes still on the room, pointedly not on him. "You don't seem to be someone who is grateful for anything let alone honesty." She took another sip of wine, gaining confidence. He bristled. But challenges came rarely. "I guess I wanted to see for myself what all the fuss was about."

"And?" This was more exciting than taking selfies with the yes-men.

"You talk how you sail," she replied, taking him off guard. "No real talent, just throw money at it, buy yourself wins."

He choked on the beer that he had picked up and was sipping. He tried to compose himself. "You're a sailor?"

"I can hold my own. I prefer one-design classes." She could tell he was measuring his next words carefully, trying to figure out what approach might crack through her armour. Maybe she'd pushed him too far already. He didn't need the hassle. But he also hated losing.

"It's Tara, isn't it." This time he took her by surprise. Much of his business success was a photographic memory for names and faces and remembering a unique detail about everyone that made them feel special.

Tara lost her composure for a second. "Which one of your assistants whispered that in your earbuds?"

"Your comment about sailing." He was less boastful now. She knew his schtick; she could read his lies. "You did the Hobart last year. Won the shorthanded trophy. Now that," he paused and looked sincere, "is impressive."

She nodded to his concession, knowing how hard it was for him to admit it, but also amused by his attempt to rescue his reputation. "Well, I guess you are heading off. The keynote usually doesn't hang around." She faltered as she thought she saw Tommo moving among the crowd.

"Oh, you obviously don't know how these things work. I am QSP. Without my influence and my billings, there wouldn't be any consulting firm left. So, I'll be at the dinner. If you want an invite, let me know." He checked himself and realised his mistake as soon as the words were leaving his mouth. "I mean. Maybe you would like to join me at the top table."

Switching back to coy, grateful corporate servant mode Tara smiled. "Oh, I'm sure those tickets don't come cheap. I wouldn't want to deprive a fan of a night with Trevor Stone." She placed her glass on the bar and walked away. *Don't look back. Don't look back...*

Tommo couldn't hear what they were saying, but he could see the body language. Tara and Trevor Stone were close, almost intimate. He watched her twirl her hair with her fingers like a schoolgirl as she smiled and laughed. Barely 48 hours ago Tommo had shared his own intimate moment at the stroke of midnight and now Tara was cozying up to the man behind the vast conspiracy that included the operations at Monaghan. And if Stone wasn't the top man, then he was probably the next one up the hierarchy from Ray Mason. Tommo's paranoia was returning. Everything since the quiz night at the Pier Hotel could be seen through a very different lens if Tara was the enemy.

He kept her in sight. She stood out. Glancing up, he noticed CCTV cameras in almost every corner. *Probably facial recognition too.* He lowered his head and made a note to choose a disguise that required a cap or other head covering. The architect's overarching vibe seemed to be creepy. The corridors were dimly lit and the thudding bass from the main event pulsed in the ceiling and the walls and the floor. Tara moved quickly; she seemed to know exactly where she was going. Tommo kept his distance as she led him into an abandoned cellblock where the air seemed to be even colder. She stopped near a feature wall incorporating the graffiti that for better or worse had become a tourist attraction in some of Melbourne's laneways. Tommo slowed his pace. Tara knew he was there, but she didn't turn. She just stared at the street art as is trying to decipher its meaning.

"We need to talk," Tommo said.

She didn't turn. Her silhouette seemed to dance. "What are you doing here? Are you crazy?"

"I thought you hated Stone," he said as he closed the distance between them. "Thought you hated everything about him."

A moment of silence stretched out before she turned. She was unreadable. "Why do you care, Tommo? What do you think you saw?"

"You looked like you were flirting," he accused her. "You had that look on your face. The one you get when you're amused and engaged."

She crossed her arms, one eyebrow arching, but it was affectation, not intuitive gesture. She was acting. "We've spent a total of about 10 hours together over the course of a week and you think you have me figured out," her smirk became a sneer. "What do you think you're going to accomplish by coming here, except pissing more people off or getting yourself beaten up or worse?"

"It's a hunch. Loose ends. Ray wasn't the King. More like a knight." He laughed to himself as he imagined Mace walking home from the Royal Oak, drunk, two steps forward, one sideways, two sideways, one forward. "I think Stone is involved." He paused and thought about whether to make the accusation. "And now, you look like you are involved with Stone."

Tara's lips curled. "You have no idea what it is like to be a woman in this business," she said slowly. "Stone is a client." She watched him as she tried different rationalisations. "He's also not very trusting, so I need to use my 'talents' to get closer to him, into the inner circle, so we can complete our mission."

Tommo reached out and touched her arm, searching her face for signs of deception, or honesty. "I thought you had resigned."

She glanced down at his hand, her expression momentarily softening into something that might have been pity. "This event is the only known semi-public appearance in his calendar before he disappears to who knows where." She was using reason now. "You can't even listen in to the keynote without being spotted. How are you going to get close enough to Stone to find out what you need?" Tommo took his hand away. He couldn't argue with her logic, and she seemed to be acting in his best interests, sticking to the plan, the same way she had bought a trailbike and rode to inspect the gate on the edge of the Monaghan property. "They are watching me. They don't trust me. If they see me with Stone, they are more likely to trust me than if they see me with you." She gave a small, bitter laugh, brushing a hand through her hair. "I can't afford to be seen with you." She paused, watching his face, studying his reaction. "Oh, by the way, did you get my present?"

His chest tightened. "The Bitcoin? That was from you?"

"Don't ask where it came from and then I don't have to lie to you." She stepped closer. "You can run now. Buy a new van. Disappear. Leave the super-hero stuff to others."

"Tempting." And it was, though in his mind he had imagined her joining him on the road. She saw it in his face and shook her head. He felt the space closing in around him.

"Take the money. Get back on your feet. Stop playing defence." She moved to slip past him. He held her arm again but then dropped it. She was right. He had no more tricks up his sleeve.

"Be careful." It was all he could think of as she flicked him a dismissive wave over her shoulder.

- # -

'Maybe this is how Ray feels.' Tommo had slipped out of the penitentiary and traipsed around Coburg looking for a pub. Not a poncy, hipster, gastro-experience with 29 local, organic IPAs on tap, but a boozer, a dive bar, a dark room to brood on dark thoughts. An old man's pub. Despite what so-called progress had done to Pentridge, there were still a couple of old-school hotels in the 3058 post code and it didn't take long to find the relic of a bygone era he was yearning for. The signs said it all. The trifecta - Carlton Draught, TAB, Drive Thru.

Tommo ordered a pint of the local brew that he'd grown up with. The barman didn't really understand why the old-timers still drank it, but he also understood that it was his job not to question what his regulars ordered. There was only one other patron. Tommo acknowledged him with a barely perceptible nod of the head, not saying a word. This was a place of sanctuary, not socialising. He stood at the bar and watched the condensation form on the side of the glass. Then he lifted the beer to his lips and sipped.

"Ahhhhh..." Tommo voiced his satisfaction, taking a slow sip of his beer. He didn't care that the audience didn't share his simple pleasure. Holding the glass up to eye level, he peered through the amber liquid, as if expecting to find the mysteries of the universe or petrified mating flies inside.

"Carlton Draught. Victorian for lager," he muttered. The young barman glanced over and slowly shook his head, wiping down the counter with a rag.

"Yeah, good choice, mate," the barman said sarcastically.

"Carlton isn't just a footy team you know. Once upon a time it was the home of the mighty Carlton United Brewery. See You Be." The barman was unimpressed with the history lesson. Tommo took another slow, deliberate sip, savouring the taste. Then, with a sudden shift in posture, he cleared his throat. Raising the glass higher, he adopted an absurdly posh English accent. "Ah, yes," he declared, "a light, malty flavour with an oh-so-subtle hop bitterness. A favourite for those who prefer a straightforward, no-nonsense, easy-drinking beer." He lowered the glass and glanced back at the bar, his eyes moving over the row of flashy taps with their overdesigned labels screaming names like Hazy Tropic, Double Dry-Hopped This-or-That, and Pineapple Crush IPA.

The barman was unimpressed. "Beer is beer."

"Not all beer is created equal," Tommo said, dropping the act. "Not like this faux-craft nonsense pretending to be independent but actually peddled by the same people who make Heineken." He waved a hand at the taps. "What's with the obsession for mangoes and passion fruit in beer, eh? The same people who think it is a mortal sin to put pineapple on pizza will pay twelve bucks for a pint of this... piss."

The barman chuckled. "You're right about pineapple. I reckon it's allowed on a burger with the lot, but not on a pizza."

"Oh, so that bit of Aussie nostalgia can stay. We can keep the beetroot and the egg and the pineapple slice on our burgers but forget about the rest." Tommo shot back "A twenty something brand manager who thinks marketing is getting likes on social media is watching MasterChef and deciding he can turn beer into fine dining." The barman took a step back, not used to such outbursts in the middle of the day. "I bet if the focus group came back and said the latest IPA tasted like 'yuzu with a hint of urinal cake.' not only would they launch it, but they would also use it in the promo."

The barman burst into laughter, tossing the rag over his shoulder as Tommo took the rest of his pint to a quiet table for one in a darkened corner.

I am turning into Ray Mason. Tommo took out his phone and opened his crypto trading app. He had an Accounting and Economics degree from the University of Melbourne. It wasn't too far from where he sat - near Princes Park, Carlton football club's traditional home ground. The classes he took hadn't prepared him for cryptocurrency. He watched as the app updated the value of his one bitcoin, the volatility making him and losing him hundreds of dollars a second. Tara had admitted that she was behind the transfer, which meant QSP had essentially bought him off. $45,098.20 in U.S. dollars. *Not the kind of gift you get from someone you barely know.* He took a sip of his no-nonsense beer, grounding himself in the familiar. He wondered how many former guests of various majesties from the bluestone prison up the road, staggered here for their first drink of freedom, were lucky enough to make it out before the term of natural lives.

Enough self-indulgence. Pull it together. Tommo looked up at a framed print of Arthur Streeton's 'The purple noon's transparent might'. He'd seen it a thousand times. It was a favourite of GP reception rooms and primary school principal's offices around the country. The original was hung in the National Gallery of Victoria on the southern bank of the Yarra River. He could wander down the road and see it if he chose. The painting drew him in, and he worked his way back through his memories of the last few improbable days.

"Tara." He looked from the phone, where the price of Bitcoin changed as quickly as the bubbles rose from the base of his glass to the meniscus, then to the painting, which was a representation of a single moment in time, at least the moments or hours that it took to commit to canvas. One was the definition of digital, the other was demonstrably analogue, but both were as disruptive as the other. The price of Bitcoin was determined by millions of market signals. The representation of the Hawkesbury River at Richmond was an interpretation of what could be seen and the rest inferred. Tommo remembered more of his art classes than he did of his high-school science. Streeton, the artist had reportedly written in a letter to his friend, artist Tom Roberts, of his intent.

> "...to go straight inland (away from the critics
> and the establishment, to) create some things
> entirely new and try and translate some of the
> great hidden poetry that I know is here but have
> not seen or felt it."

Maybe I should do the same. Tara had been right about one thing: the QSP summit was a pointless parade of pricks. There was not much else to be gleaned that he hadn't already from the name badges spread out at registration and from the faces in the audience, illuminated by phone screens at the keynote. Faces like that of the muscle - the guy who'd hunted him through the city. The guy who was probably the owner of the locker full of knives at the Mount Eliza property. A headache began to pulse behind his eyes, and it wasn't the beer. This whole caper was draining him, sapping the little energy he had left. Maybe he should take Tara's crypto and advice and disappear. Find a backpacker trying to get rid of a van, take highway 1 along the coast and let those who wanted to play their twisted games to it. *What does it matter anymore? No one cares. No one wants me here.* He could be gone, a name no one would bother to remember. The locker full of knives in Mount Eliza. Something about it gnawed at him. The beer was warming, it tasted like sand. Tara, Stone, and the muscle were going to be busy cutting their backroom deals. Tommo couldn't stop now. There was something bigger and he wouldn't be able to sleep until it was out in the open and those responsible at least exposed. Finishing his beer, he realised something else. Game theory dictated that he had to trust Tara.

- # -

Ray Mason had experienced a few bad days in his life, but none as bad as this one. Like the kind of bad that starts with... He can't remember when it started. It had all started with the fire. No. The beginning of the end was his very bad idea to drug and imprison the mouthy blonde pretending to be a real estate agent. *Welcome to the new year and the rest of your life.*

It had taken the cops most of the holiday to shake off their hangovers, drag the girl into an interrogation room, and piece together enough of her unlikely story to be convinced of her allegations. They were compelled to find out more. She hadn't held back. Why would she? She wasn't connected, she couldn't afford a lawyer, the only way she could survive the system was to lay out what she knew, and she more than Ray thought she did. Drugs, fake IDs, forged passports for starters. Then there were the machines and equipment tucked away in the outbuilding of the private grounds of an ex-politician where no one would think to look. Not until a drugged 17-year-old girl with a fake Queensland driver's licence fell out of an Uber and pointed her finger at Ray Mason. The cops didn't take long after that. The Australian Federal Police descended on Monaghan in what might have seemed like a disproportionate response if you didn't know what the accusations were. Border security was something to get a judge out of bed for, to sign a warrant, and once issued, their arrival at the property was not quiet. At least one helicopter, multiple cars and vans all with lights flashing and sirens blaring. And they knew exactly where to start searching. The girl's description of the outbuilding and its location was precise, just as her graphic telling of the way he had used his power and position of authority to coerce her into all kinds of sexual acts added up to statutory rape. He might be able to feign ignorance about the clandestine operation in the old buildings, but his DNA in the girl would not be so easy to explain away.

From the moment he heard the thumping rotor blades approaching from the north, Ray knew he was neck-deep in it. It was all a blur, but his body had lurched into motion before his mind could catch up. *Get to the study.* It was the only command his ageing synapses could convey to his heavy limbs. There might still be a way out of this, still a chance to salvage something before the cops swarmed the place. He heard the sirens closing in, designed to shame and intimidate. Minutes. That was all he had.

Upon reaching the study he slid the cryptocurrency cold storage wallet into the USB port. His pudgy fingers hovered over the keyboard already sweating. Tara had been clear - annoyingly, sweetly, maddeningly clear - about the passphrase. She'd walked him through it step by step in her kindergarten teacher's tone. Ray replayed her voice in his head, soft and measured. He entered the passphrase, his finger jabbing the keys like he was testing how well done a steak was.

```
Access Denied!
```

The exclamation point riled him up more than anything. A surge of hot anger shot through his veins, clashing with the icy grip of fear. His skin tingled, prickling with sweat and fury. *Ok. It's okay, I mistyped.* He typed again, each letter stabbing his time away. The sirens grew louder.

```
Access Denied!
```

"You sneaky little bitch?" he hissed, his breath coming out in ragged bursts. Tara. He couldn't believe it. Her face flashed in his mind: wide, doe-like eyes framed by silky dark hair, her expression always hovering between seductive and innocent. She had played him, guiding him through the setup with a professional smile as she was screwing him over. He tried again; his one-fingered typing agonisingly slow. The seconds stretched and warped, his vision tunnelling as he focused on the screen. There's no way. She wouldn't dare. He could hear the thud of boots now, in quick march.

```
Access Denied!
```

His mind twisted and spun, searching for an excuse that made sense to his world view, anything to keep him from the reality that he'd been had. But the anger seethed and boiled beneath it all. *That conniving chink screwed me.*

The pounding on the front door sent shockwaves through the house. "Armed Police! Open up!"

Mace's eyes darted to the window, quickly scanning the perimeter. The drop wouldn't have been fatal. He might have ended up with a sprained ankle if he landed wrong. The sound of the battering ram reached him, splintering the old wooden door. Ray's heart had hammered in his chest, each beat screaming, *You're a sitting duck, old man. Move.* But his feet wouldn't budge. They felt glued to the floor.

There would be no backup. The private group on Telegram, gone. His phone had no chat history, no call logs, no photos. A blank slate, like someone had taken an eraser to his digital life. His lifelines had been severed. He didn't know how they'd done it, how they had managed to wipe every trace of a connection, but then he wasn't like them. He was a dinosaur, not a digital native. Their plan had been calculated. Surgical. And he could almost hear their laughter, his ineptitude predictable, which is why they'd had a contingency. He'd been sacrificed.

He had stood dumbstruck, listening to the crunch of boots on gravel. Everyone seemed to have prepared for the worst. He didn't have a backup plan. That was a special kind of hubris. Ray had nothing to offer, nothing in his pockets worth trading, no secrets to bargain with in exchange for leniency. All he had was a surname and a voice.

The day of the fire, there was the call to Sharp, the one that broke every protocol they'd drilled into him. The Standard Operating Procedure was supposed to be tattooed on his brain - stick to encrypted messages, faceless communications that kept everyone's hands clean. Their hands clean. Now it was a sliver of a case. Sharp's voice had been clipped, professional, with just the slightest curl of an accent. *South African, probably. Sharp.* Ray clung to the name. It was all he had. As the evidence piled up against him — stacked in manila folders and Ziplock plastic bags by the uniforms now crawling through his life, turning over every cupboard, every drawer, every dusty corner for another piece of him. They already had enough to send him away for the rest of his life, but there would be some who would want to really stick the boot in, political enemies who would want the PR as well as 'justice'.

He stared at the floor, the tasteless institutional carpet patterns swimming in and out of focus. *I'm cooked.* The feeling had been gradually growing, but it was beginning to crystallise into something blunt and final, like the butt of a gun pressed into the back of his skull. The name and the voice were all he had. Sharp was out there.

- # -

"You know he has a thing for Asian girls," Bondy's comment played in Tara's mind as she got ready for the exclusive VIP dinner, the hardest ticket to get during the QSP summit. She was fairly sure they had given her a place because they needed some kind of eye candy for the lecherous partners and their guests. Given the nature of the conversations, it was not the kind of place where even the most high-class escort would be welcomed by the security suits. Tara didn't believe for one moment that Stone would elevate her to his side on the top-table. His courtiers would not like it, but they wouldn't tell him to his face. If that's what he wanted, then he would get it. Part of her wished the yes-men had more backbone and allowed her to be placed on a table of relative nobodies up the back where nobody would ask - who is the girl sitting next to Trevor Stone? She applied her eyeliner to accentuate her almond shaped eyes, it was a bit of a trope, but... *If he wants Asian, I'll give him Asian.*

The paparazzi mob was swarming already, elbowing, and

shoving in a curved amphitheatre shape arc in front of the gaudy sponsor board - logos plastered all over it like stickers on the back of a toilet door, many of them Stone portfolio companies. Tara recoiled. *Of course they invited the media.* She thought maybe, just maybe, she could ghost past them. But she was not the only one on the red carpet. She watched their postures change as if their raised photo platform had been electrified. Then a hand clamped around her bare upper arm, hard and uninvited, yanking her towards the spotlit altar. Into the glare. Into her personal idea of hell.

Trevor Stone, smug bastard, leaned in, inhaling her shampoo like a creep who'd picked up a child's toy. He pressed his body against hers, dragging her into the impromptu colosseum of flashbulbs and wide-angle lenses. "Let's give these vultures a little show, shall we?" His voice was a low growl as his arm coiled around her waist, locking her in place as a prop, a ventriloquist's dummy. Thinking too hard on that metaphor made Tara wriggle with stomach churning shame.

They were snapping, snarling, asking the same tired, brain-dead questions. "How long have you two been a couple?" Someone shouted as they jostled for the money shot, the one that would be splashed over the cover of the remaining glossy rags or turned into viral clickbait. And then, because there's always one, "Did you order her off Amazon?" That wasn't even a question. It was a jeer with a smirk and a wink and a sweaty locker-room laugh.

Stone's demeanour seemed to change once racism began to become the overriding theme of the assembled 'media'. His stance became protective, and he ushered Tara along the carpet towards the doors. "It won't last long." He pulled her to him in a reassuring hug. "Just turn your socials off for a day or so, you'll be fine." Tara looked over her shoulder. The entourage glowered as one, not used to being beyond arm's length in the shadow… of a woman… like her.

There were eight of them at the table, nine if you counted Stone. Men, every one, smirking behind their whiskey glasses and silk ties, trying to rationalise her seat at the table as ornamental. They lobbed obscure crypto theories at her like grenades dipped in patronising prejudice. Tara kept her face calm, unreadable.

"Tell me Tara," said a preppy looking oaf whose steroid filled body strained against his off-the-shelf pinstripe suit. "What do you think about MMOGs using tokens and coins instead of Fiat based currency?" He waited with a grin, assuming she'd defer to Stone or say something they could all have a laugh at.

She didn't blink. "Tokenomic based econonmies your mean?" She leant forward so he could choose to look her in the eye or down her dress. "Not so different to the US Federal Reserve is it. The central bank can control the supply and demand at will given the size of the initial issue." The man tried to rephrase his question to be more arcane, but she held up her hand and continued, "The real question is whether gamers, most of whom still like to buy their games in collector boxes, are going to fall for the smoke and mirrors of an NFT backed by a guy who identifies as a monkey." One of them snorted a laugh, which annoyed the questioner no end. "MMOGs have had their own tokens and currency exchanges for at least 20 years. There are secondary markets for most game items if you know where to look and there is the added bonus of there being actual players to play against, not just the muppet who blew all his ETH on a $40,000 spaceship that will never fly."

Stone seemed to be enjoying himself. He won either way. But she was so much better at this than he could have imagined. It was a controlled demolition. The foundations of their arguments rigged with logic that once detonated brought the whole edifice of their world view down until it lay in rubble. There were similar questions, as each of the men tried to prove they sat at Stone's table with more legitimacy than she did. The next one had that geeky, 'I'm worth a fortune, but I still can't get a girlfriend,' kind of look - bad haircut, pallid skin, and no doubt thankful for the ill-fitting suit jacket which hid the dark stains spreading from his armpits. But he was emboldened by being near his idol. "Maybe you could tell us about the ease of interoperability? When we're talking cross-chain..."

Tara cut him off. "Interoperability?" Her smile was almost kind. "Sure, let's talk about it. Let's talk about how when you used to go to Europe, you had to carry around francs and drachmas and liras and marks and pesos and now you only need Euros." She took a long gulp of her wine, but her eyes never left him. "Now we are talking not just 25,000 plus currencies, but completely different platforms and regimes. Interoperability." They kept going round the table in an anticlockwise direction. They had to prove that she was just a pretty face dragged in by Stone as decoration. The core of their being was at stake.

Stone was frowning now, not at her but at the rest of the table. The more they looked bad, the more he looked bad. That he had invited such lightweights to his table at this gathering. "Alright, boys," he needed to be as diplomatic as he could to please everyone. "You've had your fun. But I think Tara's more than held her own." His eyes gleamed as he gave her a sideways glance. The tension thickened as the men exchanged awkward looks, the realisation sinking in that they'd been outplayed. Tara looked from one man to the next and saw a new emotion. Anger. She'd shown them up in front of their hero and she was sure there would be consequences.

- # -

Tommo doom scrolled through his various feeds; He didn't want to. He yearned for easier times, when 'What happened on tour stayed on tour'. Now he saw Trevor Stone and Tara on the red carpet, again and again and again as it was reshared and commented upon by seemingly the whole world. They looked like an odd couple. He had his practised fake smile, she looked like she was being held in place against her will, paraded in front of the cameras.

The comments were the pulse of popular opinion. The 'Stoners' had gone full tinfoil hat already. It was a competition to see who could cook up the most plausible yet unhinged theory and the one that was getting traction was that Tara was a Chinese asset. According to the most vehement supporters of this theory Stone wasn't even running his own companies anymore. The Chinese government was pulling the strings, operating behind the scenes, and Stone was just a slick, sunglass-wearing puppet so that the companies could avoid all that nasty government scrutiny, sanctions, investigations, bans and the like. Tara was a drop-dead gorgeous sleeper agent, infiltrating his companies and cozying up to him under the guise of 'adviser' or 'partner,' or whatever the hell they were calling her now. She was playing the long game, a Trojan horse in Louboutins to mix Asian and Greek mythology together the way conspiracy theorists do. They had charts, timelines, 'proof' stitched together from random articles, grainy photos of Tara at events with Chinese investors from years ago, even some blurry shots of her at a Shanghai airport. It was insane, but it didn't matter. Every time someone posted about it, a new Stoner would dive in, ranting about how the Chinese were already running everything anyway. This was just confirmation.

Tommo could feel his brain cells dying with each scroll, but he couldn't stop. It was addictive, the way these idiots wrapped themselves in their paranoia, turning a tech empire into some kind of Cold War 2.0 nightmare - it was 'Reds under the Beds' all over again. Like they needed any more reason to worship Trevor Stone. Now he was practically a martyr, the front man taking the hits while the real villains hid in plain sight. And Tara? She wasn't just some woman clawing her way to the top; she was enemy number one.

The comments from women were worse. Toxic. Jealousy oozing through the labels. "Gold digger," of course, and whore. Classic. The go-to for any woman with a billionaire on her arm. But it didn't stop there. They spun her into some kind of wicked myth, saying she'd drugged him with Chinese herbs and ancient rituals. She'd forced him to ingest aphrodisiacs made from Panda scrotum and tricked him into unprotected sex. The outcome, she was already pregnant with the only heir to the Stone fortune.

It's a diversion. Tommo waited for the water in the old-school espresso pot to boil. *The oldest magician's trick. Look over there...* While everyone was focussed on Trevor Stone's exotic mystery date, they were not looking at who else was at the dinner or what they were talking about. Or maybe, the big secret he had been looking for was that the Chinese government was behind it all.

- # -

The QSP boardroom reeked of sweet vaping fluid, cheap body spray, testosterone, and a faint undercurrent of panic. Tara's skin crawled as she entered, acutely aware of the gazes from the men around the table - resentful, mistrustful, and a few who imagined her face superimposed onto the latest barely legal GIF they'd watched on Reddit. She'd rather be out dodging paparazzi than trapped in this circle jerk of corporate sociopaths, and that was saying a lot. She had been summoned. She made metal notes of the faces in the room. Most of them were recognisable from the last day or so, or past QSP projects, but there was one missing, the man she knew as Declan Sharp, a kind of security specialist, though it was unclear who he reported to. She slid into a chair, crossing her legs deliberately. Trevor Stone sat beside her, and while he protected her, she wouldn't be touched.

Stone's voice was serious now. "Gentlemen. And lady." A nod to Tara that felt more like a threat. "We've had some... hiccups." His eyes flicked to her, cold and calculating. "The contingency plan worked, but it left a bad taste. Metaphorically speaking, of course." A nervous titter rippled around the table. These men would laugh at a funeral if it meant keeping their stock options and access to Stone.

"Should've gone scorched earth on that property after the incident," a pasty-faced nerd interjected. His eyes darted to Tara like she was a bomb about to detonate. *He's the subject matter expert,* she thought. Her pulse quickened. *Monaghan?*

Stone's lips curled into something that might have been a smile on a human. "The property and the asset served their purpose, gentlemen. We cut it loose, cauterise the wound, jettison the spent fuel source and rocket onwards and upwards." The men leaned in, waiting for the how… Tara wondered if they realised how pathetic they looked. Stone nodded to a greasy supervillain henchman type with a face like a prison snitch. "Corbin. Tell us of the opportunity that serendipity had provided us."

Corbin's beady eyes were locked onto Tara, glistening with malice. His hooked nose twitched as he spoke. "The whistleblower Travis Thompson. You know the one. He who nearly brought our house down? He's back in Melbourne."

There was murmuring around the room. Tara's stomach tightened, but her face remained a mask of bored indifference.

"How do we know?" someone asked, voice trembling.

Corbin's grin widened, revealing yellowed teeth. "He was seen by our recently rumbled associate at a pub quiz, but there was someone else in this room who was there too," Tara looked at Stone. He already knew. There was a loyalty test coming.

Tara leaned forward, letting her blouse gape just enough to distract. "Yeah. I was there. I'm the only one who doesn't have a 'Stone Criminal Enterprises' tiepin." She played offence. Stone would respect it. "Let's face it boys, I don't look like you lot. He never suspected a thing."

Stone's eyebrow quirked. "If you haven't screwed him yet, then we are going to give you all you need to get it done." He stood and held the door open with his body, gesturing for the minions to leave Tara alone with The Crow.

Corbin slid an A4 envelope across the sleek, wooden table made of Ringed Gidgee from an old-growth forest that was no more. "It's all in there," he stated in a voice as smooth and dead as the wood.

"Everything you need to pin the Monaghan fire on Thompson. And implicate him in the stolen ID and passport scam. Crypto-payments, offshore accounts, even the timestamps line up. Tommo and Ray Mason, best pals." He smirked.

Tara felt a sharp crawling sensation work slowly through her whole being. It wasn't the threat in his voice, it was the lack of any emotion. The silent message was clear. We can ruin him. We can ruin you.

Corbin stood up, pushing his chair back with a slow scrape that clawed at her nerves. His hand slid down to cup the bulge in his trousers, fingers shifting it casually, obscenely, as he slowly ran his tongue across his bottom lip. "The consequences are so much worse for girls who don't play along," and then he started humming Joe Jackson's Different for Girls.

Tara's disgust was visceral, a punch to her gut she couldn't fully hide. Her hands shook as she tore open the envelope. As he exited the room, The Crow let out a low, rasping laugh that felt like an icepick to the base of her skull. Stone had left her in the room with this psychopath on purpose; this was how loyalty was bought. Terror was currency. She spread the contents out on the table, trying not to let her hands tremble too obviously. Two neat piles of paper, clipped together with the kind of spring-loaded clasp that made her shudder, given the threat she'd just received. The first set, Tommo's life in ruins, an artificial tapestry of crimes he might've really committed. Fake, but very good fakes, she could almost believe it. Hell, maybe he was playing her. Maybe he was dirty. There was a timeline of the last few days where it made a kind of perverse sense.

And then her breath caught.

The second pile was all her. Edited photos, video stills, deep fakes - her face, her body, twisted into grotesque acts she hadn't done but could never, ever unsee. The nausea hit her like a wave, but there was no time to fall apart. She couldn't even bring herself to cry, she just stared, unblinking, as her stomach churned, and she tasted bile.

Destroy him, destroy Tommo, save yourself. That was the equation.

- # -

Even if they could trace the source of the materials about to be sent into the world, all they would find would be a light-filled apartment, surrounded by greenery situated near the "shopping paradises of Chapel St and Toorak Village." If they connected the flat to the online blurb, they would find out why Tara had chosen it. It wasn't the posh postcode or the resident parking permit and it wasn't the SMART TV. Tara was only interested in one line of the online ad – "High-speed Wi-Fi is provided for your convenience."

Tara rose from the cheap IKEA desk, her body taut with indecision, pacing the confines of yet another Airbnb she'd rented under yet another alias. She could feel the weight of her next action: a decision to end the delicate balance of a quantum system and collapse it into one irreversible outcome. Click! More than one life would be irrevocably altered. Tommo had certainly flirted with the boundaries of what could be considered deserved retribution, but Tara wasn't entirely sure he merited what was about to happen.

She'd taken her time. Covered her tracks and then covered them again. The case against Tommo would traverse encrypted tunnels, bouncing between compromised routers in obscure countries - a VPN here, a proxy there. Use of the Darknet: exit nodes through the Tor network, rerouting through public and private switches. She piggybacked on IoT devices - using the IP addresses of lightbulbs and baby monitors, secured using the manufacturer's default password. This was about creating a digital ghost, one that no forensic trace would ever follow back to her. The damning dossier of Tommo's and Ray Mason's involvement in financial fraud, corporate espionage, and worse, would arrive in the inboxes of so-called journalists and influencers, each a master at the dark art of manufacturing virality.

Then, Trevor Stone, the de facto emperor of Australia's online outrage machine, would only have to retweet one of those influencer's memes with a curt, surgical line: "This is the truth" or worse yet, his favourite indictment of anything vaguely left of his ideologies - "Un-Australian". Like a casually discarded cigarette butt in a tinder-dry forest, Tara's click would set off a firestorm of anger, fuelled by social media's endless thirst for validation. Stone would be the hot north wind that fanned the flames.

She poured a slug of vodka into a tumbler that probably cost more than Tommo's last pay check. The ice clinked against the glass as she took a long sip. The vodka didn't help her decision, but it dulled the moral calculus. She hadn't seen or heard from him since their terse encounter in the service corridors of that old prison-turned-luxury-hotel complex. He'd accused her then - accused her of being capable of betrayal. She had told him to run. She hoped he had run, at least far enough that he couldn't be tracked down by the 'Stoners' about to be incited by Stone's stochastic terrorism.

She emptied the glass and poured another. She returned to the desk, fingers trembling as she clicked OK.

- # -

The multivariate testing had shown there was a photo that would rile up those parts of the media that saw themselves as not the media and get them and their talkback regulars in an incandescent rage. The photo, expertly doctored using AI, showed former politician and alleged sex-pest Ray Mason and Travis 'Tommo' Thompson standing with their feet on the head of a dead kangaroo, drinking Chinese beer, wearing T-shirts that read "God is Trans". The image ticked all the boxes - cruelty to animals, one that is featured on the coat of arms of Australia no less, racism, religion, and trans rights. Within hours of the leak, the photo had rocketed through the usual fringe digital channels without much cut-through until Trevor Stone had retweeted it with the caption:

"We must protect our country and our way of life".

And then it was on.

Doug Cain, the king of shock jocks was barely holding onto relevance in an age dominated by independent podcasts, but he still had a die-hard audience for his talkback show - the kind of people who frequented the Royal Oak Hotel. He leaned into his microphone, his voice like gravel unsmoothed by decades of nicotine and righteous indignation. The silence hung for a few beats, to let his audience's anticipation bubble. The image was already out there, plastered across social media and amplified by Trevor Stone's millions of followers. Cain's audience were not Tik-Tok types.

"You've all seen it by now. In your group chats - this disgusting, vile image of two blokes who think they can trample on everything we hold sacred in this country." Cain was psyched up for one of his signature ranting monologues. "Now, I'm not one to usually get caught up in the manufactured outrage of the day," he lectured with no sense of irony. "No, no, no - I've always said it. I'm not like the mainstream media. I'm not the fake news. I don't just report on the headlines, folks. I dive deep. I ask the questions you want answered. But this? This is different." He hit the cough button to disguise a long deep breath before continuing. "It doesn't matter if you are one of those lefty elite in Sydney or Melbourne. It doesn't matter if you are a battler, doing it tough. This is a full-frontal assault on who we are, on what it means to be Australian."

Cain imagined his audience with their fingers poised over their rotary dial phones, waiting for him to repeat the phone-in number that, in reality, they all had saved on speed dial. Cain's soapbox speech continued… "Let's break it down, shall we? First off, you've got Ray Mason and Travis Thompson. These aren't just your regular nobodies; they are repeat offenders. Mason. Well, we all know him - disgraced, corrupt and now an 'alleged' kiddy fiddler. If you don't remember who Travis Thompson is, he's the holier-than-thou 'good guy' that leaked corporate secrets and ruined the lives of hundreds of hard-working people. These two are supposed to be mortal enemies. And now… Now we see them out there, drinking some foreign beer, with their boots on the head of a dead kangaroo."

The producers were ready. While Cain took a breath and a drink of black instant coffee, they played an audio clip. "What's that Skip?" followed by a 5 second belching sound effect. Cain leaned back in his chair, smirking to himself before launching back into his diatribe. "We'll be going to the phones shortly, and I know you have something to say about this. So, you know the number." He read it out, then repeated it while he thought about the next part of his sermon. "Now if these jokers had killed a feral pig or something, I wouldn't care so much, but the kangaroo is sacred. It's on our coat of arms, mate!" Even though Cain knew that Kangaroo was predominantly used in pet food, he also knew how to use the symbology to incite anger and hatred and that meant ratings. He was on a roll. "These two degenerates are standing there, with their feet on the poor thing's head, mocking it. Laughing. I mean, who does that? I'll tell you who - people who hate this country. People who have no respect for what we stand for." He paused again, out of breath. "You know sometimes in this great country; we need to shoot a few roos. So. If that was the only thing in this picture, maybe, just maybe, I could let it slide. Let it go on through to the keeper. But… And folks, I'm really, really tryin' to keep it together here. These clowns are wearing T-shirts that say 'God is Trans'. You know what… I need to take a deep breath before I respond to this affront, so let's go to a commercial break." Cain repeated the talkback number. He sat and shook his head as he looked at the picture of Ray and Tommo. *I guess God is trans*, he mused.

The final notes of an adult diaper jingle faded, and Cain launched into the next part of his lecture. "God is Trans. Let me tell you something. This is a deliberate attempt to spit in the face of every Australian who believes in something bigger than themselves. This is about undermining the fabric of society. Look, I'm all for free speech, but this? This is blasphemy, plain and simple. This is an attack on people of faith. And why? Because these blokes want to pander to the woke mob."

Cain's demeanour changed. His excitement could be heard and interpreted by his listeners who could hear his tone go up in pitch. "Well, folks, I have a real surprise for you today. This is big - bigger than big, actually. On the line, we've got none other than… The one. The only… Trevor Stone." Cain wanted the socials to catch up. Trevor Stone was calling into Doug Cain's show. This could go viral and help with contract negotiations. "The man who's not afraid to speak truth to power…. Trevor, mate, how are ya?"

Mate? I'm not your mate, you crusty old git. "Doug." Trevor Stone was using his 'man of the people' voice. "Always a pleasure. You know, I'm just a businessman, it's men like you who speak the truth, so I felt that I had to speak up and add my voice to yours and all the decent people in Australia."

"You're so right about that!" Cain's genuflection was evident to all who were listening. "You always know how to cut straight through the noise. Now, this photo… I've been talking all morning about it, but when you retweeted it, Trevor… You've got millions of people out there, and when you amplify something, mate, it's like setting off a bomb. And let me tell you, this one? It's got people fired up. What was going through your mind when you saw that image? I mean, the kangaroo, the Chinese beer, the T-shirts. It's like they're begging to be hated."

Stone smiled as Cain took the bait. "Exactly, Doug. It's not just a photo. This is a deliberate, calculated insult to everything we stand for. You've got these two grubs - Ray Mason and that bottom-feeder Travis Thompson - standing on the body of a dead kangaroo, mocking this country. And it's not just that. It's those T-shirts. 'God is Trans.' Give me a break."

"Oh, absolutely, mate! Absolutely! They've picked the wrong fight, haven't they? People aren't just angry, they're furious. What do you think should happen next? What needs to happen?"

On the 75th floor of his tower, in his swanky pad by Sydney harbour, Trevor Stone prepared to marshal his sleeper agents. "Well, Doug, I think it's pretty simple. These people - people like Tommo think there are no consequences. They think they can mock our values and hide behind their money, their connections. But let me tell you something: there's a tipping point. People have had enough. And when the system fails to hold these types accountable, well, maybe it's time people looked inside themselves and asked - what am I willing to tolerate?"

"You're right. People need to think for themselves." Cain was skirting close to what his station's broadcasting licence and the country's hate speech legislation would cover. He waited, hoping Stone would continue his train of thought. He did.

"Look, Doug. Mate." The last word dripped with sarcasm. "People like Tommo should understand that they can't just walk away from this. They can't just shrug off the disrespect they've shown. If the people feel that the system won't protect what's sacred, then maybe it's up to the people to send a message"

"You're spot on. Spot on. Our people are tired of being told to just 'calm down' while these elites laugh in their faces. Trevor. You've said what they're all feeling but were too afraid to say."

Stone had made his point. There was enough to be cut and sliced into viral memes. "Look, Doug, Ray Mason is from a different generation. It's not an excuse, but maybe an explanation of sorts. He's going to be judged by his peers for the crimes he has been accused of." Cain murmured his agreement as Stone spoke. "Travis Thompson is a dangerous radical. He has no respect for authority, and I think that over the next few days more will come out. There is no smoke without fire." He ended the call.

"You heard it here first, folks! We'll stay on this story, but now, let's go to a break thanks to Woolies."

- # -

Tommo had run. Of course he had. He didn't have a lot of choice. The two days at Bondy's crash pad were over too quickly, and even though the apartment felt like a prison cell it did have a roof, and a bed and air-conditioning. Tara had thrown him a potential lifeline. The Bitcoin she had deposited in his wallet was part flotation device and part anchor. She had also given him advice, like the Steve Miller Band;

> *... They got the money, hey, you know they got away*
> *They headed down south and they're still running today. Singin'*
> *... Go on, take the money and run*
> *Go on, take the money and run*

He sat alone atop a sparsely vegetated dune somewhere near the Bay of Islands on the Mornington Peninsula. Looking south, out over Bass Strait, he listened to the regular boom of the shore break against the rocks and sand. His experienced eye picked out the rips between the crashing waves. The back-beach was a lot like his enemies, not to be underestimated – a picture postcard from afar, but deadly if caught in the undertow. Beyond the churned-up shallows the ocean stretched out to the horizon, empty - not a boat or ship to be seen. He savoured the vastness before him, even though it seemed to mock his predicament. Such a big, empty space, but nowhere to hide. The waves came in regular sets. Relentless. But the beach break was uneven, and a surfer was more likely to be dumped and held under rather than ride the face. *Wipeout is inevitable.* He reached down by his knees and sifted through the coarse sand mixed with twigs and shells. He let it slip through his fingers then stood, brushing burs and flotsam from his shorts in a futile gesture and began the hike back to where he'd parked his van.

The Bitcoin, allegedly deposited into his wallet by Tara, was sent to a relatively popular banking app that allowed him to convert it into Australian dollars. Once that was done, he went to an ATM and withdrew his daily allowance in cash. Not all gamblers want their families to know what they are spending their pay check on, so multiple 'solutions' have been developed to help such degenerates keep their activity off their bank accounts and credit card statements. Using the cash, he bought a bunch of prepaid 'gift' cards from a random sample of Aldi supermarkets, 7-11s, corner shops and post offices. The cards held values from $20 to $500, all able to be used where MasterCard is accepted, online and off.

Next, he needed wheels. Ordinarily he would advise against anyone buying a vehicle off a marketplace like Facebook or Gumtree, but in this case, the more anonymous he could be, the better. There was no way he was buying his new ride using AutoSettle. In a Woolworths carpark in St Kilda, Tommo took advantage of an English backpacker's urgent need for cash to fly home. After kicking the tyres, the deal was done for a 1997 Toyota HiAce. 340,000 kms on the odometer didn't matter. The van had other features that Tommo was looking for - it was nondescript white and had been set up for camping with a double mattress. On the Rosebud foreshore or Phillip Island at the height of the summer holiday season, it would fit right in.

With a few more cash Gumtree deals, he picked up an inflatable stand-up paddleboard and a sleeping bag. Then, working through various charity stores, he bought a bunch of essentials - bottle opener, coffee mug, stubbie holders, beach towels and things that he probably didn't need, but made him grin - some pulp fiction, the kind his mum used to read, Alistair MacLean, and Robert Ludlum, a fishing rod, assorted caps and hats, even a straggly pot of basil.

And then the plan had been to hide in plain sight. He secured the gear in the back of the van and headed south along the Nepean highway towards the booked-out camping grounds along the foreshore of Port Philip in places with names like Rosebud and Rye. He passed through Mount Eliza without stopping, tempted by the Stone property for a moment before continuing. Offering himself up as a sacrifice was not going to help anyone's cause, except for maybe Ray Mason. Tommo turned off the Mornington Peninsula Freeway when he saw the signs for Dromana. The 50km an hour speed limit along the Point Nepean Road was much more his speed.

"That's what I need" he said to nobody as he spotted the Ritchies IGA on the left. He parked the van. It blended in just as he knew it would. Not out of place among the various laden station wagons and pickups towing fishing boats and a few larger campervans. He'd left the stickers on the back window - Byron Bay, the Big Pineapple and Bondi beach. *What a tourist.* Walking into the fridge at the back of the bottle shop, Tommo surveyed the slabs on offer. Like the Coburg pub, there was a wide selection of new-age poncy beers, seltzers and pre-mix cans. He thought about a case of Carton Draught, but it wasn't quite the same in a can. Instead, he chose 24 cans of 6.9% Tasmanian apple juice. "Time to get off the grid."

- # -

It was a slow news week. There wasn't much to talk about except the cricket, and the 24/7 news channels needed more than WAGs to fill the time. The Tommo Tapes were just what their flagging ratings and relevance needed. But since the initial scandalous photo and Trevor Stone's promotion of it, there had been no more leaks. There had been no activity on any of the accounts known to be Tommo's either. That didn't stop the constant coverage. The bored art and marketing departments had taken the photo and created promos with increasingly bizarre headlines - 'Tommo Tapes Trans Threesome' and 'Tommo Triple Threat to Traditional Values' The live-news crews were dispatched to hunt down anyone who might be connected to the story and ended up at the Pier Hotel to the amusement of many of the regulars.

Daryl was cooked. He'd been drinking since about 1pm when he'd knocked off early because there was no-one else in the office and it was a nice day to be in the beer garden. He waved to the barman who shook his head.

"Hey. Daz. There's a news crew out there. Don't say anything you'll wish you hadn't," the barman knew his advice would not be heeded. Daz grinned as he sized up the situation. He straightened up as a young journalist and cameraman approached.

"Can we get a comment about Tommo?" Frank from Channel 12 News thrust a microphone under Daz's chin and blocked his path. "Do you know him?"

"Oh, Tommo? Yeah, mate. I knew him alright. Used to come in here all the time." Daz stifled the urge to wave to the pub patrons inside watching live.

"Really? Can you tell me more about him? Anything... unusual?" Frank was looking for a scoop. Something that hadn't been dug up by scouring social media and the rest of Tommo's digital footprint.

Daz leant in. "Well, now that you mention it... There was this one-time Tommo came in wearing a haptic suit, a diver's mask and a snorkel." His eyes were full of mischief. This Frank guy was on the hook.

"A...haptic suit you say?" Frank had no idea what that was, so he focussed on the other objects. "And a diver's mask and snorkel. In the bar?"

"Oh yeah," Daz was good at telling tall tales and now he had a national audience. "I think the mask was a kind of VR headset and Tommo was in the metaverse while also being present in the real world here at the Pier Hotel." *That should get me a couple of free drinks*, he thought before adding… "It was meant to be very hush-hush; you know. Part of some secret government program. I guess Tommo thought that no one round here would care."

"So, Tommo is part of the deep state." Frank was getting excited. This was the smoking gun, his Walkley award was in the bag. "Were the patrons of this establishment being experimented on?"

Daz could barely hold it together. This guy was a prize muppet. "Oarr. I'm not sure about that." He toyed with which QAnon theory to embellish. "It might not have been the government." Tears ran down his face and he tried to make them look like tears of sadness. "The original inhabitants of this land, they talk about giant lizards. And you know. Australia has some really weird animals that don't live anywhere else in the world…" Daz became very serious and lowered his voice. "Tommo used to talk about a portal to an alien world, where the lizards came from. That's why he wore the suit… In case he needed to communicate with earth from the other side."

"A portal to an alien planet inhabited by lizard people." Frank nodded his head. "That would explain a lot."

"There must be some collusion though." Daz couldn't believe that the reporter didn't push back, that this interview was being broadcast live. "It's hard to keep something like that a secret, but I'm just a chippy. What would I know?"

"You're right. This is just the tip of the iceberg," Frank agreed, shaking Daz's hand and turning to face the cameraman who was also teary eyed, but he wasn't sad - he was grateful the camera had a gyroscope that kept it steady or else the picture would be jumping up and down as he tried to contain his laughter.

"We focus a lot on what is happening in Canberra and our big cities," said Frank with no sense that he'd been had. "But out in everyday Australia, there are stories that get swept under the rug. We need to listen more to people like Daryl, an Aussie battler who we take for granted while we let the white-collar criminals get away with murder." He looked straight down the camera and put on a cheerful tone. "Back to you in the studio."

It was all fun and games for Daz, but he couldn't have imagined the consequences. The media descended like a flock of seagulls on a dropped Chico Roll. Within hours, the clip went viral, and every nutter wanted in. YouTube exploded with expert analysis. Self-proclaimed Xeno-archaeologists were rounded up by producers and joined by a cavalcade of conspiracy theorists who'd make Q himself look like a voice of reason.

Sceptics were labelled traitors, just another part of the grand cover-up. Those who refused to believe in interdimensional portals behind the bins of the Pier Hotel were called out as card-carrying members of the leftist elite.

The only saving grace in this circus of the absurd was that it was high season. Families were blissfully unaware of their proximity to a supposed interdimensional gateway when they booked out every hotel, B&B, and garden shed within a 50km radius. While the internet was losing its collective mind, the actual location remained mercifully free of portal-hunters trying to out-crazy each other.

- # -

In a dimly lit secure area of the QSP offices, Tara sat paralysed in front of a brand-new laptop that had never been connected to the internet. She could feel Corbin's presence looming behind her and it made her throat constrict like a noose was tightening. His hands began resting on her shoulders as he whistled his twisted theme tune, Different for Girls. Her skin prickled beneath his touch as his fingers crawled down from her shoulders, teasingly close to her chest. He didn't rush. Corbin never rushed.

"Now, Tara," he hissed, "Be a good girl. Click the mouse. We don't want people distracted by portals or aliens. We want them looking for our friend Tommo."

She could feel her heartbeat in her throat. Every fibre of her being screamed silently.

The Crow bent lower, his chest pressing into her back, His fingers reached out and down to the keyboard. He hit ALT and TAB, switching the screen. Tara's eyes began to tear up. The stick. The threat. Her face grotesquely plastered over a deep fake, a twisted scene that no doubt The Crow would delight in recreating in real life given half a chance.

His lips brushed the edge of her jaw as he hit ALT and TAB again and brought back the task at hand. "Click, click," he whispered. His hand covered hers on the mouse, guiding her finger to the button. "That's a good girl."

This time there was video, and audio. It was grainy, but it appeared to show Travis Tommo Thompson receiving a brown envelope from Ray Mason. The two men were laughing. Tommo was heard to say "Don't worry Mace, everything will be fine. No one will ever know you were involved. We get to rip off the government and the people and Stone all at once."

The video was leaked onto X by an anonymous user but quickly amplified by Trevor Stone. His retweet:

Enemy of the People!

- # -

The din of the Shark Byte café's refrigerator was the only sound. A few lights flickered occasionally from various electronic devices. The red and green LCD light fragments bounced off the shattered glass strewn across the floor. Archie stood by the till, his hand bloodied by broken shards of the front door, his knuckles white as he stared at the ignorant scrawl across the side wall: GO BACK HOME. It was smeared in blood-red spray paint across the brickwork and several of Marta's photographs of the surrounding area. He didn't need to look at his wife to know how she was taking it. He could hear her sobbing as she picked up shattered coffee cups from the floor.

"Cowards," Archie muttered, "funny how their real nature is revealed when they get a little cloud cover from an influencer."

"We need to give them Tommo," Marta said. "I like him, but I don't deserve this. We don't deserve to have to pay for his actions."

Archie hugged her close. "That's what they want. They want to isolate him." He kissed the top of her head. "And besides, I haven't the foggiest where the bastard is."

Archie released Marta, holding her hand until it dropped. and walked to the smashed windows, peering out at the empty street. A few days earlier, the town had been humming with tourists and the people who owned holiday homes, one of the weeks in the year they used the space for their own family and didn't rent it out as a holiday rental. He turned and surveyed the damage inside the cafe. *We've been through worse.* The pandemic had been the first blow, cutting off the lifeblood of tourism. Then came the storms, fierce and unrelenting, washing away roads and valuable topsoil and flooding basements full of stock. Fires were not uncommon.

"How can you be so resilient?" Marta said, her voice barely above a whisper. "Don't you get tired of being an outsider on your own land?"

Archie turned, his eyes glistening. "It's simple. I don't have anywhere else to go."

People were beginning to wake up, the dog walkers, the joggers, the surfers. Marta's phone pinged as the Shark Byte Cafe's Instagram page was tagged in a video clip from Channel 12 news. Trevor Stone had called into the studio.

"Do you take any responsibility for this incident?" The host asked tentatively.

There was an indignant tone in Stone's voice. "Absolutely not. We have no idea who did this. It could be a false flag operation to try and cause people to have sympathy for Mr Thompson. I can't be held responsible for the acts of people I have never met."

The host was on thin ice, but he continued, "The owner of the cafe was Archie Prince, a much-loved Australian sportsman and highly respected member of the local community. Do you have anything to say to Mr Prince?"

Stone was glad this was not a video call. He fumed as he was forced to address an allegation of racism as well as incitement to violence. He ignored the question entirely. "We need to come together. We need to protect our communities, our families, and our way of life. We are all looking for justice." The post cut out.

Archie shook his head and sighed. The bell above the broken door tinkled and Daz stood there sheepishly. "Reckon I caused this in some way." His work boots crunched on the broken glass on the floor. "I brought the boys. We'll have this sorted in no time."

Archie nodded, grateful for the help, slightly wary of Daz's motivations. The town was fracturing, lines were being drawn that he never thought possible. He'd grown up here, been supported by the local Holden dealership and raffles run by the Rotary Club. Even the folks who drank at the Royal Oak weren't bad people when you met them on the street, but nuance was beginning to disappear. The polarisation was real.

Marta was glaring at Daz's crew who had made an off the cuff, casually racist remark about a traditional artwork hanging behind the counter. It never occurred to him that the comment might be offensive until he saw the look on Marta's face.

Archie stepped between them; hands raised. "Guys. This is a small town. This isn't Washington or Canberra or Vaucluse. Let's not get distracted or radicalised by a bunch of city-folk."

The young apprentice backed down. Archie was a hero. A surfing legend. "From what I see on Tik-Tok, Tommo is a crim, but attacking this place is not on. Fuckin' Stone was right about one thing - we need to come together and protect our communities." He turned to Marta. "I'm sorry if I offended you." Marta could see real repentance in the lad's face. She stepped towards him and gave him a hug.

There was still tension in the room. Archie could see it in their eyes, the need for a scapegoat. And Stone had given them a target.

"Ah shit," said Daz as the Channel 12 van pulled up across the street. Frank, the interviewer who'd truly believed Tommo was using a haptic suit and adapted diving goggles to communicate with the aliens, was headed towards the door. He called out in a familiar tone that was not warranted or appreciated by those inside. "Archie. Can we get a statement about the attack on your cafe?"

Daz straightened and stepped through the broken pane he was working on brandishing a large rubber mallet. "It's not the right time guys. Go find the alien portal, it's up the road a bit, near the tip." Daz's men fell in behind him. All holding tools which could be used as weapons.

Archie moved Daz aside. "It's okay mate. I'll deal with it. Thanks." He patted the chippy on the shoulder and squared up to the reporter who shrank back a little. "It's Frank isn't it. Still on the beat eh, thought you would be the anchor by now, or have your own current affairs show." The reporter flushed as Archie casually tore his career to bits in front of the camera. "You're an experienced journalist - how would you describe the situation here? On the ground."

"Um. Well. People are obviously angry, and tensions are high," the reporter stammered, not used to being the one answering questions. He turned to the camera man and draw his finger across his neck. "Ok, let's cut… the guy at the caravan park said he was willing to go on camera, didn't he?" Frank put his palm over the lens and whispered to the operator - "We will erase that yeah."

Daz and the rest of the clean-up crew applauded as the news crew retreated. "They are so lippy when they are behind their keyboard, but not so tough when they are looking you in the eye."

Archie looked over at Marta. She made a little clapping gesture. It was a small win, but Archie knew it could go either way. Either they backed off or it would incite more of the same. At least they had a seed of a resistance movement.

- # -

Even at the height of the summer school holidays, there were deserted parts of the Australian coastline. The Mornington Peninsula was covered in a network of hiking paths, one along the coastline of the bay from Mornington to Portsea, a distance of about 43 kms, mostly flat, but also mostly without any shade. Then there was the Two-Bays Walking Track, 26kms of varied views and ecosystems - beaches, mountains, creeks, and fern gullies. Tommo picked up a couple of air-filled bullet shaped seaweed pods, he placed them side by side in the shallow eddies of the mouth of Main Creek as it emptied into the sea at the western end of Bushranger Bay. He watched the two vessels race, one taking the lead as it swept around a deeper, faster curve, only to be overtaken when it was snagged against a rock. It took him back to his childhood, when he and his cousins would spend hours racing different flotsam - leaves, plastic bottle tops, seaweed pods, and paperbark. The beach was empty. The narrow sand track from Boneo Road to the sandy shore was about two and a half kilometres. Tommo's van had been the only vehicle in the car park when he set off, but others would come.

He tilted his head as he heard voices. Sound travelled a long way, but if Tommo could hear voices over the waves breaking on the beach, the bell birds, and the wind in the Callistemon 'bottle brush' shrubs, then the walkers would have to be close. Moving behind a large basalt boulder, Tommo crouched and listened. Two people, a man and a woman, older from the tone of their voice and the idioms of the sixties.

"This Tommo bloke is all over the news." said the man. Tommo reckoned he looked like a Kevin.

"Yeah, Kev. Awful business. The world's gone mad," his companion agreed with a faint nod.

Kev slipped a backpack off his shoulders and dropped it on the sand. He took out a worn canteen and unscrewed the lid. "You can't believe everything you see on telly, but even The Age is saying the guy's bent."

"I can't believe you still read that rag. It's not the same since it was sold to Channel 9. I prefer the Guardian these days," the woman's behaviour mirrored the man's, but she spread out a small sarong style square of material on the sand before placing her backpack down and taking out an aluminium water bottle decorated in a floral pattern.

"You can't be serious, Shirl. You always were a commie." There seemed to be a close relationship between them, years of shared history. "Used to be that it was innocent until proven guilty - not trial by media." He looked out to sea, at the waves breaking against a shallow rock reef. "And now that surfer, the abor-igi-nal one, has been attacked."

Tommo stiffened. *They went after Archie. Bastards.* He pulled his cap down and slipped his wraparound sunglasses on. He coughed to let them know he was there before emerging from behind the rock. "Heya. Isn't this an amazing spot? So rugged and beautiful at the same time!"

Shirl was startled, but she composed herself quickly and took on the friendly tone that people always greeted fellow walked on the track with. "Oh! Hello there, love. Where'd you come from?".

"Oh, I was just checking out the rock-pools. Seeing if I could spot a blue ring. They always said you should look out for them in these parts, but I've never seen one.

Kev grinned. "They are in there. And you really don't want to mess with those things." Somewhere, deep down he thought that this random stranger could be the guy everyone was looking for, but what were the chances?

"I caught the tail-end of your chat. Did something happen to Archie Price, the surfer?" Tommo had not been watching TV on purpose.

Shirl laughed. "I guess you've been acting like a blue ringed octopus and living under a rock." She took a sip from her water bottle. "Some hooligans threw bricks through the windows of the lad's cafe and wrote some nasty things on the walls." Tommo tried not to show too much emotion.

"Probably just kids," Kev said, "Just a coincidence that they say he knew this Tommo character."

"Still a bit of a shitty thing to do, no matter what the motive," Tommo said.

Shirl shook her head. "Apparently his wife is foreign. A Lat-ino American."

"He's not married." Kev scoffed.

"Not the criminal, the surfer." Shirl gave Kev a playful punch on the arm.

Tommo screwed the lid tight on his water bottle and slipped it into his backpack. He had what he needed from the couple who were arguing like they were married or had been at one point. He took a step in the direction of the path. "Well, it looks like you have the beach to yourself. Have a good one."

Shirl looked down at Tommo's thongs and exposed toes. "You be careful now. There's snakes around and some unstable ground. You don't want to go over on your ankle."

"Boots are better for this kind of thing," added Kev.

"I'll be careful. Thanks," Tommo said, waving as he backed away.

"That could be him," Shirl said in a more hushed tone.

"Why would a guy being hunted by the media and all the nutters in Melbourne go looking for blue ringed octopus in Bushranger Bay?"

The conversation became fainter as Tommo put more distance between him and the couple. "Maybe he is trying to make a poison," said Shirl, a fan of Agatha Christie novels.

Tommo grinned and then his lips tightened. *They went after Archie and Marta.* His feet felt heavier as he stepped carefully over fallen branches and made his way back along the banks of the creek towards the carpark. More voices. Younger. The kind who might have seen his face in their feeds. A fugitive would hide. *Act normal*. There were 5 of them, three guys and two girls. They were talking about some Netflix series. Tommo nodded and smiled as he let them pass on the narrow track. They didn't look at him too closely. One of the guys took a look over his shoulder as they passed but was pushed forward by his mate.

Tommo scrolled through his maps app looking for somewhere he could park the van without arousing too much suspicion. If Kev and Shirl knew about the hunt for Tommo, then everybody did. Luckily, in this part of Victoria, he was just another white guy. Gunnamatta. He'd hide out at Gunnamatta.

- # -

The latest packet of 'evidence' leaked by Tara, as the 'Crow' menaced her, spread quickly as it was engineered to. Every scrap was meticulously curated to implicate Tommo Thompson in the vast array of crimes that Ray Mason had already been arrested for: forgery, fraud and human trafficking, all lumped under the heading of white male privilege.

Every network, every platform, every soapbox spouted a prejudiced opinion. The left screamed capitalist scum, the right hurled accusations of a woke takedown, the evangelical Christians dubbed him the Anti-Christ of our age, the environmentalists painted him as an apologist for the Oil and Coal industry and even the markets were offended - at least the traditional ones who were still denying the existence of Bitcoin. Everyone had a reason to hate him. And why not? Tommo Thompson was the perfect bogeyman. Once the media had run out of experts, they began to book celebrities, influencers who made their name on reality TV shows and were now milking their time to flog whatever they could. It was as predictable as it was nauseating.

Vloggers and YouTubers like Adaam, just one name with three a's, a quarterfinalist on an early season of MasterChef trying everything he could to be relevant to anyone who might stumble across his channel. "Yo fam, like, I just had to come on here and talk about something that's been really heavy on my heart, okay? This is so real and so raw, so bear with me. Like, you guys know Tommo, right? He was one of the good guys. He was one of us. Fighting for truth. But nah. It's like… I don't even know who he is anymore. He doesn't even care about our vibes, about your vibes. It's all money, money, money! Like, bro, when did it stop being about the energy, you know? The love and the healing? Ugh, I'm literally shaking just thinking about it." Adaam made sure his shake shaker was turned so his branding faced the camera and took a sip of a toxic green coloured liquid. He made a face then acted out his delight. "MMm soo good… You guys know I've always been real with you, right? It's not about the money, it's about wellness. It's about living your best life. So please, like, stay real, stay true to your truth. Don't let greed and fame win. Don't forget to leave a like, hit the notification bell and subscribe."

It was the same kind of bandwagon condemnation from every j-list celebrity and self-appointed pundit. Everyone was offended, but more importantly for the Chief Revenue Officers, everyone was entertained.

And it wasn't just the influencers who saw an opportunity. Access journalism was okay. There was nothing wrong with paying for a story if no-one else got it. Kyle Wanless was a weasel of a kid, even when he was in 7th grade with Tommo. Tommo had pitied the kid then, even stepped in to stop the bullies from taking Kyles 'frozen' money. But Kyle produced a faded photo of the 7B class where he sat cross legged at the front because of his diminutive size - the only boy in the front row. Tommo could be recognised as a youngster, his hair blonder, standing 3 in from the left on the back row with the footballers.

Kyle was on a split screen Zoom call, being interviewed by a podcaster who normally paid victims of Real Crime to vent against their enemies. "He always had a side to him that was... dark," Wanless, by name and by nature, but emboldened by being given a platform. "People like that, they don't change. Do they?"

"Go on mate, you're in a safe space," the host goaded his guest.

"Well," Kyle manufactured tears by remembering his goldfish being flushed down the toilet. "Tommo was a bully. He preyed on kids who were not as smart and not as strong. He was the guy most likely to become a serial killer." From a podcast with 7 regular listeners to the 6 o'clock news, the interview was cut and spliced and added to the pile of combustible material used as fuel for the fire. Kyle was described as brave for having the courage to speak up. Others held their hands out. It was a flywheel. Money, Fame, Ratings, Money.

Stone's team had made sure they could cash in too. The online casinos, owned by Stone's various shell companies, were now offering odds on when Tommo would finally crack, when he'd be arrested, when his trial would begin, and how long it would take for him to be convicted. On a dark web crypto based betting platform, the odds-on Tommo committing suicide spiked after Archie's cafe was attacked. It was a new game, and Stone controlled the house. Every dollar lost in these online bets trickled right back into Stone's pocket. While the people were distracted the real work could begin - the deals that would not be scrutinised, the legislation that would be passed without debate.

It was bigger than Tommo. The pandemic had seen the pendulum of power swing towards the workers. They had demanded flexibility, the ability to work from home and from Bali beaches. They had realised their bargaining power and demanded wage rises. This was an opportunity for management to regain some power by starting internal witch hunts for 'people like Tommo.' Corbin went through the anonymous emails from snitches who outed colleagues for no other reason than self–preservation. A nobody named Narin, who worked in a warehouse for the minimum wage was forced to stand in front of cameras and perform a rehearsed speech written by PR consultants to be used in an internal training video.

"No business should allow a culture where someone like Travis Thompson is hired." Narin was visibly sweating under the stage lights as he parroted the words. "A strong team is one that works together. A good day's work for a fair day's pay, not a gravy train that erodes shareholder value." Narin received a $20 gift voucher for his service.

- # -

Tommo scrolled through his WhatsApp contact list. He felt like he needed to talk to someone, but he didn't feel like burdening anyone else with his demons. They all had their own trials and were coping in their own way. It would be selfish to call any of them up or send them a text, especially when there was a chance of them being identified as a collaborator or harbouring a fugitive. He didn't dare get in touch with Archie, though he knew their friendship would be okay, he didn't want to get Archie in the shit with Marta. He hadn't heard from Bondy. Not a WhatsApp or a coded email. She'd been there when he needed her, but now she was incommunicado. *Had she been threatened? Had she been paid off?* Or did she feel she'd paid off any debt or obligation she thought she had to him.

Maybe an anonymous chat app would take his mind off things. One of those roleplay rooms where everyone was escaping the real world, pretending to be something else. Chat had always been the killer app. From MUDs to WhatsApp, there were millions of lonely people who just wanted to talk. He had inhabited these spaces for decades, since the only way to chat to others was to Telnet from one university library catalogue to another and find text-based rooms.

Then it was Yahoo, until it was shut down by prurient corporate masters, and now, thanks to encryption, there were multiple apps with names like Kik and Discord and Telegram. He scrolled down the list of 'people' looking to play out a fantasy. The world had moved on since the days of the library MUDs…

```
Coolcat923: I am your stepsister but I am the
police chief I figure out that your the bank robber
I been after.
Awoosexy: Send anything. Whatever cx
Heartme: Limitless switch looking for hung
furries/futas
Femboyhooters: Your girlfriend doesn't need to know
about me 😊
```

He closed the app and left the phone in the van, climbing the steep sand-dune between the Gunnamatta surf beach carpark and the ocean. There were other cars here, tradie pickups mostly, guys that had chosen the work because it gave them the flexibility to surf when they wanted. Looking out past the wide beach he saw the dark shapes clustered out beyond the shore break waiting for the next set. He missed the comradery of being one of the locals, even if it was just sitting silently and waiting for the next ride. He tugged a wide brimmed straw hat down over his face as a figure emerged from the water and headed for the path. Such a simple, chance encounter that happened all the time, but now he had to calculate how to act. *Nod and grunt. The most normal way to go. Ask about the waves? That would be how a tourist would act. Pretend to see something in the distance and face away as the surfer approached? That might look suspicions.*

The barefoot figure wearing a short wetsuit climbed the path. She flicked her blonde hair behind her ear and smiled at Tommo "The tide will be right for another half hour or so." Tommo could see a flicker of recognition in her face. "I gotta get to work." She sped up a little and looked over her shoulder as she crested the dune.

"Ah Shit. She knows who I am."

Maybe it was nothing. Maybe he looked like one of her ex-boyfriends or teachers. Maybe she would just jump in her truck and go to work. Maybe she would let someone know she had seen someone who looked like the guy all over social media. Either way, he had to move. Again. He waited until he heard the truck accelerate out of the carpark, watching one of the remaining surfers ride a solid face with the skill of twenty plus summers. The surfer lay flat on the board and used the smaller waves of the break to head for the beach. Tommo didn't want to greet another stranger on the path, so he turned and shuffled back down the sandy slope.

Pinching and scrolling across the map of southern Victoria, Tommo weighed up the options of where to go next. Too quiet and he would stick out as a newcomer, too busy and there were too many opportunities to be recognised. Somewhere remote, where the NBN hadn't been installed yet, where the 4 main terrestrial channels were the only source of media, where the Herald Sun was delivered at 1pm. He scrolled up and down the smaller roads and the towns bypassed by the multi lane freeways. The suburbs were spreading, and the pandemic had also impacted where people chose to live and work. The city and the CBD were not the magnets they used to be. Westernport was not as popular as Port Phillip. The beaches were muddy, with mangroves making access difficult. He zoomed in on a small man-made port shape at the end of Bungower road. Yaringa. *That will do for now.*

Driving was not the best thing for his mental health. He found himself skipping all the tunes suggested by the algorithms, apparently there wasn't a 'Hunted' playlist. He tapped the app closed, which only left him alone with his thoughts, which meant reliving the past week or so. Tara kept popping up. She had disappeared just as quickly as she had seemingly coincidentally arrived in his orbit. She was an enigma. If she was playing him, then she was playing chess, and he was playing tic-tac-toe.

He was jolted out of his paranoid wandering down short-term memory lane by a gunshot. The sound of a pebble kicked up into his windscreen by an impatient hoon who needed to get to the next roundabout 2 minutes faster than the speed limit would allow. The last thing Tommo needed was a detour to get a cracked windscreen repaired, but similarly, he didn't want some cop to judge the van as unroadworthy. The windshield was still intact, but his nerves were shot. He gripped the steering wheel tighter to stop his hands trembling and he tried to remember the exercises the surf lifesavers had taught him to cope with being dumped and held under the water. Another impatient driver leant on the horn and swerved around the van. Tommo waited for the next sound of stone against glass, but it didn't come. He looked right and saw another car in the mirror. It wasn't tail-gating him or waiting for the next overtaking lane. It just sat there, at a constant distance, a sedan, the kind the police used as unmarked highway patrol cars, or the kind that was part of a fleet used by mortgage brokers to do home visits. Tommo slowed, a courtesy to allow the car to overtake before the road thinned and the painted centre lines were doubled, but the car maintained the distance behind. Maybe it was the cops and they were checking his number plate against the registration database. What were they waiting for? The end of the road was in sight and the sign for Yaringa informed him to take a right turn at the roundabout. He indicated. The car behind didn't. He turned right, the van tilting to the left slightly. Tommo's eyes were in the mirrors. The car continued straight. The marina was only another 5 minutes ahead, but Tommo pulled to the side of the road. He took his hands off the steering wheel and looked at them. They shook visibly. His heart pounded in his chest and his skin felt clammy. He had to find a place to stay put, off the road, off the grid.

- # -

Tara shifted in her seat. She prodded the piece of sea bass on her plate with a fork and put on a fake smile as she watched Trevor Stone tear into a piece of Rib-Eye cooked blue. The restaurant's menu prices ensured a small, exclusive crowd, but the other diners, who could afford it, looked over at the couple and whispered about them.

"You're not having any fun." It seemed like a kind of catchphrase for Stone. He said it still chewing his barely cooked steak.

Tara looked across the restaurant to where Declan Sharp was standing with his arms folded in front of him. "It's hard to enjoy the food when I feel like I am a prisoner."

Stone looked up from his plate with a confused look. "There is a 3-month waiting list for a table here. The chef's only other restaurant is in some town in Norway above the Artic Circle and that one is booked out for a year."

"I think I'd prefer steak night at a pub," Tara said, pushing her fish around in a dissolving foam. She had agreed to the date in return for the fake photos and videos of her being destroyed. There were probably copies, but she had to try and protect herself somehow. Dinner with Stone at a wanky restaurant seemed like a good trade for her reputation, even if it meant the continuation of the gossip. The more she looked like Stone's girlfriend, the less likely he would be to release material that made her look like a porn-star.

Stone held out a cube of beef on his fork. "Want to try this? It melts like butter in the mouth." Tara scrunched up her face. It was true what they said, *Money can't buy class*. She wondered what the chef would think of a marbled wagyu steak not being cooked enough to render the fat. She lined up her knife and fork and pushed her plate away.

"Don't you ever do anything normal?" She wanted to get out of the heels that cramped her toes. She wanted to feel sand under her feet. She missed wrapping lava hot potato cakes in butcher's paper and throwing the scraps to the seagulls.

Stone looked even more confused. "This is my normal."

"You really think that you can win me over with a split sauce and a few bits of foraged samphire?" She felt the waitresses staring at her behind her back. "That Corbin guy is a proper creep, and you let him blackmail me."

"I don't approve of his methods, but he does have my best interests at heart… I didn't know about the fakes, really, I didn't. I never would have approved of anything like that."

Tara thought about it for a minute. Maybe there was someone else. Maybe Stone was just another cog in the wheel, like Ray Mason. Maybe they had similar dirt on him, maybe he was expendable. She lowered her voice and asked him straight out "Are you being blackmailed?" She watched his face, and his eyes darted across the room towards the man in the dark suit. But he seemed to recover his composure quickly and laugh.

"I have found that it is easier to just pay them off." He shared the remainder of the bottle of Yarra Valley shiraz between their two glasses. "My team says I shouldn't do it. That it makes me a target for repeated attacks, but it's just less… hassle."

Tara made a mental note to find something to extort Stone with, a bonus for enduring the current situation. "There must be a few skeletons in your closet that you wouldn't want to come out," she pressed.

Stone's eyes shifted and he glanced at the man standing in the shadows. "The problems that we can't pay to go away, we find other ways to eliminate." The cheery date persona was gone, and the thin sociopathic thin-lipped sneer was back. Tara pressed her knees together under the table. Long ago, growing up in the country, she had adopted a dingo as a pet. This felt like a similar relationship, never knowing when the animal would revert to its wild nature.

- # -

Tommo parked the HiAce as far as he could along the piece of forgotten land they called Point Pud. He checked the windscreen. His luck was holding. There was an almost invisible mark where the stone had hit the glass, but there was no danger of it cracking. No need to find a fix. His hands were still shaking from the drive - he didn't want to get behind the wheel for a while.

Packing a few morsels of food into a backpack he'd picked up from a pile of unwanted items left on a nature-strip, he wandered towards a couple of wooden picnic tables sectioned off with white rope in a quaint nautical wedding photo opportunity kind of way. No bride would remember this place. To his left, the mangroves provided sanctuary for crabs and other mud-dwelling creatures while doing some heavy lifting for the climate by taking carbon out of the atmosphere. Stretching out into Westernport in front of him were two lines of pylons - one set topped with green paint, the other with red defining the narrow channel. The channel was the entrance to a long, narrow port harbouring a mishmash of waterborne vessels, each one with a story of misplaced opportunity and redundancy.

Tommo stood and studied the 63-foot Miami-class Air-Sea Rescue Boat moored alongside the opposite floating dock. It seemed amazing that it was still afloat. Designed by the Miami Shipbuilding Corporation, of Miami, Florida, but built by Fellows & Stewart in Wilmington, California, as hull C-26683[4], the craft was an 80-year-old shell now. The only thing to associate the hull with its past was the lettering RAAF 02-109 stencilled on the bow. *I wonder how it ended up here.* The trawler 'Tamure' was similarly stranded. It was hard to tell where the red primer paint ended, and the rust began. The catch was not enough to sustain the price of fuel and a crew anymore, so the boat lay idle. His eyes drifted to the double masted, ocean-going yacht named Double Moon. It was set up to be sailed shorthanded, with a windmill for power and the kinds of toys required for enjoying more tropical climes. Perhaps it had been bought with the dream of sailing around Australia or even the world. *Surely this place wasn't the idyllic destination the voyagers had in mind.*

It was a place where people and things ended up through

misadventure at the end of usefulness. Tommo cracked a can of hard cider and gulped it down. One would not be enough to lower his heart rate or his underlying stress level. Footsteps. Behind him on the gravel. He jerked his head around. Nothing. He grabbed the edge of a table as his head spun, and his vision blurred. There were whispers, coming from the mangroves. Hushed voices. *They are speaking about me. They are giving away my location.* The ground vibrated as the low rumble of a marine diesel engine started in the direction of the boat-ramp. *I'm not alone here.* A pelican took off from its perch atop a broken flagpole. Tommo watched it bank to the right and soar towards the civilization of Hastings - only 8 kilometres away as the pelican flies. *They use dolphins. They attach cameras to their fins and use them as part of the military industrial complex. They could do the same with pelicans. It's not real. It's a robot. A drone disguised as a bird, low on battery, taking its surveillance of the harbour back to the powers that be. The insects. The cicadas. Bugs. Airborne listening devices. Advanced animatronics adapted to spy on the Luddite activists who would come to a place like this.* Tommo sank to his knees in the grass under a lone eucalypt at the end of the point and held his head in both hands. He needed to sleep.

- # -

Tara was glad to be back in her own place, even though she resented having to share a floor and walls with others. She would prefer to have something detached, but standalone properties with a view of the sea were rare at this end of the bay. The large balcony made up for the body-corporate bullshit. The Spirit of Tasmania didn't dock at Port Melbourne anymore, but it was busy - kitesurfers and cruise ships and car carriers and container ships stacked with Chinese ecommerce orders. She combed through the evidence that she had been forced to disseminate about Tommo. There was just enough information to demand further investigation, but probably not enough to make a criminal case. She had appeared as an expert witness for both sides of various white collar and financial crime cases over the years, usually helping clients who had been caught exploiting loopholes 'get away with it.' From what she understood of the case against Ray Mason, there was physical evidence connecting him to the alleged crimes - most had happened on his property, and there were credible witnesses willing to testify to Ray's involvement. The materials she had been coerced into making public about Tommo contained circumstantial accusations and the deep fakes would be exposed by a professional. Nevertheless, the shock-jocks and the tv commentators continued to call for justice to be done.

One aspect of the plan that Stone, or his masters, had failed to anticipate was the unexpected support for Kelpie Prince. Surfers, often dismissed as layabouts and bludgers, were estimated to number 2.5 million in Australia and formed a deeply tribal community. Beyond those who owned a board and surfed, millions more identified with the lifestyle and dreamed of riding waves. The tribe had united around the ex-pro, urging their favourite brands to withdraw advertising from channels that had promoted the narrative of Kelpie being one of Tommo's co-conspirators. It was one thing to have a go at a suit with white privilege, it was another to use it as an excuse for a take-down of an Aussie sporting legend whatever his racial background. Archie himself had been silent since the attack on the Shark Byte Cafe, but Marta was enraged, using her own podcast as a platform to speak her truth to a small but influential group of supporters. Tara's fingers played over Marta's contact listing and debated the merits of reaching out. *Too soon perhaps*. Marta was a quiet voice being drowned by the firehose of misinformation and weaponised rumour.

The large social networks, based in the United States, under the cover of Section 238 legislation that relieved them from being held liable for third-party content, used freedom of speech as a mantra to rationalise their behaviour and made no effort to remove the various posts that doxed Tommo and others who may or may not have been in his orbit. The only reason Tara hadn't been included in the hunt was her proximity to Trevor Stone. *Soon, he will expect more from me. More than I am willing to give.* She didn't want to be part of this anymore, whatever this was. She still didn't know.

The worst part about having to share a floor and walls on a summer night, with neighbours who preferred an open door with a flywire screen to air-conditioning, was that everyone could hear everyone else's life. The arguments, the passion, the dropped plates, and the rat-tat-tat of video game machine gun fire. Someone had the TV on.

"The nationwide manhunt for the whistleblower and cyber-terrorist Travis Thompson, aka Tommo intensified today with officials linking a series of data breaches to an account used by the fugitive." A news anchor read off a prompter with no apparent care for the veracity of the truth of the content, only the ratings that it would bring.

Cyber-terrorist. That's a new one, thought Tara as she scrolled through the source material, she had been provided. She couldn't see any references to the new accusation in her files.

"Millions of ordinary Australians have had their lives turned upside down," the newsreader continued with an almost breathless tabloid lilt. "Many have had to replace their driver's licences and other important documents after companies like Optus and Medibank Private were hacked and personal details stolen by hackers."

Looking up at the waning gibbous moon, bright, despite the light pollution of the city, Tara took a mental picture of the board in her head. Stone was playing some kind of schoolboy chess – his strategy seemed to be to capture the queen, and she seemed to be his queen in this game. She was playing something more akin to Go. She had never learned the game of her ancestors, so she couldn't say with any certainty, but the game she was playing felt more complex than chess, there were too many players, too many motives, too many hidden agendas. Maybe this was more like Risk. She had been good at that as a kid.

Tara asked the lunar body responsible for the tides out loud "How do the data breaches fit?" The moonlight illuminated the bay like the Risk map. It was perfect projection. While the vigilantes were motivated by publicising Tommo's location so he could be punished, the laziness of Australia's corporate IT teams in protecting personal data could be ignored and blamed on someone else. It was the QSP of old. The data breaches happened on their watch, while they charged million-dollar retainers they failed to deliver a solution that couldn't be beaten. Two things had to happen. A scapegoat had to be found, and the incidents needed to allow the lobbyists to push for legislation that would need consultants to ensure compliance. Rather than lose their contracts, the consultants could bill for hundreds of millions of dollars of more work.

- # -

Bondy leaned against the balcony railing of her seaside villa overlooking the grubby brown beach on the shores of the Gulf of Oman. There was a faint hint of a waning gibbous moon washed out against the blue sky. It was too hot to be out at this time, even in winter. She took a long drag from a local cigarette, grimaced and spat, stubbing the end into a leaf of the frangipani that provided a hint of shade. *Why would anyone come here willingly? To this slice of manicured paradise. This manufactured oasis of stultifying boredom.* Her eyes drifted to the pool, an absurdly long, improbably blue rectangle, double the Olympic length. She was thankful for that architectural dick measuring feature. Her muscles still hummed from her earlier swim, lap after lap of back-and-forth. She'd pushed herself to the brink of exhaustion, hoping to drown out the restlessness caused by inaction.

The job had come out of nowhere, which was not unusual, but the timing was a bit too much of a coincidence. Bondy wasn't quite done, but she did get a day off, and so, she was stuck in 7-star limbo which did nothing to keep at bay the nagging voice in the back of her mind. *Who took me off the board? Not Declan Sharp, or if it is, he's not acting alone.* He'd hit on her as he shepherded her away from Monaghan, and in another time and another place, she might have been tempted by his ex-military vibe, but she had the distinct impression that the mercenary security man wanted her to be close, to use the rescue as leverage against Tommo somehow. He wouldn't have sent her 13 hours in business class to the north and east.

Poor Tommo. Even if she was back in Melbourne, there wasn't much she could do for him. The sharks were circling and even though she loved the bastard, she wasn't going to use up all her owned favours and wasta on this fight. She had kept tabs on various message boards on the dark web. There were no official bounties or hits out... yet, but the chatter was growing louder by the day. There would be rewards, even if it was a pat on the back from Trevor Stone.

She pushed herself away from the railing. She had the same need as the sharks, to keep moving, but the heat forced everything indoors where the entertainment options were sparse - read a book, watch France 24, mindlessly scroll through social media. Bondy paced around her air-conditioned cage, over to the bar, pouring herself a good glug of the single malt she'd picked up at duty free on the way in. She lifted the bottle to the light to see how much was left. *Not enough.*

Was it Tara? She's a strange one. Was she that jealous of an ex that she would orchestrate a very specific consulting job on a mega yacht in the Gulf? The girl seemed to have a weird fixation on Trevor Stone too, and now, according to the parts of the media who truly believed Stone's love life was more important than climate change or the geopolitics of the Middle East, Tara was dating him! 24 hours of relaxation and peace under the waving palm fronds might be some people's ideal getaway, but it was Bondy's idea of torture. She poured another drink and stared out at the empty sea, then checked her watch, then paced again. Something was off, but there wasn't anything she could do about it. She tuned into Triple M Melbourne via the Listnr app on her phone.

- # -

"Authorities want to question the cyber-terrorist Travis Thompson who goes by the online alias of Taipan. Tompson has been linked to several high-profile data breaches where millions of personal records were stolen from some of Australia's most high profile and trusted companies. Thompson was last seen in the Coburg area of Melbourne…

And in other news - billionaire socialite Trevor Stone has been spotted having dinner with his new Chinese girlfriend. Sources at the exclusive concept restaurant 'Stoic' say that the power couple seemed very close but could not confirm if the bad-boy entrepreneur popped the question."

The bulletin was syndicated around the nation to radio stations that had tradies and footy fans as their core market, including Triple M Melbourne. Tommo tuned into 105.1 on the van's radio as he plotted how to get lost. The outer edges of sprawling suburbs were not far enough. He needed to go bush, disappear into a dense eucalypt forest, a day's walk from the nearest car park. Somewhere the mountains had no names. But he needed resources. Supplies. Which meant one last encounter with civilisation. One more roll of the dice, to shop without being recognised and outed. He turned off the van radio and took a left, back onto Bungower Road, which ran in a dead straight line all the way back to Mornington, though that was not his destination; a right at Jones Road, another left at Eramosa Road, and into a small shopping centre - small compared to the giant Westfield malls with their own postcode. Everything he needed was available: a Target, a Coles, a shop that resold everything in the Ali Express catalogue, a discount chemist, an independent butcher, and a Maccas.

He tugged his BCF hat down so the brim obscured his face. Just another bloke who was into fishing and beer. The Target would have all the camping stuff he needed to hike into the wilderness. The barn-like variety store was empty, no one who knew how to use Temu or the other big Chinese ecommerce sites would shop here. It was the same range of products; there were even apps that allowed you to find the high-street store item, buy it directly from one of a thousand white-label factories, and have it shipped to your door for less than the sticker price. But these products were marked up to cover the $7 million salary of the CEO and ensure the pension funds' investments were protected. Tommo picked through the bins of clothing, brought in specifically to create the illusion of a discount, while his eyes scanned the floor for disaffected staff or socially media-savvy customers. He couldn't see either, but the longer he stayed still, the more chance there was of someone having to pause Candy Crush and ask him if they could help. Shoulders hunched, head down, he worked his way through the camping section of the store, checking for anything that had a security tag and placing it back on the shelf. Self-checkout was his friend. The same technology and processes designed to increase profits, reduce entry-level jobs and make older customers feel estranged made it easier for him to perform his prepper act without making eye contact or speaking to another human soul.

The variety store teetering on the brink of redundancy was one thing, the supermarket would be different. Tommo walked back and forth behind the first row of cars parked outside and scanned the entrance for the greeter wearing a cheap suit and a scowl. Swapping his hat for an unbranded trucker cap, he assumed the persona of a local. There would be a few farms around here that did a big shop infrequently, so a trolley full of supplies shouldn't seem too out of place. The people who needed to fill a pantry would want things that were long-life, the kinds of things he needed to feed himself in the bush - things like 2-minute noodles, mac and cheese and dehydrated pasta Alfredo. He stifled a laugh as he turned the packet over in his hands and read the blurb that reeked of someone trying to stay just inside the lines of the advertising standards act:

```
Providing endless possibilities straight from your
pantry. Use to create a wide range of mouth-
watering meals today. Boasting a crowd-pleasing
taste, it's great on its own or as a side dish that
will elevate any meal.
```

"The fusilli's on sale." Meredith adjusted the name badge pinned into her polyester vest emblazoned with the garish logo of one of the foreign food giants. "Three for the price of two." Tommo was suddenly tuned into the buzz of the faulty fluorescent light directly above that sounded like angry wasps trapped in jars, which is how he felt. He ignored her, pretended he hadn't heard her. "You know," the part time merchandising rep said with a knowing inflection, "I've always found rigatoni to be... 'criminally' underrated." She definitely knew who he was. The weekly update email that listed how many facings the stock keeping units had to have, and on which shelf they should be placed to ensure they were in the eyeline of shoppers, also included a description of a man who might be trying to purchase specific items. The corporate AI had identified lightweight supermarket items that had a high probability of being bought by someone on the run. There was a high overlap between the company's dry goods and the list, so there was a high chance of Tommo being spotted in the aisles patrolled by the mums who made sure the pasta, protein bars, and jerky that barely contained enough meat to meet the labelling laws were being displayed according to the shelf layout, which was also designed by the same AI that had alerted the POS posse to be on the lookout.

He knew she knew who he was. He could see the look of

recognition in her face, hear it in her voice, her choice of words, intentional or not. "A few of the carbonara are close to their sell by date," Tommo said. Once upon a time he had worked for companies like this and knew what buttons to press. "You know the customers never blame the store. Always the brand. Better get the grocery manager down here. The stock rotation needs to be looked at." The tactic was designed to keep Meredith busy for a while. She'd have to go through all the products and find any that were close to their sell-by date and then she would have to find a manager who was probably hiding out the back or in the break room. Tommo threw a few random packets of pasta into his trolley and headed towards the tills. "We wouldn't want another poisoning scare, would we?" he called over his shoulder.

As he scanned his items and the self-checkout area simultaneously, Tommo's anxiety levels ramped up. Every beep of every barcode sounded like an alarm. He cursed the user experience designer who, instead of just listing fruit and vegetables in alphabetical order had created a system where the shopper had to guess which category the produce belonged in. *Where are the bloody tomatoes?* Each press of the touch-screen was a second he didn't have.

"Would the grocery manager please go to Aisle 5?" A youthful voice screeched over the tinny public address system. "Would the grocery manager please go to Aisle 5. Thank you."

Tommo maxed out a prepaid Mastercard as he hurried out of the store. Head down, he stowed his bags and started the van. There was no time to plan. No time to look at a map or make an informed decision. He had to get on the road and away from Somerville as fast as the 60 kilometre an hour speed limit would allow. *East. Then North. Into the mountains.* The quickest way would be through the city, but the risk of being spotted was too high. East towards Moe, then north. It would add 3 hours to the drive, but it was the best plan.

- # -

The 'WINNER' screen flashed on Declan Sharp's tablet; it should come with an epilepsy warning. It did come with an epilepsy warning. His fifth Battle Royale victory in a row was a tedious achievement. Of the supposed 100 players, at least half were NPC bots, their movements as predictable as the position of the Southern Cross in the January night sky. His other opponents? Teenagers, their squeaky voices betraying their youth when he played in team-up mode to mix things up. His finger, calloused with real-world firearm use, swiped through the gaudy parade of achievements, bonuses, and prompts to share his success with the wider world. Looking up, through the windscreen, he checked the front door of Bondy's apartment, the last known location of Tommo before he'd been seen at the QSP summit. Sharp's jaw clenched at the memory of being outwitted, though the wits on his deputised security team were dimwits and nitwits and fuckwits. Despite the full press media hate campaign, Tommo remained elusive. A small part of Sharp couldn't help but admire the bastard's resolve. The tablet pinged, an ad for another game that was already installed on the same device. He turned it off and threw it on the passenger seat beside him, switching his attention to his phone. His whole life was lived behind a screen.

Sharp's 'AI powered' scraper wasn't as sophisticated as it sounded. It searched through social media posts and the deep-web, corporate intranets, and edge computing networks, for keywords like Tommo and Travis Thompson and seen or spotted. There were a lot of red herrings, some of which might even have been created by Tommo himself to throw people off the track. Most of the results were clickbait, influencers trying to get likes, but there was a new one that was different. On an unsecured chat group, used by casual supermarket workers, there was a report of a man fitting Tommo's description in the outer suburb of Somerville. According to the source, the man was buying items that were consistent with someone who was intending to go camping or hiking including the ingredients for scroggin, a mix of dried fruit and nuts and chocolate. Sharp asked for his app to calculate the drive. 47 minutes from his location in the current traffic. Tommo had at least an hour's head start. Moving the map around with his finger, Sharp tried to put himself in the mind of the fugitive. The most obvious place would be Wilson's Promontory - but there was only one road in and one road out and all the official campsites would be booked out for the summer holidays. That left the Yarra Ranges National Park, 760 square kilometres, with the longest path being 50 kms, or further north there was the Alpine National Park - 6,474 square kilometres, just a bit smaller than the state of Delaware. *If someone wanted to get lost, that would be the place to do it.* He did another distance calculation. A 4-hour drive would get him to the southernmost border of the area. If he was right, there wouldn't be many of Trevor Stone's mob out that way. Maybe he could get to Tommo before anyone else. He sent a text.

```
DS: Credible sighting of T in Somerville Vic. Best
guess to start search: -37.66183, 146.69313.
Rolling.
```

- # -

Tara couldn't help beaming as she looked down at the blue haze that made the eucalypt forests of the mountains blur. Trevor Stone's helicopter pilot could fly a lot lower than the commercial 737s that shuttled people between Melbourne and Sydney on the same general flight path.

Stone watched her. "I promise you, there will be no media at Mount Buller." His suggestion for their next dinner date had surprised Tara, but it meant he was trying. The mountain in summer would not be empty, but it would be home to hikers and mountain bikers rather than the 'snow crowd'. "Probably not a lot of influencers or groupies either."

"Not until your first Instagram story reveals where you are," she said into the headset that allowed them to speak and be heard under the rhythmic pulse of the rotor blades.

Stone held up his empty hands. "No one will know. The pilot is very discreet, as is the private chef who will be cooking dinner. A BBQ. Steak cooked to your liking." He watched for her reactions. She wasn't convinced yet.

"It's better than heritage carrots done 12 ways." She was exhausted by the events of the past few weeks, and she was not in the mood to put up a fight. "It's still pretty random though."

"Which is why it's the last place anyone will be looking for me." He could see the resignation in her face, and he didn't like it. "You shouldn't feel like you have to spend time with me."

Turning away from the window, she made eye contact and held it to make sure he knew that the next words were deadly serious. "And you shouldn't feel like me agreeing to a private dinner in a mountain chalet means I am going to be an addition to your body count."

"I'm not the person that the media says I am."

He sounded sincere, but he was a practised libertine who would only put up with the 'hard to get' attitude for so long before he moved on to someone more unprincipled. "Well, let's play it by ear then shall we." She looked back out the window. "No expectations."

The pilot interrupted the tension. "Do you want to go over The Bluff? It's pretty spectacular and if you get the chance to see it from the air, you might as well."

Tara's mind flashed back to seeing 'The Man from Snowy River'. Despite the title, the film had been shot on the mountains below them. Her concerns about Stone were briefly forgotten. "If it's not too much trouble."

"Great idea 'Temple', there's no wind around. No signs of storms or bad weather. Let's do it," Stone said enthusiastically. The helicopter banked and passed low along the ridge as if lining up an aerial shot from the classic Australian movie. Tara looked out over a cleared area where a traditional cattleman's hut made from corrugated iron provided refuge from the snow in the winter.

"That's Bluff Hut," said Temple, reading her thoughts. "It's the third highest hut in the country. But that's not the original. The first one burnt down in the 2007 fires."

"Wow," Tara exclaimed as The Bluff came into view. *The people of the Kurnai nation must have had a name for that*, she thought, as her breath was taken away by the place which, like much of the Australian bush, was awesome in the non-American sense of the word. The prehistoric wilderness was both intimidating and, at a deep spiritual level, beautiful. Somewhere in a bag, a phone could be heard to ping, but no-one in the helicopter thought much about it as the pilot turned towards the helipad on the summit of Mount Buller a few clicks away.

- # -

Once on the road and well away from the Melbourne suburbs, Tommo had pulled into a roadside picnic area and studied the map with the same logic that Declan Sharp had used. He had briefly considered The Prom, but once past Yanakie it was too easy to get cornered. He thought about towns he had been to as a kid with names like Metung and Tamboon, but anything near the coast would be busy. Which left the mountains, which was not his natural habitat, but he did enjoy the vastness, and the unpredictability of the weather made the Alps a less popular summer destination.

His initial intuitive plan had been sound. He'd passed through Moe where he took a left and headed north to Woods Point - not so much of a town as a pub, a phone box, and a general store. He'd stopped to stretch his legs and take photos of the old bowsers and the faded Golden Fleece sign at the log cabin petrol station. He'd been tempted by the sign for McMillans track - Woods Point to Omeo, a distance of 220 kms. Had he done so, he might have found Declan Sharp waiting for him in Licola after a 13-hour hike. Pushing slowly onwards, following the broken lines, living on borrowed time, the van often struggling with the steep incline, he smiled to himself at the place names, the literal expression of the feelings of the white explorers, places like First Fish, Frenchman's Gap and Mount Terrible. It was a shame he was in such a rush. It would be nice to take a few weeks to do the drive that had taken him over 6 hours.

A couple of 4WDs had passed him going the other way as he had approached his first choice of stop. His luck was holding for now. The car park was empty, as was the campsite. Even though daylight saving time meant the sun would be up for a couple more hours, it was unlikely there would be anyone in this place until the morning. Once the van's tired engine had been turned off, there were no manmade sounds. No cars, not even in the far distance. No generators or music playing through speakers, no human voices. Tommo pulled a folding chair and an Esky out of the van and wandered towards a cleared lookout area. In the distance he could hear the modern world approaching. Helicopter blades. He wasn't worried. It was highly improbable that they would be using helicopters up here to try and track him. More likely that a hiker was lost or injured. The sound became louder as the chopper banked and lined up to make a low pass over Bluff Hut. Tommo crouched under a snow gum; his paranoia was back. He kept trying to rationalise the situation in his head - *It's just a sight-seeing trip. A joyride. They' have better things to spend resources on than helicopters scouring the high country looking for some alleged white-collar criminal.* He felt like he could almost reach out and touch the skids of the helicopter as it passed overhead moving in the direction of The Bluff. He didn't even realise he had been holding his breath until his lungs began to burn and his vision began to blur. Then his shoulders slumped in relief as the mechanical bird turned for the summit of Mount Buller, just 9 or so kilometres away in a straight line. *No need to worry. Just some rich asshole looking for a respite from the heat, a hypocrite who doesn't understand or care that his use of a helicopter for such a journey is a contributing factor to the temperatures being 4 to 5 degrees warmer than normal, and the extinction of the ski season, the sort of person who thinks the rules don't apply to them. A person like Trevor Stone.*

- # -

Declan Sharp was sitting on the banks of the Macalister River. He had just handed over $150 for a night's accommodation in a porta-cabin. He'd had to pay extra for a towel and bedding, but he was "lucky" because there had been a last-minute cancellation. Unlucky would have resulted in driving 57 kms back to the Heyfield Railway Hotel. It had been a bad decision to come all this way on a hunch, but now he was here, he could maybe have a night off. The first in a long time. He cracked a can and watched the eddies on the surface of the river. There was no cell-signal. But there was Wi-Fi. He sighed as his moment of contemplation was disturbed by a message that came in on an encrypted chat app.

T: Target within 10km of Mount Buller summit.

8

Tommo squinted as he woke with the sunlight streaming through the open windows of the van. A full day of driving had taken its toll; yes, that was the reason he felt rough, not the bottle he had drunk, tumbler by Tumblr, as he watched the darkness inch down to the horizon and the stars appear. There was no light pollution. Almost every star that could be seen from the southern hemisphere could be seen. At some point he must have climbed out of the folding fisherman's chair and clambered onto the mattress in the back of the van. The site was still empty, but that could change quickly. The 6 or so hours of sleep, 50 percent deep, 40 percent light and 10 percent REM, according to his watch, had been free of panic and second guessing, but now he was awake and the reality of the world, as beautiful as it was in this corner of the earth was tinged with the underlying fears of a hunted man.

He filled his various water containers from the tank. It has been a while since he had tasted rainwater, not glacial water stored in a plastic bottle, or tap water that had travelled through miles of pipes, but H2O straight from the sky, though when it had rained up here last, he couldn't judge. The water hadn't collected in a stone pool, but in a corrugated iron tank, and so, it had a unique taste. Tommo guessed that tank water was like French wine in a way, each with its own terroir. He brushed his teeth under a gnarled, stunted Snow Gum and marvelled at its resilience. The Mountain Ash that grew further down the mountain stood tall and straight to height of over 300 feet. They didn't have to adapt to snow and frigid winds. This tree was just as old as its cousin eucalypt but had only managed to grow to 12 feet high. Neither variety had the option of running. They put down roots and they dealt with whatever came along. Tommo didn't know how to feel about that.

One of the reasons that he had bought the van on sight was the technology the previous owner had kitted it out with, specifically Starlink. It is the kind of technology that was built for Australia, with hundreds of thousands of kilometres that could not be wired up, where satellites were the only way to get digital signals. Perhaps it would have been better if he was totally off the grid, starved of information about the rest of the world until he managed to get to a post restante or a telegraph office. *Does Post Restante still exist?* He fired up the link, not wanting to see what was being said on social media or the so-called news sites, he just wanted to check his email, make sure he wasn't overdrawn on any accounts, see how much the remainder of his Bitcoin was worth, that kind of thing. Not important, not urgent, but he was as addicted to his digital umbilical cord as most people. There was mail. Ordinarily he would have binned it, but the title was unusually specific:

```
Stone Seals the Deal.
```

He opened it. Probably the first mistake, but helicopters notwithstanding, he was over 75 km away by steep, winding, often unpaved road from the nearest habitation that could be classified as civilised. The sender's address gave nothing away, a Gmail account with a randomly generated string of characters as a username - he would have done the same, had done the same. There was no message, except for a thumbnail from a video that clearly showed two people in bed. Both appeared to be naked and, by the looks on their faces, engaged in an activity that gave them equal pleasure and pain. Tommo felt his heart begin to beat faster. He felt like a cocktail shaker at one of those bars where a mixologist has decided he is the bartender equivalent of Salvador Dali adding ingredients that have no place together without creating jarring, distasteful effects for no reason other than notoriety. Tommo leaned in. It was Stone's face, his neck muscles taut in a rictus of exertion and determination. The other face he knew just as well, if not better. Tara's eyes rolled back in her head, and she was screaming silently. Tommo knew that if he clicked the triangular code for 'Play' there would be sound, and he didn't want to hear it. He paused. The frappe he had made from instant Nescafe and tank water was causing his heart to pound in every artery in his body. The peacefulness of the layered blue mountains stretching away forever was ripped away by his addiction to being online.

Who filmed this? Who gains by filming this and who gains by sending it to me? A soft voice of reason spoke up from the back of his mind. He left the laptop open and slid out of the van, jogging towards the lookout position where he spent the night before in an alcohol induced denial of reality. He stood at the edge of a cliff and asked the universe to help him.

He spoke out loud "Tara wouldn't do this. She is too private and even if she decided she wanted to have a sex-tape of Stone, she wouldn't send it via anonymous email. Would she?" There was a noise behind him, and he almost shrieked with fright. A wallaby stopped and turned its head and seemed to raise one eyebrow. Then it loped off, unperturbed by the ranting human. "Stone would definitely do this. He would want to have a trophy of his conquest, and he would love to rub it in." Tommo wandered back to the van, his head spinning with new conspiracy theories. He sat before the screen and hovered the arrow shaped cursor over the play button, indicated by a triangle pointing to the left, it had signified play since the days of reel-to-reel tape audio in the 1960s and it was still universally known what happened when it was pressed. He leaned in. If it was a fake, it was a very good fake, but then, the materials that had been leaked about him were very good fakes. *Just delete it. What happens if you don't see it? If the video is never watched, did the event even happen?* He clicked the link.

It began with a creepy stalker vibe. The sort of gonzo porn film that makes the most depraved aficionados either cringe or harden a little. The opening shots were there to establish the location. The video seemed to have been filmed within eyesight of Tommo's current location, on the summit of Mount Buller. Fade to black. The couple sitting on a comfortable couch on the balcony of a chalet, their gaze in the direction of Bluff Hut, then Stone's arm rested around Tara's neck and her head dropping onto his shoulder.

Tommo hits the two vertical rectangular bars that represent the command to pause. It was real. There were no edits that look out of place, no continuity errors or irregularities in the timestamps. But his questions remained. *Who stands to gain by filming this and why did they send it to me?* There was no reason to imagine that the answers would be revealed by watching the rest, but he wanted to know. *Did she sleep with Stone consensually?* Was the image etched into his brain by the thumbnail a real scene? He didn't want to know. He did.

He was feeling unusually jealous and possessive. Tara had led him back to her Airbnb the first night they had met, and he'd enjoyed it. *Did I?* She'd gone to bed with a loser that she met at a pub quiz in a seaside holiday town between Christmas and New Year. If she had done that, why wouldn't she want to sleep with a rich, powerful, good-looking celebrity who could give her anything she wanted? But then he watched the last twenty seconds of the video again. The sound had been isolated. The POV had changed just a little and there was a sense that the tables were turned. Trevor Stone looked uncomfortable, scared even. Tommo had the power balance all wrong. Tara was in control. She had him by the balls. Tommo skipped back and watched it again. Tara lifted her head and whispered into Stone's ear and his eyes widened and she seemed to laugh.

- # -

The Bluff summit was 4.2 kms from where the van was parked. Using a formula only known to the National Parks and Wildlife Service, that was 2 hours away on foot. Tommo knew from experience that it would take nearly half that time to walk to a spectacular spot with a sheer drop into nothingness. He packed a daypack with a few items, things he hadn't really wanted to be found in the van when someone finally decided the owner wasn't coming back. He made a mental note to throw them in the opposite direction from the one he was going to jump. His only play had been to trust Tara, but the more he looked back, the more he saw reasons that he shouldn't have. It wouldn't be so bad if she had just been an agent of QSP, a drone acting out her corporate wage-slave responsibilities and doing what was right for her employer, but this was something else. She had looked him in the eye and said that she hated Trevor Stone, that he was a reprehensible human being that she would never give the time of day to, yet here she was, spreading her legs for him. "… and there ain't nothing like the kisses from a jaded Chinese princess."

- # -

Tara stood doubled over. Freezing sweat caused her to shiver as she tried to fill her lungs with thin mountain air, but the perspiration was not the reason for the chills running down her spine. She'd woken early and alone in a strange bed. The silence of the alpine environment was not one she was used to. She had rolled over and turned on her phone out of habit to check her email. She had mail. Ordinarily she would have binned it, but the title was unusually specific:

DISCARDING DECENCY

It seemed to have Corbin's grubby fingerprints all over it. The thumbnail of the video was enough to make her shudder and gasp out loud, then, perhaps in shock, she spent a moment thinking about how the act of making a sketch with the nail of one's thumb became the terminology for a video still representing the longer piece of content. Then she noticed something else. The email had been cc'd to Tommo, at least it was highly likely that tt@antipodeon.com was Tommo's email address. She had blacked the screen of the phone and thrown it across the room as she felt tears begin to well in her eyes. She knew the video was not a fake, she could remember Stone making that face as he did what the subject line of the email so succinctly described.

Standing up and taking a deep breath, having rested to catch her breath after a punishing run along a track designed for mountain bikes, Tara took in the expansive 360 degree view from the top of the mountain. Perhaps here she could get some perspective. Up until now she had been in control, at least it had seemed like she had been in control. Even while what was recorded by the hidden cameras was happening, she had told herself that it was all part of her plan. She had been sure that Stone was the one she wanted, but the footage of them together was a wrong'n, the cricket equivalent of a curve ball. *Is this why oracles and monks live on mountains?* She wondered as she gazed at The Bluff that Stone's pilot Temple had flown over on the trip in. Lifting her hand to her brow to shade her eyes, Tara squinted. There was a solitary figure on the summit of the cliff. Is there? Or was her mind making up shapes? It wasn't a tree, the summit was barren except for tundra grasses and bushes. It was moving, like a person pacing one way then the other as if deep in thought.

Whoever set up the camera, whoever sent the email, whether it was Stone or some other sociopathic puppet master, Tara had to find Tommo. She had hoped that he would have responded differently. She had hoped he would have been guided by the traits which had led him to blow the whistle on the sordid dealings of QSP and Ray Mason and Trevor Stone, that his core belief in doing the right thing would make him take the fight to Stone. But instead, faced with the onslaught of corporatised cancel culture, Tommo had fled. Tara remembered the first time she saw him, shuffling and stumbling and slurring at pelicans. He'd be in that state again now and this time she was responsible. She had to find him. Her mind flashed back to the low pass over The Bluff, the magic of the place perhaps one of the reasons she had let her guard down after the private dinner for two. If Tommo was going to jump, that escarpment would be a fitting place for a final breath. She opened her messaging app, the one that had a 'people nearby' function. Tommo was last seen within 10 kms. She sent a message

        T: Come and get me. I know where he is.

- # -

Tommo began to tramp up the path towards the top of The Bluff wearing only thongs, shorts, a t-shirt, and a floppy wide-brimmed hat. He didn't care if he went over on his ankle, he didn't care if his skin became red and sore and burnt from the sun. Everything he was being told was that 'the meek will not inherit the earth,' that there is no shame, that it's every man and woman for themselves and the good guys are suckers. The scrub opened out as he climbed, the exposed ground too inhospitable even for the Snow Gums. It was like being alone in the middle of a mountain top ocean, a profound experience of solitude and connection to the vastness of the planet and the space it orbits. He took a long, deep breath. The air was different, crisp, and pure, with less oxygen than sea-level. He could feel it travel through his body, down into his lungs and spread through his bloodstream like a transfusion. His body became lighter, the climb became effortless, like he was being pushed from behind by an invisible hand.

The view from the top was endless, layer upon layer of random wavy lines of blue, each sheet a slightly lighter hue until the mountains became indistinguishable from the sky. This was the kind of place where the concept of Gaia made sense - the mountain itself is a living being, ancient, and indifferent to human presence. Tommo wondered how far away the sound of him opening his water bottle could be heard. He looked out at the arced horizon and tried to reconcile the theory of quantum physics that suggested the act of opening his water bottle caused all the other atoms in the universe to rearrange themselves. That there was significance to his actions and existence while the immensity of the scene suggested the opposite.

He shuffled to the edge of the bluff and looked down. His vestibular system in the inner ear, regulating his balance and spatial orientation disrupted by the change in visual perception triggered a sense of vertigo, a self-defence instinct, an in-built survival mechanism like a snow gum reducing its surface area to protect against the frigid winter winds. The earth would not miss him. He shivered. The wind had changed. It was stronger, from a different direction. Even in early January the weather was unpredictable. The storms came from nowhere. The height of the mountain meant that the summit would be engulfed in thick cloud, visibility would be reduced to almost zero and there was no protection from the elements. He laughed into the void before him "Bit of a cliche isn't it?" A low rumble of thunder replied from the distance, and he was put back in his place. Granite pebbles made a soft scratching sound as his feet shuffled and dislodged them and sent them over the edge and a new feeling came over him. He wanted to stand defiant and watch the storm build and come at him. He wanted to stare down the tempest, lean into the squalls and feel the sleet lash at his skin. One last act of hubris before he gave up.

- # -

Wrapping a borrowed jacket around her shoulders, Tara looked up at the sky. If she had been on a boat, she would be quickly reducing sail and preparing to get wet. There was a green light that she knew all too well. A storm was coming. She paced around the white van parked discreetly away from the Bluff Hut. The hut was built to provide shelter at times like this, though the corrugated iron sheets didn't look as if they would stay nailed down in a strong wind. The van was almost identical to the one that had blown up in the surfside carpark in the explosion that was supposed to happen while Tommo was in her bed. He was supposed to get angry, but he'd been in the van as it burned and instead, he had been scared off. Tara traced her finger around the shape of the Giant Pineapple sticker slapped casually onto the tinted rear window of the van and then was snapped back to the present by a whip-crack of lightning and a thunderous boom. She grabbed a backpack out of a rented car.

"Give me a 20-minute head start," she said over the wind to her companion. "If he sees you, who knows what he will do." She shook her head and started along the path as the first drops of rain began to fall.

Tommo raised his hands towards the sky, daring the fizzing electrostatic massing in the clouds to use him as a conduit to the earth. He thought about the hollow people, the ones who got mad about a Tweet or a comment on a blog, the ones that thought proving their point about the ending of a reality show or the price of a meme coin while hiding behind an avatar and a pseudonym gave them purpose. In that moment he thought people should be forced to stand alone on a mountain in the teeth of a gale, to be enveloped by clouds so thick their movement can be felt against your skin. To be humbled.

"COME ON," he roared in the centre of the tempest, but the sound was instantaneously equally dissipated and consumed by the tumult.

And then, he could see the horizon again. The mist and fog and sleet thinned to drizzle and then that was swept across to the next rage as the sun reappeared. The air became thick with humidity as the groundwater began to evaporate and return to the sky from where it had just cascaded. Tommo felt better. He was dripping wet, shivering, moments away from hypothermia, but the spirits of this place and the universe had decided that today was not his day to be vaporised and turned back into pure carbon. A thin smile spread across his face for a moment and then vanished as he watched a figure appear over the crest of the ridge.

"Tara?"

She could see the moment he spotted her. His stance changed. He had seemed to be at peace but now he was tense and on edge, right on the edge, his flimsy footwear providing no grip. He stood with his back to the drop and raised his arms like a competition high diver. "Noo. Wait. Please. Tommo please" She broke into a run towards him.

"Come to finish the job, have you?" He spat. "Stone's most covert and soulless assassin."

Tara held up her hands, palms towards him in surrender and then realised it looked like she was going to push him over the cliff. She didn't know what to do with her hands, so she jammed them in the pockets of her jacket. "I'm sorry. I didn't mean for it to happen like this."

"How was it supposed to happen?" Tommo studied her face. He still couldn't read her. "Stabbed in a gang-related incident in the Docklands?"

"Okay, okay. Meeting you at the Pier Hotel Quiz night was not a co-incidence," she blurted out and he almost stumbled off the precipice in dazed confusion. "Please Tommo, come away from the edge and I'll explain everything."

He turned and looked at the gully far below and took a small step onto firmer ground. "You look different. You have a glow about you." The jab hit home, and she reddened and glared back at him. "Did he choose to have you on your knees from behind, or was that you? I guess it depends on who placed the camera, so it framed both your faces together. Very convenient." He wanted to humiliate her.

"I think he filmed us," Tara said softly, "I underestimated him. But I also overestimated you." Her body was trembling now as she built up to telling him her true motivations. He waited. And waited. The next words out of her mouth would decide more than one fate. "I want justice. For Raya and for Maryam." She dropped to her knees on the wet grass and held her head in her hands.

He knew the names. They were burned into his psyche.

"You're part of the cover up. You know what happened to them." Tara wept. "You threw the others under the bus to try and protect your own ass, but you never revealed what happened to Raya and Maryam." There was anger in her voice now.

Tommo padded over to her and coaxed her to stand. He helped her out of her jacket and placed it on a boulder, sitting beside her, numbed by her accusations. "I don't know what happened… I wish I did."

Tara pushed back her shoulders and sucked in a deep breath, holding it before she let the next part of her confession rush from her mouth. "I thought that if I pushed you hard enough, backed you against the wall, took you to the very edge that you would give up the secret." She rubbed her eye with her balled fist.

"How do I know that you are not just working with them? To see what I know?" Tommo's paranoia was returning. She'd played him so many times. She was good at it, very, very good. He had helped 'Them' silence Ray Mason, one of the only other people who might know the fate of the two girls. Someone was getting rid of loose ends.

Tara took out her phone and scrolled through her photos. She showed him the screen. A picture of ghosts. A family scene, at a banquet table in an Asian restaurant. Tommo barely recognised Tara. She was younger, happier, and innocent. She hugged a girl to each of her sides. They were even younger, even happier, even more innocent. "These are my nieces." She pointed to them one by one. "This is Raya.

And this is Maryam." Tara looked up and looked directly into Tommo's face through tears. Her voice became grave. "And if I thought you were directly responsible for whatever happened to them, I would have personally slit your throat already."

"I have some clues," Tommo shrugged. "But the answers are at Monaghan. Maybe." He looked down the path and then looked back at her. She looked down the mountain, following his gaze. Tommo was back on the back foot, guard up. "Well, I guess they didn't think you could go through with it." Declan's Sharp's gait was unique. Tara grabbed Tommo's wrist and urged him to remain seated. She took another deep breath to signal yet another revelation.

"Declan Sharp works for me."

Tommo pulled his hand away from hers and sprung forward. He paced up and down along the edge of the drop as the mercenary approached in a quick march. Everything Tommo thought he knew was unravelling, but if Tara was telling the truth, then her plan had been very thorough. If she was telling the truth.

"I needed a backup plan," shouted Tara. "You're not exactly predictable or dependable."

"So, he's here to make sure I don't get off this mountain." Tommo knew he wouldn't win that fight. Sharp was dressed for combat.

"He's here to make sure you DO get off this mountain, you fucking idiot," Tara screamed in frustration. "He's the one who rescued Claudine from Monaghan. He's here to protect you." *That's one mystery solved.* Bondy's escape from Ray Mason had been miraculous. "And while I am being honest, I am the one funding Claudine's current project in the Gulf. I needed to isolate you. I needed to think you had no way out."

Declan Sharp had made it to the summit. His heart rate was the same as someone who had just woken from an afternoon nap. He reached slowly into a backpack and took out a hipflask, offering it to Tommo who nodded towards Tara.

"She should take the first sip I think."

Sharp laughed. "If you end up at the bottom of that ravine, I don't want them to find any poison in your bloodstream at the inquest," his voice was deadpan. "That is if they ever find your body."

Tara took the flask and sipped from it, coughed, and screwed up her face. "Did you bring that in case you needed to light another fire?"

"The Licola General Store does not have a great range of spirits," Sharp explained. Tommo watched the interaction between the two. Tara didn't seem to fear him, and he was respectful towards her, the way an associate would be.

- # -

Wandering off along the ridge, Tommo tried to process what was happening and what Tara had told him. Sharp could have just taken three steps forward, grabbed him by the shirt and ushered him over the edge to certain death and that would be the end of it. Tara had now learned that there was no smoking gun, nothing had been held back. So far Tommo had proven to be completely ineffective against Trevor Stone and others further up the chain, if there were any, so she didn't need him. She had Sharp to do the things that Tommo didn't have the stomach or the training for, so why come and try to talk him off a cliff? He felt a presence behind him.

"Think about it from my point of view," Tara said. The hip flask was still in her hand. "I saw the evidence. What they said about you in the media." She took another sip and poked out her tongue in disgust. "Part of me knew it was fake, but there was a part of me that couldn't trust you. I still can't trust you. I saw that email this morning and I actually thought that you did it. I thought that Bondy had worked out a way to bribe the chef to hide the camera. I actually thought that you are the mystery mastermind, the Verbil Kint of the operation. You're the one they are all scared of." She put her hand on his shoulder. "Up until right now, when I watched you look at that picture, I didn't know for sure. And now I think I do. Now I think I can trust you."

"You did overestimate me."

"You want to know why I hiked up this bloody hill in a storm to save you?" Tara pressed against him. "Because, apart from me, you are the only person in the world who tried to stand up for those two girls." She sobbed again. "I don't think they are alive. But I want to be sure. And I want justice for those who were responsible. And I want you to finish the job you started."

"You're a much better strategist than me," Tommo said. He loved the view, but he was being tugged back towards the sea. "But maybe you're overcomplicating it. There is only one person with the resources to pull off a cover up that he is implicated in, and that is Trevor Stone. And we all underestimated him."

"Um, so…" Tara had a sheepish grin. "Now that we are being honest with each other. I should let you in on the next part of the plan."

"You mean, now that you are being honest with me." Tommo prepared for whatever bombshell she was about to drop.

"Ray Mason is broke. Not only have his bank accounts been frozen, but just before he was arrested, he decided to donate all of his cryptocurrency to a good cause…. Anyway, his legal defence will not be cheap. He has already sold his Airbnbs. He was given a cash offer he couldn't refuse." She reached into her pocket and pulled out a keyring and jangled it.

"You have been busy."

"It might be a small victory, but WE found where Mason was weak, and we exploited that weakness." She looked up at a wedge tailed eagle soaring in circles. "I'm not done with Ray Mason either. He will be forced to sell Monaghan next."

Tommo wandered away from her again. "I think you are getting over your skis a bit." He thought it was a good analogy given their location. "Mason might have had enough Bitcoin to buy a couple of beachside cottages, but I'm sure there isn't enough left over to buy the mansion."

"It's not important right now," Tara said. "Trevor Stone is the next target. We dig, we find where he is vulnerable, and we apply pressure." She took another swig from Sharp's hip flask as Sharp himself sat on the boulder and whittled a piece of eucalypt into a sharpened point.

"We go to war with Trevor Stone."

"I have the resources to do this right. To play offence." She was making an argument. "But I can't do it on my own. I need a team. I need Sharp and I need you."

Reaching into his shorts, Tommo took out the small USB drive he had rescued from the burning van. It contained a single file with all his notes and research, all the articles, all the things he thought he knew but couldn't prove. He held it out to Tara. "You'll need this."

9

Thanks to Daz and a team of local tradies funded by an anonymous Bitcoin donation, the Shark Byte Cafe was back in business. Some of the bright red graffiti had been left in-situ as a reminder of the attack on decency and common sense which had caused most of the town to rally around Archie and Marta and their local business. The town's independent stores told sales reps from large brands who did not criticise Trevor Stone for his comments that there would be no orders. Once the products sold out, the shelves would be left empty. No-one really thought that the Brand Managers in their cubicles in Sydney would care, but someone had to make a stand. Sales of Archie's Pilote branded surf wear were up, both in the store and online via the teampilote.com website. Ever since Rip Curl had been sold off to a Kiwi company, surfers had been looking for something more homegrown.

Marta watched a sandy haired kid inspect the boards in the rack. "The black mini-mal is not for sale. It's already been reserved. I should have put a sticker on it, but things have been a bit mental around here."

"No worries." the kid said, grinning. "I'm looking for something that I can use when it gets over 6 foot at Kelpies. I might need a custom." Ever since the spotlight had been put back on Archie through his arms-length relationship with Tommo, there had been renewed interest in the surf spot around The Point.

"If it's over 6 foot at Kelpies, you're gonna need a custom coffin," Archie joked, looking up from his laptop. An offended look came over the kid's face before he understood that Archie was teasing him. "Nah. It's all good. I saw you ripping off the point the other day, Sevvo. A custom is the way to go. I'll WhatsApp you Neptune's number. He'll sort you out with a gun."

"Wicked." Sevvo high fived Archie and bounded out the door.

"Someone is going to get hurt round there," Marta said, shaking her head. "Sevvo and the locals might know what they are doing, but some tourist…" She stopped mid-sentence as three figures cast a shadow from the doorway into the cafe. Archie put down his laptop and stood, shoulders back. The handful of customers who were enjoying a coffee by the brand-new plate-glass window noticed the change in the mood.

"I'm so sorry," Tommo said as he stepped through the door. "I really never thought they would go after other people in my life." He watched Marta's face. It didn't change. She held him responsible for everything that had happened to her and her husband in the previous days. But she wasn't looking at Tommo. Her eye line was fixed on Tara and Declan Sharp. Tommo turned. "Ah guys. Maybe you should do a lap around the block or check out the pier for a bit…hmm?"

Archie did exactly what Tommo thought he would do. He wrapped his arms around him and gave him a solid hug. "So you went and got yourself cancelled."

"It's not over," Tommo warned. "Stone might have dialled down the rhetoric a little bit, but there are a lot of people who are still looking for a scapegoat for all kinds of shit."

"So, you thought it would be a good idea to come here." Marta snapped. "And put us in danger and bring your nutcase lover and her pet Nazi."

Tommo took a deep breath. "There are a few things I need to bring you up to speed on. Just hear me out." It was a plea. "If you don't want to be a part of it, then we will leave you alone, but you both have skills that we need." Marta backed away from him as he took a step in her direction. "Tara has some skills too." He patted the new high-end Italian espresso machine. "She can source funds. You know, like the kind needed to get a cafe rebuilt during the holidays with a shortage of builders and material."

Marta nodded her head slowly in understanding "I see."

"And the pet Nazi is the one who apparently rescued Bondy from Ray Mason's place," Tommo explained. He watched Marta's eyes widen. "Yeah. Crazy right?"

"What are you doing back here?" Archie asked. "Shouldn't you be up in Sydney if you are going to try and take on Stone and his crew?"

Tommo spoke in a more hushed tone. "Monaghan." The word hung there. "We need to get access to the whole place. Every inch of it. We need to solve the mystery of what happened to those two girls at the party once and for all."

"That's what this is all about?" Marta was softening. "The ones who disappeared after the party?"

"Yeah. But I'm not the one who has opened the can of worms." Confusion crept over the faces of Marta and Archie. "That's Tara's story to tell." He laughed. "Seems the quiz night wasn't such a random encounter after all."

"No shit? She had me fooled," Archie said. "I mean there was something off about her – an offshore sailing, trailbike riding crypto genius? That's a special kind of crazy."

"I will take that as a compliment Archibald," Tara said, reappearing in the doorway. "I'm also sorry, for my part in the attack. I never thought they would come after you or this place." Her head was slightly bowed in contrition. "And I know that this is not your fight. But I could use some counsel, someone who understands this place and the people in it."

Marta fiddled with an order-taking notepad on the counter. "What do the girls mean to you Tara?"

Tara slumped against the doorframe. Tommo helped her to a sofa while the others stood around with a mixture of wariness and concern. "They are my nieces. My brother's daughters. And they have names - Raya and Maryam."

Marta noticed that Tara was using the present tense. "I will never forget that time," she said. "But it was a long time ago. So how are we going to find more than they did then." She sat down beside Tara and put her arm around her shoulder. Tommo opened his mouth to talk but then stopped.

"It would have been inconvenient for the wrong people if they had found anything," Tara said softly. "I was sure that people like Tommo knew more than they were saying. I was sure that once we brought down Ray Mason, he would cave, but maybe he doesn't know the truth either?"

"We believe that the answers are still on the Monaghan property," Tommo said. "So, we need to get in there somehow. Maybe it will be easier now that Ray is gone, but we will need time to properly explore." Marta smiled as Tommo's attitude changed from defence to offence. "Archie, I need you to think about any old stories from your people. Anything about caves or underground water. Maybe there are maps from when the property was first sold or subdivided. You enjoy that shit."

"You know I do." Archie agreed.

Tara straightened her back and pulled back her shoulders. "There is another way to get access to Monaghan." She let them wait. "We buy it." There was silence. She shrugged. "Why does everyone look at me like I am crazy when I say that? People make offers on properties all the time, and we already know that Mason was open to the idea, and that was before he was locked up."

"He fought hard to get Monaghan back in his family," Archie

said. "Even if he was tempted to sell, and even with his desperate situation, I'm not sure there would be much change from 20 or 30, maybe 40 million."

Marta stood up. "I wonder what would happen to the share price of Trevor Stone's stocks if there was a sex tape of him with his Chinese spy girlfriend." She giggled. "I wonder how much money one could make by shorting the stock?"

"That would be insider trading, wouldn't it?" Archie was always the voice of reason.

"I wonder what would happen to the value of certain meme-coins if there was a sex tape of Trevor Stone demonstrating the right of the patriarchy to use women as they choose." Tara hypothesised out loud.

"Thousands of crypto bros would pile into the coin, because Stone was the GOAT," Marta was on the same page. "And the whales would want a piece, so they would ride it up, but not too far because there would be an inevitable MeToo style backlash and the pasty kids who will never get a girlfriend anyway will be encouraged by the women in their lives to dump the coin."

"Now you're the one talking Chinese," Archie said.

"You never listen to my podcast do you," Marta looked to Tara for support. "I've been talking about this stuff for years." Tara just shrugged. Marta continued. "Basically, it's the same scam, but because it's not regulated by the Australian Stock Exchange, there aren't any insider trading laws."

"I am going to leave that up to the brains-trust while I get lost in a dusty analogue archive," Archie said.

Declan Sharp had quietly entered the premises while the others were in discussion. "I've established myself as a relatively well trusted lieutenant in part of Stone's operations." As Sharp spoke, Tommo thought back to the locker at the Mount Eliza property, and then back to the Mount Eliza t-shirt that had seemed so incongruous at the time. He filed it away as something to ask when he got the chance. "Now… Admittedly I was focussed on the passport and identity theft stuff at Monaghan, but I know a bit about the crypto. I know how to access the treasury."

"Mount Eliza," Tommo offered. The others looked at him quizzically.

Sharp continued. "Yes. There is a data centre and a blockchain node down there. We may be able to manipulate the supply and demand and influence the price from the inside."

"Right," Tara said. If you guys are on board, then we should divide and conquer." She seemed perkier now. "I need to go back to QSP. I can work from home to an extent, but it will look suspicious if I don't go into the office." She looked around at the slightly dishevelled group. "Archie and Tommo can focus on Monaghan, and Marta and Declan can collaborate on the crypto plan."

"I think we will need Bondy," Tommo added. "She's a lot more valuable to us here than benched on a superyacht somewhere."

Marta nodded and smiled. "She's on her way. Check her Instagram she's in the Emirates lounge at DXB sipping on something dark."

- # -

Bondy sat in the artificial silence created by her noise-cancelling headphones. She'd been craving action and adventure, but now she needed to create thinking space. The high-paying job that had materialised then evaporated just as quickly as it had been offered had been engineered by Tara leaving Tommo as chum tossed into the churned-up waters to lure the sharks. She clenched her jaw as she pondered the new information about Tara's machinations. The logic was there, the motivation understandable enough but the methods ruthless. Stone was a beast, a predator, and if he was responsible for causing harm to family, then he should pay. And yet, the collateral damage, people she cared about, was beginning to mount. Marta and Kelpie didn't deserve to be roped into or tangled up in this ambitious plan. *Yeah. Let's go with ambitious.*

Truth be told, she wouldn't mind spending a bit more time with her rescuer, the man with the endearing 'Sith Ifrican' accent, and those arms, those biceps, that still made her bite her lip if she thought about them too long.

Tommo suddenly seemed to have purpose. Tara's regime of psychological torture had somehow unlocked a sense of dignity, maybe even given him a new chance at redemption. If the right Tommo showed up, if the version of him who was more than just the inebriated impersonator of Tommo, if that Tommo arrived, then maybe he'd walk out of this mess with his pride intact, maybe even with a glimmer of validation.

But could she trust Tara to let that happen? That was the crux of it, wasn't it? Bondy stared blankly at the glass wall ahead and the blurred movements of planes on tarmac. Tara. The woman was reckless. A danger to herself and everyone else around her. Revenge was her real fuel, a dangerous incendiary emotion that did not mix well with rational thought. Revenge had a way of blinding even the cleverest of minds. There would be more collateral damage. That much was clear. The plan was already too much of a big swing. Someone she knew and cared about was going to get hurt. Maybe Marta. Maybe Kelpie. Maybe Tommo. And all because Tara was so hellbent on destroying Trevor Stone that she'd throw anyone and anything into the flames to see him burn. *Can I work for Tara?* The question spun like a hologram in the centre of her mind. She rose from her seat, her body on autopilot, legs carrying her across the room to the self-serve bar where a newly opened bottle of some exclusive, obscure brown spirit had been laid out. She poured herself a generous measure, the dark amber liquid swirling in her glass. She lifted the glass to her lips, inhaling the rich, smoky aroma before taking a sip.

Tara and I need to have a little chat. Not just a casual chat or one of those clever exchanges that Tara liked to dominate with her intellect or her 'I'm just a suit' act. No, this would need to be a confrontation. One where she would have to force Tara to admit there were risks and consequences and blame assigned accordingly.

- # -

"How does anyone fall for this stuff?" Marta said as she scrolled through the tokenomics white paper for Trevor Stone's crypto based coin – 'Dinkum'. She was sitting in the passenger seat of a Hilux, bringing herself up to speed on the vagaries of how name-coins worked.

"FOMO," said Sharp as he drove the pickup through the gates of the horse racing facility on the shores of Port Phillip. "All the people who missed out on Game Stop think that they can be on the next rocket… to the moon."

Marta looked up from her phone and gasped. "This is a nice setup. No wonder that they all think that Trevor Stone can turn horse shit into gold."

"A lot of normal people are going to lose big on this deal. Like hairdressers and customer support representatives and people who stack shelves in supermarkets."

"They are the same people who lose their rent money to poker machines or betting on the footy, or buying scratchies and Tatslotto tickets, either way Stone is the bookie. The House always wins." She watched a very expensive looking bay thoroughbred being led towards the training track. "Hopefully, if we do it right, they can get out before the whole thing crashes and Stone is left holding all the worthless coins." Marta scrolled back through the document. "There are only ten million, and either through luck or Tara's grand plan, Stone's ever-increasing publicity means that trading volumes are up, and the price is more volatile. That should mean we can acquire a fair chunk without it being too noticeable."

Sharp shrugged in a kind of 'if you think so' kind of way and handed her an ID badge. "This will give you access to the NOC. The trainers won't bother you. Most of them don't even know the server room is here. And I'll keep a lookout." He beckoned her towards a heavy unmarked door. "Only use the computers connected via a cable…"

"And only use encrypted chat. Yes. I got it." Marta said, weary of the details of Tara's plan being repeated over and over again. "You really must be used to working with muppets."

"I'd prefer muppets."

- # -

Tara had been working on the Reddit post for 40 minutes. She had written various versions and used several AI tools to suggest language and hashtags to get the tone just right. She couldn't really believe she was going to proactively send the video out into the world. She couldn't really believe that these subreddit groups existed and were allowed to exist with names like FacistMisogyny and PatriarchyBros. The video was mercifully short. Just long enough for both Tara and Stone's faces to be visible and identifiable. *At least I am not outing some other poor girl.* Tara had a long list of rationalisations. There might be a longer version out there somewhere, but it wouldn't show Stone in as good a light - he hadn't lasted long. Tara shuddered as she read the post one more time. It was engineered to trigger. It was designed for a small, targeted demographic, a place on the Venn diagram where oppressed white man overlapped with crypto-bro and MAGA cult member. She had a picture in her mind of the kind of person she was manipulating through a few keystrokes.

She changed tabs, inspecting the candles on the chart of the historical price of the Dinkum token. There had been a slight increase in volume caused by the actions of Marta, Tommy, and Bondy in the last few hours. A few automated trades using her own wallets and accounts added to the position. The trades hadn't alerted the bot algorithms yet, so the price was within normal limits. 16:31. Her targets would be knocking off work or on a smoko. The Dubai crowd would be awake, and it was primetime in LA. This needed to be global.

"Fuck it." She pressed the button on the mouse and lit the blue touch paper of the next battle in the culture wars.

- # -

Tommo shook his head as he looked at the still from the video on Twitter, or X or whatever it was called today. It had taken exactly 7 minutes from the time an anonymous user posted the video on various subreddits to screenshots being shared on Discord and Telegram and then modified to meet user guidelines of the more mainstream platforms. Predictably, the twittering classes had divided into two polarised tribes, but that wasn't really the point of the exercise. The team had to stroke the egos of Stone and his cultists in such a way that they would embrace Dinkum as a talisman for an ideology, a digital token of resistance for those who feel disenfranchised by diversity. Bondy was right, the outcome was a coin flip. But Tommo's role was to help herd the sheep. He liked and reshared the posts from various accounts and kept the narrative about Stone as the leader of a movement, which really wasn't too hard. The Stoners bought it without question.

- # -

Marta gasped in shock when she finally saw the image. Her stomach tightened with a wave of nausea. Her heart pounded. She wished she could unsee it. It was so raw, so painfully revealing. *Is Tara incredibly brave or completely out of her mind?* Marta didn't need to seek out and watch the accompanying video. The still image alone, paired with the provocative post, was powerful enough to turn her insides. Stone's face expressed power and contempt, and it would motivate a group who had been alienated by years of political correctness. She shivered and forced her focus away from the moral implications. She had more important things to do.

The post was the signal she'd been waiting for. This was the moment to start buying up Dinkum in volumes that would make the token surge. The strategy was simple. Hype. Get Dinkum "in play." She had to create enough momentum for the crypto influencers and the day-traders to pile in, driven by the scent of fast profits. Marta executed the next trade with her eyes locked on the price chart. She watched as the price ticked up in response, enough to indicate that the move had been noticed. The size of the subsequent trades would begin to draw more attention from the algorithmic traders and bots. The pump was beginning.

In the dimly lit Network Operations Centre, Marta's eyes darted across the multiple screens in front of her. The hum of servers and the quiet buzz of machinery created a weird comfort, but it also gave her the chills. The simplicity with which someone who knew what they were doing could manipulate so many people and have so much impact scared her. Multiple alerts were being triggered by the surge of activity. Algorithms were set to manage the token's circulating supply to keep the price within predetermined limits, but Dinkum wasn't behaving like the little-known vanity coin it had been up until that point. The treasury lead would be aware now, he might have even notified Stone of the activity. She messaged Tara

```
M: They will be onto the NOC activity by now. I
need to get out. Your move.

T: Thank you. Get out of there. We will take it
from here.
```

Suddenly Sharp was standing beside her. "We need to go."

- # -

High above Sydney Harbour, in his pretentiously decorated penthouse, Trevor Stone paced back and forth. The harbour sparkled below. He said he could never tire of this view, but today it didn't give him the ego boost and sense of superiority it usually did. For the first time in decades, uncertainty gnawed at his psyche.

How dare they? The video was meant to be a trophy of sorts, for a very private collection. He still couldn't work out who emailed it to Tara and Tommo, or why. He let out a long sigh as he recalled how Tara had fled their alpine tryst before he'd even crawled out of bed. *Somewhat dramatic.* But according to the PA at QSP, Tara had turned up for work at the office in Melbourne today as if nothing had happened, no doubt wanting to forget about the whole experience. He really did like her, thought that maybe he could make it work, but it was unlikely she would trust him ever again.

Now that his personal memory aid of his latest conquest was public on the internet there was no way that genie was going back in the bottle. Three phones lay scattered across his imported marble countertop, all powered down. He knew they could be turned on remotely, they could be used as listening devices, so he didn't speak his thoughts out loud. His spin doctors and publicists and personal brand advisors would be apoplectic by now. No doubt their voicemails and emails and WhatsApps would be counselling him to deny the authenticity of the video and call it a deep-fake, but until he could figure out who had released the footage and their potential motivations, he would stick with 'No comment.'

"Footage." He said the word out loud, as he pondered its derivation. So many of the nouns from the analogue past would be meaningless to the digital natives, but what else would you call it? Film? No. Movie still worked.

The context of the post to Reddit made no sense - it painted him "as a legend", "a man's man who knew how to treat a woman properly," though the language the author had used was obscenely crude.

Tara has nothing to gain. Not even the most vapid influencer would release a video like that of themselves and certainly not in that forum with that caption. She probably deleted it on sight. He felt sorry for her. She would be horrified given the treatment she had already suffered from the media. He wanted to call her, but he was sure she would not pick up. Try to forget the girl.

Tommo had the most obvious motives, but why would he bury the video deep in a forum for such extremists? *Why not send it to some pinkie journo at the ABC?* Tommo was a woke wimp, a pitiful creature who had disappeared when the pressure was applied. He was probably at the bottom of a bottle, or a cliff.

There was only one other credible answer, though he didn't want to admit it. *Corbin?* Stone's lips twisted into a sneer as he conjured the image of the sweaty, perpetually dishevelled creature who wore Hugo Boss suits because of the brand's heritage. Corbin had made an art form of knowing exactly how much filth people would tolerate before their squeamishness gave way to pragmatism. He'd been known to brag about his barely legal tastes during their private meetings, trying to establish some twisted form of camaraderie. He was useful though, and he was desperate to prove himself worthy of Trevor's inner circle. The more Trevor thought about it, the more sense it made. *Perhaps he thought he was doing me a favour.*

His thoughts were interrupted by the video doorbell. There was no front door to knock on, the private elevator brought him straight to his keep, here at the top of the citadel. He jabbed at the button and peered at the screen. It was one of his more junior advisors, maybe in the crypto team, visibly and audibly out of breath.

"Mr Stone? It's important. It's Dinkum. It's up 52% already this morning and it's not slowing down. We need to make some decisions about supply and when we take profits and… "

"Thank you for letting me know... Mark is it? Get the right people in a room." Trevor abruptly ended the exchange and smiled. "Maybe Corbin did me a favour after all."

- # -

"This is some fucked up shit," Bondy said as she scrolled through the subreddit where the video had been posted. "I thought Twitter was the toxic waste dump of the opinions of some of the world's scum, but this stuff makes Patrick Bateman look like a saint."

"I don't even use Facebook anymore," Archie said. "I don't mind Instagram. There is some cool surfing content and a good vibe, but all the others, I don't want to know."

Bondy shook her head. "Imagine. A much-loved game show host gets kicked off a network and can never appear on TV again because he called a contestant 'luv', and there are forums on the public internet with names like GenZTraumaSluts." She groaned with frustration. "There are women on here! Rape-BaitBitch. What the actual fuck? I mean half of the US is going mental because of a decision to make abortion illegal and then there are these people."

"Outrage sells," Archie said. "The more people get fired up, the more time they spend online and the more ads they can be sent."

"What do you sell to someone who calls themself BangMyBully?" Claudine continued her rant.

Archie smiled. "Well hopefully, if this grand plan works, we sell them a phantom currency and we won't feel bad when we do the rug-pull, and they lose all their money because it was karma."

"Rug-Pull?"

"Yeah. I finally got around to listening to Marta's Pilote podcast."

"How's the Monaghan research going? Need any help? If I spend one more minute in this rabbit hole, I'm going to turn into Donnie Darko."

Archie spread out a document atop a pile on a table. The map was stained and torn and had been repaired in places with tape that had darkened. "This is how I always imagined a treasure map would look like." He pointed to a line that represented the creek that seemed to begin on the Monaghan property and then flow out to the sea near the Kelpies break. "Tommo might be onto something with the underground water theory. The creek seems to begin here, in the middle of nowhere, which means it might emerge from the ground as a spring, but there is too much water in the creek, even in summer for it to be just a spring.

"Which means if it has flowed underground for any distance, it might have created caves through erosion over millions of years." Bondy caught on fast.

"There is no name for a cave or a cave system on any map, but there is a story of my people that mentions a perridak, which is a platypus in modern day Strine."

Bondy looked confused. "Strine?"

"It's phonetic," Archie grinned and tapped his ear, "Listen again. Str-ine" he said the world more slowly and put on a more stereotypical outback accent.

Bondy nodded. "Got it."

"Anyway, perridak. The creek has that name on a couple of maps. Here." He pushed the top map aside to reveal another, faded and ripped along the lines where it had been folded over and over again over time. "See this one. Perridak Creek."

"Have they ever opened up Monaghan for the day?" Bondy asked. "You know those open garden things they do, where you get to wander around rich people's backyards? You'd think that Ray Mason would be selling tickets to see the caves and the fauna."

Archie was online, seeing if he could answer the question. "There were the parties of course, on Australia Day, back before the…" He paused, looking for the right word. "Infamous one. The locals used to be invited, but according to this map, the source of the creek is a hike from the main house and there are no photos of that part of the property. Nothing on people's socials."

"I'm guessing the aerial shots don't show an entrance." It was becoming clearer that they would need to physically be on the property to find the cave, if it existed at all.

"The presence of water means the trees are dense, and there is no significant change in elevation, so yeah, 2D is not going to work for us. Someone needs to get onto the land, legally or illegally." He scratched his head. "We could use the drone. It was part of the plan to survey Monaghan before you got yourself abducted."

Bondy decided not to throw her new iPhone at him. She poked out her tongue. "It was an okay plan when Ray Mason was in residence, it's a better plan now that the place is empty."

"And we don't need to go as far. We can fly in from the beach to the source of the creek," Archie said. "A drone flying near Kelpies won't raise too much suspicion now that it's full of day-trippers. We need to wait for Marta to get back from Mount Eliza though. She is the pilot."

- # -

Twenty years ago, Trevor Stone might have been ruined by a sex 'tape', but the world was a different place now. Australia was a different place now. Now there was money to be made from bad behaviour. His courtiers were gathered around a rented WeWork boardroom table. Corbin had not been invited. They were there to nod and cheer his decision to lean into the controversy, to go global by tapping into the MAGA crowd and Donald Trump's media enablers.

"We can definitely get you on Joe Rogan," said a thirtysomething guy who had never really worked a day in his life - right school, right degree at the right uni, right internship at the right bank and now, to say the right things to vigorously support whatever Trevor Stone wanted to do. "Fox News is already taking your side."

"Rogan is good. He's got a bunch of the crypto crowd that listen to him, that's who we need to focus on." Stone sat at the head of the table. "Let's not get distracted by the death of civil society stuff. Concentrate on Dinkum."

"You need Musk or someone to tweet it," another man said. Stone didn't even know his name and wondered how he managed to get into the room.

"No. We want the smaller guys who don't really understand the scam and are open to having a punt, the ones who use CashApp and Crypto.com. Get TripleM talking about it. What's that drivetime show…?"

"The Rush Hour?" another guy said, one who Stone might have bullied at grammar school. "They only talk about sport and play ads for CarpetCall and Rheem."

"Yeah. Perfect. We want guys who think they just got a hot tip on the 3rd race at Randwick that nobody else knows about." Stone didn't really care who got hurt. He was going to make a lot of money from this one. "Not a bad little plan, hey. Leaking out that vid." He waited for the fawning compliments. And they came in fast.

"You're playing chess, and they are playing checkers sir"

"Nice one boss"

"Only you could have thought of it Mr Stone. Brilliant move."

Stone threw out his hands in a gesture of dismissal. "Ignore the dykes and the noise around the so called 'New Patriarchy.' Focus on the money boys." Stone was having fun. "Oh, and make sure you trigger the seppos. Big market. Lots of clueless rednecks who will love this shit."

- # -

Tara was also having fun. Her psyop was working. She sat back and watched on two screens, one for the crypto pricing graph and one for the deluge of content and comments and babble. She was alone, in a room that had the ambience of a mortuary, but she suddenly felt like singing as Trevor Stone broke his social media silence and posted…

```
#Dinkum. #tothemoon 🚀 $DNKM #FOMO
```

"Blue Horseshoe loves Anacott Steel," Tara said under her breath to no-one. She was tempted to comment the same words, but it might give the game away. Stone probably wouldn't know what she meant, but others would. The next post from Stone's X account made her smile even wider.

```
The Deep State is coming for your dollars. You're
being lied to. Protect yourself. #MAGA #Trump2024
$DNKM
```

She executed a few more trades to keep the activity and the price rising. She wanted to be noticed now; she wanted to acquire as much Dinkum as she could. Stone's personal involvement and messiah like image would help fuel the greed, even the sceptics would want to be along for some of the ride, but they thought they were smart enough to know when to get out before the dump came. Tara knew, because she would be the instigator of the sell-off.

- # -

Marta and Tommo were being thrown around in the back seat of Bondy's 4WD on the way towards the coast. Tommo was practically airborne in the back seat, bracing against the side door while Marta clung to the headrest in front of her. She kept one eye on her phone screen, scrolling through the town's WhatsApp group, a collection of messages where every event, however minor, was analysed from the point of view of people who only ever left the postcode to visit the Gold Coast or Bali for a week a year.

"I bet none of them have actually WATCHED the video." Tommo leaned over to try and read what was on Marta's screen. "They've only seen the thumbnail or been told about it."

"If it wasn't Trevor Stone, nobody would care," Marta said as she closed the chat, feeling queasy from the lurching motion of the vehicle.

"Okay back there?" Archie glanced over his shoulder from the front seat, also holding on tight. "We're almost at the coast. Got to warn you, though… it's packed."

Bondy slowed. Word was out. A line of cars stretched along the rugged track, spilling out from a small car park that barely fit five vehicles but double that were squeezed wherever they could find room. "I hate Instagram."

"The council's going to have to do something about this." Archie shook his head. "If the break doesn't end up killing someone, that climb down the cliff will."

"I bet Sevvo and his lot just take the shortcut across the point," Marta said, nodding in the direction of the rocky outcrop.

Archie shrugged. "Yeah. I can't say I blame them; they'll be alright. Maybe get a fine, but who's going to go through the hassle of booking some kids who just want to surf?"

"Whereas We," Tommo raised his hands in mock surrender. "I. Need to stay squeaky clean."

Bondy pulled up in a spare space. "Alright, we'll unload here. This is close enough to the creek, isn't it?" She nodded towards the edge of the cliff, "It's about equidistant and a few less prying eyes."

Marta peered over the edge. The wind tugged at her, and she enjoyed the smell of salt and drying seaweed for a split second before taking a step back, feeling the pulse of her heartbeat quicken. "I'm not hauling this kit down there," she muttered, grabbing a camera bag from the back of the car.

The cliff face loomed, jagged and unforgiving, with the wind coming off the ocean in salty gusts. "What are we supposed to do while you do your James Bond stuff?" Tommo asked, realising that he was a bit redundant.

Bondy shot him a look, climbing onto the running board of the car to retrieve her board from the roof racks. "I know exactly what I'm going to do."

Archie's eyes widened with horror as he watched her secure the board under her arm. "You are not about to take that brand new board down that… that… it's not even a path. Bondy, come on."

"Oh, I am," Bondy replied, unapologetic, as she slipped a backpack over her shoulder. After lounging in the flat, salty Gulf she wanted to be reinvigorated by the waves of the Southern Ocean. "You didn't bring your boards?"

"We're here to work," Marta said, hands on her hips. She couldn't help but feel like the scolding mother of the group.

Bondy smirked and adjusted her grip on the surfboard. "It doesn't take four of us to do this job. I played chauffeur, my work is done until y'all are. ta-ta."

Without waiting for permission or protest, she turned and began the descent. Archie closed his eyes, unable to bear the idea of the board's flawless, glossy fibreglass being dinged. "Be careful!" he called after her. Tide's on the way out, and the rip will be…ripping."

"Her funeral," Marta muttered, although She did like Bondy's 'try and stop me' attitude.

Archie looked around the carpark rubbing his arms. It was colder by the sea, nothing to block the wind. "This place can't handle a fraction of the visitors it's getting right now. It's not just the carpark, the reef won't stand a chance."

Marta sighed, glancing back at the line of cars that seemed to stretch endlessly down the road. "Add it to the list of collateral damage in Trevor Stone's wake." She launched the drone, and it swung out over the edge of the cliff and then swooped down with Bondy in shot. The blonde stuck up her middle finger and laughed.

Marta squinted at the small screen, her fingers lightly adjusting the joysticks as the drone buzzed forward, moving steadily along the creek, a wide-angle HD camera capturing the complex ecosystem of the winding waterway. White Ibis stalked through the reeds, and native Coots paddled near the banks. She gasped and made the drone hover in place when she saw movement. A blue-tongued lizard looked up from where it was basking in the sun and seemed to ponder the danger of the machine for a split second before scampering for cover under a rock.

"Alright, Tommo," Archie said, his eyes fixed on the laptop screen where the images streamed in real-time. "Let me know if you spot anything that Marta should take a closer look at." The two of them huddled over the screen, shielding it from the glare as the drone's camera panned over the water. The creek narrowed, flanked by thick reeds, and gnarled eucalyptus roots. "Stay high," Archie called out to Marta "We can drop down if we need to."

"Everyone's a pilot," Marta muttered with a smirk, nudging the controller to keep the drone on course. "Just a sec. We're about two hundred metres from where the map says the source is."

The feed flickered as the drone veered slightly. Marta frowned. That was weird. The camera captured a shelf of rock partially submerged in the murky water. Marta slowed the drone, moving it in closer, and they leaned in to see what had caught her attention. The creek disappeared underground at this point.

"There." Tommo pointed at the screen. "That crack in the rocks… Could be a cave behind there."

Archie zoomed in on the screen, his voice low with excitement. "Maybe. But it looks like any entrance would be underwater, which means we need to go diving and that increases the level of difficulty somewhat."

"Alright, I'm going to see if I can get closer," Marta said, carefully manoeuvring the drone toward the area of interest. The lens picked up details of the rocky ledges as she tried to avoid the tree branches.

"Well, the hypothesis was correct" Tommo whispered, leaning in closer. "The geography suggested that there could be an underwater source, and it might be big enough for people to get inside."

Marta inched the drone forward, tilting it slightly to try and get a view of what might lie underneath the water's surface. The screen flickered and glitched and suddenly she was flying blind.

"Uh, what's happening?" Archie asked, glancing at her, worry creeping into his voice.

Before Marta could respond, the drone's image froze entirely. The din of the drone's blades could still be heard. It was still airborne, but then there was silence. A heartbeat later, the device dropped out of the sky, the video feed kicking back in just as the drone splashed into the creek.

"Shit." Marta cursed, her hands white knuckling the controller. "It was a brand-new battery."

Tommo shook his head in disbelief. "A jammer of some sort? That doesn't make any sense all the way out here, no matter what Ray Mason and his crew were up to."

Archie was already closing his laptop, shoving it into his bag with a grimace. "Well Tara owes us a new drone out of the Dinkum caper."

Marta took a deep breath, fighting back her frustration and then laughed. "Maybe it's a secret submarine base." Marta tucked the controller into the bag. "Well, we found your cave Tommo. What's the next part of the plan?"

"Same as it always was," he said. "Get onto the property. Get into the cave."

Archie shook his head. "That's a lot of risk to take on a hunch. What gave you the idea about the cave anyway, you don't strike me as a geologist."

"There are some things," Tommo said evasively "that I am keeping to myself, to protect you." He put his arm around Archie's shoulders "They attacked the cafe and that was before you knew about the cave stuff. So, I don't want anyone to have to answer questions about what they knew when and have to lie, or feel pressured to give up certain information."

"But you think that the cave could be part of the story of Tara's nieces somehow." Marta said. "Like their final resting place."

"We can replace a drone. We can't replace one of us if we die in a cave diving accident." It was a warning.

- # -

Tara's heart was pounding. Her pupils dilated as she watched the visuals strobe across the displays. 44.7% ownership. That was more than she thought she would have ever been able to get. Stone's early-money suckers had scattered like a dog had been let loose on a beach full of seagulls. Many of the very early investors who had only bought because of Stone's apparent business success had already bailed out once the price hit 50 cents, some of the biggest cryptocurrencies in the world had never reached 50 cents. The small early investors, some of whom had only put in a few hundred bucks when the price was a few cents, would make a good profit at 50 cents, but they would be disappointed already. Dinkum's treasury actions seemed to be being done by bots harvesting profits at predetermined intervals. If they were selling, she was still buying. Up and up the price climbed, a mathematically perfect curve that would've made Euler weep.

Despite his billionaire status, Stone gave off everyman vibes and his coin, Dinkum, which began as a bit of an inside joke among ex AFL players and cricketers was today mainstream news. The result was that Tara felt some guilt come and go in waves. Somewhere out there, night-shift nurses and gig workers were YOLOing their rent money into this digital Ponzi, their phones buzzing with push notifications from influencer prophets screaming "HODL", a phrase created in a sense of denial of missing the top of the peak. There would be losers, but she needed the money to buy Monaghan, because

Tommo and the others had found the cave and there was no other way to get onto the property to conduct a thorough investigation. This Pump and Dump play had to succeed.

Short interest was ticking up - digital canaries in the blockchain coal mine. Someone, a co-founder perhaps, had just dumped 1.5 million coins into the market at $1. That was strange behaviour. *Has Stone blinked?* She thought about it for a second. *No. Stone wouldn't want to trigger a collapse like that.* Someone had just made $15 million bucks, but they were also giving her an opportunity to take her stake to more than 50% and that should get Stone's attention.

- # -

Trevor Stone was not happy. He felt like he'd been conned. And he had been. Dinkum had been a bit of fun, but it was about to become a very expensive exercise. The guy who had promised to make it all happen had, in the last few hours, disappeared. According to one of Stone's team, one who seemed to know about as much about crypto as Ray Mason, 'Taipan' had cashed out all his founder's tokens and most of them had been acquired by a previously unknown address on the blockchain.

"In other words… what you are telling me," Stone was fuming. "Is that we now own a minority stake in this thing? Where the fuck is the guy who looks after the… The data centre thing down at the stables? Sharp, is it?"

The lackey cowered, "Mr Sharp resigned last week, Sir. I believe he was on the security team. I don't think he was involved with Dinkum."

"What about the QSP team? Get me their top crypto…" He stopped. He looked like he had been hit across the head with a bat while taking a full toss with a cricket ball to the nuts.

Phone in hand, the hapless aide asked softly "Should I call an ambulance? Are you having a stroke or a heart attack?"

"No." Stone's fists were clenched. His nostrils flared as he snorted air. "I want Tara from the QSP team on the phone. Right. Fucking. Now." He was hyperventilating. "And find Corbin and bring him to me. I don't care if you have to hogtie him and drag him in here kicking and screaming."

- # -

Tara's heels click-clicked across polished concrete, each step a metronome counting down to Dinkum's digital armageddon. Timing was everything - hold just a little longer until even Stone's greed peaked. The door whispered open.

"Excuse me," the PA's voice trembled. "Trevor Stone. Says it's urgent. Work, not..." A blush spread across her face. "Not... pleasure."

"Put it through here," Tara said. She was still thinking through the large transaction that had given her effective control of the token. A little bit of research into the chat surrounding Dinkum's creation revealed that Stone was just the face of the coin. He'd outsourced most of the work to a mysterious London based consultant who hid behind a pseudonym – 'Taipan'. The phone bleated for attention. Tara let it ring out. Her mind decided at that moment to recall the sun-bleached evening at The Pier. Tommo relaying the story of his vintage Napster shirt

"I was advising Trevor Stone's company about some namecoin he wanted to create, you must know Trevor, he's all over the news these days, Sydney socialite who got lucky with other crypto early on, anyway..." Tommo had revealed. The timeline was off, but...

The phone stopped and started again. "Hello Tara." Stone's words were precision-engineered for fake civility. "I... would like to apologise and have a larger conversation about the other night and the... other stuff. But right now, I need someone who can stop me losing a shit ton of money."

"Hello Trevor," she put on a faux politeness that he had heard her use with people she had contempt for. "Yeah, I hear that Dinkum is doing well. Congratulations."

"I need out. Above ten cents. Make it happen."

"You don't think it will go that low. Do you?" She teased in a mean way.

"You're QSP. That means you're mine." The mask slipped.

Tara smiled. She put him on hold. *One algorithmic massacre, coming up.* She started dumping and her short positions kicked in, turning the price collapse into a beautiful symmetry of profit. The digital winds changed direction. She'd just jettisoned enough tokens to create a singularity in the price chart. The greater fools rushing in to buy the dip were already toast - they just didn't know it yet. She'd make damn sure that this was the absolute historic all-time high. "Sorry about that. I just needed to… oh it doesn't matter. What were you saying, Mr Stone? Oh yes. Well I guess I could help manage the treasury through this period, but I would need the root access codes for the admins, and if the whole thing is done through bots and smart-contracts, I won't be able to stop them doing what they were set up to do, they will just execute in line with the wishes of the DAO." She knew he didn't understand a word.

"Please." He stared at his own screen as the candles changed from green to red as the price began to plummet as large chunks of Dinkum were sold off. He was desperate, and she was his only lifeline, but he knew that because of the video being leaked she would not lift a finger to help him. He tried something he'd never done before. He begged. "Tara, please."

"I'll pass on your message to the Crypto team, but it's a bit late. Good Luck Mr Stone. Goodbye." She said it with finality, and she meant it.

- # -

The man known as The Crow sat squirming in a chair designed for aesthetics rather than comfort, his eyes fixed on a coffee ring stain that marred the cheap pine tabletop. Across the table, Trevor Stone sat with a casual menace that made the pay-by-the-hour office feel like a kangaroo courtroom. But there were no witnesses and no cameras.

"I don't know if it was you who wrote that post and leaked that video, and right now, I don't really care." Stone said menacingly "You have one chance to stay employed, to be useful and not be jammed into a compost bin with the worms where you belong."

Corbin kept his eyes downcast, studying the wood grain patterns where the planks were joined together and interrupted the natural swirls. He was not used to being submissive, even in Stone's presence. "I understand Sir."

Stone leaned forward. "You exist in the gutter, so I don't have to get dirty," he continued, reinforcing the true pecking order. "But don't think for one moment that I can't go low when it's my money at stake."

Corbin's teeth ground together hard enough to send shooting pains through his jaw. "Yes Sir. What would you like me to do." The question emerged flat, a statement of surrender rather than inquiry.

"I have a new enemy." Stone's tone changed slightly and became like a Batman villain in a Saturday morning cartoon. "An individual who hides behind an online alias. Taipan. He stole $15 million from me today, and I want it back."

Something stirred in Corbin's sense of self – a desperate need to demonstrate value, to prove his worth. He raised his head a fraction, just enough to show engagement without risking eye contact. "I guess you can't go to the police." He knew it was a stupid thing to say as the words left his lips. The Crow, master of the analogue underworld, suddenly felt every one of his technological shortcomings. Web3 was for kids. The kind of kids that in the school yard got hooked on fads like Yo-Yos. "I can try, but..."

The slam of Stone's palm against the table echoed off the walls and made the glass partitions shake. His voice dropped to a register that made the room temperature seem to plummet. "Try?" Stone co-opted the phrase from the Star Wars universe and added his threatening twist. "There is no try, you piece of shit. DO find this Taipan character and work out a way to convince them to repay the money they took from me." The chair legs grated against the floor as Stone pushed back from the table. "Get out of my sight."

Corbin remained frozen as Stone's footsteps receded, the door clicking shut. A vacuum cleaner droned on in the distance and The Crow saw himself as a night shift cleaner. He realised that vacuum cleaning was now done by autonomous robots and didn't need his old school talents. *What a wanker.*

- # -

The wind carried the tang of fish and the low rumble of the diesel engine of the trawler making its way back into the safe harbour. The gulls cawed and squawked as they circled around the back of the fishing boat, hovering in expectation, waiting for scraps to be discarded off the stern. Tara and Tommo stood at the end of the pier and watched the boat return with its catch. There was a playful smile on both their faces.

"Well," Tara started, with a languid stretch of her arms, her tone that of idle banter, "imagine my surprise, Tommo, when, at a critical point of our well planned out caper, a large portion of Dinkum was sold off." She leaned in, just enough for her words to be heard over the increasing chorus of seabirds. "An amount that could have only been amassed by someone who got in… very early."

Tommo's face might as well have been a neon sign, but he played dumb. "Lots of folks got in early," he replied, running a hand casually along the cracking paint of the pier railing. "Celebs, finance types, that bloke who's on twenty different TV shows."

"No." She purred, her eyes narrowing as she closed the distance between them even more. "I looked at the transactions. That's the thing about the blockchain, they never go away. It was someone involved with the founding of the project. An advisor, maybe… or a technical consultant who did all the heavy lifting while Stone smiled for the camera."

Tommo didn't answer straight away. His fingers tightened on the rail as he watched the well-practised docking routine. The expert throwing of mooring lines around the bollards, the timing of the captain's changes in throttle and gear, from forward to reverse. "That would mean they've been sitting on those coins for ages. Years."

A flicker of admiration or amusement, something knowing, passed across Tara's face as she watched him. She reached up and placed a hand on his shoulder. "Let's suppose that our actor was issued Dinkum at, what? A cent a piece? Half a cent? That person made at least $15 million today." There was a hint of accusation in her voice now. "And if that person had inside knowledge of the little scam, we had planned…" Her voice turned silkier, "there was another fifteen to be made on shorting all the way down. That's a thirty-million-dollar payday."

"I guess you're right." The grin on Tommo's face widened. "A 30-million-dollar payday you say. Not a bad day's work." He turned and looked at her. "And how much did our little syndicate make today? Hmmm?"

It was Tara's turn to look away. The pier creaked beneath them and was remixed with the rhythmic percussion of the waves against the pylons below. Well, WE had a higher buy price," she chuckled, "but I reckon we walked away with," she turned back towards Tommo, the tears in her eyes were testament to the intensely emotional day. She dropped her head and mumbled. "About 48 million."

"That seems low, given the investment." He took Both her hands, their fingers entwined in a brief moment of understanding. They'd won today's skirmish, but they both knew it was far from over.

Tara let go and punched Tommo in the shoulder playfully. "That's 48 million profit Tommo." She looked up, held his gaze. "Or is it Taipan?"

The playfulness that had been a theme of the conversation was over. Tommo's face hardened and he spoke gravely. "If you can work it out, so can others," he said. "This is a big win for us, but it's a drop in the bucket for Stone. He still has vast resources at his disposal and his pride is at stake."

"I know. And we are both on his radar already. I know that."

"So, it's a race. We need to be able to prove that he was responsible for whatever happened to Raya and Maryam, and we need to do it before he ruins us, or worse."

- # -

"I don't know if it was you who wrote that post and leaked that video, and right now, I don't really care." Stone had said as he read the riot act to Corbin *"You have one chance to stay employed, to be useful and not thrown on the garbage heap of worms where you belong."* The conversation played over in Corbin's head as he tried to solve the puzzle - who was Taipan? He kept coming back to the first bit of what Stone had said. Stone hadn't leaked the video, and he didn't know who did. *Was the video leak linked to the Dinkum pump-and-dump?* It now looked like it had been engineered to be the trigger for the sudden interest in the token that had bubbled along at below 10 cents for nearly a decade or more after the initial launch frenzy. Corbin pushed his laptop away and rubbed his eyes. He couldn't make head nor tail of this Web3 world. He needed a way into it that had fewer zeros and ones, so he would start with flesh and blood instead. People were a lot easier to put pressure on than computers.

He slid a manilla folder towards him, opened it and spread out its contents. "I bet the OG wankers don't know why a manilla folder is called a manilla folder," he said to the empty room. "Probably couldn't even find manilla on a map." He leafed through the papers and printouts, working through the personnel who were involved with the Dinkum project. There were no red flags - why would there be, he had personally vetted each one of them before they were read in on any confidential information and they all had iron-clad NDAs. He scanned chat logs and unusual behaviour, but the guys, all guys, on the Dinkum team were rewarded above market rate and received perks, like VIP access to clubs on nights out with Stone and tickets to the F1. These guys were not about to try and stop the gravy train.

"Hmm." He ran his finger down the entry log for the crypto facility south of Melbourne. "That's weird."

Declan Sharp had, up until last week, been one of the better members of the security team. Corbin had found a few skeletons in the man's history, but what soldier of fortune didn't have secrets? Sharp's handling of Ray Mason and the subsequent fallout had ensured that the wound had been cauterised and there was no real impact on other parts of the organisation. He'd been present at the QSP Summit and kept order, despite being unable to apprehend Tommo, something Sharp had explained in a debrief was due to being saddled with temps and casuals and not well-trained security professionals. Sharp's exit interview upon his recent resignation also made sense - having been partially responsible for not keeping Mason in check and the winding up of the business at Monaghan, he was falling on his sword and would seek out new projects. Corbin had written a glowing reference and not thought much of it. Sharp was a mercenary, and a good one, and he was probably bored babysitting when he could be in a conflict with more job satisfaction.

So how, and why, was Declan Sharp swiping into the Dinkum facility in Mount Eliza on the 31st of December, when he was managing the meltdown of Ray Mason and the compromised operation at Monaghan? And why had Sharp re-issued two badges for contractors on his last day, badges that had a clearance level that would allow access to the NOC? And why had those specific badges been used to gain access to the NOC at the exact same time the video was released to social media and Dinkum was put in play?

"That's not nothing," said Corbin as he dragged his laptop back in front of him so he could access the various systems that allowed him and by extension Stone to spy on anyone in the wider organisation. He typed with two fingers, D e c l a n S h a r p. He looked for deviations in Sharp's behaviour that might explain the aberrations he had already discovered. Nothing. Sharp was a soldier. He obeyed orders, even distasteful ones, without objection.

"Wait a minute," Corbin followed the text with his finger of an email requesting that Declan Sharp be present at an afterhours meeting. The first date between Trevor and Tara. The email seemed to suggest that Tara had requested Sharp specifically by name. He was going to follow that lead.

"Hello?" Gail was Trevor Stone's personal PA, the one that dealt with anything in his personal life outside of his various businesses and sometimes there was a very thin line between the two. She thought Corbin was a creep and her skin crawled just thinking about who was on the other end of the line.

"Hello Gail." He let her name linger, coating it with a smooth veneer of sleaze. She'd hear it; she always did. The young athletic blonde had slept her way to this position, Corbin knew it, had it over her to use in case she ever decided to go public with any of Stone's intimate secrets. "Do me a little favour, won't you baby girl? Tell me how it came to be that one Declan Sharp wound up on security detail for Trevor's little soirée with Tara."

The event was a sore point with the PA. She didn't like Tara, didn't trust her, and was a little bit jealous, but after recent events she could imagine how her own night with Trevor Stone could be turned into a global internet meme. "Tara liked the way that Sharp conducted himself at the QSP event, particularly how he handled the media on the red carpet." She paused. "Said she'd feel better if there was someone to intervene."

He chuckled, low, letting the sound slip through the line. "Thank you, Gail," said Corbin breathing heavily down the phone like a stalker in a bad horror film. "Dream of me." He licked his lips and shifted in his seat as she hung up on him.

There was no reason for Gail to lie. In fact, Corbin had made it known to her on several occasions that there were many reasons why she shouldn't. Her on-the-spot answer rang true. The timelines made sense. Stone's infatuation with Tara was not a surprise, but the fact he let it be made public was unexpected, it was not standard operating procedure. It was probably a good thing that Sharp had been there that night, but that didn't explain Sharp's badge being used down at the stable complex days before Stone had even spoken with Tara. *Sharp might be a mercenary, but he's not a race traitor.*

"This is a waste of time," Corbin grunted in frustration. He was chasing his tail. Sharp was a grunt, not some crypto cowboy. Tara had been tracked into the QA offices on CCTV. She couldn't have used the re-issued badges. Sharp was still his best lead for now. CTTV! He clicked and clicked his mouse down through directory after directory, smiling at how the icons were designed to represent cardboard folders that used to sit in filing cabinets, wondering if that imagery would ever change. *How else would you represent a file?* He kept clicking, going back in time until he found the recordings for the CCTV for the 31st of December. His hands shook a little as he played the file. "Come on, come on." He sped up the motion capture video. "No way." He skipped back and halved the playback speed. "No. Fucking. Way," he shook his head and skipped back and played the video frame by frame. Watching a familiar figure pass through the camera's field of vision for less than 2 seconds. Pausing the video, he enhanced the image. "Hello again Mr Thompson."

- # -

The two women sat side by side on a wooden seat facing the ocean. Each had a cardboard tray wrapped in butcher's paper on their lap. There was an awkward silence between them.

Bondy began. "A fair bit has happened since we sat here last. Not much of it good." There were fewer tourists around, the workers were back at work even though the schools wouldn't go back for nearly a month.

Tara's fingers worked at the butcher's paper. "You could say I have some trust issues." She made sure Bondy caught her meaning as she demonstrated the proper way to tear a protective strip harking back to their first shared meal in this place.

"Schooling me again?" Bondy's laugh had no humour in it, but she copied the motion anyway. The paper crackled. "This isn't a simulation, Tara." The white cockatoos screeching in a flock in the Norfolk pines caused her to pause, which allowed her to look up at the sky and put the right words in the right order. "This is personal for you. I get it. I really hope that you find out what happened to your nieces, but we have no idea who we're going up against, and what they're willing to do to protect their secrets."

"You can walk away at any time." Tara was finding it harder and harder to stay motivated. She didn't need a lecture. "And there's not much more that they can do to me at this point."

"Just because you're on some kind of suicide mission doesn't mean you should endanger others." Bondy tried for reasonable, achieved strained. "Others like Archie and Marta who have nothing to do with this."

Tara was distracted as a cricket began to chirp in the couch grass. She pushed back. "You weren't here when it happened." She really didn't want this to become a confrontation, but it already was. "Marta was here. Archie was here. They were part of the community that was affected by what happened at that party."

"Thank you for the rescue by the way." Bondy wanted to remind

Tara of the close calls, that she had already been in physical danger in the course of Tara's mission so far. "But what if Declan isn't there next time?"

"Declan? You on first name terms with the lug now?"

"I think he may have saved my life." The frustration in Bondy's voice matched the cricket which seemed to start, then stop before really getting into its song. "Someone is going to die."

"Good. Someone needs to die."

"Not someone that I love, Tara."

The paper crinkled as Tara wrapped what remained of her dinner. "I can't stop now. You can walk away, Marta and Archie can walk away, I haven't asked them to do anything illegal. Tommo can do what he wants, he's got enough cash to disappear for the rest of his life if he wants to." Standing, she dropped the package into the bin. "I have more money than I can ever spend, but what use is it if I walk away from this now knowing that I could have done something and got justice for my family and I gave up?"

Bondy's voice changed to convey the promise she was about to make. "I want you to understand that if something happens to any of us, I will hold you personally responsible." She upended the box on her lap and threw her unwrapped chips into the air. They scattered across the grass, drawing a squadron of five then ten then twenty silver gulls She rose and pointed a finger at Tara, and in that moment, she looked dangerous and threatening. "You have your family, and I have mine. So, you keep that in mind."

Tara headed towards the surf club, leaving scalloped patterns from her desk shoes in the sand still warm from the day's heat. The coastal breeze always allowed her to think better. Bondy's words had hit home. She'd scraped through so far, but her luck was stretching thin as a fishing line. Stone was wounded, which made him unpredictable, domesticated wild animals are still wild animals.

The USB stick in her hoodie pocket was smooth and cool against her fingers. Tommo's gift from The Bluff had filled in some gaps, including those references to the cave. They'd found what looked like an underwater entrance, but that was only the first hurdle. Even if they could get in, and that was far from certain, the dive would push the limits of safety. Bondy was the only one qualified for something this technical, and after today's conversation, she seemed about as keen as a surfer who'd just spotted the fin of a great white.

Something caught her eye out past the break. She turned, but there was only the chop of waves against the reef. Then she saw it, a dorsal fin cutting through the water in a smooth arc. Just a dolphin. Her dolphin? Sunlight caught its skin as it surfaced again, and despite everything, Tara felt her shoulders relax. Maybe it meant something. Maybe it didn't. She was in control, so she took it to mean that she was in the right place.

- # -

The Shark Byte Cafe had just received its weekly drop of the local rag. Until recently, the paper was little more than a pamphlet for local real estate listings, with the odd story thrown in about Beryl's soggy rugs after last month's water main disaster or the persistent graffiti battle at the bus stop. Even the local lawn bowls club had moved to email for their weekly score updates. But things changed after the explosion in the surf beach car park, the suspicious fire that torched the ancient oak, and the high-profile arrest of former MP Ray Mason. Now the paper's small team was flat out, covering beach access snarls, dangerous crumbling trails, a recent attack on the Shark Byte Café itself, and the ongoing storm of controversy surrounding local surfing legend Archie 'Kelpie' Prince.

Today's headline was the one that Marta knew Tara at least had been hanging out for:

"Fire Sale. Mason Puts up Monaghan to Pay Legal Bills."

The details of Mace's ongoing court action filled the article beneath, but the sub-editor had done their job well and the headline itself told the story. Marta flipped past reports of another NIMBY protest against the new phone tower and a rundown on the latest changes to pier parking, until her thumb reached the glossy real estate insert tucked inside. On the cover was a glammed-up shot of an imposing old mansion, the burnt-out tree now ashes Photoshopped back into the picture. The headline was predictable but apt: "Once in a Lifetime Opportunity to Own an Iconic Landmark." The digital link directed readers straight to the listing on one of the local agency sites. Marta fired both the links to the group chat. "Be careful what you wish for…" she whispered.

- # -

Tara scrolled down the listing and swore as she hit the obstacle she hoped wouldn't be there. "Dammit. It's going to be an Auction." She and Tommo were camped in the Airbnb she'd snagged from Ray Mason, ironically paid for in part with his own cryptocurrency. They were in separate rooms, a world of tension between them, and it nothing to do with romance.

Tommo, rummaged through the barren fridge. "Bet they're open to offers." He glanced through at the empty shelves. "You really do get everything delivered, don't you?"

Tara let the comment slide, she was laser-focused on completing the final phase of her plan to get Monaghan into her name and lay her ghosts to rest, once and for all. "You and I can't just walk into Sotheby's Real Estate. You enemy of the people number one and me, the harlot who seduced Trevor Stone and leaked a sex tape."

Tommo knew where she was going. But offered a different point of view. "If you are the kind of person who Trevor Stone would be seen to publicly date, you are the kind of person who would have the means to buy a place like Monaghan."

Tara considered the logic. "If it does go to Auction, we don't want the world knowing that it's happening. No. I can't be seen to be involved. We need someone else."

"Archie?" Tommo was trying to be helpful. "He bid last time it came up for sale."

"I'm not trying to be harsh." She was about to be harsh. "But nobody's going to believe Archie has fifty million just lying around. We don't have any other credible proxies." She knew what the solution was, she just had to get Tommo to make it happen. "We've already set Bondy up as the front for an anonymous overseas buyer."

Tommo shut the fridge with a groan, his hunger unsatisfied. "What about Sharp? Mason thinks Sharp's tied to Stone's network. Maybe Stone would buy it to show solidarity and hold onto it for Mace until he's out."

"Mason's not getting out. With the charges against him, he'll be lucky to make it through his first week inside." She closed her laptop with finality. "And Sharp? That bridge is torched. He can't go back in there."

Still on the hunt for a snack, Tommo opened one cupboard after another, finally pulling out a packet of 2-minute noodles. He checked the date and wrinkled his nose, five years past its prime. "After what Mason did to Bondy, drugging her, tying her up, leaving her in that stable, she's not exactly going to waltz into a real estate office with a grin."

Tara tossed him a pink lady apple from the fruit bowl, her aim was precise. "The agents don't know about any of that. She's a pro at playing her part, and she'll pull this off just fine."

Tommo caught the apple and looked at it as if it was injected with polonium. He sighed with resignation. "Alright, alright. I'll talk to Bondy."

- # -

Claudine Seaton-Bond sat in the reception area, coolly sizing up the girl at the front desk, who greeted her with the same enthusiasm she'd have for a dick pic.

"Has there been much interest in the Monaghan property?" Bondy asked. It was a multimillion-dollar estate with National Trust listed building on it and nearly a kilometre of undeveloped beachfront. If there had been interest, it would not be from people walking through the front door of the office.

The girl barely looked up from filing her nails. "Oh. Um. Dunno." She shrugged. "That's my dad's area."

Now it made sense. The partner's daughter. A GenZ who could probably only get a job like this through nepotism. "Has anyone at least called about the ad in the paper?"

"A couple, maybe. It's, like, really exie."

Claudine raised a brow. "Exie?"

The girl tapped a finger to her temple, as if she was talking to the dumbest kid in her class. "Derrrr…. Ex-pen-sive. Like, millions."

An estate agent from central casting strode out from the back of the store. It was 35 degrees outside, but he wore a three-piece Italian suit and a yellow tie that was in fashion when he started in this game. His first job was working for Ray Mason, back in the day when Mace was an agent. He thrust out his hand, "Simon."

"Claudine." She dialled up her posh British accent.

"Glad you could drop by Claudine. I hope it wasn't too much trouble; this property is truly unique on a global scale. We already have several bids lined up." He had the same supercilious expression his daughter did.

Claudine's inner voice urged diplomacy, but she decided to throw in a dash of "bimbo" just to test him. "Well, the ad said, 'price on application,' so here I am, applying. What's the reserve price for the auction... Simon?"

The provincial agent looked momentarily thrown. "Are you the buyer yourself, or just representing someone else?"

"That's not relevant right now... Simon." She assumed he liked it when women called him by his name. She went for a number low enough to test his nerves but high enough to hint she was serious. "Twenty-five million?"

Simon's grin faltered, though he quickly replaced it with a condescending smile. "Let me just say, I do hope you didn't come all this way for... your clients. It seems you've got a bit to learn about the market here."

"Thirty," she countered. Claudine knew Tara's target and was willing to push high enough to avoid a public bidding war. Simon's brief hesitation told her what she needed to know.

"Well, then," Simon recovered, wearing an expression of strained politeness. "We'll be delighted to see you at auction, Ms...?" He hadn't been bothered to remember her last name, but his focus was all on his commission now.

Claudine kept her voice measured, pressing her advantage. "Thirty-point-three million. You're obliged to present that to the seller."

This was the first time he'd ever been involved in a deal of this magnitude; he was used to 1 month holiday rentals and McMansions. He was out of his depth on a deal this big. "I'm fully aware of my obligations, Ms. Seaton-Bond," he said, rearranging his tie as a nervous tick. "I will pass on your offer, though I'd recommend bringing a bit more if you hope to be in the running."

- # -

In a frigid room that he wished was ten degrees cooler Corbin sat, feeling the sweat spread under his black suit jacket. On the table in front of him was a beige folder stuffed with printouts and transcripts, a lifeline he'd pieced together in hopes of impressing Trevor Stone. He went over his lines like a defendant acting on his own behalf without a lawyer. "Tommo is Taipan." Too direct. He corrected himself: "There's a very high probability that Taipan is actually Travis Thompson." It was clean and logical, a step away from assumption. But he knew the evidence was thin.

The door clicked open, and Corbin tensed at the familiar scent of Stone's signature cologne as the man took a seat across from him. "This had better be good," Stone said, cracking open a can of full fat Coke. "When I asked you to find Taipan, I expected you'd only darken my door with hard proof. Hope you've got it."

Corbin took a steadying breath, mentally rehearsing his closing line. "There's no one else it could be… sir." The last word was affected. "Travis Thompson was a senior consultant with QSP when they bid to develop your namecoin, Dinkum." He nodded subtly toward the Coke can on Stone's desk hinting at his own thirst. Stone ignored him, waiting for something more concrete.

Corbin cleared his throat. "The advisor known as Taipan, was engaged after responding to an RFP that was circulated to a very select group of people. Public records put Thompson in London then, though Taipan's emails showed a Melbourne IP." He paused, conscious he was just echoing the script he'd drafted with AI assistance, not entirely confident it would hold up.

Stone didn't blink. "And?"

"IP addresses can be spoofed," Corbin said, feeling his voice wobble. "So, someone in London could make it look like they were in Melbourne."

"No kidding. How do you think I juggle so many women at once?"

Corbin forced a chuckle. "Right, right. But take a look at this." He slid a CCTV printout across the table, the timestamp visible in the corner. "That's him. At the Network Operations Centre. December 31st."

Stone's expression stayed flat. "Did anything unusual happen that day? Server glitch? Blip in the system? You're telling me Thompson had full access to our blockchain node and did... nothing?"

"He was there," Corbin insisted. "He could have planted a trojan horse that was activated later."

Stone crushed the Coke can flat with his fist, punctuating his impatience. "The 'Australian Financial Review' did a 2-page spread on that facility. Everyone knows Dinkum runs from there. It's not exactly a national secret."

Corbin pushed on. "Two contractors were issued badges the day before the Dinkum 'heist'. They made trades on the network at the exact time the video went viral on Reddit." He watched as Stone leaned in; interest piqued. "But the CCTV footage from that period's gone. Based on what we saw on New Year's Eve, there's a very high probability that it was Tommo."

"Who issued those badges?"

"Declan Sharp, sir."

"The same guy whose badge Tommo used to get in. Where's Sharp now?"

Corbin swallowed, feeling sweat prickle along his neck. "Sharp resigned last week, right after the events at Monaghan. He was out of contract. There's no indication he's Taipan."

"And nothing saying he didn't help Thompson FUCK ME," Stone erupted, fury rising. "A couple of badges and a blurry photo, is that all you've got?"

Corbin's career hung by a thread. He played his final card. "Sharp and Thompson were seen together. Today. Near the Monaghan property."

"Talk about burying the lead... You're fired."

"Do you really want to do that....... Sir?" Their relationship was built on mutually assured destruction.

"This all went down on your watch, Crow. Own it."

- # -

The Monaghan auction was a spectacle from the start. It was held in the formal gardens behind the grand estate, surrounded by weird geometric topiary and rose bushes that had been hurriedly trimmed. The agents had chosen a Tuesday morning on purpose, to make it hard for the riffraff to come and have sticky, but the crowd numbered about fifty, locals and outsiders alike.

Most of the locals were there to spectate rather than bid, though it was nearly impossible to tell who was serious. There were a few city slickers in their uniform of khakis chinos and blue chambray shirts, retirees in country-style attire, and then the wild cards, people who looked like they'd just rolled out of the pub. It was all very laid back until you caught a glimpse of a few shadowy types who were likely Ray Mason's people, planted to push up the bids.

Archie and Marta's presence was not questioned. As a pro-surfer Archie had won a few big purses in his day, and it was not a secret that Marta had invested it well. The couple couldn't match Ray's bid last time around, but if this was a true fire-sale, then there was a chance they could pick it up cheapish. That's what the locals would think. They knew how high Tara was willing to go and it was way out of their budget. Their role was to be Tara's eyes and ears.

Marta shook her head as she looked at Archie leaning up against a Japanese maple in a wide brimmed hat, a Pilote t-shirt and shorts. "You could have made an effort my love."

"I bet you that the richest people here are the least well dressed," Archie said, "look at what Zuckerberg and Musk wear. The dot-com crowd aren't really into appearances, unless it's to wear a Patagonia gilet as a bit of virtue signalling."

"You might be right. There isn't anyone here that looks like they have 30 million dollars to spend."

As if on cue, a helicopter dramatically banked over the point and flew low over the crowd. Trevor Stone didn't just show up, he wanted to make a point of his entrance. The pilot found the patch of grass that had been freshly mown, just in case anyone decided to arrive by air. Marta laughed as Stone strode towards the gathering as if posturing on a catwalk. *Does he actually believe he is the embodiment of a real man?*

A younger guy who had parked a gaudy mirrored pink Lamborghini in the driveway applauded Stone's arrival. Everyone else murmured their opinions in hushed tones to the person next to them. Stone scanned the crowd. His eyes fell on Bondy, and it took a second to spin through the mental rolodex of contacts in his head. She smiled at him, and he put the face to the name and the place. The last time he had seen her was on Constitution Dock at the end of the Hobart Race. Corbin had vetted her before she stepped aboard the boat, she had checked out but was before she had been seen deep in conversation with Tara on several occasions. Bondy was there to bid for someone else, but who?

The auctioneer, who was a bit of a character, adjusted his bright red suit jacket and matching bow tie and took his place up front. He had a friendly, weathered face that looked like it'd sniffed a few corks in its time "Righto you lot. Settle down. Time to get this show on the road." He nodded a greeting to Trevor Stone as if there was no one else in the crowd. "She's a beaut ain't she? Hopefully this place ends up in the right hands, if you know what I mean." The crowd chuckled and shuffled forward a little, their voices lowering. "The reserve is 20 million." Marty dared the crowd to show they could meet the starting price. "This one features a beachfront longer than yer granddad's bedtime stories, and for all we know there is a goldmine under us. Do I hear 20?"

A young couple at the front conferred with their advisor who nodded. The man tentatively raised a hand in a way that suggested it might be the only bid he was going to make.

"I have twenty. Ned Kelly would be proud of that level of stealing." Marty winked at the crowd, prompting another laugh.

Bondy looked over at Trevor. He smirked and mouthed "after you".

"Twenty-Five" Bondy said confidently, loud enough to be heard, but not shouting. She looked back at Stone.

Marty picked up their interaction. "Will we be hearing from you today, Mr Stone? Twenty-five mill is about 6 decent nags, isn't it? Pocket change for a man such as you."

"I can do thirty I guess, just to keep it interesting." It was clear there were only a few real bidders present.

Marty conferred with a girl that Bondy recognised as the receptionist at the agent's office. She had her earbuds in. She flushed red as Marty whispered something in her ear and then the auctioneer called out. "We have thirty-two point five on the phone. New bidder." The increments were getting smaller as the buyers who knew the true market value attempted not to overpay.

Bondy held her ground. Tara had let her know where their limits were. There weren't any, but she didn't want to give that away just yet. She made a show of rubbing her chin.

Stone nodded at Marty. "Thirty-three point five." Before the Dinkum event, thirty million would have been a bad night in Vegas, but he was a bit short on liquid assets right now. Maybe he didn't want to win this auction anyway, maybe it would draw too many questions, but also didn't want to be outbid by Tara if she was one of the other bidders - the one on the phone or the one Bondy was representing.

It was both. Tommo, through a voice modulator, put the next bid in by phone. The receptionist, giddy at the thought Trevor Stone was watching her, relayed the amount to Marty who raised his eyebrows. "Thirty-four million, against you Mr Stone."

"Fine." Stone was good at this game. He'd watched the other bids tick up in smaller amounts. He was bored now. "Thirty-seven five" He turned and waved his hand as if to say, 'get in touch with my people to sort out the details.'

It was Bondy's turn to turn the screws a little. "Thirty-seven, seven fifty." The hint of a smirk appeared on her face before she slipped back into character.

Stone turned back and glared at Bondy and then looked at the auctioneer as if appealing to the umpire for a marginal LBW. "Really? Come on Marty, are we really going up by two hundred and fifty K at a time?"

Marty was a professional at this if nothing else. "My job is to get the best price for my client." He looked towards the girl taking the phone bids. She shook her head. "The bid is thirty-seven million, seven hundred and fifty thousand dollars. Do I hear anything more?"

Sneering in the direction of Bondy convinced that Tara was on the other end of the call, Stone was incapable of acting rationally. He could sell something or work out finance. Marty was right, the amount was akin to a few good runners at the yearling sales. He wasn't looking at Marty, he was looking at Bondy whose expression was one of the best poker faces he had ever seen. "Forty million." The crowd gasped.

Archie had been in conversation on the phone with Tara the whole time. He knew that forty was the upper limit of what she wanted to pay. He could hear Tara and Tommo talking and his eyebrows raised as listened in on their conversation.

"I'll put in ten," Tommo offered.

"How's that going to work?" Tara was more grateful than she sounded.

"Or we go halves. Twenty-two point five each and we bid forty-five."

At the auction, the crowd was restless. Marty was restless. Stone was restless. Bondy was a picture of calmness, but she knew what was coming. Marty raised his gavel, but he couldn't resist being the centre of attention. "Imagine what you could do with this place." He moved his arm around to convey the vastness of the property. "Plant some vines, make a nice pinot. Maybe Greg Norman could design 9 holes that would challenge the world's best."

"Bid 45 Archie," Tara instructed.

Stone was moving. Walking towards Bondy to shake her hand as Marty rambled on. "Just drop the hammer, old man."

"The bid is forty million, going once." The auctioneer was staring at Bondy. She didn't move. "Forty million, going twice. Come on luv, you could turn this place into a spa, and it's only 22 million of your great British pounds…"

"Forty-Five." Archie called from his position up the back, languishing against a stone plinth where a statue of Eros once stood. The whole crowd turned. He waited until he was sure he had their full attention. "Forty-five million dollars," Archie repeated more loudly.

Marty was stunned. He looked at Stone and fury was projected back at him. He looked at Bondy who casually took her earbuds out and put them in their case. She shook her head. She was out. He looked up at Archie who was grinning like he'd just won the world surfing championship. He stammered. "We have a new bidder. Welcome Mr Prince." He looked back at Stone who was not grinning. He was incandescent with rage. "The bid is forty-five million dollars." He lent on the flimsy lectern, and it nearly collapsed under his weight. "Anyone else waiting in the wings? No more surprises?" He was not sure his heart could handle much more. "Right then. Going once… twice… "He paused for Stone to come back in, but he knew from the whine of the rotor blades warming up there would be no more bids from that party. "Three times, sold to Mr Prince for forty-five million dollars."

10

The story fed to the press was that Archie, a descendant of the land's original inhabitants, had purchased the property with the assistance of silent partners who wanted to keep Monaghan in Australian hands. It was an angle that Trevor Stone couldn't really push back against. The reality was that Monaghan had been bought by a consortium, the identities of which were obscured by various trusts, shell companies and vehicles designed specifically to obscure who the new owners really were.

At the edge of Perridak Creek, Bondy was checking Declan Sharp's diving equipment. He was checking hers. The dark water, stained brown by paperbark gave nothing away about what lay beneath. "Do you have any money left to pay us for this platypus chase?" Bondy quipped, addressing Tara.

"Plenty. And there is a bonus too if we can finally put this all behind us, depending on what you find in that cave." Tara replied solemnly.

"You're all set. We've got plenty of air and it's not going to be deep." said Sharp in his no-nonsense way.

Bondy gave Sharp a quick kiss on the cheek. "I'm pumped. No one has ever dived this cave. Who knows, maybe we can turn it into a tourist attraction."

"If only we knew the owners." Declan smiled at Tara.

"Be safe you two." Tara watched as they walked backwards into the creek."

- # -

The headlamp projected weak circles of light through the murk, barely penetrating the silt their fins had stirred up. Bondy led the way, her movements precise and economical. Sharp followed, keeping the safety line taut between them, his breathing steady through his regulator despite the growing unease in his gut. Bondy pointed to the bottom where the wreck of Marta's Drone sat in the mud. The first passage was tight, barely wide enough for their tanks, Bondy could understand why Archie's mob believed such a tunnel could be made by a snake or a serpent. Their bubbles gathered in silver pockets against the ceiling, temporary mirrors that distorted their reflections into grotesque shapes before finding hairline cracks to escape through. The tunnel widened. She signalled to Sharp, pointing upward where the passage opened into what looked like a larger chamber. They ascended carefully, their computers showing they'd been under for seven minutes.

Sharp could see the amazement in Bondy's eyes through her mask as she swivelled her head to take in the chamber. A galaxy of soft stars created by hundreds of glow worms covered the ceiling.

Bondy removed her regulator, but she couldn't speak. She was mesmerised by the sensory overload of the place. The sound of water dripping was not random, more like a Mandelbrot set transliterated into a percussion piece. Declan didn't say anything either. The hard man that he was, he was also affected by this place. They pulled themselves out of the water onto a ledge and stood still. Sharp turned Bondy's chin, leaned in and kissed her. He'd been wanting to since he'd found her tied up in Ray Mason's stables. She didn't pull away.

They shared the moment until Bondy sighed, "We have a job to do. But hold that thought…"

Sharp pointed to where a beam of light shone down through the darkness like a laser. "That means there is access from above, but we didn't find anything when we did the reccy."

"It's a small hole. Not much wider than a fist. We could have easily missed it."

They edged themselves along the wall of the chamber towards the source of the light. Delan explored the walls with his torch. "This is as far as we go. Even if there is more through an underwater tunnel, there is no way someone is dragging two bodies in there. This is a dead…" He checked himself.

"Oh my God!" The beam of Bondy's torch carved through the darkness, catching something that made her throat constrict. "Over here." She managed, her voice barely above a whisper. The unnatural arrangement of shapes ahead screamed wrong. The light trembled across bleached bones draped in rotting fabric. Bondy's stomach lurched as empty eye sockets stared back at her. She stumbled backward.

Declan moved in, his neoprene and rubber boots crunching against the cave floor as he crouched by the remains. His gloved fingers brushed over the scraps of remaining clothing fabric. "Early 1900s," he muttered, studying the degraded jacket. "The cut, the material... this guy's been down here for a century."

"Christ." Bondy's voice cracked. She forced herself to look up at the skylight. It was barely wide enough to drop a skull through, let alone a whole corpse. "How the hell did someone get a body through that?"

"Maybe they didn't." Declan's flashlight beam traced upward. "Opening could've been bigger back then. Or..." He let the thought hang. "Maybe they covered the hole with something like a tree trunk, we won't know 'til we get back up there." He studied the skeletal hand, a gold band still circling one bony finger. "Male. Married." He glanced at Bondy. "I wonder if Archie knows who it could be."

Bondy was moving and searching again, sweeping her light across the cave's recesses, her breath coming in short bursts. "Someone could've brought the girls down here, without using the creek entrance." The thought sent ice through her veins.

"There is only one other way in and that's the hole in the roof." Declan caught himself. "Any other bodies would be lying on top of this one… Hang on. What's that?" His light caught something, a metallic glint that didn't belong. "There."

Bondy kneeled and brushed the accumulated dirt away from a small object, turning it over in her still trembling hands. "It's a Rolex."

"Yachtmaster?" Declan was a bit of a timepiece nerd.

"Yes. It's not a teenage girl's watch." Bondy brushed the dirt off the case back. "Every Rolex has a serial number. Which means we can trace who the owner is or was."

"I hate to play black hat, but a watch in a hole is not proof of anything."

Bondy looked up at the vent in the roof of the cavern and pushed out her bottom lip in thought. "This watch doesn't belong to the body. It's highly unlikely it dropped here by accident. But if someone knew the hole was there, they would also know that the chances of this watch being found were about the same as a million monkeys on a million typewriters creating the entire works of Shakespeare."

Declan couldn't help laughing. "Better a witty fool than a foolish wit."

The dripping seemed louder now and less random. "We need to bag this," Bondy said finally. "Maybe there are some skin cells caught in the band, maybe the serial number will help." She slipped the watch into a Ziplock bag, secured it and then grabbed Declan, spinning him around and kissing him hard. "No matter what happens, they can't take this away from us."

- # -

A noisy miner chirped from somewhere in the scraggly coastal banksias, probably eyeing the wrapper from Tara's four-n-twenty that had escaped her pocket and was doing cartwheels across The Point. She swore. "Shit." She couldn't go after it. She hated that she had contributed another piece of single use plastic into the environment. "I think they use beef these days," she said in the direction of the silver bird.

She'd won so many battles, and yet she seemed so far away from the closure she craved. She'd humiliated Trevor Stone in ways he'd never forget. She'd acquired this land, beautiful in a wild, untamed way, and it hinted at countless possibilities, but peace still eluded her. Without knowing what happened to her nieces, she knew she'd never truly have it. And, if it came to that, she'd risk losing every inch of this place to get there.

A more thorough investigation of the property above ground revealed that the fallen-in roof of the underground tunnel had been covered over with corrugated iron sheets and branches and soil, either to stop people from falling to their death or to hide the final resting place of Alfred Mason, which solved a century old mystery, but didn't make Tara feel any better.

The watch they'd found in the cave turned out to indeed belong to Trevor Stone, at least he was the one it was awarded to as a prize for a yacht racing regatta in the US Virgin Islands. But as Sharp had said, with all the emotion of a parking inspector writing a ticket. *"A lost watch in a cave means jack shit."* Stone was the kind of guy who might have given it to one of the crew or gifted it to a politician in exchange for favours, a politician like Ray Mason, the descendant of the dead man in the cave and the owner of the property. Stone wasn't the kind of guy to wear something as boring as a Rolex. She remembered him wearing a Hublot on their first date, and in the infamous video, eagle eyed horologists would have spotted a Ulysse Nardin on the bedside table.

Her phone buzzed in the pocket of her hoodie. Archie. She let it go to voicemail, but then came the text:

Archie: Please call me. It's important.

She was weary, it was in her voice. She could barely manage a single word. "Hey."

"I've got something," he said. He sounded excited and cautious at the same time. He'd been working back through the evidence Tommo had gathered, pouring over texts between anonymous users that talked about a cave, written in some obscure code.

"What is it?"

"Well..." Archie took a deep breath. "In Latin, cavus means hollow, which is where we get caverna. But it was dumb luck that we found the cave or Alfred Mason or the watch. Total fluke."

"You rang me for a Latin lesson?" Despite her daily Wordle addiction, Tara wasn't up for games.

"Hang on, hang on. You might want to park yourself for this one. Tommo got the translation wrong. It's not cavus, it's corvus." He wanted to drag it out like a reality tv show host announcing the episode winner but knew better. "Corvus means rook, or raven... or crow." He could tell where she was from the sound of the wind as it blew across The Point, it drowned out everything, even her breathing. "Tara?"

Her bloodstream froze like she'd finished a Zooper Dooper too quickly. Her hand could barely keep hold of the phone. "Thank you, Archie. I mean it. Thank you so much." Her blood went from Antarctic chill to boiling in a moment. Her need for revenge surged. A smile tugged at her mouth as she spotted the tip of a dorsal fin breach the surface of the ocean fifty metres out. It was not a graceful arc. The triangular fin cut through the water with intent, hunting. "I'll see you at the cafe."

- # -

"Maybe we should get back to the task at hand?" Tommo was eager to get the details of the plan sorted. "The Aquarius is the place we are going to lure Corbin 'The Crow' to convince him to tell us what he knows once and for all."

Through the steam of her third coffee, Tara traced her finger along the resort's faded brochure. "I've been to that place recently and it doesn't look like that anymore."

"Yeah, and it might never look like that again," Archie said. "Place was shuttered last week after the last guests left and word down the Pier is that it won't ever re-open." He looked directly at Tara. "Some developer is gonna turn it into a Four Seasons or something."

"It would be a great location for a movie version of GTA Vice City. Pink and turquoise everywhere, glass blocks catching the sunset. Pure 1980s cocaine dreams."

Tommo scoffed. "There have never been drug pool fuelled parties at The Aquarius. You're way off. It's got a post-apocalyptic thing going on now. Funky old neon signs, broken windows, that weird green pool that looks radioactive. Tell me that's not straight out of Fallout 4."

"Fallout 4?" Archie asked, squinting at them both over his reading glasses. "How can there even be a Fallout 2. You'd think the first one would have wiped everything out."

"Yeah, fair point, there is a bit of creative licence when it comes to games, but that place might as well be run by ghouls…" Tommo started.

"No, no, no." Tara cut him off. "The fountain with the dolphins? Pure Vice City vibes."

"Vice what now?" Archie's knowledge of video games began

309

with Outrun and ended with Afterburner, which he'd wasted too much money on in the arcade at The Aquarius."

"Grand Theft Auto" they said in unison.

"You think an Australian timeshare can be described through the lens of some game studio in LA?" Archie said, placing his glasses on his head.

"Fallout was developed in Maryland I think," Tommo offered.

Archie was not impressed. He pointed out of the window in the direction of the resort. "That's not Fallout or Vice City. It's not enough that previous generations were brainwashed by yank cultural imperialism through Hollywood, now you guys frame your nostalgia in the context of a video game narrative."

Tara studied the brochure with fresh eyes. The resort smiled back at her from 1982, a temple of leisure rendered in pastels and promises, all of them imported from somewhere else. "Maybe the guy who designed it had watched a few too many episodes of the Love Boat."

"Guys, the plan." Tommo tried to being them back to the task at hand. "We are going to use The Aquarius for the boss level, yes?"

"Yes, the 'Ocean View', I mean Aquarius is perfect." Tara said.

"And I'm the bait." Tommo wasn't too comfortable with the idea, but he couldn't see any other way to tempt Corbin to meet. They knew Corbin had come to the same conclusion that Tara had; Tommo was Taipan.

"If things go sideways, we can get you out via the water on the jet-ski," Archie said.

"And we know the layout," Tara added. "We can create a kind of gauntlet, using locked doors and barricades to make sure he ends up where we want him." She jangled a ring of keys and grinned.

"You guys better be right. There are no respawns."

- # -

Corbin stepped through the sagging gate as his eyes scanned the abandoned resort grounds. *Give the boy credit, this is a good place to hide-out.* Even though The Aquarius had only been closed a week, it was already in a state of romantic decay. The loungers sprawled across the cracked pool deck looked like they'd been dropped mid-evacuation. A few were stacked near the gate, haphazard and sagging like flimsy barriers against some imagined invader or a tsunami. Empty cups and the odd plastic flamingo floated near the edge of the pool.

He tried the front door. It was locked, but a small gate in the chain wire fence had not been chained or padlocked. He slipped the bolt and followed a quaint paved path complete with kitsch signposts that showed the distances to key locations, Tennis courts 200m, Spa 50m, South Pole 5801 km, Beach Club 100m. *That's where Tommo will be.*

The entrance to the beach club was flanked by two artificial palm trees, their paint faded and chipped. Corbin paused. He knew this was a setup, Tommo had been too easy to find. The man who had evaded capture with every news bulletin and social media post talking about him had suddenly popped up on Corbin's radar. No. Tommo wanted to be found.

Corbin moved through the beach club in silence, creeping across the mosaic tiled floor, the only sound the faint wash of the waves on the beach. He slipped from room to room, noting the old posters advertising the annual Mussel Festival and the Air Supply tribute band. There seemed to be no pattern to which doors were locked and which weren't, but there was a pattern. It was like a level in a so-called open-world game designed to feel vast and free but crafted to guide the player along a single, predetermined path. The maze offered the illusion of choice, yet every twist and turn subtly funnelled the player in one direction, ensuring they followed the route intended by the game designer, in this case Tara.

Corbin ran his thumb over the pistol tucked into his waistband, flipping the safety off. It wasn't loaded. If he did his part right, no one would know it was harmless. Intimidation was all he needed.

The trail included subtle breadcrumbs, like a dimmed light that led him deeper into the club, past the games room featuring a table-tennis table and nothing else, toward the deck by the main bar. He felt a trickle of sweat at the base of his neck. *You've taken down bigger game than Tommo, stop psyching yourself out.*

The deck's sliding glass doors were already cracked open. When he stepped out, he wasn't expecting what met him. It wasn't Tommo's smug grin and lazy slouch, but Tara Kwong, leaning back at a table with her legs crossed, her face lit by an electric candle. Her fingers were resting casually near a Rolex Yachtmaster. He recognized instantly. It was the one he'd been given as a bonus, the one he had dropped into a bottomless hole in the earth to be lost forever. He could not imagine any universe where that watch would or could reappear.

Tara's eyes had the look of a starved she-lion. He took a step forward, pulling the gun from his waistband, aiming it level at her. "Where's Tommo?" he asked, his voice steady. But the next thing he felt was a grip like iron on his wrist as Declan Sharp appeared from behind him, twisting his arm effortlessly until the gun slipped from his hand and clattered onto the deck.

Pinned in place, Corbin cursed, trying to wrench free, but Sharp barely flinched, his hold firm and precise, professional. Corbin stopped struggling enough for Sharp to usher him into a seat where his wrists were bound to the arms with commercial grade zip-ties. His ankles were similarly fastened to the legs of the chair. Sharp then moved behind Tara, arms crossed.

Corbin's first instinct was to lash out and threaten, but he'd seen what Sharp could do to a man with his bare hands, let alone a weapon, like a knife. He'd be fish food in minutes.

Tara's eyes hadn't left him. She smiled as if she could read Corbin's mind. "If you don't give me what I want…" She didn't even look at the gun on the ground. "You will wish I had fed you to the sharks."

Suddenly, everything that Trevor Stone could do to him also

seemed trivial.

"It's a lovely evening." She looked out at the lights of the town down the coast on the horizon and then back to her captive. "Why don't you tell me a story about two young girls who went to a party and never came back."

Up until the moment he saw the watch, Corbin had assumed that Tara's motives were financial. The cozying up to Stone, the video for blackmail, the revenge play of taking down Dinkum. He glared at her, jaw clenched, refusing to speak.

Tara wasn't in any hurry. She stood up and Corbin flinched. She walked over to the jukebox and plugged it in. It hummed to life, and she pressed the combination for the song she wanted. "You've got a choice, Corbin," she said as the opening bars of 'Different for Girls.' played. "You can tell me the truth about what happened to my nieces at the party…" She paused, letting the song play, using his own tactics against him. "Including the character that Trevor Stone plays… or my friend here," she nodded to Sharp, "will drop your body into the cave where we found this watch and leave you there. Alive."

Corbin glared at her, his jaw clenched, refusing to speak., he was trying to work out how much she really had. The watch connected him to Stone and to Monaghan, but not much else. "You don't know anything," he rolled the dice, trying to summon any scrap of defiance he had left. "You're bluffing."

Tara's gaze didn't waver. "Maybe you won't be alone in the cave. We could give you some company, a taipan perhaps, or something more indigenous this part of the world, a brown snake, tiger? Red belly black snake has a nice ring to it, and they are on the property."

"Look… we can work something out. I can give you Stone. But I need guarantees. I want to be able to disappear."

"In case you hadn't worked it out already, this is not a negotiation." She picked up the watch and turned it over in her hands. "I don't really need you, Corbin," she said. "I will get the truth eventually, whether I get it from you or someone else. This way you get to rot in a jail cell instead of a hole in the ground with a venomous reptile as a companion."

Corbin felt the walls closing in. He tried one last desperate gambit. "Trevor Stone will come looking for me. He'll lawyer up, he'll never be convicted."

Tara moved in close, her face mere inches from Corbin's, her eyes unflinching. He could smell the Wrigley's Juicy Fruit on her breath. "If you want to negotiate," she said, her voice a low, lethal whisper, "you can make a bargain with the authorities for your evidence. Maybe they will give you a deal, find a nice life for you in witness protection."

Corbin's face drained of colour. "I can't do that. I can't be a rat. Stone's reach is too long. I'll be found hanged in my cell Epstein style."

"The alternative is starving and shivering in the darkness." Tara sucked the gum against her teeth, so it made a soft popping sound. "Your body lost for a century in a cavernous grave, a Schrodinger's mystery - did you die from a snakebite or not?"

Dropping his head down against his chest, Cordin sighed with resignation. "Build your opponent a golden bridge to retreat across."

Tara straightened, folding her arms as she glanced at Sharp, who remained a silent enforcer behind her. "Ah. A little bit of Sun Tzu. I prefer Machiavelli myself - Everyone sees what you appear to be, few experience what you really are."

- # -

Trevor Stone watched the police officers on the screen of his video doorbell. His lips curved into the kind of half-smile he'd used a thousand times to talk his way out of sticky situations. But he was about to be blindsided again. The officers waiting outside his door might have been part of his fan-club in the not-too-distant past, but not now. Not once they heard the evidence against him. And, deep down, Stone knew he was done. With a deep sigh, he pressed the button and allowed them inside.

He barely put up a fight as they cuffed him. The officers moved him with swift efficiency, ignoring his murmured objections as they led him down the polished marble hallway, through the private lobby, and outside to be paraded in front of the photographers and live TV crews that had been tipped off. His tame media, who had held him up, were ready to bury him, or at least capitalise on his notoriety. They yelled questions at him as if he would incriminate himself for their pursuit of ratings and clickbait. An AI would do better.

"Did you do it?"

"What do you have to say to your fans?"

"Are you the victim of cancel culture?" Their cumulative stupidity rang in his ears as he was ushered to the paddy wagon, handcuffed and grim.

Corbin's confession had broken it all open, all the secrets Stone had paid to be buried had clawed their way to the surface. The allegations were that he had personally forced the two girls into a twisted night of debauchery in a dungeon style cellar beneath the Monaghan main house. There had been an element of revenge involved; the father of the girls had stolen 1000 Bitcoin in the distant past when the cryptocurrency was worth cents. But it didn't really matter to Stone who the sisters' family was, they were merely a night's entertainment. At the end of it one girl lay cold from a cocaine overdose, and the other sprawled alongside, her last breath choked out by Stone's own hands. In his mind, they were nothing. No one would miss them once discarded.

Corbin thought he was confessing his part in return for leniency, perhaps he was doing it for redemption, but given the part he had played, there was no guarantee of either. As he had predicted, Corbin had been found dead in custody, hanged in his cell shortly after he had given Stone up to the police. That story had not been given any coverage. Despite an endless aisle of news sources, there was no room to dedicate to just another prison suicide. The talking heads were too busy with Stone's disgrace and reinventing themselves as critics. The same people who'd fawned over him were now tearing him to shreds, claiming they had "always seen through him" or that "the signs were there all along." Their hypocrisy filled the screens, each taking the moment to remind viewers they'd been "ahead of the curve" on Stone's character.

- # -

Tara didn't have any sympathy for Corbin. Hearing the truth from him had been a thousand degrees worse than she'd imagined. She'd been physically ill as she listened to Stones's fixer's story. Every horrific detail from the ordeal of her niece's final night on earth to the grim particulars of how their bodies were disposed of.

She sat on the end of The Point and watched the surfers squabble over waves at Kelpies. The truth hadn't set her free. She wouldn't really be free while Stone was. Despite the evidence against him, bail had been granted. With Corbin, the key witness gone, the case was circumstantial.

One of the surfers whooped as he dropped in on a 6-foot face. Tommo had stood by her, admittedly coerced for much of the mission, but he'd been there when all the powerful men looked the other way.

Maybe there was a way to be free.

EPILOGUE

Kelpie's break looked like hammered slate under the winter sky. Marta looked out to sea from the new and improved Shark Byte Café, constructed from old shipping containers on the foreshore of Kelpie's Beach. The two-story coffee joint, surf shop, digital nomad hangout and the Taipan Bar could be reached by a new access road through the Monaghan property. There was a small donation box at the end of the driveway, but only the tourists contributed. In the relative comfort of the café, behind double glazed windows with the heating cranked up and steam rising from her Fairtrade Americano Marta still shivered as she watched the brooding Southern Ocean. A brutal wind dragged heavy clouds across the horizon as the constructive interference of waves colliding threw water skyward in a violent coming together. There were only 3 dark shapes in the water.

Tara took a deep breath of oxygen and DMS. Everything, the water, the air, even the salt on her lips felt raw and keen Waiting for the right gap, she paddled out, one stroke after another, using her movements against the cold to keep her core temperature up. She wore Archie's latest wetsuit; a custom prototype he'd designed just for her. It was a thick, layered affair: five millimetres on the chest to lock in warmth, but even with all that neoprene, the cold still sliced through. Her fingers ached on the edges of her board, and her face tingled as she duck-dived under an oncoming broken face of a wave.

To her left, Tommo kept pace, his eyes steady on her as he paddled. "You're crazy, you know," he said. "This is about as close as I ever wanna get to actual frostbite." He was shivering too, despite the bravado. They both were. This break wasn't a place to go in winter if you wanted warmth or comfort. It was for the ones who didn't know how to back down. And it was the place where, for the first time in her life, Tara could breathe.

She had feared it at first, the way Kelpie's waves rose so fast, the razor-sharp reef lying only metres below the break. Today, though, she felt something else, something close to joy, a feeling that was half release, half surrender.

"Ready for the next set?" Archie called out from where he sat astride his board in the lineup out past the whitewater. He looked completely at ease. He'd been the perfect, patient tutor these last few months and if Archie's face said, "Everything is alright," it probably was.

Straddling her board, Tara leaned over and gave Tommo a kiss before she moved into position. She felt the adrenaline pump through her fingers, her toes, her spine. It was an old friend, a familiar charge that prickled under her skin and demanded she stay sharp, stay alive. She'd once thought this feeling would fade, but it never had. Not even after all these months. Archie called it the 'Blue Mind' theory. She caught a glimpse of the oncoming set. Instinctively she wanted to take the first wave, but Archie had coached her - choose wisely. She let the first two waves of the set roll under her. The swell lifted her up, up, and then down in a slow descent. She watched them turn into churning foam as they approached the beach, but she didn't have time to watch them all the way onto the sand.

She kicked and paddled as the ocean kicked up where it met the shallows, and then she was moving, pushed forward by the power of the underlying mass of water. She felt her board lift, balancing her weight so she didn't nosedive or fall off the back of the wave until she was on her feet, dropping down the face, weightless before making the rail catch so she could make a bottom turn. She could feel the cold bite into her cheeks, her breath fogging the air as she rode. It was the kind of feeling she could never explain to anyone who hadn't been out here, who hadn't felt the full weight of the ocean behind them. The water hissed and thundered as she rode, and she caught a glimpse of Tommo and Archie watching her, cheering her on, their shouts swallowed by the waves. She felt her body start to numb, the cold seeping into her bones. She waved back at the guys to signal she was paddling in.

Tommo hummed as he dangled his feet in the gelid water… "And there's nothing else could set fire to this town."

"Are you okay mate?" Archie was setting up for the next set. He pointed. "This is my last wave I reckon. Don't stay out here too long on your own." He paddled quickly as the face rose up. "Oh and…" he grinned.

"Something makes me think that she WILL be around."

THE END

THE END

About the Author

David Fuller remembers summers on Kunyung Beach and the curious intricacies of corporate life in Australia, long before embarking on a journey that took him across continents. After backpacking through Asia, he joined an internet startup in London, setting off a career spanning marketing, sports writing, and sailing blogging. His work has taken him across the USA, Europe, and the Middle East, where he built websites, led training sessions, and delivered talks as a public speaker. In addition to creating and presenting podcasts, David also launched his own casual clothing brand, Pilote.
Discarding Decency is his debut novel.

@DMFREEDOM
dmfreedom.com/links

A c k n o w l e d g m e n t s

Thanks to all those who have helped and offered encouragement and their honest opinions. Thanks to Paul DeVos for challenging me to write a screenplay which was too hard, so I wrote a novel instead. Thanks also to my dad – Neil Fuller who acted as copy editor. Thanks to my mum – Susan Fuller for laughing at some of my jokes and observations. Thanks to Simon Dean Johns for some clarification on legal matters. Shout outs to Christina Ioannidis, James Ditzell, Mike West, Andrew Sampson, Simon Darling and Richard Osman.

9 781763 859128